HITTING THE WALL

A STONECUT COUNTY ROMANCE

CATE C. WELLS

This book is a work of fiction. Names, characters, places, and incidents are the product of the author's imagination or are used fictitiously. Any resemblance to actual events, locales, or persons, living or dead, is coincidental.

Copyright © 2021 by Cate C. Wells. All rights reserved.

Cover art and design by Clarise Tan of CT Cover Creations.
Photograph by Wander Aguiar.
Edited by Nevada Martinez.
Proofread by Kayla Davenport.

Special thanks to Kara Paquin Meredith and Jean McConnell of The Word Forager.

The uploading, scanning, and distribution of this book in any form or by any means—including but not limited to electronic, mechanical, photocopying, recording, or otherwise—without the permission of the copyright holder is illegal and punishable by law. Please purchase only authorized editions of this work, and do not participate in or encourage electronic piracy of copyrighted materials. Your support of authors' rights is appreciated.

※ Created with Vellum

1

SHAY

Ten minutes ago, three men rolled up in a brown-and-tan sheriff's cruiser. Grandpa's out front talking to them now.

I'm in trouble.

My hands wanna shake, but I force them steady so no one notices I'm peeking through the blinds. Grandpa's lady friend, Connie, is shuffling around at the sink. She's spying, too. Bet she's steaming mad. She knows this has to do with me. Ever since I came up from South Carolina to stay, she's been praying for me. And she makes damn sure I can hear.

I know these men. Everyone in Stonecut County does. I see them all the time in the diner where I wait tables.

The tall man in muddy boots is Mr. Wall. He owns the horse farm where Grandpa works. The businessman in the pleated pants is Mr. Price. He tips well and gets handsy. And then there's the sheriff. He's straight from an old cop show—ruddy nose and cheeks, bushy mustache, and a star on his chest. Connie says he's a fine-looking man, and I guess he used to be. He's got that swagger.

The sheriff claps Grandpa on the back. Guess they're done talking. Grandpa hangs his head and ushers them into our trailer.

My belly clenches, and I burst out in clammy sweat. This is it. Time to pay the piper, as my grandma used to say.

I didn't think three old guys would show up, but they do things strange in Stonecut County. This place is unbelievably old-fashioned. Everyone is upstanding, and everything is picture-perfect, neat and tidy, and just so. And if it isn't, everyone pretends they can't see it.

"Shay!" Grandpa hollers.

I tug an oversized sweatshirt over my tank top as quick as I can. No time to slip on shoes. Connie's gonna give my bare feet the evil eye; I can feel it coming.

"Shay!"

I slip through my bedroom's folding door and step through the kitchen. I come to a stop where the linoleum turns to carpet. The men have completely taken up the living room. Grandpa's trailer is small—a single wide—and we're cheek by jowl when it's only the three of us. Probably why Connie's not so keen on having me.

"Grandpa?"

"Sit." He waves at the couch.

All four men wear stone faces. I scuttle past the sheriff and sit. They loom over me, blocking the door and the window. Mr. Wall moves so he's between me and my bedroom. A knot coils in my guts.

Grandpa's holding his hat in his hands, worrying the brim with his fingers. He never takes his hat off inside.

The other men are holding their hats, too. Except Mr. Price. He's doesn't wear a hat. Not with all that product in his thinning hair. He keeps his aviator sunglasses on, and he folds his hands in front of his midsection like he wants to make sure he doesn't accidentally touch anything.

"Shay," Grandpa starts, and then his words seem to fail him. His rheumy eyes take on a shine like they do when he's overcome.

I flash him a sad smile. I didn't mean to screw things up so badly. He really saved my ass when Mama said I'd have to pay my share of rent if I wanted to keep on living with her. I would've had to drop out if he didn't take me in.

He gave me a shot, and I blew it. My heart aches over that.

"Shay," Mr. Wall awkwardly clears his throat and takes over. He looks like his son. Handsome. Blue eyes so pale they're unnatural. Muscular and weathered from hard work outside. "We're, uh, here to talk to you."

He pauses. Waits.

What am I supposed to say? Eventually, I kind of nod.

He nods back and begins again, gruff and uncertain. "The other day—uh—my boy, Cash, he came to me with a—uh—very disturbing rumor."

Mr. Wall focuses awkwardly over my shoulder out the bay window. Nothing to see out there except the cans where we burn trash, and the creek that floods when it rains.

"Shay," Mr. Price interjects. His voice booms. Confident. Irritated. "There are rumors going around the high school—and we're not accusing you of spreading these rumors, necessarily, but we need to put this to rest because rumors like this can destroy lives. Do you understand that?"

Connie glares at me from the kitchen. Grandpa's face is crestfallen. I'm his favorite. He loves me almost more than the horses. Of all his grandkids, I'm the one he calls when a mare foals or the Walls buy a new stud. I don't care much for horses, but I will never let on; he loves them, and I love him.

When I don't answer quick enough, the sheriff takes over. "If this rumor was true, and obviously it ain't, but if it were, one of my men, a stellar, up-and-coming young officer—" The sheriff flashes Mr. Wall a prodigiously butt-kissing look. "Well, he could lose his job. His livelihood. His future."

"Why?" I know the rules are different in Stonecut County, but come on. The town golden boy is gonna lose his job over loose talk?

"Because if the rumor is true—and it's not, of course—but if it *were* true, I would have to arrest Kellum for statutory, uh, offenses," the sheriff stutters, avoiding the other men's eyes. He's treading very carefully. Everyone knows that Mr. Wall and Mr. Price own this county.

They breed derby winners at Stonecut Farms, and horses that foreign princes buy for hundreds of thousands of dollars. Everything new and nice in this county has a plaque on it thanking the Wall or Price families.

"If an officer is accused of that kind, of, uh, crime—he can't be a police officer," the sheriff finishes, falling silent.

No one speaks.

Everyone stares at me.

My cheeks flame. Well, shit. I didn't know that.

I have a rock lodged in my throat. I cram my hands in my sweatshirt pouch. There's an old lollipop in there that Pandy gave me days ago. I twirl the stick in my fingers.

The men cast stern looks in my direction. The sheriff shuffles in place. Mr. Price coughs to prod me along.

"I'm seventeen," I say.

Connie sniffs in the kitchen. Outside, a vehicle skitters down our asphalt road. Pandy's husband, Lonnie. His truck door slams, and his boots pound up the steps to their trailer. There are only four units here for people like Grandpa who work at Stonecut Farms, but they're close together. You can hear everything.

After a minute, it gets quiet again.

Finally, the sheriff breaks the silence. "See, uh. Miss Crowder. There's a corruption of minors statute in this state. Age of consent is sixteen, yes, but not if the, uh, fella is twenty-four."

Kellum Wall is twenty-four? I knew he was older than me, but I figured he was closer to twenty, although twenty-four makes sense if I stop a minute to do the math.

The first time I saw him, I was a kid. Mama was between places to stay, and she'd foisted me off on Grandma and Grandpa for a few weeks. It was fall. On Friday nights, they religiously attended the Stonecut County high school football games. Everyone in town did.

Chapter 1

Kellum was the star quarterback, even though he was only a freshman. He sprinted up and down that field like there was a force field around him. No one could touch him. I've never seen anything like it since, and the high school back home regularly makes it to state.

The sheriff draws in a deep breath, and I shake off the cobwebs. "Not sayin' that Kellum did what the rumor mill says. That's why we're here. To clear this up, before lives get ruined. These kinds of accusations...they can take on a life of their own."

"Listen," Mr. Price interjects, sliding off his sunglasses. Kellum's uncle is what Grandma would have called a cool customer. "I think we can be blunt. Miss Crowder, we all know that Kellum Wall did not get you pregnant. We've all known him since he was a baby—even your grandfather here has known him his whole life."

Grandpa's ruddy cheeks flame a deeper red. He better have been taking his medicine. Oh, Lord. My heart skips and my palms slick with sweat. The lollipop in my pocket keeps slipping from my fingers.

"Varsity his freshman year, took us to state three years in a row. He got offers from Ohio, Mississippi, everywhere." Mr. Price lists out on his fingers. "But Kellum decided to stay in his hometown to serve his community. This is a good kid. Always has been. He's got himself a really sweet girlfriend. He's getting ready to settle down and start a family. You might think you're just getting yourself some attention, young lady, but he has a future. You're playing with fire."

He has a girlfriend? My heart sputters and sinks until I'm weak-kneed and trembling. Thank the Lord I'm sitting.

How can he have a girlfriend? No one at that party said. And people would have talked. We were dancing so everyone could see.

And not just a girlfriend, but a woman he's gonna marry. 'Cause he's twenty-four and a cop. And he has a *future*.

My ears ring. I'm in trouble. Trouble, trouble, trouble. And I was *so* stupid.

"Van, please." Mr. Wall puts a hand on Mr. Price's arm, urging him backwards. Then Mr. Wall squats down, inches from my face.

I have no room to breathe at all now. I press my spine into the back of the couch.

"It can't be easy making your way in a new place. People make mistakes. It's what they do after the mistake that's important." Mr. Wall's pale blue eyes bore into me, fixing me to the spot like a bug on a pin.

It's boiling hot in here. So stuffy. It's early fall, but we're having a heat wave, and it's in the high eighties. Sweat trickles between my boobs.

I can't breathe, and I'm being cooked to death.

I'm so screwed.

The men have shifted, edging Grandpa out to the kitchen with Connie. Her face is scrunched and sour. She won't meet my eye.

Neither will Grandpa.

"All we want is the truth." Mr. Wall lays his hand on my knee. I want to knock it off. I don't dare.

"You tell the truth, this ends here. Buck is one of our best hands. We don't want to lose him," Mr. Price says. Mr. Wall shoots him a look over his shoulder.

Grandpa sucks in a short gasp and stiffens.

Oh, shit. Oh, shit. Oh, shit.

Grandpa can't lose this job. It's his life. He loves those horses more than anything in the world. And if he loses the job, he'll lose the trailer. Where will he live?

These men are all too close. And they *reek*. I smell two different types of cologne and tobacco, and the sheriff had Italian for lunch. My stomach heaves. I swallow hard.

"We have to consider that there is a point where spreading rumors is slander. And slander is against the law in Stonecut County." The sheriff tucks his thumbs in his belt and sways on his feet.

Mr. Wall shoots the sheriff another agitated look. Mr. Wall wants to play this nice, but his friends aren't going along.

Chapter 1

That slander thing's an obvious lie. If rumors were illegal, everyone in America would be in jail. That's not saying the sheriff wouldn't find something else. Back home, if you get on the wrong side of the guy who rides around the trailer park in a golf cart looking to hassle people, he'll get you towed. And he's only a guy in a black T-shirt that says SECURITY.

Mr. Wall turns back to me, holding me fast again with those strange blue eyes. "Young lady, all we want is the truth. If my son did what he's accused of doing, we will make it right. If he committed a crime, he will face the consequences like a man. But if this is a story, if you had anything to do with spreading it around, you need to do the right thing. Tell the truth. My son could lose his job, the woman he plans to marry, the respect of this community. I'm asking you, one person to another—tell the truth."

What does he mean "face the consequences"? Could Kellum go to jail? They'd never arrest him. Would they?

Back home, the rich kids get away with everything, and from what I've seen so far, that's how Stonecut County works, too.

But I don't want Kellum Wall to get arrested. Even after everything, I still have a stubborn sweet spot for him.

My gut churns.

There's a patch in the couch next to my thigh where the upholstery has worn through, and you can see the orange cushion underneath. Grandma would have been absolutely mortified. All these important men in her house, and there's a hole in the couch. Not to mention Connie in her kitchen. She's turning over in her grave.

What am I gonna do?

I'm in such big trouble.

And where's Kellum? His father, his uncle, and his boss are here. Where's he?

Goddamn Pandy Bullard. She's the one who got me in this mess. She convinced me to get all dolled up and go to that bonfire. She told Kellum Wall that I was her cousin from Pyle when I caught his eye. Made up a whopper about how I'm a hairdresser. She's the one running her mouth all over town now.

My fist clenches around the lollipop stick in my pocket.

The sheriff breaks the silence. "Maybe we should take this conversation down to the station. We are talking about a crime here. We're trying to settle this privately, but if you're not going to cooperate Miss Crowder..."

Grandpa shuffles in alarm.

Connie sneers at me, victory in her eyes. She knows. After this, I'm out of her hair, one way or the other.

These men can do anything they want. They can walk in this house like they own it. 'Cause they do. All these trailers belong to Mr. Wall. He's the landlord. Doesn't matter that Grandpa has lived here my entire life. They could put him out tomorrow.

The sheriff could arrest me for slander or anything he can make up. Who would stop him?

And Mr. Price. That man has grabbed my ass or grazed my boobs a half-dozen times down at the Over Easy Diner where I work. Because he can. He's got his own helicopter and flies in for weeks at a time from the city, and then flies out again whenever he wants.

If I say anything, I don't work at the diner anymore. That's for sure.

I'm a problem to these men.

I'm a threat to their golden boy.

"Young lady, we *know* Kellum Wall never touched you. That never happened." Mr. Price drops his good manners. His black eyes glint. "We aren't going to let a girl like you ruin an innocent man's life."

My heart pounds. The living room shrinks. The hot air is thick and suffocating. My eyes flit from face to face then settle on the far wall above the TV. Connie hasn't gotten around to taking down the pictures yet.

There's Grandpa with his favorite horses over the years. Itchy Bramble. Geodesic. Frampton Lee.

Chapter 1

There's an old picture of Mama and her four brothers and sisters, like stair steps. Grandpa's standing off to the left. Grandma's in the middle, hugging Aunt Donna and Mama close to her sides.

Grandma raised five children on her own while Grandpa raised horses for the Walls. *Five.* And except for Mama and Uncle Pete, they all turned out more-or-less fine. They live all over the place now: Texas, Kansas City, the Carolinas. They all made their way.

Mr. Wall is right. It's what you do after you make the mistake that matters. I can't reverse time. I can't take anything back.

"Where's Kellum?" I ask, but I'm stalling now. I know what I have to do.

There's a pause, and then Mr. Wall says, "If he did this thing you're accusing him of, it's not appropriate that he be here." His gravelly voice is strangled, and his face flushes dark.

I'm not accusing Kellum Wall of anything. I never did. Goddamn Pandy Bullard's the one who can't keep her mouth shut.

"Miss Crowder, I have to insist you answer the question. Are you saying you're pregnant by Kellum Wall?" The sheriff rests his hand on the butt of his pistol.

My breath stills in my lungs.

"No, sir," I say, my voice reed thin and unnaturally high. I take a deep breath and try again, making it firm. "There must have been some mistake."

Every person in the room sighs in relief.

Mr. Wall rises to his feet. "Young lady, you need to set this right."

I swallow. My mouth is bone dry. "I'm actually planning on goin' back to South Carolina. To finish out the school year."

"That's not good enough." Mr. Price looks at Grandpa meaningfully, the threat clear on his face.

No.

That's not how this works. Grandpa can't lose his job.

"Mr. Price." I don't know how to do what they do. Talk and say one thing, and make sure people know that you mean something else. But Grandpa can't pay for my stupid mistakes. I have to try. "As soon as I'm gone, the rumors will die down. Grandpa goes back to worrying over horses and not over me. And I'll finish school in South Carolina."

I catch his gaze and hold it. I try to put everything I mean into my eyes.

I'll go quietly. I won't be a problem. I understand what they're saying.

They are big. I am small.

What they say is possible, what they say is true, *that's* what happened. That's the truth.

I understand how the world works.

They don't need to fire Grandpa and kick him out of his home.

"All right, Miss Crowder. I see we understand each other." Mr. Price nods, dips his head to Grandpa and Connie, and ducks out the front door. The sheriff follows him. Mr. Wall stares at me a few moments longer, a question lingering in his pale-blue eyes. Then he leaves, too, shutting the door carefully behind him.

Connie's massive bosoms rise as she sucks in a deep breath, getting ready to rip me a new one.

I bolt for the bathroom. Like I did for the first two months or so, I turn on the fan and flush the toilet as I puke.

Grandpa and Connie's voices rise in the kitchen. They're having it out.

I slide to the floor, resting my head against the wall and drawing my knees to my chest. In this position, I can feel her. The baby. It's like soda pop bubbles really low in my belly. I've only been able to feel her for two weeks or so.

"It's all right, little one," I whisper so low I can hardly hear myself. "You're okay. Little bit of a change in plans, but when God closes a door, he opens a window."

Grandma always used to say that.

I don't believe in ghosts. Not all the way. But ever since I figured out the condom must have broke and I'm expecting, I swear I feel my grandma. Out by the line when I'm hanging up the wash. Walking next to me during the quarter mile to the school bus stop.

Lord knows, Mama and Uncle Pete turned out as disappointments to her, but she never stopped loving them, and she loved her grandkids so fiercely that we all know what a mother does, regardless of whether we had a good one or not.

Grandma would have never let those men near me. Grandma would kill Kellum Wall.

"We'll go back to South Carolina. I'll get a job. Everything'll be fine."

That's what a good mother does. She tells her baby everything is going to be okay.

Even if it's not.

I unwrap my pocket lollipop and stick it in my mouth. It's butterscotch. It takes away the awful vomit taste in my mouth, but my heart's still racing, and my fingers tremble.

I'm scared.

"Everything's okay, baby." I wind my arms around my knees. "We're gonna be just fine."

And to comfort myself, just for a minute before I have to haul my ass back up off the floor, I let myself remember. One last time.

Music blaring from a Jeep, Kellum shuffling his boots off beat, hands wrapped around my waist, smiling and chagrined, the flames from the bonfire making his blue eyes sparkle like sapphires.

"I can't dance a lick," he said, sheepish, smiling softly.

"Then why'd you ask me?"

"I wanted to touch you. Seemed the likeliest bet."

His hand holding mine in the woods full of night sounds, laughter and music in the distance, the silver moon round and impossibly big, hung over the river by magic. How could something so big and low not fall?

Kellum's rough fingers, gentle on my cheek. "Don't look at the moon. Look at me."

His kiss, so scorching and ravenous that it scrambled my brain, and everything flying by so quickly—my breasts bare, his hands between my legs, his hot tip nudging my core and then plunging to the hilt—I couldn't catch my breath. I could only feel.

And then after, when I was sticky and sore on the mossy bank, the water babbling past, bull frogs honking, his smile tender and warm, his gaze unwavering, taking me in, he said, "Come on. Let's swim."

"I can't."

"We'll stay close to shore. I won't let you go." *I'd believed him. I'd clung to him, trusting him not to let me go.*

The water—cool but not too cold—lapping my calves, then my knees, then the juncture of my thighs, soothing the burn as we waded deeper and deeper, right into the moon's reflection.

"You're so beautiful."

His lips soft and firm. Still hungry.

His friend calling out from the bank. Something happened. They needed help.

His strong grip as he led me back to the bank, saying, "Wait here. I won't be long."

Waiting, shivering in the night breeze, my wet skirt stuck to my thighs. The soreness between my legs throbbing. A crack in the woods. My heart leaping.

But it was nothing. An animal, maybe, or the wind.

I've been holding on so tight to the memory, sneaking it out every night, every spare moment, admiring it like a jewel, a treasure easily stolen, easily broken.

I suck down a breath, and I force myself to keep remembering.

I waited by the river until my teeth were chattering.

Until the moon had shrunk to its usual proportions.

Then I trekked back to the bonfire, following the muted sounds of drunken shrieks, panties ripped, palms red and raw from where I'd braced against a tree.

Pandy was leaving. I didn't see Kellum Wall anywhere. I got in her car, and it hurt to sit.

On our way out, we saw Kellum and some others towing a

truck out of a ditch, the front end crumpled from where it hit a tree.

I'd raised my hand. He didn't see.

He never called.

I did. He cut me off. He blocked my number.

That night wasn't magic. This isn't a fairy tale.

I'm huddled on the warped tile floor of a trailer bathroom, knocked up, and screwed.

There's no more time for pretty stories. Kellum Wall isn't coming back to save me. He's no knight in shining armor. He's a prettier version of all the men who've tromped through Mama's life, all sweet talk until they get what they wanted, and then they're gone.

I grab the edge of the vanity, haul myself to my feet, and splash cold water on my face.

I need to pack and get the hell out of Stonecut County.

2

SIX YEARS LATER

KELLUM

I almost don't see him.

My eyes are dry and bleary, and my head's pounding.

I'm cruising down Main Street across the Old Mill Bridge, going fifteen miles per hour. I needed to get out of the station.

Del is locked in his office with the Feds. Last night, over a bottle of whiskey at Birdy's, he finally came clean to me. Admitted he's been asked to answer some questions. The Feds got wind of that article Ken Dobbs' girl wrote for the paper, and they opened an investigation.

He might need to step back; I might need to step up. It's nothing; it'll blow over, but it's gonna be a pain in the ass until it does.

I'm not excited about doing the public relations work. That's not why I signed up. Ever since that night on the Albanstown Road when I was thirteen and John and I helped Del pull that SUV out of a ravine, I wanted to be a cop. Not a politician. I don't give a shit what's pinned on my chest. That was one of the bones of contention in my marriage.

Elizabeth called the office this morning. She wants to talk about the Harvest Day Parade already. It's on the list, but the list is long, and it's months away. I'm thinking about how to get out of it when I notice the man on the bridge. I'm already a few yards past when I jerk the wheel, pulling onto the shoulder.

It's Billy McAllister, high as a kite, weaving around on the waist-high wall, a baby in his arms. The river's fifty feet below.

His thin ankle bends, his sneaker wobbles on the edge of the stone wall, and the baby wails.

Fuck. Fuck.

I fumble for the radio. "Dispatch."

"Go ahead."

"Thirty-three. Ten-eighteen. All units. Old Mill Bridge." Does anyone even remember the codes? "There's a man with a baby on the bridge. He's gonna jump. All units."

"Shit, Kell. Is it Billy McAllister?"

"Affirmative."

"Nancy's on the line with Mindy. Hold on—"

There's a muffled conversation in the background. "Kell, he has the baby. He has Alyssa."

"Affirmative. Get Del down here. All units."

"Oh, God. Kell, that baby's not even a month old."

"I'm out. Send everyone. No sirens." I exit the vehicle as slowly as I can with my adrenaline spiking and my heart slamming in my chest.

Billy stumbles, swaying. He cackles to himself.

I'm nowhere near close enough.

"Hey. Billy. Whoa." I sound like my brother Jesse with the damn horses.

I edge closer to the wall. Will he let me get up there with him?

He's staring past me to the cruiser. I vault up on the wall, and ease slowly from a crouch to my feet, hands raised high where he can see them.

His eyes find me and widen. His pupils are blown.

"Stop there. Don't come closer."

"Okay, man."

There's seven feet between us.

He shuffles his feet, not looking where he's going, and his heels hang over the edge again. He's clutching the baby to his chest. Way too tight. The baby's too young to hold her head up, so it's lolling to the side.

Dispatch told me the baby's name. Damn. What was it? Alicia? Alyssa.

"Why don't you let me hold Alyssa? We can talk."

"Fuck you, man. That bitch sent you, didn't she? Did she tell you she's fucking the neighbor? She's been fucking him for years. This baby probably ain't even mine."

This isn't just drugs. I've seen him high. I've been busting him and his buddies for blazing up behind the Gas-and-Go since he was in junior high. He mouths off, but he goes quietly.

He's got to be off his meds. Probably when his Gram passed a few months back, no one bothered filling the prescription anymore.

"Billy, let's talk this through."

"She's always on the porch. Always on her phone. What's she doin' on her phone, huh?"

"I don't know, man. But this isn't the way."

"This isn't the way," he mimics, voice high, edged with hysteria. His gaze wanders to the river below.

If I lunge, he'll have more than enough time to jump. The bridge is high. Five stories above the Luckahannock. A few years back, an older man jumped. A vet. We fished him out at the shallows where the river bends east.

He'd been in the water too long to know what killed him, whether it was the force of impact or drowning. His lungs were filled with water, but he had a dozen broken bones as well.

Either way it was a bad death.

"Listen, Billy. I get it. Let's talk it through. What's the plan, brother?"

He snorts. "I ain't your brother. I ain't a *Wall* or a *Price*." He drawls the words. "Wasn't born with that silver spoon. Don't got my name on half the shit in the county."

Point of fact, there's a bronze plaque at the entrance to this bridge. My family's name is etched on it above Van's.

I've found my name opens a lot of doors, draws a lot of attention, but it does shit-all in moments like this when the chips are down.

The baby cries. She's so small that the wind whips most of the sound away.

"Please. Billy. Alyssa didn't do anything. Let me hold her. We can talk."

Sweat trickles down my back, itching like a motherfucker.

These aren't the right steps. There was a workshop. Two years ago. In Pyle. I can remember the room, the hotel overlooking the park. There was a presentation. A guy from the FBI field office. He was wearing a teal sweater vest.

What the *fuck* did it say on the slides?

I can picture them in my head. What were the words?

"Please, man. We can fix this."

"Fix it?" He cackles. "I told you. I ain't a Wall. I don't roll with the sheriff. Millionaires in black ops helicopters don't fly into town to rain cash on me so I can prance around town like I'm the king." He does a little mocking dance, knees high, and the baby's head bounces.

I raise my hands higher, my gut cramping. Too far. He's too far away.

"I got *real* problems." He stops, teetering, his ankle bending again.

Is it now? Is this the moment? My body primes, every muscle impossibly taut.

"You don't even know what real people go through, man."

"So talk to me. What's goin' on, Billy?"

He huffs. "But you got real problems, too. Don't you? I heard the lady from Channel Thirteen put you out," he crows. "News at eleven. Deputy Dumbass kicked to the curb."

Empathize. That was one of the slides. Empathize.

"Yeah. My wife and I split. It was hard, man." His weight is on his heels. He's not going to jump. Not right this second.

"Yeah, so hard. Like there ain't a line of bitches forming to take her place. I bet Beth would pay to fuck you. Did you fuck her? Fuckin' whore."

He rocks back, the heels of his sneakers see-sawing over the edge. I brace. Prepare. He shuffles forward. I exhale.

If I tackle him, twist to the side, he'll hit the concrete. Maybe crush the baby. Dash her head against the stone. If I get the angle wrong—if the velocity is off—I push him off the bridge.

The baby's face is bright red, and her eyelids are drooping. She's cried herself out. She's in a pink onesie with an elephant holding a rainbow umbrella in his trunk.

There are finger marks on her thin arms.

Oh, God.

I need words. What do I say?

I go to church every Sunday. Sit in the family pew. Dutifully repeat the words.

But until this moment, I never really prayed.

Please, God. What do I say?

Billy flashes a toothless grin. "She's gonna be sorry after today, boy. Lemme tell you. She's gonna regret *all* the shit she's done." He pats the baby on the back. "You got regrets, Deputy? Or do you really think you're the good guy? I'm gonna tell you something—"

He leans over, as if to tell me a secret. That's it. Come closer.

"You're no better than the rest of us at the end of the day. A grade-A fuck up who doesn't know what's really going on." He laughs. "Later, asshole."

His feet don't move.

He doesn't jump.

He throws the baby.

Hikes her high in the air. She's a ragdoll, floppy against a bright blue sky and a glaring mid-day sun.

I'm too far away.

Chapter 2

I run. Two steps to get speed before I leap. Arms extended, obliques straining, reaching, stretching.

My eye isn't on the ball. It's on where the ball is going to be.

My fingertips graze soft skin.

There's only time to tuck, and then I fall, slamming through the surface, my limbs slicing through the water, knocking the breath from my lungs. I shoot to the bottom, the freezing cold raking my skin, an electric shock to the system.

I gasp without thinking, sucking down a mouthful of gritty river water.

Pain explodes in my chest.

There's no up. I can't see. My brain's a jumble; my muscles have seized. It burns. The cold, my bones. Energy is leeching from me, second by second.

Where is up?

I fight. Kick my legs. My utility belt drags me down. My boots drag me down. There's no direction down here, only freezing fire in my lungs and chest, and a rushing roar in my ears.

Everything is unmoored. I secure the baby to my chest and thrash through the murky dark with my other arm. Am I dragging us further down?

Is this it?

Do I die now, and at the end, is this the thought I have? Everything is wrong. Upside down. Over too soon and pointless.

What have I done that was worth doing?

What do I have that means anything?

I'm going to lose it all, and in the end, it's not much at all.

The river is cold, and it's too late now to choose more wisely. I press the baby closer with a numbing hand. I don't want her swept away in the current.

I am so sorry.

My feet jolt on the rocky bottom, and I push straight up. I kick with every ounce of strength I have left, every bone and nerve in agony.

We break the surface.

I've got her. I've still got her.

There are distant shouts overhead. I gulp crisp air, choking, and I struggle to my back. I have to stay afloat.

Oh, God. Where's the baby?

She's here. Right here, on my chest. Limp and quiet. But she's breathing. Oh, Lord. She's breathing.

Thank you.

She's so small. I can cover most of her with the palm of my hand.

Sirens wail in the distance. Far overhead, a hawk glides on an updraft.

"Oh, my God! There he is! He's caught the baby. He has the baby!"

"Is she alive?"

"She's alive!"

I breathe out.

Everything in my life is messed up. My marriage is over. From what Del told me last night, the Sheriff's office is in trouble. I might lose my job, or end up in court, testifying against my own godfather who raised me.

I've broken at least a few ribs. Maybe my collarbone.

Everything is wrong. I can't find the way up.

But the baby is safe.

There is one thing right in the world.

3

SIX MONTHS LATER

SHAY

"Miss Crowder, you need to calm down," Principal Rice says.

No, I don't. My daughter's not safe. I don't need to do shit.

I push back in my chair and stare down the folks around the table, one-by-one, forcing them to look me in the eye. Everyone and their mother is here for this meeting 'cause I've become the squeaky wheel. The school psychologist. Principal Rice. A lady from the central office who everyone defers to even though she's never even met Mia and keeps calling her Mya.

Mia's teacher and her caseworker shift in their chairs. They know this is crap, but they're outnumbered and outranked.

"Shay." Mia's teacher, the only one not shrinking from my glare, reaches over and touches my wrist. "This is an IEP *team* meeting. We're going to work together to figure out what's best for Mia."

Mrs. Ellis has done a lot for Mia this year. Mia even spoke to her a few times.

I unclench my fists, take a deep breath, and try again. "Y'all are talking like Mia doesn't know what's happening around her. Just because she won't talk to you doesn't mean she can't talk. She talks all the time at home."

Slight exaggeration, but I'm making a point here. "She says this little boy is hurting her, and she comes home with the bruises to prove it. And y'all won't do anything about it."

Mrs. Ellis explained to me on the down low that the teachers aren't allowed to talk about the other children. And she explained about something called "manifestation of disability."

What she means is that since Bryce Adams has special needs like Mia does, he can punch and kick and pinch her all he wants, and they can't put him out. It's against the law. Of course, they could get Bryce a one-on-one helper like the Pruitt boy has, but they don't want to pay for that.

"Miss Crowder, we want to assure you that we do everything in our power to provide a safe and appropriate learning environment for all the children at Back River Elementary." Principal Rice casts a sidelong glance toward the lady from the central office. She wants to make sure her boss is getting this.

"We are, of course, compelled to abide by the provisions of federal law and local policies when it comes to the delivery of instruction and administration of consequences, but we will do everything in our power to provide the support to make sure Mia meets with success." She finishes, flashing a fake smile and checking her watch. Just in case I haven't gathered that she's an important woman with places to be.

Principal Rice likes to lay on the big words until you get tired and give up. She tries to confuse you, make you think you're the dumb one, and that she knows her business, so best leave her to it. Mia's only in kindergarten, but it's far from my first rodeo with this woman.

Principal Rice was my guidance counselor in high school. She's the one who convinced me it'd be easier to drop out and take the G.E.D. than to finish school with a newborn. I don't know if she was right, but I don't have a diploma, and I never got the G.E.D.

Chapter 3

That's water under the bridge, though. I regroup and try again. "Bryce Adams is hurting my child, and you're letting it happen. If you won't stop him, move Mia back into the normal class."

The lady from the county tuts. "Mrs. Crowder, we don't have 'normal' classes in Fairview County. We provide differentiated services to meet the needs of our diverse learners. This team decided the functional support program was the most appropriate learning environment for Mia. You agreed to the placement." She starts rooting through her papers as if she's gonna show me my signature.

I signed it. I remember. And I regret it every damn day.

Principal Rice said there would be fewer kids and more adults. Mia would get more attention and help on her language skills. When she has her meltdowns, they're trained to handle it so she doesn't hurt herself.

They didn't say anything about the boy almost two years older than Mia and fifty pounds heavier who terrorizes that classroom—including the teachers—on a daily basis. Bryce needs more help than they can give, and Mrs. Ellis keeps asking, but no one listens to her.

"Mrs. Schaeffer's class," I say, although Principal Rice knows damn well what I mean. "Move Mia back to Mrs. Schaeffer's class."

"That's not on the table for this meeting."

I grit my teeth. They've got lots of rules for the meetings. Meetings to get permission to test. Meetings to go over assessments. Annual meetings. They start late, go long, and nothing gets done except I get docked half-a-day's pay, piss off my manager at Food Fiesta, and lose hours on my schedule until she decides to stop being mad.

I called this meeting, though. Don't that mean I say what's on the table?

"What *is* on the table then? We can't talk about Bryce hitting Mia. You won't do anything about it. Why are we here then?"

"We're here for Mya," the lady from the central office says.

"Mia," I say between clenched teeth. Mrs. Ellis lays her hand on my forearm under the table and pats.

I suck down a breath. More than one way to skin a cat. "Well, how about you get Bryce Adams one of those helpers? I know his mama; she says she's asked for one."

"Mrs. Crowder, we are not permitted to talk about other students."

"Then get Mia a helper."

"That's not on the table."

For the number of people *around* this table, there is a remarkable lack of shit *on* it.

Principal Rice sighs, long-suffering. "Dr. Anderson. Perhaps you could share your perspective?" She throws the ball to the only man in the room.

Dr. Anderson blinks and rustles in his chair like we woke him up. He's over sixty with bifocals and a rumpled tan suit. He shops at Food Fiesta. Never puts his cart back.

"Ah. Yes. Let me see." He flips through a thick folder. How can a six-year-old have a file so big?

Mia's not that messed up. She was born six weeks early, and her lungs weren't the best. She has asthma, but it's only bad in ragweed season.

She didn't start talking when she was supposed to. She didn't say anything at all until she was nearly four, and then only to me, but she knows the words for things.

Storms and crowds and too many noises freak her out, but if you give her space, let her do her thing, she calms down.

She's an odd duck, but she's crazy smart. She knows the name of every critter that lives in the swamp behind Mama's trailer, and their calls, and what the calls mean, and if they migrate, when they're due to leave and come back.

I'd like to meet another kindergartener who can tell a muskrat from a vole with only a glimpse at its hindquarters.

There's nothing wrong with my child. Plenty of folks are a lot worse off.

Chapter 3

Dr. Anderson hacks into a genuine fabric handkerchief and adjusts his glasses. "Well, to be honest Mrs. Crowder, it was very difficult to conduct the assessments. As you know, Mia is nonverbal."

"She talks fine," I interrupt. "She's shy at school. I've told y'all."

Everyone is silent. No one calls me a liar, but it's written on all of their faces. Even Mrs. Ellis.

Dr. Anderson clears his throat and plows ahead. "Nonverbal or selectively mute. Because Mia was unable or unwilling to engage, many of these assessments are inconclusive. I can say her visual-spatial skills fall in the above average range. She can identify objects and patterns. It continues to be her communication skills that we're all concerned about."

"I'm worried about the little boy beating her up every day." I cross my arms.

Dr. Anderson shoots me a look of disapproval. "Miss Crowder, we have to face the facts if we want to help Mia. We have to focus on her needs."

She needs that boy to leave her alone.

I have to drag her into this school every morning now, and Mrs. Ellis has to physically pry her off of me so I can go to work. And this is a child who hates touch. Hates snuggling. Always has, even as a baby.

"The functional support classroom is the most appropriate placement for Mia at this time. Have you talked to the pediatrician?" he asks.

There is no pediatrician. I take her to the clinic in Wylie. Different doctor every time. One said she's fine, give it time. Another wanted me to take her all the way to Charleston for testing.

A third gave me a checklist, but when I brought it back, there was a new doctor, and he put it in her file, and then the next time it wasn't there. So now I've got a new checklist filled out and sitting on my desk for her next appointment.

"How about I worry about Mia, and y'all worry about Bryce Adams hitting the other children?"

"Miss Crowder, it is important that we all keep a civil tone so that we can have a productive meeting," Principal Rice interjects, preachy as ever.

She sounds exactly the same as when she was Mrs. Rice and she called me to her office, scowling at my round belly as she handed me the withdrawal papers.

Like I said, not my first rodeo.

Principal Rice likes problems to disappear.

It'd be different if I *was* Mrs. Crowder like that lady from the central office keeps calling me. If I had a man sitting next to me, someone else on my side. It might be "yes sir, yes ma'am" then. But I'm on my own.

And this is going nowhere.

"Miss Crowder, we are trying a new thing during morning circle. It's called social-emotional learning, and—"

I scrape my plastic chair back, cutting Mrs. Ellis off. I feel bad, but I'm done.

"Pardon, Mrs. Ellis." I stare down Principal Rice. "I'm gonna tell you what. You do what you need to do. Mia comes home with one more mark on her body that wasn't there in the morning, I'm pulling her from this school. And then I'm gonna go on down to Appleville to the legal services and tell them about how y'all are out of compliance with Mia's IEP."

Every one of them straightens in their chair. Mrs. Ellis told me to say that. *Out of compliance.*

"On that paper I signed, it says Mia gets an hour of speech services every week. And she hasn't had speech in months."

"Mrs. Crowder, we explained to you that the speech pathologist is out on maternity leave," Principal Rice stands too, glowering at me over the wire-rimmed glasses perched on the tip of her nose. "As you are well aware, we've been making all efforts to secure the services of another speech pathologist."

"That's your problem, Principal Rice. Just like Bryce is Mia's problem since you won't give that child what he needs. The paper is law, and it says one hour of speech per week." I poke my finger at the packet in front of me. It's Greek to me, but Mrs. Ellis told me what's in it.

"This is not the way to resolve the issue." Principal Rice draws herself up, boxy shoulders nearly to her ears.

I hike my chin. "I've said my piece. Ball's in your court."

I grab my purse and sail from the room, nose in the air. I keep it there until I'm a quarter mile away, turning onto Route 12 where the sidewalk ends. I tromp along the road, cornflowers and thistles whipping at my ankles, baking under the late afternoon sun.

For this meeting, I borrowed Mama's khaki slacks and a pastel pink button-down shirt. The elastic hardly holds up the drawers, and the shirt strains and gapes across my tits. The fabric is made of some space age material that's impervious to moisture, so as I walk, the pants slap against my sweat-slick thighs.

I tug my purse higher on my shoulder. Maybe someone from Blazing Trails will drive by and give me a ride. Hopefully not Willie Smith. Mama's newest live-in has a 90s sedan that still runs, but that's all he's got going for him. He's a drinker and a leech.

On second thought, I'd be happy to see Willie. That would mean he's not at home. Mia's already there by now—the last bell rang while I was in the meeting, and she's on the first bus wave—and she and Willie don't get along.

Willie figures she's being ornery when she doesn't talk and won't meet his eyes. Mia figures he's garbage. At least that's what I gather. I don't disagree with her. He's been working his way from trailer-to-trailer, one lonely woman to the next. Only reason he didn't cozy up to Mama sooner is 'cause we live all the way at the back of the park on Twelfth Street.

I trudge along, no cars pass, and I'm thirsty as hell with a pounding headache when I reach the turnoff to our trailer park.

I hope with all my heart that the school decides the juice isn't worth the squeezing, and they move Mia back to Mrs. Schaeffer's class.

Appleville was a bluff. How am I gonna get there? And I can't get Mama her rent if I miss any more shifts this month.

She hasn't followed through on her threats to put me out when I've been short before, but she didn't have Willie before to make up the difference, either.

All of this is whirling through my mind when I finally reach our dusty dirt road. The crickets are chittering, and the air is thick with humidity.

And Willie Smith is passed out in his dingy boxers, half-on and half-off the bottom step to the porch.

The front door's wide open. Mia is standing there, stuffed rabbit in one hand, her other hand fisted at her side. She's got one of her plastic critters in there.

I sprint the rest of the way, haul myself over Willie's carcass, and hustle Mia inside.

"He touch you?"

I'll murder him where he lies.

Mia shakes her head.

"He been there long?"

She nods.

"Was he there when you got home?"

Another nod. The bus drops her off on the main through road, but I guess the driver didn't bother to turn her head. Willie isn't hidden from sight. At all.

"How'd you get in? Climb over him?"

She wrinkles her nose and jerks her pointy chin toward the back. She let herself in the other door, thank the Lord.

"Is Grandma here?"

She shakes her head. I didn't figure.

I heave a sigh and shoo Mia to the kitchen. It's boiling hot. Mama must have unplugged the air conditioner again. Cash is tight early this month.

Mia hops up on the stool at the breakfast bar, and I pour milk in her red plastic lion cup.

I check the cupboard. No granola bars. Someone left the

empty box, though. I rummage in my purse and find a pack of peanuts at the bottom.

"Is it an ostrich?" I guess.

Mia solemnly shakes her head.

I dump the peanuts in a plastic bowl and set them between us.

"Is it a bird, then?"

Mia inclines her head.

The way her fist is bulging, it's a big one. "Flamingo?"

Mia rolls her eyes.

"Don't sass me, child. This is a difficult game. I deserve credit for getting the type of critter right on the first guess."

I nudge the peanuts toward her. She ignores them. I sigh. She won't eat at school. She needs her afternoon snack or she gets hunger headaches, and then she won't eat dinner. She's being stubborn today.

That's fair. Willie Smith in his dirty undies killed my appetite, too.

"Eagle?" I guess.

Silence.

"Duck."

Nothing.

"Duck."

She waits.

"Goose?"

Not even a twitch of her lip. I thought that was a good one.

I shake out my blouse, try to get some air on my sticky back, but it must be over ninety degrees in here. It's not gonna get bearable until past midnight, and Mia's a furnace. Maybe I'll sleep on the sofa tonight.

Crap. I can't do that with Willie in the house. I'm a light sleeper, but I can't risk him wandering into our room "by accident."

I close my eyes.

This can't go on.

How long 'til that boy at school really hurts her? What if there's no mark, and she doesn't tell me?

What happens when he goes after Mia, and she hides again? She's done that three times now, and once, it took them hours to find her. She was behind some boxes in the boiler room. She could have burned herself.

Those teachers can't be everywhere at once. They've found her so far, but what if she starts running instead? They might not be quick enough to catch her. That street in front of the school is two lanes and always busy.

Even if by some miracle Principal Rice agrees to move her back to Mrs. Schaeffer's class, how long before drunk and naked Willie stumbles into our room? He hasn't yet, but what are the odds he won't? Not good.

How long before Mia gets home and there's no one else here but him, and he's drunk and awake?

I prop my elbows on the counter and lower my head to my hands.

"Swan?" I say, blinking away the prickle of tears.

We can't stay here, but you need a one month's deposit to sign a lease.

Everything is a goddamn *can't*.

Can't save money 'cause I can't get enough hours at work.

Can't get a new job 'cause I don't have a car.

Can't get Mia out of Bryce Adams' class 'cause I signed a paper.

But I absolutely, positively cannot let Mia grow up thinking it's normal to step over drunk old men passed out on the front stoop with their limp dicks peeking out of the stained flap on their boxer shorts.

That's not a can't. It's a *won't*.

But there are no options.

Or are there?

What about Stonecut County?

My nerves come alive, jangling at the thought. I can't go back there.

Chapter 3

But there's an empty trailer. Grandpa passed two years ago, but Mama and Connie still talk. Connie's taken up with a man from town. She's moved in with him. The Walls said she could stay in the trailer—rent free—for as long as she wants. She's tryin' to figure out if she can rent it on the down low. So far, she's decided it's not worth the risk of the Walls finding out, but she's keeping it empty in case things don't work out with her new man.

In my experience, once Connie gets her foot in the door, she stays.

I'd only need a few months. I'd find a job. Save some money to start over somewhere else. I wouldn't stay in Stonecut. Mia could have a brand-new start in school. Normal classes. I wouldn't sign a paper this time.

Mia casts me a stinky look and starts rocking on her stool.

"All right, don't get impatient. I'm thinking." I try to picture the tube of animal figurines I bought with the birds in it. "Parrot?"

She snorts.

"Not a parrot. Lord, Mia, this one's tricky. Can't you give me a clue?"

She raps her knuckle on the countertop, impatient.

I cock an eyebrow.

She raises hers right back.

"Pigeon."

Mia rolls her eyes.

"Keep doin' that with your eyeballs, they'll roll right out of your head."

She grins. She always finds that amusing.

I can't move us to Stonecut County. What if I run into Kellum Wall? What if he sees Mia? It's a small town. We're gonna see him. It's unavoidable.

Will he walk by and pretend he doesn't know who I am? Who Mia must be to him?

Shit, has he forgotten?

I was nothin' but a cheap fuck, after all. I choke off the bitterness before it blooms and sours everything. I don't have time for it. Didn't then, don't now.

What if he sees her and realizes I could go after him for six years of support?

What would the sheriff, the big city millionaire, and the man who owns the town do if they decide they don't want Mia and me darkening their doorstep after all this time? They don't have Grandpa to threaten this time.

A retching sound floats through the screen door. Willie's puking on the steps.

Mia blinks at me.

"Parrot."

She tilts her head, frowning, nose scrunched.

"Crap. I said parrot already, didn't I? Okay. Penguin."

That earns me a small smile. She didn't think I'd remember that penguins are birds.

There's a groaning and grunting from the porch.

That's a lot of *what ifs*, but are any of them worse than *what is*?

We can keep our heads low. Are the rich folks really gonna remember me after all this time? I don't flatter myself. Grandpa knew how to get a hold of me, but I never got a call. Not when Mia was born. Not after. They knew, and they didn't care, or they didn't want to know. I didn't keep her a secret.

I bet I could sashay down Main Street with Mia, and none of them would look at us twice. Poor folks don't matter to rich folks like the Walls. I haven't been a problem to them this whole time, so there's no reason they'd bother with me.

A few months of living cheap, and we can come back and get our own place. Maybe in Chamberlain so Mia can go to a new school—no Bryce Adams, no Principal Rice.

It's a risk. It might end in disaster. I honestly don't understand people like the Walls well enough to predict what they'd do.

Willie staggers up the stairs and leans against the doorframe, panting as if he's run a mile. He belches and swipes drool from his mouth with the back of his hand.

Chapter 3

Mia gazes steadily at the space above my left ear, expectant.

There is nothing I wouldn't do for this child.

I love her—her bony elbows, her knobby knees, her big blue eyes that remind me of cotton candy. I love her odd ways and how, if it's peaceful, she doesn't seem to notice the wider world at all.

I bet she has no idea Willie's slumped against the doorframe there, scratching his balls. He doesn't register.

That's fine. I've got this covered. There is nothing I won't do for this child.

Even buy a bus ticket back to Stonecut County.

"Emu," I say.

She unfurls her fingers, blanched white from clutching the small plastic toy so hard for so long. She sets the emu very carefully on its tiny clawed feet.

"That's a big bird," I observe.

"Third biggest," she says in her tiny voice.

"You don't say?" I nudge the peanut bowl until it's right in front of her, and she pops one in her mouth.

Willie staggers to the couch, collapses with a groan, and turns on the TV.

"Get me a beer, would you?" he calls over.

I reach over and tuck a loose curl behind Mia's ear. "When you finish your snack, we're gonna embark on an adventure."

Mia doesn't pay me any mind. She's munching away and squinting at that emu.

"What's the biggest bird in the world?" I ask, just to hear her voice again.

She blinks and chomps away on her peanuts.

"On my own on that one, am I?"

That's all right. I can figure it out on my own.

I always have.

4

FOUR MONTHS LATER

KELLUM

I took a long lunch. Knew it was a mistake. Every time I take a long lunch, when I come back, the station's on fire. We share the building with the Stonecut Volunteer Fire Department. Once they brought some embers back on the truck. Didn't realize. That day when I came back from the diner, the place was literally smoking.

Usually it's metaphorical, though.

I try to come in with my head down, but the only thing Nancy and Bev at the front desk like more than gossip is busting my chops.

"You're late, Deputy," Bev sings as she grabs the ringing phone.

Both ladies swivel in their padded chairs. Nancy dyes her hair gray and Bev doesn't, and if not for that, you couldn't tell 'em apart from a distance. Both are pushing seventy. Both are never gonna retire.

"You get waylaid rescuing a lady tied to a railroad track?" Nancy chuckles, hand pressed over the receiver of her phone. I can hear the music. She's on hold.

I'm still getting press from the incident on the Old Mill Bridge. It's almost died down, but not quite. Nancy used to have to help

Chapter 4

me with my duty belt when I first started on the force. She's not impressed by me yet.

"I didn't get the call, Nance. You sleeping on the job?"

"Now, how could I sleep when this place is going crazy, and you're off gallivanting around town, looking for kittens to fetch out of trees."

I wouldn't say the place is going full-blown crazy. Del's door is shut. He's probably still in there with the lawyers. The guy who delivers the water jugs is waiting for a signature, and the guy who maintains the copier has it in pieces on the back counter.

There's a couple waiting in reception. Sarah Evans is nodding off in a chair. She must be using again. Ed Houser is with her, playing on his phone. They're an odd pair. He works down at the parts factory—has for decades—and it doesn't seem to bother him that she comes and goes.

"Ed here to report a robbery?"

Bev hangs up, signs for the water, and shakes her head. "Not this time, no." She leans forward and lowers her voice. "Sarah wants to talk to Del about her girl. Del says he already talked to her. Nothing he can do. She says she ain't leaving 'til he takes a report. He says he already took a report. We're at an impasse."

"Del tell you to hand it off to me when I came back?"

"He did." Bev smiles and winks. "You do have a way with the ladies."

Both women crack up. They find this very funny.

"Oh, that reminds me." Nancy rummages around on her desk until she finds a message slip under her keyboard. "Your ex called. She wants you to call her about the Harvest Day Parade."

"Aren't you divorced?" Bev asks for the hundredth time. We are. More than two years now.

"You can be friends with your ex," Nancy says, passing me the message. I shove it in my pocket. I'll probably forget it's there, and it'll end up in the wash.

Bev snorts. "I suppose. If they're the friendly type."

I make a show of peeling my sweaty shirt from my back. "It's a hot one."

I have to cut off the conversation before they get themselves started.

Bev narrows her eyes, assessing my damp pits. "It still a hundred degrees out there?"

"Feels like it."

"You've got a fresh shirt hanging on the door."

"Much obliged."

Bev gives me an indulgent frown. "Don't drop the dirty one on the floor like Del."

"Wouldn't dream of it. Give me a minute to settle in, then bring Sarah and Ed to my office?"

"Yes, sir." Bev gives me a saucy salute, and swivels back to her computer.

"You want coffee?" Nancy asks. "I put on a fresh pot a few minutes ago."

"Not now. Thank you, Nance."

As I head for my office, Sarah Evans is still conked out and listing over in her chair, and Ed's still deep in his phone. I take a minute to hang my hat on its hook, change my shirt, and scroll through email.

Since Del's been dealing with the investigation, he's forwarded me a lot of his obligations. Community meetings and planning committees and all sorts of business that must be dealt with at a desk. I hate being stuck behind a desk.

There's nothing urgent in my inbox, so I'm ready to go when Nancy brings Sarah and Ed back. Del mentioned the situation briefly the other day.

Sarah's daughter Rory finally had enough and left town: no notice, no note, no forwarding address. Sarah insists the girl is missing, but she's eighteen. Del ran her through the system. She's living in New York. He called, and they had a chat. She got herself a job at a restaurant and a place in Brooklyn.

Chapter 4

Good for her, getting a fresh start. Sarah's not taking it well, though.

Nancy shuts the door after my visitors shuffle in. Both have steaming Styrofoam cups of coffee in their hands. Sarah's is shaking slightly in her yellow-stained fingers.

Ed grunts as he lowers himself into a chair and stretches his legs.

"Deputy," he nods. He sips his drink and makes himself comfortable.

"Ed. Good to see you. Sarah."

Sarah has crossed her thin legs, and she's leaning forward, all bones and angles. Del says she discovered pills in high school, and she's been lost ever since. Heroin. Fentanyl.

Before she took up with Ed, she spent a lot of time in the holding tank. Racked up charges for prostitution, possession, public intoxication. Ed keeps a roof over her head, and if she's out of her mind, he'll come and get her.

I don't pretend to understand the relationship, but I'm not one to judge. My marriage was its own kind of mess.

"Del pawn us off on you?" Ed asks good-naturedly, scratching his belly.

"He did."

Ed chuckles. "Surprised you got time for us. Ain't you due for an interview somewhere?"

After the bridge incident, I was highly sought after. On local papers and TV stations, but also national programs. Apparently, I'm photogenic. Del asked me to do the interviews. The sheriff's office needs the good press. Bev and Nancy gave me a script of what to say, but I was still awkward as hell. I don't have the gift of gab.

"I'm yesterday's news." I force a smile. "Now, how can I help you folks?"

"My Rory is missing." Sarah swings her crossed leg and tightens her grip on her cup. "I told the sheriff, but he won't do anything."

Ed casts me an apologetic look. "He says she's eighteen, and he looked into it. She's fine."

"Then why won't he say where she is?"

"You remember, Sarah. He said he couldn't. Privacy."

Sarah snorts. "Bullshit. I'm her mother. And Rory wouldn't leave without saying anything."

Ed and I share a glance. Sarah herself has disappeared plenty of times over the years. She always turns up, but we've all fielded the calls. Before Ed was the one hunting her down, it was her parents.

"Del's briefed me on the case." Slight exaggeration. I'm remembering that he vaguely mentioned it in between bitching about the F.B.I. investigation and the ever-increasing number of nuisance complaints we get each day. "He ran her through the system. Everything checks out. He spoke to her. She left town of her own accord."

"Someone's got her." Sarah drums her fingers on the arm of her chair. "They could be making her say she's okay."

Ed rolls his eyes.

"Is there a reason you believe this?" I'm careful with my tone. I've learned a lot since I started this job. Half of the time, you don't know what you think you know. Truth is stranger than fiction.

"She had that good job up on the hill."

That's right. She cleaned for my folks and Van. Actually, I think she was friendly with my sister Dina, too. Dina's not like other folks. She doesn't take to people. But she liked Rory; I know that. She mentioned her, and she never mentioned people. I bet she's bummed that Rory left town.

"Is there anything else that has you concerned?"

I maintain eye contact, watch my tone. People won't tell you anything if you act like you've already made up your mind.

"She would have said goodbye." Sarah's eyebrows spear down. "And Pandy Bullard knows something."

I school my features. Pandy Bullard stirs up more drama in this county than any ten other people combined. She's the one

Chapter 4

who told me the girl at the bonfire, the one with the auburn hair, was her cousin from out of town. I was wasted that night. I didn't think to question her age. Turns out she was a minor. I didn't know 'til years later when Cash was reminiscing on a hunting trip.

Apparently, there'd been gossip at the time. Cash got coy and wouldn't spill all the details—he said it was total bullshit—but apparently, it could have turned real ugly. Especially since that night happened right before Elizabeth finally decided she wanted to stop doing the on-again, off-again thing and get serious.

The girl moved back to where she was from, though, and if Cash hadn't gotten drunk, I would've never known how badly I'd fucked up.

The old sick feeling of guilt creeps into my chest. The girl was so sweet, and I was a jackass.

Shit. Now is not the time. I shake my head to clear it, and I refocus. "Why do you think Pandy Bullard knows something?"

"Rory was staying with her before she went missing. I asked to see her room. Pandy wouldn't let me past the front door."

"Where does Pandy say Rory went?"

"She won't tell me anything. She says—" Sarah stops and scrubs roughly at her eyes. "She won't talk to me."

"She says that Rory left town," Ed volunteers.

"She'll talk to Ed, but she won't talk to me." Sarah starts jiggling her knee.

"Why was Rory staying with Pandy?" I'm careful to keep the accusation out of my voice, but Sarah bristles anyway.

"She'd graduated, hadn't she? She had a job. Pandy's place was closer to work."

"Rory is eighteen, correct?"

Sarah jerks her chin and stares past me out the open blinds of the window behind my desk, her eyes shiny with tears. "I know what you all think about me, but Rory wouldn't just leave. She's lived here her whole life. Everyone she knows is here in Stonecut County."

"Del spoke to her. She left town. There is no evidence of foul play."

"What did she say?"

"I don't know the specifics."

"Someone could have been making her say she's okay." Sarah rises abruptly to her feet. Ed blinks in surprise, but he lumbers up beside her. "Listen. I know you don't believe me. None of you do. I should have figured. That's how it is in Stonecut County."

I stand, too. Sarah's gripping her cup so tightly her fingernails dent the Styrofoam. "If you're hot shit in this town—if your name is Price or Wall—whatever you say goes. And if you're regular folk, you're on your own. I should have known."

She sets her coffee on the edge of my desk.

"At least you're consistent." She shoots me a scathing look, turns on her heel, and leaves.

Ed lingers, his face flushing red. "Uh. Sorry about that, Deputy."

He gulps the rest of his drink and tosses the cup into my wastebasket. "You, uh, gotta know, though. Rory didn't ever talk about leaving town. She didn't have any money. Del said she's using her credit cards, but she didn't have no credit cards. She got paid under the table for cleaning your folk's houses. She couldn't get one if she tried."

He stands there, phone in hand, stained T-shirt and jeans worn through at the knees, and he meets my eyes.

"Something happened. Here—" He scrolls through the phone, and then he holds it up for me to see.

It's Rory. She's holding an enormous pumpkin. Thirty pounds, easy. The sun glints off her reddish-brown hair, and she seems caught by surprise, but she's still smiling shyly. In her overalls and pink headband, she doesn't look like a woman. Not at all.

"This was last Halloween. She might not have told Sarah she had plans to leave town, but she would've told me. She's a good kid."

"I'll talk to Del."

"Look into it. Please. I just want to make sure she's okay. She ain't had an easy go of it. I wouldn't blame her if she left. But—just make sure she's okay."

I nod and step around the desk to offer my hand. He shakes it in his meaty grip and shuffles out.

By the time I sit back down and open my email, Nancy has forwarded me the report Del ran. According to this, Rory is working at Franco's Italian Grille. She's shopping at a pharmacy and a corner store. No one's kidnapped her and wracked up charges. It's all ten dollars here, twenty dollars there.

There's no current address, but if she's new to the city, she's probably renting a room. No phone, either. She could be using a disposable.

How did Del get a hold of her?

Pandy Bullard probably had a number for her.

I need to talk to Del. He's already talked to her, and I don't want to hassle the kid. If she's trying to get a fresh start, good luck to her.

I'll just double check, dot the Is and cross the Ts. Can't hurt.

I shoot Del an email to holler when he gets done with the lawyer. In the meantime, I can drive up to the trailers and have a chat with Pandy Bullard.

There's nothing else that needs doing around here, and it'll at least get me out of the office. While I'm there, I can swing by the barn and get the extension ladder. I've got no plans for the weekend. Might as well flush out that bat. The attic's gonna be a hundred and ten degrees, but the forecast isn't calling for it to get much cooler anytime soon.

I should call Elizabeth before I head out. She's gonna ask me about the damn parade again. She wants me to be a judge—ride in the back of a convertible, wave, pose for pictures, act like I'm King Shit. There's no way.

I'll call later. Or conveniently forget.

I grab my hat, tell the ladies where I'm going, and head out of town, blasting the air conditioner, cruising slow, careful to scan methodically and notice everything. I learned a helluva lesson when I almost drove past Billy McAllister on that bridge.

Mr. Henry is supervising as his oldest boy power-washes the awning of Stonecut Drug. It's a losing battle. The green fabric is threadbare in places and sun-bleached to gray. The awning runs the whole block. It's gonna cost a pretty penny when he goes ahead and replaces it.

Bob and Sue Acheson are riding their matching bicycles down the sidewalk. They wave, and I nod. Mr. Henry is gonna holler at them to get on the road when they pass his place. Nancy will likely be letting me know tomorrow that Sue called to report Mr. Henry for harassing her in the street.

Miriam Dutter's girl is huddled with a friend, vaping in the alley beside the library. Miriam was a senior—head of the cheerleading squad—when I was the only freshman on the varsity team. I remember her blazing up behind the bleachers before a game. The more things change, the more they stay the same.

The sun is high, baking everything, heat waves shimmering off the roads. Most folks are inside. Everything is calm. If it isn't exactly as it should be, it's as it always is.

I'm so damn tired. Maybe I won't grab the ladder. Let that bat live in peace another week.

After talking to Pandy and taking a few more laps around town, I'll go home, sit on the porch, and stare out at the fields and the mountain in the distance until the stars come out. I've been doing that a lot lately. Besides work, just doesn't seem like there's anything I care to do.

I turn off onto Route 7 and head out of town. The speed limit goes up to fifty-five, but I stay at a cruising speed. There's no one behind me on the road.

I'm not thinking about much of anything when I see them ahead, walking side-by-side on the wide shoulder.

A woman and a little girl.

The woman has reddish-brown hair and a slight build. Like Rory Evans. She's carrying a laundry basket on her hip.

Chapter 4

My interest is piqued.

The girl is maybe six or seven. Same colored hair. She has both of her skinny arms wrapped around a smaller basket. They're trudging along the road, kicking up dust. There's no shade. No breeze. They must be miserable.

It's not Rory. The height and age aren't quite right. But that auburn hair. That's familiar for some reason.

A child so young doesn't need to be walking along a highway on such a hot day.

They're headed away from town, and the closest houses are another two miles or so. They're not doing anything wrong. But still, I turn the wheel and pull off onto the shoulder ahead of them.

They stop in unison about twenty feet behind my cruiser. I glance into the rearview mirror as I reach for my hat on the passenger seat, and I freeze.

Holy shit.

It's her.

The girl with the auburn hair. From the night at the bonfire.

My heart slams into my ribs, adrenaline surging through my veins. My hand is on the door handle. She's standing there, skin glistening with sweat, hip cocked, foot turned out, in a pale pink blouse and brown patterned skirt, shading her eyes.

It's her. There's no doubt. Those round hips and trim waist. That stubborn chin. I swallow past a lump lodged in my throat, and I get out of the car. I remember my hat a second too late.

What's she doing back here in Stonecut County? By the side of the road?

I wipe my hands on my thighs. Square my shoulders. The heat hits me like a brick wall, stealing my breath.

I see the moment she recognizes me. Her entire body goes rigid. She grabs the little girl's upper arm and tugs her close to her side. The action draws my eyes down.

Holy. Fucking. Shit.

It's Dina.

The kid is an exact replica of my little sister at that age. Identical. Same pert nose. Same arched eyebrows. Same bow mouth. Both skinny. Even the stiff way she holds herself.

The little girl blinks owlish clear blue eyes at me. Same exact expression. Same exact shade of blue.

Dina's eyes.

My eyes.

She's six or seven years old.

The bonfire was seven years ago. A lifetime ago.

Holy shit.

"Is she mine?" It comes out as a deep croak.

The woman drops her basket in the dust and moves in front of the girl, blocking her.

The little girl peeks out at me.

All those years ago, she said her name was Shay. Was that true?

The girl drops her basket and reaches for her mother's hand. She's scared. They're both scared.

A truck zooms past doing at least fifty. The little girl slams her hands over her ears. Shay reaches behind her to press the girl to her back.

They're not safe here by the side of the road. Fuck.

I slowly raise my hands. "Shay. It's Shay, right?"

The shoulder is wide, but Shay's gaze is darting everywhere—down the road, the field past the guardrail. She's looking to run.

The girl moans, wordless, distressed. Exactly like Dina used to right before she had a freak out.

"Shay?"

Her face hardens until it's etched in stone. Her jaw tightens. Her cheeks hollow, and she reaches for the girl, swings her onto her hip, and staggers back a step. She's getting ready to run.

What do I do?

Shit. I let her. I raise my hands higher. I'm not chasing her into traffic. I don't have any plays here. Patience. That's it.

I wait for an answer. A chorus of crickets swells from the field beside us and then fades to quiet.

Chapter 4

After a long moment, she inclines her head.

"Shay, it's not safe here by the road."

"Then get back in that car and drive away." She jerks her chin at the cruiser.

Her voice. I remember it now. Husky. Tough. A gruff purr.

"I can't do that. Let me give you a ride. You're coming from the laundromat?"

If so, they've walked two miles already in this heat. I don't see a water bottle. Shay's wearing flip-flops for Christ's sake. At least the little girl's wearing socks with her sandals.

"We don't need a ride."

The girl is peeking at me, head cocked ever so slightly to the side.

"What's her name?"

She's beautiful. Like a pixie.

That's my child. My daughter. I didn't know.

Why the fuck didn't I know?

Fury rises in my chest, but I roughly shove it back. Not now. Won't do any good now.

Besides, maybe she's not mine. She's a Wall, though. There's absolutely no doubt looking at her. Did Shay fuck one of my brothers, too? Cash is making his way through the single female half of town. Jesus. My stomach churns, the rage surging again.

Doesn't matter. I can't ask. Not here. Not now. I need them to get in the car.

An eighteen-wheeler rumbles past. The little girl burrows into her mother's back, hands flying back up to cup her ears.

Shay glares at me. She's trying to look tough, but I can see the rapid pulse in her neck from here, and under her tan, she's blanched white. She's terrified.

Of me?

She should be. She had my child, and she said nothing. She disappeared.

But that's not exactly right, is it?

She did call me. Once. A few months after that night.

Elizabeth was with me.

Shay wouldn't get to the point. Lots of "ums." She sounded like all the other shy girls who screwed up the courage to talk to me. Elizabeth was getting more and more pissed, and I felt like a sleaze. I cut her off. Told her I wasn't looking for anything. Elizabeth had me block her number while she watched.

A truck honks as it whizzes by. Fred Burnham's behind the wheel. I wave out of habit.

Shit.

How long have we been standing here? Shay's gnawing her bottom lip with her teeth. The little girl is staring at me.

"Why didn't you say? When you called me?"

It only takes a beat for her to follow what I'm saying. "I did try. You hung up and blocked me."

It's an admission.

Jesus.

The little girl is mine.

And it is not safe here.

"Please get in the car. I'll drive you where you're going. It's dangerous standing here."

My gaze flies to the girl. I shouldn't have said that. I don't want to scare her.

If I rattled her, she doesn't show it. She's on edge, clenching a handful of her mother's skirt and worrying it in her fingers, but what I said didn't trigger her.

She's pretty. Too thin.

Is she okay? She hasn't said a word. Dina didn't talk 'til she was older. Is she autistic?

Her mother's stonewalling. She glares, giving nothing away. Like a perp. A hardened one who's not gonna break.

If I push her, she'll fight me. I've got at least eighty pounds on her, and I'm armed, but I'm powerless here and now.

I draw in a deep breath.

"What's her name?"

Chapter 4

For a moment, I think Shay's going to refuse me even this, then she raises her chin and says, "Mia."

"Mia," I repeat. The little girl blinks, yanking on the skirt she's been kneading.

Shay glances down. "He's the police. Don't worry. We didn't do anything wrong."

Nothing wrong? She didn't tell me I had a child for six years. I'm the deputy sheriff of Stonecut County. My email address is on the county website. You can search me up on the internet. Mail a letter. I'm a public servant. You want to tell me something, I'm not hard to find.

You don't try once to tell a man he has a kid and then give up.

Shay shuffles a step back. My rising ire must show on my face. Shit. I need to keep it together.

What will it take to get them in the car?

I lower myself into a squat until I'm eye level with Mia. I force a smile. "Your mama's right. You didn't do anything wrong. But I don't want to leave you two walking on the side of the road in this heat. I'd like to give you a ride home. Have you ever ridden in a police car before?"

Shay snorts.

The little girl blinks.

"Neither of us have been in the back of a police car before, believe or not," Shay says. "But it sounds like an adventure for another day. We're fine. You can continue on your way."

"I'm not going to do that, Shay." I stand and rest my hands on my duty belt.

Her golden-brown eyes darken. Not with anger. With fear.

My gut tightens. Why is she afraid of me?

"I'm not gonna make trouble for you," she says softly. "Let us go. We won't bother you."

I don't understand.

"There's no bother."

Another eighteen-wheeler rattles past, doing at least ten miles over the speed limit. Mia moans. Her palms go to her ears. She's starting to fidget.

"Let me give you a ride. I'll take you where you want to go. That's all. You have my word."

My father taught all us boys that our word is our bond. He drilled it into us since before we could remember. No matter how messed up the world becomes, your word has to mean something. When shit is falling down around you, it means everything.

In this town, folks know that about the Walls.

A motorcycle roars by as Shay glares at me with nothing but wariness and suspicion. Mia begins to rock on her feet. I guess my word doesn't mean shit to this woman.

I only have one move left.

I turn slowly and walk to the passenger side, boots crunching. I'm drenched in sweat again as the sun beats down on the top of my head.

I open the door and wait behind it. "Leave the baskets. I'll put them in the trunk."

They are so small, alone, by the side of the road. Mia's flowered sundress and Shay's hair whip in the hot wind as another truck blows past.

I need them in my car. I need them safe.

I could wrangle them both into the back. Shay has curves, but there's not much else to her. I'm twice her size.

It's an idle thought. I'd never risk it. So I wait.

They both stare at the open door.

And then Mia slips her fingers around her mother's wrist and tugs.

Shay glances down, eyebrows raised.

Mia cocks her head.

Shay sighs. "Well, if you say so." She lifts her shoulders and then—thank the Lord—walks forward, dropping her basket behind the car. She grabs the handle of the back door. "We'll sit back here if it's the same to you."

Whatever she wants.

Chapter 4

I shut the passenger door and move to help, but she's already buckling Mia. There's no car seat. Mia's no more than forty pounds or so. She'll need a seat with a harness. She's too small for a booster.

I pop the trunk, stow the baskets, and then ease into the driver's seat. I adjust the rearview mirror.

Shay and Mia are both stone-faced and tense, their faces flushed and shiny. They need hydration. I've got nothing in the car.

The belt cuts between Shay's breasts. Her knees are pressed tight together, and she's tucked her sweat-dampened hair behind her ears.

Her gaze darts from Mia to me to the radio to the floor. Her hands are resting deliberately, one over the other, on her lap. Her fingers tremble.

Nerves riot in my stomach. She's stunning. The kind of striking where you can't stop looking. And prickly as a porcupine.

Beside her, Mia stares out the window.

"Ready?"

No one answers. I turn the key and ease onto the road.

Something inside me uncoils.

They're in my car. For now, they're safe. They can't go anywhere.

I have a child.

And I didn't know. How did this happen? How did I fuck up this bad?

Elizabeth and I had planned to have a family, but the timing was never right, and then the marriage was over.

This whole time, there was a child. My child.

And I wasn't there.

An impotent rage floods my chest.

How dare this woman keep this from me?

My grip tightens on the steering wheel, and I glare out the windshield.

"You know where the trailers are at Stonecut Farm?" she asks.

She's been staying on the property? My house is on the other side of the farm, further up the hill. No more than a mile away. Do my folks know about her and Mia?

"How long have you been staying there?"

"A few weeks."

"My folks know about you?"

"No."

No explanation. I force my voice even. Keep my eye on the speedometer. I don't have much of a temper, but she's pricked it.

"Who are you staying with?"

"Connie Murphy."

"Buck Crowder's wife?"

"His lady friend."

"I thought Connie was staying in town these days."

"She is."

So she's staying alone in Connie's old trailer?

"How are you related to Connie?"

"I'm not. I'm Buck Crowder's granddaughter."

Shit.

I knew Buck. I knew him my whole life. He worked in the stables. He was a man of few words, but he taught all of us boys how to care for the horses and the tack. Passed a year or so ago.

That makes Mia his great-granddaughter.

My brain spins, trying to connect the pieces.

"You were staying with Buck when you were here? You're not Pandy's cousin?"

She gives a slight nod.

"You didn't say you were a minor."

I watch her in the rearview. She presses her lips together and glowers out the window. "Didn't come up, did it?"

"I wouldn't have—" I stop myself. If Mia is anything like Dina, she's listening, even when it seems she isn't. Now is not the time.

Shay chews the inside of her cheek, keeping her eye on the passing scenery. "Well, you did."

"Takes two."

"That's what I'm told. Been managing just fine as one."

Has she?

She has no car. No washing machine. Her clothes are obviously secondhand. Her blouse is cut too tight, and her skirt hangs loose. Mia's sandals are made of plastic. Plenty of kids wear shoes like that, but taken all together, I'm inclined to disbelieve that things are going just fine.

A weight, brutally heavy, settles across my shoulders.

My child was walking along the highway in plastic shoes, hauling laundry in ninety-eight-degree heat.

Whatever led to this, I made the wrong call.

I missed something.

Everything's out of place. Nothing is what I thought, and I *should* have known. As furious as I am at the woman in the seat behind me, I'm twice as enraged with myself.

A man is responsible for his own business. Period. End of story.

I tamp down the anger. Shay and Mia are safe in the back seat. For now.

As I turn onto the narrow lane leading to the trailers, my pulse kicks up. How am I going to convince this woman to let me in her house?

I'm not walking away, and I sincerely doubt she'll let me in.

I've been accused of being stubborn in the past. I suppose I'm about to find out just how stubborn I am.

5

SHAY

Kellum drives like an old man. The speed limit is forty-five, and we're doing forty-five.

My knee jiggles.

He looks the same only more so. More muscular. More rugged. More confident, although I don't know how that's possible. He always had a swagger, the kind that isn't cocky so much as calm certainty that his way is the right way.

On the football field, of course, he'd catch the ball. At the bonfire that night, of course, I'd dance with him.

Of course, I'd get in this car.

It's perturbing, such conviction. Seems unfair you can be born to confidence like you can be born to money.

At least we're in the air conditioning. Mia left her water bottle at the laundromat, and by the time I realized it wasn't in her basket where I put it, we were halfway home.

As the cool air dries my sweat, I'm getting chilled. I'm not gonna complain. I'm gonna keep my mouth shut, thank him when we get to the trailer, and maybe life will break my way for once. He'll ride off into the sunset, good deed done, can of worms left unopened.

Based on the sharp line of his jaw, that's wishful thinking.

Chapter 5

Guess he didn't know about Mia.

I know plenty of liars and fakers, but none that could pull off that look of pure surprise.

He's angry, too. Righteous indignation.

So his daddy and his uncle and his boss and his brother never let him in on the "gossip?"

Back home, someone farts on Second Street, the folks on Twelfth hear about it damn near instantly. Are rich folks really that different?

Of course, they are.

I didn't really understand this place when I visited as a kid or during those few months I lived here in high school. It vaguely registered that there were two Stonecut Counties, but now that I'm older, it's clear as day.

There are the Victorians with turrets and gingerbread trim and huge potted ferns on their wraparound porches. The cutesy shops on Main Street. Along the river, grand old buildings from a hundred years ago have been rehabbed into an arts center and something called a "gastropub" and condos for seniors.

And literally across the railroad tracks, slapped together houses with moss on the siding lean against each other to stay upright. Lots with uncut weeds, knee high. Discount liquors. The suboxone clinic.

You can make out the white fences and huge barn of Stonecut Farms on its hill outside of town, the mountain soaring behind it. And if you turn the other direction, you can see the garbage collected in the bend of the river, and the pier with missing planks where folks drop crawfish traps baited with scraps of ham leftover from dinner.

There are the older couples who retired here from the city. The banker and organic grocer and restaurateur. And there are the townies and the hicks.

Dry Cleaners for one. Laundromat for the other. The only things they use in common are the roads in and out.

It's just bad damn luck that Kellum and I ran into each other.

I wish he'd turn the radio on. My nerves are jangling.

What is he gonna do?

He could make a world of trouble for us. I underestimated the risk when I made the decision to come back. He's the law. Not an officer anymore, but a deputy. Says "SHERIFF" right on the side of his vehicle.

I can't read his eyes. They're pale blue, like Mia's, and like hers, they don't give anything away.

He keeps checking on us. Each time he does, my belly swirls. Part worry. Part something else.

He'll probably demand a paternity test. Call his lawyer. Isn't that what folks like him do?

I told myself that if he saw us, he wouldn't notice. Or he'd keep driving. His people were clear. Especially Van Price when he came back with cash. Get gone. They probably expected me to take care of it, but I was too far along and way too clueless besides.

I didn't really grow up until I had Mia. And then I grew up fast.

I'd never have given her up. She's the most beautiful thing life's ever given me—maybe the only beautiful thing. No one is taking her from me.

I curl my fingers around the seat belt strap, the edge biting into my palm.

"What are you gonna do?" I ask, breaking the silence. I aim for cool and calm, but my voice hitches at the end.

His eyes meet mine in the rearview. His Adam's apple bobs as he swallows.

"I'm gonna take you two home."

"What then?"

He draws in a deep breath and flips on his signal as he turns onto the dirt road leading to the trailers.

"We'll talk."

My muscles tense. The closer we get to home, the harder my blood pounds. Mia's still staring out the window. Probably trying to catch sight of some birds. She's found a raccoon and a

Chapter 5

groundhog at our new place, but she misses her bitterns and grebes.

However this goes down, Mia doesn't need to hear it.

When we pull up to Grandpa's trailer, we're the only car. Everyone's at work.

I unbuckle Mia, grab the handle and push, but it's locked. I have a heart-stopping beat of panic before Kellum gets out and opens the door for me from the outside.

I grab Mia's hand, and we both scoot out. The heat blasts me in the face. It's almost worse when you've been in the air conditioning.

I don't want to invite him inside. The trailer's too small. He's too big.

He pops the trunk, stacks the baskets, and nods at the trailer. "Get the door?"

I reach for the baskets. "I can take those."

"I already got them."

Kellum waits expectantly, and there just isn't anything else to do. I open the screen door for him. Mia snuggles behind me, peeking at him.

She's curious. She doesn't give a fig for most people. She's more of an animal person, but occasionally, someone will strike her fancy. She studies them like she does her critters. I imagine she's cataloguing them. Their habits. Characteristics. Which tube they'd go in if they were one of her plastic figurines.

What does she make of him?

She's wary, but not scared. He's an imposing figure in his uniform with all that gear, tall and broad in the shoulders, hair trimmed perfectly neat, no stubble, boots polished. Everything is strong—jaw, chin, nose.

He doesn't look like the kind of folks we know. He looks like he strode off a newsreel from the fifties when policemen wore those peaked caps, not the wide-brimmed ones they do now.

He eases past me with the baskets into the gloom of the living room, setting them on the carpet, scanning the place, every inch a cop. A thread of guilt worms its way through my belly. I have nothing to be ashamed of. The place is clean.

But it's hot as the seven hinges of hell.

There should've been a puff of chilled air when I opened the door. In this heat, I keep the window unit running low even when we're out 'cause it's cheaper than cooling the place once it's got up past a hundred. But the air is still and thick with humidity, and there's no hum from the fridge.

I flip a light switch. Nothing.

Oh, no.

The power's out?

I glance over to Pandy and Lonnie's. They keep their porch-light on twenty-four seven. It's on, and in the quiet, I can make out their AC cranking away.

Oh, crap. I check the breaker box. Everything's fine.

I bet the power company cut the electric. Connie's been complaining about how high the bill has been since we moved in. I give her cash to cover it, but she has this idea that I'm running it up on purpose to mess with her or something.

Kellum's squinting around the place, brow furrowed. He noticed.

"Power's out?" He strides to the door.

I scuttle back, out of his way.

"The neighbors have power." He frowns down at me.

I move to the kitchen, and fill Mia's red lion cup with water from the tap.

"Come drink this." I pat her stool. She hasn't moved. She's still in the entranceway, craning her neck up at Kellum, blinking her blue eyes.

He notices her looking and goes stock-still. Arms relaxed at his sides. Face somber. Feet hip-width apart.

He lets her study him.

She can't possibly know. My stomach knots.

She's never asked about her father. I've never said. I'm not sure how much she understands about it all. I don't have a father. Plenty of her cousins are being raised by stepfathers, or in Pete's case, their mama's parents. A father's not a given where we live.

She watches TV, though. Even the cartoon animals have mommies and daddies. She knows how people think it's supposed to go.

A long time ago, I decided that if she ever asked, I'd say he lives in another state, and it didn't work out. It's close enough to the truth that I'd be able to say it straight-faced. And I suppose I thought eventually, if she didn't ask, I'd have to tell her something. Mia's an iceberg. What she says is the very tip, but what she thinks goes for miles below the surface.

Kellum shifts his weight to the other foot. The moment stretches. Mia can go on like this for hours, but most folks can't.

Eventually, Kellum curves his lips in a careful smile.

"Hi."

Mia narrows her eyes. Hah. She wasn't done.

She drops her gaze and scampers over to me, climbing up on the stool. I slide her cup over.

"Finish all of that now, or you're gonna get a headache."

Kellum's brow knits, and he goes back to poking around at the place. The more he sees, the blacker his expression. My shoulders tense.

"You walked all the way to town, and you didn't bring water?"

I don't curse in front of Mia, so instead of telling him to fuck himself, I stalk to a window and tug at the sash. It's swollen shut.

It's getting hotter by the minute in here. With the windows down and no power, the trailer is a sweatbox.

So far we've been lucky with Mia's asthma, but with no air circulating, you can smell the mold. It's probably under the trailer, seeping up through the floor.

I yank harder, but the window's not budging.

Kellum strides over, flips the lock with his thumb, and slides the pane up with one hand.

Besides being able to hear the creek and the birds, there's no difference. No breeze. Except he's closer now. Right beside me. My heart kicks up a notch.

I scowl. "I would've figured that out any second."

"Glad to be of help." The corner of his lip quirks up. It's replaced almost instantly with a frown. "Why is your power off?"

I retreat behind the breakfast bar. Mia's finished half her water. I refill the cup.

"Couldn't say."

"Can't or won't?"

"It's not your business."

He bristles, drawing himself up. His face turns hard. Shivers zip down my spine. Mia darts a glance up at him.

"It is my business. Make no mistake."

I sniff.

He stiffens.

A hawk screeches, and Mia turns to peer out the window.

I take a deep breath.

I don't need to bait this man. The basic facts from seven years ago have not changed. I'm not the one with the power. What him and his people say goes. I can make it easy on myself or hard.

Bitterness clogs my throat, but I don't have the luxury of indulging it.

"My best guess is Connie didn't pay the bill."

"Stonecut Farms doesn't pay the utilities?"

He means doesn't his daddy pay the utilities. "No, they don't."

I've been here almost two months, and I've given Connie thirty dollars a week. I can't get the electric in my name 'cause she's keeping it in hers. The money's supposed to cover water and electric, but if she's used it for something else, there's not much I can do.

"Maybe something triggered the breaker." I'm hoping he didn't notice that I already checked.

He scans the wall until he sees the fuse box. He opens it and scowls. Then, he sighs and shakes his head.

What am I gonna do?

Chapter 5

There's meat in the freezer. Milk in the fridge. That's money down the drain. And this heat shows no sign of breaking. Mia's okay now, but if I have to keep the windows open, with the dust and the pollen—a hard lump rises in my throat.

She has an inhaler, but it only has a dozen or so puffs left.

I twine my fingers, wringing my hands.

Maybe Pandy will let Mia sleep on her sofa. Lonnie's loud and blowsy, and he freaks Mia out, but maybe if I talk to her, she'll be okay. Or I can have her wear her headphones.

Kellum crosses the room in two strides to the other side of the breakfast bar, facing Mia and me. I wish he would go. He's too close.

He rests his forearms on the counter. He's rolled up his sleeves. His arms are all hard muscle, veined, lightly dusted with hair. His huge hands rest on the linoleum, intentionally still.

I have to figure this out, and I can't with him staring.

"Why don't you go pack a bag? We'll go to my place."

What? No.

"We're not going anywhere with you."

Mia's gaze flies up to my face. She doesn't like it when I get upset.

"This isn't a safe place to be."

"We'll manage."

"It's not safe for Mia. And it's too damn hot for her."

Anger flashes through my chest. "You let me worry about Mia."

Kellum grits his teeth. A tic pulses on his left temple.

"You need to come with me."

Those hard blue eyes bore into me. I'm rocked by the full force of his presence, that natural authority. Of course, I'm going to do what he says. There's no choice.

My nose tickles. I'm not going to cry. Not in front of this man.

I know I need to get Mia out of this hot trailer. I know he's my only option, but I don't trust him.

I will always do what's best for Mia, but what is best?

I glare straight ahead, and since he's there, I stare at the muscular plane of his chest and the tan shirt with buttoned pockets. The radio and the curled cord. The gold star and the gold pin with his name, K. Wall.

He's bound to know people at CPS.

He would know exactly who to call and what to say to take Mia away. Unsafe living conditions. Neglect, maybe.

Would he do that?

Almost seven years ago, when that delegation of big shots crammed into this living room to show me exactly who I was dealing with, there was no doubt in my mind they'd do whatever it took to get their way.

Why would I think this man is any different? Same uniform. Same name. I chew the inside of my cheek; it'll be raw tomorrow.

Mia sips from her cup.

He clears his throat, and it echoes in the silence. When he speaks, he hesitates over the words. "When Dina was little—she had to have things a certain way. She had a blanket. And she needed a fan on to sleep."

He pauses, then he starts again. "That sounds like all kids, but it was a hundred things, really. Everything had to be just how she liked it."

"Dina's your sister?"

"Yeah. My younger sister. Mia looks exactly like her."

So that's how he knew.

He takes another breath. "What do you need to make it okay for her?"

"Air conditioning."

He exhales. Those blue eyes spark. I'm surprised he's kept his temper this long. He can't be used to hearing no.

"I tell you what. The electric company office is already closed for the weekend. Come with me now. We'll go there first thing Monday morning and settle the bill."

"I don't want your money."

His fingers curl into a fist, but he catches himself and straightens them.

Chapter 5

"Shay." He lowers his voice. "She can't stay here."

He says it like it's the undeniable truth. Because it is. I blink back the tears. I don't have a choice.

His shoulders ease. He knows he's won.

"What does she need?"

Oh, hell no. He doesn't get to root through our things. I point to the sofa. "You sit there. Gimme a few minutes."

He raises his hands, nods, and takes himself over to the couch. He doesn't sit, though. He stands there, watching Mia as she takes her little bird sips, an inscrutable look on his face.

∽

THERE'S GOING to be a storm tonight. Mia doesn't do well with storms.

Thick thunderclouds rolled in on the short ride up the hill to Kellum's place, blackening the sky so that the setting sun burned red-orange like a coal in contrast.

While I watch and worry, Mia can't tear her eyes from the horses. She strains against her seatbelt, angling to keep them in sight long after we've passed.

She's always been into smaller critters and winged things, but maybe that's due to lack of opportunity rather than interest.

Kellum notices, and he drives slower until the white fences end at the turnoff to his house.

Everyone knows the layout of Stonecut Farms. It's on postcards in the shops on Main Street. It's what you see every day when your eyes are inevitably drawn to Stonecut Mountain, towering behind the farm to the west.

The base of the hill is thick with trees—that's where the trailers are—setting off the stretches of manicured fields and their bright white fences. A huge, red octagonal barn is nestled smack dab in the center, overlooked by a house they call the "Lodge" where the Walls live.

Grandpa got invited to the Lodge on occasion for dinner or a meeting with John Senior. He said it's like a fancy hotel, made to look down-home but chockfull of gadgets like a fireplace that lights when you say "light the fire."

Even higher on the hill, on a ridge at the very top, is the mansion they call the "Cabin." That's where Mr. Price lives when he flies in from the city. It's all glass with a steep-pitched roof and an infinity pool that winks in the sunlight. Pandy told me all about the Cabin. She used to clean it before she took the job at General Goods and passed the job on to a younger girl from town.

And then there's the old homestead. From down in the gully, you can only make out the crimped metal roof. It's perched on the north side of the hill, facing the mountain.

When we were catching up, Pandy said Kellum's been living there since he split from his wife.

The old farmhouse is a hundred-and-fifty years at least. It's all red brick with a huge wraparound porch and a cupola with a rooster on top, spinning and creaking as the wind whips up. The temperature has dropped a good ten degrees. It'd be a relief if I didn't know what we're in for. Mia's gonna have a hard time tonight.

The place is well-kept, but if I'd just driven by, I'd think no one lives here. There are no flowers in the bed along the front of the house. No rockers or glider on the porch.

Kellum opens the car door for us and goes to grab the bag I packed from the trunk.

Mia makes no move to get out of the car. She stares up at the house. No, she's staring at the black clouds gathering behind it.

She's figured out what's coming.

"Thunder is only a noise. It can't hurt you." I always remind her. Doesn't make a difference.

"I packed your headphones." Mrs. Ellis recommended them. They help in crowds. Not so much in storms. I don't think it's the noise, per se, that sets her off. It's almost a phobia.

She keeps her eyes on the storm, her little body going taut as a wire.

Kellum waits at the bottom of the porch stairs, watching us. Nerves spark in my stomach.

We're alone here. No one for at least a mile.

I don't have any minutes left on my phone, and no one knows we're here. I don't think Kellum would hurt us, but I don't like having no way out.

Was this a mistake?

Well, if it was, I already made it. We can't stay out here in the car all night.

"Mia, it'll be better to be inside when the rain starts. Right?"

There's a low grumble in the distance. She unclicks her belt and bolts for the house. I hustle to keep up.

Somehow, Kellum gets ahead of her, unlocks the front door, and holds it wide. Mia zooms past him and disappears inside.

By the time I get indoors, she's nowhere to be seen. Kellum frowns down at me.

"Where did she go?" he asks.

"Bathtub. Closet maybe. Someplace small where there are no windows."

"She's really scared of storms?"

"Yeah."

"What do we do?"

We?

"I'll go find her. Where are we gonna be sleeping?"

I swallow. Until I asked, I hadn't thought quite that far ahead. No reason to be nervous, though. Whatever this is, it isn't *that*.

I remember how he looked at me that night. Hungry. Starving. Like I was everything he wanted. Me. Shay Crowder.

Maybe it's the uniform, but he seems so much older now. Almost grim. If I met him now, I would never believe he's the type to go off into the woods with a woman like he did.

He must be angry, right? If he really was in the dark? But if he's angry, it doesn't show. He's as cool and collected as if he pulled me over for speeding.

"Shouldn't you get Mia?" he suggests.

"You got guns or traps or something dangerous lying out?"

"Of course not."

"Then she'll be fine for a few minutes. She needs to be alone to collect herself. If you crowd her before she's ready, she'll start wailing on you."

He peers deeper into the house, his brow furrowed.

"She never goes far."

"You sure she's okay?"

"I'm sure."

He has trouble letting it go, but eventually says, "I have a spare room. This way."

He heads up wooden stairs worn to a shine, carrying our bag. I follow, listening for Mia. She's generally a quiet kid, but when she's about to have a meltdown, she moans. And then when she loses it, she shrieks, and everyone can hear her then.

It's the worst sound in the world. She hurts, she's in pain, and there's nothing you can do but wait it out.

Kellum stops in front of an open doorway. Inside, there's a four-poster bed covered in a red and blue Amish quilt. Between two wide windows, there's a waterfall dresser from the '50s and a chifforobe with a full-length mirror on front. No pictures on the wall or knick-knacks, but it's clean. Someone dusts and vacuums.

"I can run over to my folks' place. Get a cot for Mia. I've only got the one guest room furnished."

"We can share." We always have, ever since she outgrew her Pack-n-Play.

"Should I—uh—help you look?"

"Best you don't."

His jaw tightens.

I smooth my palms down my rumpled skirt.

He steps into the room, setting the bag on a rocking chair. I scoot past him and head back downstairs.

I hope he stays where he is. I don't want him to see this, to think Mia's worse off than she is. There's nothing wrong with her. She's smart. She's learning, faster than folks thought she could.

Chapter 5

I had nightmares when I was little. I woke inconsolable and cried so hard my face ached the next day. I grew out of it. Mia will grow out of this, too.

"Baby girl," I call out softly. "Where did you get to?"

When Mia freaks out, she operates on instinct. She runs and hides. I start my search at the front door. To the left is a parlor, clean, dusted, and unlived in. To the right is a dining room. There's a huge oak table that would seat twelve. No tablecloth. An empty hutch.

Straight ahead is a narrow hall to the kitchen. The path of least resistance. I go that way, poking my head into a half-bath and a closet tucked under the stairs. It would have made a good hiding place, but the closet has built in shelves. Although they're empty except for some paint cans, they're a bit too narrow for Mia to wedge herself into.

In the kitchen, there are finally signs of life. A mug in the sink. Mail on a Formica table. All the stainless-steel appliances are new. They look completely out of place.

There's a door beside the refrigerator. I ease it open a crack. Please don't be the basement. I hate basements in old houses.

I exhale as I peek inside. It's a pantry. There's a narrow, high window letting in a yellowish light.

There's a rustle in the back.

Bingo.

"Baby girl? Come on now. There's a nice room for us upstairs."

Nothing.

I can see Mia in the corner, tucked as tight against the wall as she can get. The pantry's mostly empty, but a few shelves are stocked with food. Tin cans. Glass jars. If she starts windmilling, this could get messy quick.

I need to get her out of here.

"Let's go get Bunny. He's in the bag upstairs."

She doesn't budge.

In the distance, there's another low rumble of thunder.

She quakes, a low moan rising from deep in her chest.

If I grab her now, she'll fight me. Last time, I ended up with a bloody nose, and she almost put her fist through the trailer wall.

She does better left alone, but she's too damn close to those canned goods.

A sharp crack causes the windowpane to rattle, and she screams. My pulse pounds. I can stand in front of the shelves, but I can't block everything.

"Mia, baby, please come to me."

She plasters herself further into the corner, wedging herself halfway under a shelf, her moan rising. A gust of wind batters the house.

Oh, sweet Lord.

I lean in and grab an armful of mason jars. Cucumbers, pretty mixes of peppers, peaches. I dash into the kitchen, set them on a counter, and come back for more.

Kellum's there, standing awkwardly by the stove. He's taken off his duty belt. At least if he interferes, she won't be able to grab his gun.

I dart back for more jars. Why does he have all these? The rest of the pantry is protein bars, boxed meal kits, and packages of nuts and jerky.

Mia's rocking harder, her curved back jostling the shelf. Thunder growls. No lightning yet. The shit will hit the fan when the lightning flashes.

I reach for more jars, but Kellum's on my heels, reaching past me.

"I got these."

My face burns. I want to explain. You can't explain.

Besides, I don't care what he thinks. We all have quirks.

I kneel beside Mia, close, but not too close. Thunder booms. She startles, kicks a leg. I stay frozen.

"It's only a summer storm. It'll be over as soon as it came."

Kellum efficiently clears the rest of the jars, and then he looms behind me in the doorway. I want to tell him to leave; he's making her nervous. But the truth is, at this point, Mia's oblivious to whoever's around her. She's inside her panic.

Lightning illuminates the room.

She screams, slamming her back into the wall.

I know words don't help, but I still try them. "It's okay, baby girl. It's going to pass soon. We're safe. I promise."

Thunder claps, dragging on, echoing against the mountain. Mia scrambles, but there's nowhere to go, so she throws herself against the wall again, as if she can force open a hole to hide in.

Her head wobbles on her thin neck, thunking against the wall.

"Oh, baby. No."

Kellum steps forward.

I hold my hand up to stop him. "No. Stay there. You'll make it worse."

Mia's scream is a constant now, rising and falling with the storm outside. There're a series of flashes, and she works herself up, jerking forward to fling herself against the wall.

There's my opening.

I dive forward, wrap my arms around her, drag her to my chest, and plop back on my ass, legs splayed wide.

She fights, bucking with all her strength, but this ain't my first rodeo. I've got her now, and even though she's kicking the hell out of my legs, she can't headbutt me 'cause I've got my face tucked in the crook of her neck.

"It'll be over soon, baby," I murmur, over and over. She's yowling, furious with fear, trying to get leverage by digging her sandals into my shins. I hiss and grit my teeth. That's gonna bruise.

"How can I help?" Kellum asks, squatting in front of us, gauging the scene, looking for an in.

"Go away. You'll make it worse." I have to shout to be heard over Mia.

"I could hold her legs."

No. He's too strong. Mia's all sound and fury when she's like this. It's easy to think you need more force than you do, but she doesn't weigh hardly anything.

"Don't touch her. Go away."

He sets back on his heels, hovering, watching. Why can't he leave us in peace?

Rain beats against the window. Mia emits one of her ear-splitting howls of terror, the kind that drive Mama to throw up her hands and barricade herself in her room or head for the bar.

My heart breaks like it always does, but it's not an intolerable sound to me. Some days, if you cracked me open, it's the exact sound that would come from my chest.

I cuddle her closer, gentling my voice as much as I can. "It's a terrible storm, but it'll be over soon. We'll be fine. I promise. It can't hurt you. I won't let it."

I plaster my cheek to hers, streaked with hot tears, and we rock. She stops kicking me.

The thunder is rolling off now. It booms low and long from the distance.

Kellum lowers himself to his butt, arms around his knees. It's so out-of-place, a grown man in a tan-and-brown uniform, tall and broad, sitting on the floor of a pantry as if he's at a picnic.

I suppose I look a sight, too. Skirt pushed above my thighs, my blouse popped a button. And I lost a flip flop.

"You don't need to be here. When the thunder and lightning is over, she'll be fine."

"She doesn't mind the rain?"

I shake my head. Mia's moaning now, and she's limp against my chest. She's fading fast. There was our long walk to the laundromat and the excitement by the side of the road, and she hasn't had dinner. The storm was the icing on the cake.

I resettle my arms around her, looser. She only really lets me hold her when she's sick or after a meltdown. Otherwise, she just tolerates it for a few seconds to humor me.

I wish Kellum would leave.

I know what he's thinking. The same thing everyone thinks. Something's wrong with that child. Bad mother. No home training. Sad story.

"You can go now," I repeat. "She's calming down."

He makes no move to go. Instead, he stares at us with those blue eyes. It's dim in the pantry, and I swear, they're glowing.

"Dina did this all the time. Not storms so much as crowds. Every year, she lost it at the Fireman's Carnival." He chuckles, shaking his head. "She wouldn't let us even talk about leaving her at home, though."

My skin prickles; my breath shallows. "Dina is—she's like this?"

He nods, slowly. "Yes."

I close my eyes. Something inside me wants to burst, but I can't afford to let it. I have my arms full.

"Is she okay? What does she do? She works?" The questions spill from my lips. *Can she pay her bills? Does she have friends? Is she happy?*

"Yeah. Dina's brilliant. She works with computers. She lives with my folks. She doesn't have to, but she has no interest in moving out, and Mom's happy not to have an empty nest. Dina does really well for herself."

Tears scald my eyes. There's no holding them back. I cradle Mia to me. She's got hiccups.

"She could take care of herself if she had to?"

"Yes." He gazes at us intently, as if he wants to come closer, or wants to say more, but he holds himself back.

"Does she have a doctor?" he eventually asks.

I stiffen. "I take her to the clinic. She has all her shots."

Mia whimpers and wriggles. I force myself to relax my arms.

He sighs, glancing up to the window. The sky is lightening. "We should talk about this later."

"Yeah."

"It's dinner time. I'll make something."

"Okay."

"Will she want to eat?"

"In a few minutes. We'll go wash her face. She'll be fine." Mia's drooping. She might not make it to dinner, but if we sit here much longer, she's definitely going to fall asleep.

Kellum hauls himself up, scanning what's left on the shelves.

"Macaroni and cheese?"

Mia perks up a little, straining against my arms so that she can sit upright.

"That's fine."

Kellum offers us a hand. Mia ignores it.

"I saw peaches in one of those jars." I say, jiggling Mia a bit. She blinks and stirs. She's coming back to life. Mia loves fruit.

Kellum glances over shoulder towards where we stacked the jars. "Yeah. My Mom cans. She's always bringing stuff over."

"Peaches are Mia's favorite."

Kellum's lips rise. It's a soft smile. Tentative. A flutter comes to life in my belly.

I didn't say it to make nice with him. It's just true. And Mia needs to eat.

"Macaroni and cheese with peaches, then." Kellum leans over 'til his hand is closer. It'd be rude to ignore it.

I take it. It's rough. Strong. It envelops mine. I find my feet and let him ease me up as I haul Mia upright. As soon as we're standing, he steps back.

"You know where your room is. There's a bathroom attached. Towels are in there."

I nod, suddenly bashful. Mia's sniffling, clinging to my side. There's only a light patter of rain against the window.

Uneasiness swirls in my stomach. What is he thinking? He says Dina is like Mia, but that doesn't mean anything. In Mia's class, every kid has something. That doesn't stop parents from looking askance at each other. Judging. Pitying. Wondering. What will become of this child? What will become of mine?

Dina works with computers. Dina's brilliant. Dina does really well for herself. I hold onto that. Squeeze it hard and tight.

Mia and I are on the second-floor landing when Kellum calls

out from the bottom of the stairs. He's thrown a dish towel over his shoulder.

"Shay. What's your favorite?"

I stop. What?

He holds up a jar of peaches. "What's your favorite? I've got all sorts. They don't get eaten soon, they're gonna go to waste."

What? Canned food lasts forever.

I'm still struggling to even wrap my brain around the question when Mia pipes up, her thin voice husky and raw. "Mommy likes apples."

He's still a moment—probably processing that she spoke—and then his somber face transforms with a bright, white smile that wrinkles the corners of his sky-blue eyes. My breath catches. He's impossibly handsome.

"Apples." His smile grows impossibly wider. "I've got some sliced apples in a sugar syrup. They're my favorite, too."

I swallow past a stupid lump in my throat.

"This all should be ready in twenty minutes," he says.

I nod and hustle Mia up the stairs, unsettled, that heart-stopping smile tickling my memory.

It's a dangerous smile.

It means nothing.

It means trouble.

I'd do well to remember that.

～

AFTER A MOSTLY SILENT DINNER, I wipe Mia's teeth with a washcloth—I forgot to pack our toothbrushes—and I tuck her into bed. She goes out like a light.

On our way upstairs, Kellum asked me to come back down once she's asleep. To talk.

My belly's been sour ever since. Churning.

I take my time, changing out of my grimy, sweat-limp skirt and blouse into gray yoga pants and a worn turquoise top I've had forever.

I probably had it when I was here the first time.

In the three months I've been back, it's clear—this place is different, but it hasn't changed at all. There are some chain restaurants now on the big highway that cuts through the county, and a supermarket whose name I actually recognize.

But unlike back home, all the small shops on Main Street are still open. In Stonecut, high school kids still walk to Pizza Haven after class, and they park their trucks together in the feed store parking lot late on Friday and Saturday night, revving their diesel engines and pissing off the locals to the point they write scathing letters to the paper.

I never read the local paper when I was in school, but I buy it from the grocery for a quarter every week now to search the job listings. That's where I found the elder care position. It was great for a few weeks until the man's daughter finally dropped by and saw I brought Mia with me. The son didn't mind, but the daughter felt I couldn't watch them both.

That was a few weeks ago. I'm down to my last fifty bucks, but school starts in a month. Once I get Mia enrolled, I'll have a lot more choices.

Of course, there's the electric.

And the man waiting downstairs.

My stomach cramps.

I've put this off long enough. I wipe my sweaty palms on my pants and head for the kitchen.

Kellum's leaning against a counter, sipping a beer. At some point, he changed into blue jeans and a black T-shirt. It's tight across his broad chest. His feet are bare.

My gaze skitters from the hem of the sleeves cutting into his bulging biceps to the large hand wrapped around the neck of the bottle. My face flushes. I cross my arms.

"You want one?" He lifts his beer.

I shake my head.

"Want to sit?" He nods at the little square table pushed up against a wall.

"No, thank you."

He exhales, rising to his full height, setting his drink down with a clink. "We can do this like civilized adults."

Do what? My pulse races, and my mouth goes dry. "What do you mean?"

"Talk."

"Go ahead. Talk."

His face darkens. "Is she mine?"

"Yes."

All his muscles bunch, but his carefully controlled expression doesn't change. "Is there a chance she's one of my brothers'?"

"Your brothers?"

No. The answer's no. I didn't have sex with Cash or Jesse Wall. Kellum is the only man I slept with in Stonecut County. Hell, he's the only man I've slept with *ever*. But what the hell kind of question is that?

"Did one of your brothers fuck me against a tree by the Luckahannock, and the condom broke, and when I called, he hung up on me and blocked my number?"

I stalk to the fridge and swing open the door with a bit more force than I intend. I've changed my mind. I do want a drink.

"You don't need to be vulgar," he says to my back.

"True. I should be a civilized adult. Like you and your folks."

There's hardly anything on the shelves besides beer and condiments. I don't like dark beers. There are bottled waters. I grab one.

When I turn, he's standing at attention, wired. I guess there is a temper under there somewhere. Maybe I should tread carefully. I am alone in his house. There's a gun somewhere.

But it's been a long damn day. My head's aching. And I'm so tired. I'm just not afraid enough right now to watch my mouth.

I take a swig of cool water, and then level a glare at him.

"You know, Mia looks so much like your sister that you knew

her immediately. She's six. We fucked six years ago. What makes your brain jump to 'could be one of my brothers'?"

I lift my eyebrows and wait, but he has nothing to say.

That's the way of it, though, isn't it? For people like him. They make the rules; they enforce the law. There can't possibly be consequences for them. Consequences are for other folks.

I inhale, force down the lid on the boiling pot inside me. I can't afford to be so mad that it makes me stupid. This is an opening. I have to be smart.

He wants this not to be his problem?

I can make that happen.

"Fifty thousand."

His eyes narrow. "What?"

"Fifty thousand, and Mia and I go back to where we came from, and we never darken your doorstep again."

He kind of sputters. Was fifty too high?

"She's my child," he bites out through clenched teeth.

"You sure about that? Could be Cash's."

There's a war on his face. Oh yeah, he has a temper. It's not a quick one, but it's rising now, flashing in those blue eyes. He's not so calm anymore. Not so in control.

Good.

Adrenaline pumps through my veins. I crack my neck. I want to fight.

"Why didn't you tell me?" he growls.

"I called you. Remember? *I'm not interested. Click.* Like I was tryin' to sell you an extended warranty on your car."

His eyes flick, fast, as if he's searching up the memory. Is it even there? He's probably turned down dozens of girls over the years.

"You didn't say you were pregnant."

"You didn't let me get a word in edgewise."

"You could have tried again."

"You blocked my number."

"You could have come to the house. To the station."

I snort. "Didn't need to. The house and the station came to me, didn't they?"

"What do you mean?" His brow furrows, but it's not all confusion. There's dawning suspicion there. His stance shifts almost imperceptibly. He's bracing himself.

My anger ebbs a little.

"You didn't know, did you?"

He's silent, waiting for me to go on.

"Your dad, your uncle, and the sheriff paid me a visit. They told me to get gone."

I wait for him to say that's a lie. I wait for the scoff. The instant denial.

Instead, his face blanches white. His pupils constrict to tiny dots, the blue swallowing them up, and he slowly lowers himself into a chair, shaken. His expression is raw, unguarded.

I can see the gears turning in his head, the second he fits another piece together, every realization sapping strength from his spine.

I glance down at the hardwood floor. Looking at him in this moment feels like an intrusion.

"They definitely thought I'd get rid of it," I offer, as if it's consolation. It's not. I'm not really sorry for him. But I can't watch a man take a body blow and not wince on the inside. I'm not that hard.

I peek up at him. His shoulders curve as he stares at the old Formica table.

"They didn't tell you," I say, but it's obvious.

"No."

I watch while he collects himself. It's like he's putting on his uniform. His back straightens. His chin lifts. He inhales and hardens his face until it's cold and unreadable again.

He nudges the chair across from him with his foot. "Won't you come and sit down?"

I'd rather not. I feel better standing over here. I don't want to get closer, or take a seat, or talk about this like two civilized adults.

I don't want to make myself small on a couch while men with all the power tell me how it's gonna be.

Maybe I would have if he'd asked a second ago, but I've got his measure now. I know exactly how long it takes for him to pick himself up off the floor. And it's seconds. That kind of control makes for a dangerous man.

"I'm happy where I am."

He casts me a carefully even look, oozing restraint, that suggests I'd like to reconsider. Probably works well on criminals, that subtle suggestion that his patience isn't endless.

I'm not a crook. I haven't done anything wrong.

After a few seconds stretch into painful silence, he grimaces. With a huff, he turns his chair to face me, not the table, and braces his hands on his thighs.

"Will you tell me what happened?" He closes his eyes, and then opens them again, finding mine, pinning me where I stand. "Please."

"When your people came to visit?"

"The whole story."

Well, maybe I should have taken the seat. Makes my entire body bone-tired just thinking about where to begin. It's not a story I've really told before. I figure it's better to make it brief.

"I got pregnant. Your people heard and ran me off."

"That's it?"

"Of course not."

"What else then?"

"What exactly do you want to know?"

"Everything."

A crushing sadness squeezes my chest. *Everything*. What does that even mean?

Does he want to know how when I finally got myself to the clinic, and they did an ultrasound, the older lady doctor smoothed my hair from my face so it didn't get wet as I cried while we listened to the ka-thunk, ka-thunk, ka-thunk?

All the problems and the C-section and how I didn't know for years later that I should have been scared shitless?

How Mia came out bright red and then turned yellow, and I was terrified she'd stay that way?

How the woman at the hospital asked me was I sure when I left the space for father blank on the birth certificate. Was I *really* sure?

But I didn't know if Kellum spelled his name with a "C" or a "K" and was it a "U" or an "A" and getting it wrong seemed worse than leaving it blank.

How afterwards, as the years went on, and the drama faded, none of it mattered much at all anymore?

He must get tired of waiting for me to speak.

"I remember when you called," he says. "You must have found out a while before then."

I fold the sadness and tuck it away in a corner. He doesn't want to hear *everything*. He wants to figure out who's to blame.

"Not really. I left it longer than I should have to find out for sure. Wishful thinking, you know? I called you the day I took the test. You hung up. I was thinking over what to do, and then your dad and Mr. Price and the sheriff showed up."

I take a breath. He's listening hard, those cold, blue eyes assessing every word I say.

"How did they know?" he asks.

"Pandy Bullard. She can't keep her mouth shut. Your brother Cash heard. Told them."

"Cash knew?"

I shrug. "Cash heard."

"Was he with them?"

I shake my head no.

"What did they say?"

I don't revisit that memory often. It sneaks up on me, but I slam the door quick if I catch it coming.

I inhale. "They called me a liar and told me I'd better stop spreading gossip about you. You could be in real trouble on account of being a cop, and me being a minor. They said my grandpa would lose his job, and that would mean he'd lose his house. I said I'd go back to South Carolina, and they didn't need to worry."

"You told them, though? You said you were pregnant."

"I didn't say anything. I said I'd go back to South Carolina."

His shoulders relax, and his hard gaze lightens a touch. "They didn't know. They thought it was a rumor."

I shrug. "Not sure about your dad and the sheriff. Mr. Price came back the next day when Grandpa was up at the barn. He gave me two hundred dollars cash and told me to get rid of it."

Rich men have no concept of what things cost. And what can be bought. I used the two hundred on a bus ticket and rent so Mama would let me move back in.

Kellum winces, sucking in a breath so fast, he hisses. His muscles tense again, straining against his shirt.

I'm waiting for him to deny it all. Turn it back on me somehow. The woman gets the blame, that's the way it goes.

When she gets pregnant, it's the woman's fault. When the man doesn't stick around, it's because of her: she picked badly, or she couldn't keep him. If she has trouble making ends meet, well, she made her bed, didn't she?

It's like the entirety of the world is women's responsibility, and when we hold everything together, we're not strong, we're suckers. We're letting men take advantage.

Bunch of crap. People need to pick.

I swig from my water bottle. It's silent in the house except for the gentle whir of the air conditioner. I've never seen this type before. Instead of blocking the windows, the units are mounted high on the wall.

Kellum follows my gaze to the white plastic rectangle above the doorframe, and then he seems to brace himself.

"I'm sorry," he says, squeezing his eyes shut for a second. "You were seventeen?"

I nod.

Chapter 5

"I wouldn't have touched you if I'd known."

I'm sure he's only telling the truth, but the words still feel like a blow. I wrap my arms tighter around my body.

This is what I am never going to let Mia feel. She is not a regret. Not a mistake. Not trouble. Not a problem in need of fixing or a bad choice.

"Same," I say. I ignore the twinge of guilt in my gut while I watch ire flare in his eyes.

Then, in an instant, his face is cold again, lips pressed thin with determination.

"What are you going to do?" I steel myself.

He doesn't answer right away. He stares at me, searching for something. I unconsciously straighten, tugging down the hem of my shirt.

Then he nods to himself as if he's come to some conclusion, balls his hands into loose fists, and very deliberately meets my eye.

"What do *you* want to happen?"

I blink. "What?"

I wait for him to go on, but he doesn't. He sits there, tense and still.

What do I want to happen?

That's a crazy question.

The plan was to get a job, save some money, go back to South Carolina. Find a place in a different school district. Maybe near my cousins.

I guess I figured if I didn't seek out Kellum Wall, I wouldn't run into him.

But that's a seventeen-year-old's way of thinking, isn't it?

The cool kids and the rich folks exist on a higher plane. They don't notice you. Not really. That's why it felt like something close to magic when Kellum Wall noticed me that night at the bonfire.

But people are people, and this is a small town. When I started at the high school back in the day, I was the object of curiosity for weeks. Did I really think I'd enroll Mia in the elementary school and no one would ask questions?

Pandy stirred up a whole hornet's nest when I got pregnant. Did I really think she wasn't gonna tell the whole town when I moved back next door with Mia in tow?

But what do I want?

There's so much. If I start thinking about it, I'll never finish.

I skim the condensation beaded on my water bottle with my thumb, collecting the drops.

Why won't he say something?

Offer me money. Threaten me with lawyers. Throw out a half-baked plan so he's not the bad guy. Kind of like how Uncle Pete always promised to swing by and take my cousins out for burgers.

But Kellum's not saying a word. His hands are fisting tighter now, the veins in his forearms popping.

My heart quickens, but it's not fear. I know what a man looks like before he throws a punch. And Kellum doesn't look like that.

This thumping in my chest? It's closer to stage fright. When is the last time someone waited to hear what I had to say?

I can't remember.

Nerves swoop in my belly.

I could never say what I really want. So what do I want for Mia?

"I want to get Mia into school when it starts back up. And I don't want her in a special class. I want her with the other kids."

"Okay." His brow knits.

"If you're asking what I want to happen with you, it doesn't matter to me."

I draw in a deep breath, focus on my tone so he has no doubt that I mean what I'm about to say one hundred percent.

"If you or your people mess with us, we will be in the wind. I don't care how much money you have, how many lawyers you know, how many cops are your friends, how many judges you play golf with or whatever. I'm not a kid anymore, and I'm not stupid. We will be gone. Believe that."

He goes rigid, his eyes bright, maybe with indignation. I don't know. I don't know him.

"She's *my* child," I say with all the force I have in me.

"I'm not going to try to take her from you," he growls.

"Good."

"You don't believe me."

"You said you won't."

"I keep my word." His voice rises.

"So do I." I let it hang there in the air.

Eventually, he leans back in his chair. "I want you to stay here."

"We're here."

"Not just until you get the power back on. I want to go get the rest of your stuff tomorrow."

"No."

"Mia is my responsibility, too."

Mama slapped eye-rolling out of me early on, but I can't stop myself. *Responsibility*.

"We don't know you."

He stares up at the ceiling, the cords in his neck straining.

"I want to get to know Mia."

"That's fine. You can come over and visit."

"That trailer should be condemned. It's no place for a child."

"Tell your daddy."

He huffs in exasperation and shifts in his chair. You can see the urge to stand in him, the instinct to loom and swell his chest. I don't know why he's still sitting there like his mama put him in punishment.

"I will," he says. "He can't know how bad it is."

"Yeah. Like he didn't know about Mia."

"I cannot believe he knew."

"Right."

"He's a good man."

"So everyone says."

"If he'd known, he would have helped you."

"He heard the truth—your brother told him—and your dad brought his two closest friends to bully a seventeen-year-old girl into keeping her mouth shut." My voice is rising, too, anger flaring to life in my chest.

I never got angry back when I first had Mia. Fear took up all the room. And then one day when she was almost three, I was at the clinic, and the doctor was saying she had concerns, and on the way home, I got pissed.

It's like a switch flipped. I couldn't be scared anymore 'cause anger took all my energy. Anger at the doctors who tell you that you have to do things you can't afford at places you can't get to with time you don't have. Anger at the bosses who don't want to give you time off and then cut your hours when you have to stay home with your sick kid. Anger at Mama who had all the advice in the world, but not an ounce of patience.

There was so much to be angry about.

It eased over time. Mia didn't talk much, but she could. She followed stories, and she knew her left from right. She could tell time at five years old. There was a show about explorers who discover new animals each episode, and two minutes before it came on, she'd come find me to see if I could convince Mama to switch the channel.

So I got less scared and the anger faded, but I saw things a different way. When I was seventeen and knocked up, I felt like I was in trouble because I'd done something wrong. I screwed up. Whatever happened, I had it coming.

But Mia is not a crime. She's the best thing I ever did. No one wanted her to even exist, this beautiful *person*. *No one* thought she was anything other than trouble.

Like me.

I'll be damned if the world is gonna do to her what it tried to do to me. It took a few years, but I got it straight—who the bad guys were, and that I was not one of them.

I'm so lost in thought, it doesn't register that Kellum hasn't replied. He's staring at his lap again, a tic pulsing in his temple.

He almost seems more shook than he did on the side of the

road when he recognized Mia. There's shame in the bend of his neck.

I don't have any comfort to offer him, but my chest aches. I know what loss looks like, and I know how it feels.

But he's not the victim here. And if he is, he's not *my* victim.

Sure, I could've gone by his house. Or the station.

And his people could have fired Grandpa, and kicked him out of the home where he raised his kids.

They're Kellum's family. He has to know what they're capable of.

I don't owe him any comfort. Certainly, no more than what his folks offered me.

Oh, crap.

I cross the room and plop down in the empty chair across the table. He rouses, surprised. He fixes his chair so he's facing me. I set my water bottle on the table between us.

"I'm sorry," he says.

The words sting like antiseptic on a cut, not a balm. There is nothing I can say to that. I am, too.

"How do I make this right?" His voice has dropped, and it's rough. Broken.

I lift a shoulder.

"I want you to stay here."

"We can set something up. Visitation."

"That's not good enough," he answers, his cop voice re-emerging. I bristle. He stops. Sighs. Leans back in his chair, and stares out the window into the dark. "When's her birthday? I don't even know her birthday."

"March twelfth."

"My birthday's in March."

"She came early."

He listens, intent, a crease showing between his brows.

"I had this condition. Preeclampsia. My blood pressure went nuts. They tried to keep her baking longer, but it got too risky, so they popped her early."

"How early?"

"Six weeks."

"Jesus. Is she okay?"

"Asthma. That's all."

"Are you okay?"

I blink. My blood pressure went right back down after I delivered her. I had a killer headache and my vision got blurry, but it cleared up. Frankly, no one really fussed too much about me. I was young. I was gonna be fine. We all worried about Mia; she was so tiny.

"Yeah."

"Is the asthma bad?"

"Only when the pollen count is super high."

"Is she on an inhaler?"

"Yeah."

"You packed it, right?"

"Nope. Left my child's life-saving medication back in the trailer."

He bares his teeth. "You don't have to be a smart-ass."

"You don't have to be condescending. You don't know more than me about taking care of my child."

"I don't mean to imply that I do."

"Yet, you keep on implying."

"Are you always this prickly?"

"Pretty much. You always this high-handed?"

"Pretty much."

We fall quiet, glaring at each other. The corner of his lip twitches. I bite the inside of my cheeks so I don't crack a smile.

"I want you two to stay here."

"Why?"

Earlier, he said Mia was his responsibility. He can fulfill his responsibilities if we're in the trailer. I'll take a child support check. Happily.

He inhales, and his eyes darken. "Because I don't want to miss any more time."

Chapter 5

He swallows. There's a crack in his façade. My heart rate quickens.

"Shay, I know you think I have all the power here, but I don't. I only have what you'll give me. I want to get to know my child. I don't want to lose anything else. I know you have no reason to trust me. But that's what I'm asking for."

From another man, it'd sound like pleading, but Kellum has that natural confidence. Part of you already agrees with him before you totally process what he's asking.

Pump the brakes, though. We're not moving in with Kellum Wall. That's crazy.

But isn't going back to the trailer crazier if this place is an option? There's no dank stench here. No Lonnie bellowing, drunk and belligerent at all hours. No scary dog running loose, getting in the garbage cans. There's not much in the pantry here, but more than I have. The cash I have left could stretch further. I could make it until school starts.

But I don't know this man.

I do know his people. Not a scruple between them. But that's a very flimsy concern compared to black mold.

Kellum attempts a cajoling smile, but it comes off sad. Heartbroken.

"We can bring Mia to see the horses. She was really taken with them on the ride here. Has she ever ridden?"

Is he serious?

"A pony ride at the carnival maybe."

"There's a really friendly mare we all learned on. She's getting older, but she still has the sweetest temperament."

I nod. "Orange Blossom."

His head tilts, and then that bright smile breaks across his face again. Changes him entirely.

"Yeah. Orange Blossom." His eyes crinkle at the corners. "How did you know?"

"She was one of my grandpa's favorites."

"Did you ride her?"

"We weren't allowed to touch the horses. But Grandpa would always take us grandkids up to see them when we'd visit."

He stiffens. The smile's gone.

"Shay, I am so sorry."

I willfully misunderstand him. "I was never interested in riding anyway."

I'm too tired to keep going. I yawn, make a show of it, and clamber to my feet. Kellum rises with me.

"I think I'm gonna head to bed now."

"Will you stay?"

"We can talk about it tomorrow."

He opens his mouth to argue, but he must think better of it. Instead, he ambles off toward the sink. He rinses out his beer bottle and drops it in the blue recycling bin.

"Okay. Do you need anything? More blankets?"

I shake my head, but then I remember. "Do you have a spare toothbrush?" I forgot mine, too.

"Upstairs."

We walk up together, careful to be quiet, the stairs squeaking under our tread. There's a faint patter of rain and the steady whir of the air conditioners. The house smells old, but it has all the good old house smells. Polish. Wax. Wood.

I follow Kellum past the cracked door where Mia's sleeping to the end of the hall.

"This is my room," he murmurs. "This is the master bath." He ducks into the next door. I see him rummaging in an old-timey medicine cabinet, the kind with a glass pane instead of a mirror.

He emerges with an opened multi-pack, two toothbrushes left. "Does Mia need one, too?"

I nod, taking them both. "Thanks."

He's close. The hall is narrow, but still—he's close. I have to crick my neck to meet his eye.

He jerks his chin toward the other end of the hall. "That's the door to the attic. You might want to leave it shut."

"I'm not gonna poke around your house."

Chapter 5

"There's a bat."

"We won't bother him."

"You and Mia can explore all you want. My brothers and I used to love poking around this house when we were kids."

"You lived here when you were little?"

"No. It was my grandparents' place."

"They passed?"

"Some time ago."

"I'm sorry."

"Thank you. The house had been empty a few years. When my, uh, wife and I split, my folks offered me the place. I took them up on it."

Oh, yeah. The ex-wife. Pandy filled me in. She was Kellum's childhood sweetheart. They were on-again, off-again. Right after the night at the river, they got back together for good. She's the daughter of the man who owns the Stonecut County Bank. A newscaster on Channel Thirteen. They were the perfect couple, and no one knows why they broke up, so everyone figures she cheated on him, and he's too much of a gentleman to say.

At least that's what Pandy says.

"You divorced or just separated?"

"Divorced."

"How long have you been living here?"

"Two years."

"Are you gonna stay here? It's big for one person."

I don't know why I'm being such a busybody. Especially here and now. We're almost whispering, and the hall is dimly lit, edged in shadows. The only light is what spills out from the bathroom and a weak glow from an old sconce on the wall at the top of the stairs.

And he's standing so close. His bare feet are inches from the toes of my flip-flops.

"I love the place. Besides, I didn't want to look into anything else until everything was settled. There was a lot of back-and-forth with the split."

"Back-and-forth?"

"It's amicable. You don't have to worry. There won't be any scenes."

I snort. "There's gonna be so many scenes."

He grimaces. "I suppose there will." He sobers, pinning me with those blue eyes again. "I won't let any of it near Mia."

"Neither will I."

I expect him to put his back up, but instead, the half-smile sneaks back. "You're a fierce one, aren't you?"

And there they go again. My eyes roll. "Prickly? Fierce? Like a porcupine?"

"You're not unlike a porcupine."

I shake my head, a real yawn garbling whatever smart aleck response I was mumbling in reply.

"You're tired," he says.

"Yeah."

He jerks his chin toward the door to the spare room. I pivot, expecting him to turn in the direction of his room, but instead, there's the lightest pressure against the small of my back. Shivers skitter up and down my spine.

We only take a few steps before he reaches around and gently pushes the door wide.

The curtains are pulled back, but there's no moon or stars, nothing but blackness visible out the window. The only light comes from a crystal nightlight plugged into the wall. Mia's a shadowy lump under the thick quilt.

"Is she okay?" he whispers.

"Yeah."

"She's not gonna get too hot?"

"If she does, she'll kick the covers off."

He stands in the doorway, hand on the knob, brows knit, staring at the bump on the bed.

I hold up the package of toothbrushes. "Thanks for these."

His gaze breaks. "If you need anything, I'm down the hall."

"Okay."

He doesn't move, and neither do I.

"Do you think she knows who I am?"

A lump swells in my throat. "We'll tell her. In due time. Then she'll know."

"Shay—" He doesn't finish it, whatever he was going to say, but I guess he doesn't need to.

"Goodnight," he says, and slowly draws the door closed.

There's a moment or two before I hear him tread down the hall, step heavy in the near silence of the old, creaky house.

6

SHAY

I sleep like the dead, deeper than I usually do. I think it's the quiet. No assholes burning rubber late at night or drunks howling at the moon. Even the rain eased up. It's bright and shiny now. The sun's streaming in the window, and I smell bacon.

Mia's already awake, playing with her critters on the carpet. She's in her nightgown with the mermaid princess on it. She's had it for years. It hits way above the knee now, but she won't let me put it out when the park has the community yard sale.

"You hungry?" I ask, scrubbing my eyes.

She shakes her head.

"Well, I'm hungry." I hoist myself out of bed and scoop her up to swing her like a clock. She squeals and ducks her face, but I smack a kiss right on her cheek. "Get decent, kiddo. Put some shorts on."

I go pee, and then I snatch my bra from the rocking chair beside the bed where I hung it before I passed out. That bacon smells ready now. A shower can wait.

Mia grabs a huge fistful of forest animals, and she's considering another when I take her free hand. "Come on, my love. Let's see what's for breakfast."

Chapter 6

I feel strangely light this morning. I trip down the stairs, and even though nerves spring to life in my belly, I'm not worried.

For this moment, the basics are covered. Food. Shelter. Electric.

When we hit the kitchen, the table's set, but there's no Kellum. There's bacon heaped on a plate, a dish of peaches, and another dish of cinnamon apples.

Next to the stove, there's a bowl full of pancake mix and a carton of eggs.

Mia hops into a chair and starts lining up her animals. I grab a slice of bacon. No sense in letting it get cold.

As I munch, I catch a low, angry murmuring from the back porch. I take the seat beside Mia, and sneak a peek out the window. Kellum's stalking back and forth, ranting into his phone, pissed.

Mia turns full in her chair to stare at him, too.

This morning, he's in a different pair of faded jeans, low on the hips and tight across the thighs. He's wearing a forest green T-shirt. It looks soft. His hair's wet and tousled as if he's been running his fingers through it. His hair's thick, the color of polished wood. That same shine.

He pauses for a moment, bracing his arms against the white railing, staring out at the impossibly green, rolling fields accented with groves of sugar maple and dogwood, too pretty and perfectly placed to be natural.

Horses graze in the distance near the huge red octagonal barn. Mia spots them and crawls onto her knees, leaning as close as she can get to the window, pressing her fingers to the pane.

"Yeah, they're something, aren't they? My grandpa would take us up to that barn. Each horse has his own stall with his name on a sign, hanging on the door."

Mia flashes me her "go on" look.

"It smelled so good. Like wood and straw. Only a little like poop."

Mia gifts me with one of her split-second giggles.

"Those horses would stamp and snort and whinny. Reminded me of all of us at Aunt Carol's on Thanksgiving. Eating and carrying on." I make a *nom nom nom* noise, and Mia giggles again.

She's generally unsettled by new places and things. It's a relief, and a minor miracle, that she's rolling with all of this.

On the porch, Kellum starts his pacing again, even more agitated, almost spitting out his words, and then he sees us. He stops short, barks a curt word, and hangs up, slipping the phone in his back pocket.

He stands there a moment, and then he slowly raises his hand in greeting.

Mia splays her fingers on the glass.

They both stay like that for a few beats. Whatever pissed him off fades from his face while Mia studies him intently.

Does she recognize him?

A shiver races down my spine.

I always figured I'd never know it if I ran across my daddy. But who could really say? I'd know Mia anywhere. If she were taken from me, I'd know her. No doubt in my mind.

And that's what happened, isn't it? She was taken from him. In a way.

If I set the hard feelings aside for a moment, if I look at the past from where I sit now—he didn't get to decide. And who knows what he would have chosen? He might have been the one to hand me a wad of cash.

He might not.

It's a brand-new thought. *He might not.*

It's too big to wrap my head around so early in the morning. I'm relieved when he tramps in the back door, stomping his boots on the doormat.

"Your back porch that muddy?" I ask, sliding a few more slices of bacon onto my plate.

He smiles, chagrined. "Force of habit."

He walks to the sink to wash his hands. "I thought the peaches and apples might be good on pancakes."

"Or on their own." I nod at Mia. She's almost done with the serving dish of peaches. She dug in when she lost interest in the horses.

"Does she like pancakes?"

"You can ask her."

Mia is capable of making herself understood. He'll learn.

He stiffens, but he shakes it off quick enough. "Want pancakes, Mia?"

She holds up three fingers.

"She can have two." Three would make her sick after all those peaches.

"What if I make them small?" Kellum's eyes sparkle.

"You can, but it seems cruel to make them small if she can only have two." I lift my chin.

"Mama is a tough customer, eh?" Kellum casts Mia a conspiratorial smile.

She's watching us both from the corner of her eye as she rearranges her critters. Her expression's noncommittal.

I don't dignify his comment with a response. I am a tough customer. He needs to learn that, too.

When he realizes no one's biting, he changes tack. "How many pancakes do you want, Mama?"

"I'll have two, thank you."

"Coming right up." He's smiling, bemused, as he opens the fridge to take out the milk.

We're all quiet as he lights the range and heats the griddle, testing the heat by flicking water on it to see if it sizzles. My Grandma used to do that.

I stare out the window, admiring the view. It really is as pretty as a postcard. Stonecut Mountain is dark with pines, and mist still clings to its peak, even though the sun is high in the sky now. People live up there, on the mountainside. Real backwoods folk who only come to town to stock up.

Connie warned me off them when I first came to town. She said they're not Christian. I don't see how she could possibly know, and I don't know why it would possibly matter.

"Here we are," Kellum says, sliding plates in front of us.

Mia has two pancakes, reasonably-sized. I have three, and they cover the plate. Kellum has a stack.

"I'll never be able to eat all this."

"I'll finish 'em off if you don't. No worries." He winks at Mia. "Or Little Bit here can clean your plate for you."

Mia already has the maple syrup open.

"Just a drizzle," I say.

She gives me a look. Yeah, I don't know why I'm fussing either. With Mia, I'm always nagging her to eat.

I sigh and settle back in my chair.

I'm probably fussing 'cause I don't know what to make of this. If someone's making breakfast, it's me. And Mia and I eat and run, either because I have work and she has school, or because we're trying to make ourselves scarce before my mother wakes up and launches into her bitching.

At some point while he was cooking, Kellum started coffee. When the pot hisses, he pauses cutting up his pancakes into perfect squares to pour two cups.

"Do you take cream and sugar?" he asks.

I shake my head.

"Me neither."

He hands me a steaming mug, and we both sip. It's good. Strong.

Mia and I are facing each other. He's seated between us. He fills his entire side, corner to corner, his legs sprawling underneath the table. Every time I move, I knock into his shin or his boots.

"Guess the table's not built for three," he says when I give up and draw my legs up to sit cross-legged on the chair.

"You've got long legs." It just kind of comes out. A second later, my face flames.

He glances at me, amused, chewing his pancakes.

"Like a spider?" he asks after he swallows.

Chapter 6

"Giraffe," Mia says, her mouth full.

I snort at his look of surprise.

"I look like a giraffe?" He rests a hand on his chest, feigning indignation.

My nerves jangle. Sometimes Mia doesn't get when a person is fooling around.

"Giraffe *legs*," she says, shoveling more pancake in her mouth. Maybe she could have finished three.

"As long as I don't have that freaky tongue." Kellum shudders.

Mia nods. "They're prehensile. That means like a monkey's tail."

My heart leaps in my chest. That was two sentences. In a freakin' row! My baby girl is having a *conversation*!

I told 'em so. I told *everyone* so.

Kellum's giving me a strange look. He doesn't know that was one of her goals on that damn IEP Forming sentences. Taking turns in a conversation. She's nailing 'em. One after another.

I want to get up and dance around the kitchen. I want to call that school, get Principal Rice on the line, and shout, "They are prehensile. That means like a monkey's tail, bitch!" at the top of my lungs.

I know she knows what prehensile means. We watch nature shows for hours a day. And I know she can speak in sentences. She doesn't often, but she has. Only to me, though.

I'm grinning, barely restraining myself from leaping out of my chair, picking her up, and swinging her around the kitchen.

"Yeah," Kellum says, serious and apparently oblivious to what's happening. "I know what you mean. My tail's prehensile, too."

It takes a beat, but then Mia lets out a peal of giggles. "You don't have a tail!"

"It's a small tail."

"Uhn, uhn." Mia shakes her head. "Tails are in proportion to the size of the body. So you'd have a long tail. You're telling a lie." She thinks a minute. "A fib. You're fibbing."

She's grinning, she's so satisfied with herself.

I'm losing it. The beginnings of tears are burning my eyes, and I don't know if it's because she's having an actual conversation with someone who isn't me or 'cause she told him he must have a long tail, and the effort in keeping a straight face is almost painful.

I squirm in my seat. I have to be cool. Mia freaks out when I freak out, and I don't want this to stop.

"I do fib sometimes," he says.

"About tails," Mia concurs.

"Only about tails."

"You shouldn't fib."

"Noted." Kellum chews his pancakes, and then he casually changes the conversation. "Do you want to go see the horses today? Maybe ride one?"

I've lost track of how many times they've gone back and forth, but it's way more times than the IEP says, and way more than she does with me.

Hold up. Ride horses?

My stomach knots.

The horses are by the barn. The barn is by the Lodge. Where his parents live. And who knows if his uncle's around? The whole town generally knows when Van Price arrives 'cause his helicopter flies in over the river, obnoxiously loud and low, but I haven't been noticing it lately. It's become a part of the soundtrack again.

Kellum's frowning at me. Mia hasn't answered him.

"It'll be just us," he says. "I called up to the Lodge this morning. Some hands might be around, but no one else."

Mia stares wistfully out the window at the horses and squirms in her seat.

I fold my arms. "I don't want to put people out of their own property." And I don't want to be anywhere near his family.

I sure as hell don't want them anywhere near Mia.

Kellum studies me, narrowing his eyes at my crossed arms. "You know, I own an interest in Stonecut Farms. Through the trust."

Chapter 6

He pauses, but I'm not sure what to say. I thought he was the sheriff's deputy.

"All the grandkids have a stake in the trust. My grandfather established it. We all own an interest and a stud."

"You own a stud?" My lip twitches.

"Dundalk Nice. He's not what he used to be, but he's still going strong."

"I don't know what to make of that."

Kellum's eyes twinkle. "You want to swing by his stall?"

My heart sinks, the brief distraction over. I don't want to get any closer to those people than I currently am. Based on his body language on the porch earlier, Kellum's already had words with them. What are they gonna do?

I can't begin to guess, but my belly aches. Every fiber of my being shouts to keep Mia far away from them.

They didn't want her or me to exist back then. What will they do when they find out we're back?

"Rather not, if it's all the same to you."

"It'll just be us."

"So you say." My stubborn's shaking itself off, getting ready to rumble.

Kellum searches my face, sets down his fork, and leans back in his chair.

"Shay, I'm a man of my word."

He says it with such perfect assurance it borders on mild irritation. How can I doubt his word? How could I even need reassurance? He said it. Therefore, it is.

"I wouldn't know."

He pushes his plate away. "If I say it'll be just us, it will be just us."

"You say so, so that's the way it is, eh?" Bitterness creeps into my voice.

"Yes."

"I need to trust you?"

"Yes," he repeats, more emphatically.

I check Mia. She's bored with the conversation, and she's back to playing with her critters.

"'Cause you're the man. Nothing happens that you don't want."

His muscles tense all at once. His face darkens. I wait, but he seems at a loss for words.

We sit there, glaring at each other in silence, until Mia clip-clops one of her little plastic critters past my plate. It's not a horse, but it's the closest thing she's got. A donkey.

"Mama? Please?"

Clip-clop. She bops the donkey closer until it's on the edge of the table, staring at me with its round white donkey eyes.

"Mama? Horses?"

My shoulders slump. She never asks for anything, let alone twice. I touch the donkey's little nose. Mia nudges him against my fingertip.

"Nothing will happen that you don't want." Kellum's voice is low. Rough. Firm.

I don't believe him. Hell, he probably doesn't even realize what a lie he's telling. I bet that's a promise he actually thinks he can keep.

But this is the road I put us on when I agreed to come to this house. Maybe even when I had the idea to come to Stonecut County.

We're in for a penny now, and these people are gonna do what they're gonna do. But this time around, I'm not seventeen and terrified. It's gonna play out different when it goes down.

"Gimme a hundred dollars."

"What?" His upstanding officer expression drops, and his eyes narrow, suspicion creeping in. I don't care. He can think what he wants.

"I need a hundred dollars."

"For what?"

"For a ride share to the bus station. If we need it. If something happens that I don't want."

I don't think a ride share would even come out this far—and I have no clue how much they'd charge if they did—but I'm making a point.

Kellum glares at me.

I glare back.

He pushes back in his chair and stands. "Come on then."

Mia blinks up.

His voice softens. "Everything's okay. You stay here, Little Bit. Finish your breakfast."

She glances at me. I nod and force a smile, and she goes back to her critters. She's arranged the cutlery into fences, and the creatures are grazing in clusters, just like the horses outside. She'll be occupied for a while.

"Okay." I drop my napkin on the table and follow Kellum to the front of the house.

I haven't gotten the tour yet, so I'm a little surprised that there's another room through the parlor. It's definitely a parlor, not a living room. There's no TV or coffee table. There is an old-timey sofa on carved wooden legs, a matching chair, and a rocker facing a fireplace. A grandfather clock stands on the far wall, and a gold-framed painting of a black stallion in a stall hangs above the mantle.

Kellum leads me through a doorway to a study. Unlike the parlor, this room seems lived in. There's a big desk with mail stacked in a tray and a computer. Everything is dark wood and leather. More horse paintings hang between bookshelves. It's a man's room.

Behind the desk, there's a black metal gun safe, the tall kind.

"You can have a seat." He gestures to one of the overstuffed leather chairs facing the desk.

I stand.

His jaw tightens, and he turns to enter the combination. I look out the window. You can see the barn from here, too. There's more movement now. Two hands are standing in a yard, chatting, and a frisky black mare stamps, impatient at the end of her reins.

My grandpa was never one to stand around. When he'd take us

to see the horses, he'd still be pitching hay and raking crap. Never idle a moment. My heart twinges, and I rub my chest. I miss him.

"Here."

Kellum pulls out a metal strongbox. He flips it open and takes out a stack of twenties. It's way more than a hundred dollars.

He flips through it with his thumb, and then sets it in front of me on the desk. "That should be two thousand."

He stands at attention, chest puffed, hands on his hips. Pissed and lordly.

Behind him, the gun safe door is wide open. He's got a bunch of rifles, a few handguns. Boxes of ammo. It's a big safe, and it's full. I guess he *is* in law enforcement. Still. That's a lot of firepower.

"Why do you have stacks of cash in your gun safe?"

"It doesn't matter."

"Do you run drugs or something?"

"I'm the deputy sheriff." He bristles.

I purse my lips. I said what I said. "I'm not an idiot. You've got a lot more stacks in that box. Do you gamble?"

"Do you need to know?"

"Yes."

"It's not my business to tell."

"Holding it for a friend, eh?"

"Just take the money."

"Nope. I know trouble when I see it. Stacks of cash in a safe full of guns is trouble."

He draws in a breath, and his gaze drops. I'm right, and he knows it. He stares out the window a moment. Seems to wrestle with something.

"I don't have a checking account at the moment," he finally says.

Neither do I, but I figure he's got different reasons. "Why not?"

His jaw tics. "My ex. She spends too much."

I'm not entirely following.

"She ran up debt." He exhales. "She's still probably running up debt. More than can be paid back. We had to declare bankruptcy.

She still tries to open credit in my name. Dina set me up with a service that checks so I can shut it down."

I've never had a credit card. I've gotten offers in the mail, but the math didn't work. I'd be too tempted to max it out to bail myself out of one jam or another—there's never been a shortage—and I'd only ever be able to pay the minimum. I'd be sending them twenty extra bucks a month forever for doing me the favor of lending me five hundred bucks one time. Donny on Sixth Street has much more favorable terms.

"So why can't you have a checking account?"

"I thought closing it would be a deterrent when we were married. I haven't gotten around to opening another."

"Is that why you broke up? The money?"

His face hardens. For a second, I don't think he's going to answer. I guess it isn't my business, really.

"In a way?" He's quiet a moment. "She never saw anything wrong with it."

"I don't understand."

"It would have been one thing if she had a problem. If she couldn't stop herself. And, for what it's worth, I don't think she can stop herself. But she doesn't see anything wrong with it. She thinks all the stuff—she thinks she needs it."

Not a problem I'm familiar with, but I've heard it's a struggle for some.

"The divorce would have been final a lot sooner, but she felt she should get more."

"Like the stacks of cash in the gun safe?"

He winces. "Those are my paychecks. I'm not hiding assets."

"So you went to court?"

He shakes his head. "Not in the end. We're actually civil. We run in the same circles. If we'd taken it to court, there'd have been talk. Our families go way back. It didn't get that far. We settled."

"What was she holding out for?"

"A stake in the trust, but it's clear that only biological issue get a cut. Legally, it's not a marital asset."

"So, she tried to take your money, and you both kept paying lawyers, but you didn't actually take it to court, 'cause your families are tight, and you see each other all the time?"

He shrugs a shoulder.

"That's nuts."

I grab the cash, flipping through it like he did. It's a wild feeling. I've never held this much money in my hand.

Two thousand solves a lot of problems. It's enough to do the plan. I could bail and get a cheap place back home in the school district over. It'd definitely see us through the summer.

How much would a judge give me in back support? More than two thousand. It's not like I'd be taking something I'm not owed.

There's no reason not to take the cash and move along.

Except Mia.

It hurts so bad I can hardly think it, but I want her to have more pancakes. More back-and-forth conversations about tails. I want her to have memories, so even if it all turns out sad and messed up, she knows she came from somewhere.

It doesn't seem actually possible. Like winning the lotto. Other people do win, but what are your chances?

Still. I'm not taking away Mia's chances. At anything.

I huff a sigh and peel off two hundred, placing the rest back on the desk. There are no pockets in my yoga pants, so I roll the cash and tuck it in my bra.

Kellum's confused. "You can take it all."

"I don't need it all."

He lifts his brows.

I toss a shoulder.

"I owe you. Much more than that," he says.

I liked the room when I walked in, but now, it feels uncomfortable. The light streaming in the window is too bright. Too many horses on the walls.

"You don't owe me. You owe Mia."

"I owe you both."

"Don't worry about me. Worry about her."

"I can worry about you both."

He edges closer. He's standing beside the desk now, his hand resting near the corner, inches from where I'm standing. My heart speeds up.

We both stare down at the stack of twenties.

My eyes flick up to his face. I catch his gaze, flicking down to mine. I swear there's a sizzle like when lightning burns the air.

My belly warms. His chest rises and falls, quickly.

I forget to breathe, and when I remember, I cough to cover the gasp. What am I doing?

"I'm not your worry." I fold my arms.

He nods slowly. "No, not my worry."

"If you feel obligated, don't."

"I don't feel obligated." He speaks slowly, and there's a thread of uncertainty in his voice, as if he's trying to work out in his own mind what he means to say.

I curl my toes in my flip fops. Why am I still standing here? I have the cash. Why don't I turn and go?

He reaches out, but then stops, his hand hovering in the air between us.

Butterflies flutter beneath my ribs.

What's happening?

It's so quiet. I can hear the grandfather clock ticking in the other room and the blood rushing in my ears.

His hand falls to his side.

His eyes are so blue you get confused. You think he's gazing at you intensely, with feeling, but that's just the color. I learned that the hard way. My body's being stupid, that's all. He wasn't going to touch me.

He's handsome, and when I was a girl, I had a silly crush. Of course, my palms are sweaty. It doesn't mean anything.

"Shay," he says. "Let me take you horseback riding. You and Mia."

I've already decided to go. I took the money. But I'm a damn fool, 'cause my heart lifts, and it feels so crazy good. Being asked.

"Okay," I breathe.

Some of the tension leaves his body. His lips curve ever so slightly.

"So, you've never ridden before?"

"Nope."

"Scared?"

"Never."

His smile widens, and the corners of his eyes crinkle.

"You'd never admit you're scared, would you?"

My cheeks warm. I should go before he notices I've lost my damn mind. But I stay, arms crossed so tight I'm crushing my fingers in my elbows. "Who'd I admit it to?"

His voice drops. He leans over until he's inches from my ear. "*I'm* scared."

Nerves zing around my belly, leaping like they want to get out. I stare at the desk. The floor. His tan carpenter boots.

"Why?" I ask. It comes out a whisper.

"I don't want to fuck this up."

He lets it hang there, in the air between his lips and my cheek.

He smells like soap. The green kind. And a little like maple syrup, too.

My skin tingles. I'm breathing too quick and too shallow. My brain is creaky slow, as if it's under a spell.

I stare at the shiny hardwood floor. "I'm scared of what your people will do. When they find out."

"Shay." He touches my chin, gently, lifting my face, and the little air that's left whooshes from my lungs.

The pads of his fingers are rough, but his touch is light. A hundred memories flap and flutter in the back of my mind.

"No one is allowed near you or Mia. You are both safe here. What you say goes. Understand?"

The last word has a ring to it. A demand. Shivers race down my spine.

"I'm in charge?" I mean to say it jokingly, but it comes out squeaky.

"Yes, ma'am."

His lips lift, easy, natural, no effort at all. Lord, I remember that smile. By the bonfire. His impossibly handsome face cast half in shadow, half in firelight. I was done in by that smile, and even now, I can't stop my lips from curving in response.

"Shall we go?" He sweeps his arm to the door.

A small twinge of disappointment pricks my chest, and my heart lurches.

I'm a fool.

I know better than to be disappointed. To want things.

That's what leads you into the woods against your good common sense.

It's dangerous, and I am too well-versed in consequences to make myself stupid again over a pretty face. I square my shoulders and sail out of the room, leaving Kellum to follow when he wants.

I need to get Mia dressed.

I guess we're going horseback riding.

∼

I THOUGHT we'd head out in a half hour or so.

I showered in the huge clawfoot tub, braided my wet hair, threw on a pair of jeans, sneakers, and a black tank top, and I was ready to go in twenty minutes.

And then Mia had a meltdown.

She didn't want to put her animals back in the plastic tube. She didn't want to wear long pants, and she didn't want to wear shoes with socks. And when I told her she couldn't be around the horses in her sandals, all she heard was "can't be around the horses," and she burst into tears.

Sometimes, all you can do is sit and wait.

I plopped myself in the rocking chair, resigned. Kellum knocked on the door five minutes later, just as she was calming down, to ask if everything was okay. Gave her a nice, long second wind.

I hollered "fine." Eventually, he walked off.

She doesn't have this kind of meltdown often. I call it "yanking the brakes." She'll do it after hectic days—doctor's appointments with shots, days when she has a substitute at school, when we moved here to Stonecut. It's like the world unfolds too quickly, and she's compelled to put her foot down.

No more changes. Time *out*.

No, she will not get dressed. No, I cannot brush her hair. No and no and no. Not gonna lie, I completely commiserate.

All you can do is give her space and time. Sometimes she's done for the rest of the day.

Sometimes there are horses waiting up the hill.

When she's worked herself out and the hiccups come, I go to the window and peek out the curtains.

"Ooo." I round my eyes, give her the "you won't believe this" look. I don't have to say anything else.

She glowers up from the floor, thin chest heaving, totally onto me, but she still hauls herself to her feet and trots over to see what I'm looking at. Two sleek black horses race in a distant field, one chasing the other. You can't hear the nickering or neighs, but they toss their manes, and it's something to see, even soundless and in miniature.

"Ready?"

She slips her hand in mine. I squeeze.

"Let's go see the horses."

When we come downstairs, Kellum is sitting on the edge of the fussy flowered sofa. He jumps to his feet, twisting his baseball cap in his hand. It reminds me of commercials where the girl comes down, and her prom date's waiting.

"Hey," he says.

We stand in the foyer. He's in the parlor, scanning us head to toe. I flush. Mia sniffles and wipes her nose with the back of her hand.

"Is she—" He catches himself, and steps forward through the doorway. "Are you okay, Little Bit?"

She clings to my side. She's shy again.

"We're ready," I say.

He searches my face. I keep my expression blank. I decided a long time ago not to apologize for Mia's meltdowns. She doesn't hurt anyone, and apologizing for yourself when you haven't done wrong is a great way to teach people to treat you like garbage. She's not gonna learn that from me.

I raise my chin. Kellum tugs his hat on and folds the brim.

"Let's go, then," he says.

He ushers us out the front door, and we head around back. He leads the way, his stride all easy confidence and swagger. Any trace of prom-night jitters is gone. Must've been my imagination.

He leads us to a narrow, worn path that runs along the fence edging the backyard and then turns up toward the barn and Lodge. The rain cut the humidity, but it's still August, and there's not a cloud in the sky. There's a slight breeze, though, that cools your sweat every so often, so the heat's not as unbearable as it has been.

It's only a fifteen-minute hike to the barn, and like Kellum said, it's quiet.

Mia's eyes are round, taking it all in. There are two chestnut brown horses cozied up to the fence near the gate to the yard, stretching their necks to reach a clump of grass on the far side. Mia stops in her tracks, entranced.

"That's Patty and Rose. They're old girls."

Kellum squats to pick some grass and then offers it to the one with the swayed back, palm flat, fingers bent back.

"This is Patty."

He grabs some more and offers it to the smaller one. "This is Rose."

Both horses snarf it up, and he stands, wiping his hand on his jeans. He pats the one he called Patty on the nose.

"Let's go get some sugar cubes from Mr. Bill and spoil them, eh?"

"Mr. Bill's still here?" He was Grandpa's boss. Growing up,

there were only two people who could do no wrong in Grandma and Grandpa's eyes, and they were Mr. Bill, the barn manager, and Jesus Christ.

Kellum flashes me a glance. He seems so surprised every time I know something about his world. As if the Walls and Prices aren't on display for the whole town. Stonecut Farms is the town's version of Real Housewives.

"He sure is. He's training a replacement, but he keeps pushing his retirement date back."

He was set to retire when I left expecting Mia.

Kellum opens the gate for us, and we trek in. Mia's vibrating with excitement. She clutches my hand and gapes at the back end of the horses, no fence separating us now. They swish their long brown tails, and she rocks on her feet.

"Big up close, aren't they?"

Patty stamps and shuffles, and Mia startles.

Kellum comes to stand at her side, so she's between us.

"Patty was an escape artist when she was younger. She was never quick, but somehow, she'd outsmart the hands. We'd find her grazing by the road. Sometimes a mile away."

Mia frowns, craning her neck up at Kellum. "She get in trouble?"

My breath catches. She's talking again. She's never chatty after a meltdown.

"Oh, no. No trouble. She didn't do anything wrong. She was our responsibility. We messed up, not her. It's our job to take care of her and keep her safe."

He watches Patty and Rose swing their tails while he talks. There's no reason I should read between the lines. He's talking about a runaway horse, not us.

He casts me a glance from the corner of his eye. "We got lucky that she's so smart and tough. That she handled everything so well when we didn't."

My chest tightens. I clench my teeth so my chin doesn't wobble. He's not talking about me.

Chapter 6

Kellum reaches over Mia's head and tucks a flyaway strand of hair behind my ear. Shivers race down my neck.

"She's strong, but she's not alone anymore," he says.

"She has Rose," Mia says.

I don't know what to say. I'm stuck. If I speak, my voice will break. If I move, I'll fall apart.

I *did* handle things. Don't know why someone acknowledging the fact should make me want to cry.

"She has Rose," Kellum agrees. "They make a great pair."

We watch them chomp away a little longer, the three of us in a row.

Is this what it feels like? Families?

My chest fills until it aches.

I'm grateful when Kellum says, "Let's go see about sugar cubes. I know where Mr. Bill keeps them."

We follow him into the barn. The doors are pushed wide open, and it's bright inside. Light filters down from the windows around the cupola. The doors at the opposite end of the barn are open, too, and huge industrial fans create cross ventilation.

I check Mia, but she doesn't seem bothered by the dull roar. We walk down the wide central avenue, and she peeks into the stalls. Like I told her, the horses' names are on plaques. I read them for her as we go.

"Button. Eliza. Fairweather Duty. Pumpkin. Sherman's Electra."

The barn is still except for the thumps and snickers of the horses. It smells like straw and sunshine. And only a little like poop.

A flood of memories well up. Summers when I was growing up, and Mama would send us to Pennsylvania for a few weeks. Grandpa would wake me early, before the sun came up. We'd tromp up the hill and feed the horses. He didn't trust me in the stalls, but I could help haul the buckets. It was a chore to me then, but worth it for the time with him.

He worked in a steady, silent way. He got the job done, and

afterwards, he'd give me a soda from the mini-fridge in Mr. Bill's office and send me back to see if Grandma needed help at home.

It was always so calm. Not hectic like Mama always managed to make home, even though it was only ever the two of us, or three if she had a man at the time.

It's calm now despite the occasional whicker or stamp.

"How come some of the horses are named Pumpkin and some of them are named, like, George Washington's Cherry Tree?" I ask.

Kellum chuckles. "The horses that raced have their Jockey Club names on the doors. The ones who never raced have their real names."

"So Sherman's Electra isn't his real name?"

"Nope. That's Buzz."

"Buzz?"

"He got stung by a bee once, when he was a colt. Buzz."

"Poor guy."

"It was memorable. He ran like hell for an hour. Only Jesse could get him to simmer down. It's how we knew he was gonna be a champion."

"Ferdinand," Mia pipes up. She's peeking into a stall, fingers wrapped around the metal bars.

"Ferdinand." I nod.

Kellum raises an eyebrow. We're side-by-side, behind Mia. Inches apart.

"It's a children's book. A bull is stung by a bee. He gets misunderstood."

A shadow passes across Kellum's face. "I don't think I've read that one."

My heart twinges. Mia loved Ferdinand. She made me renew it as often as I could from the library. They had a limit, but they also had a few copies, so I'd return one, and check another out. That was last year, though. She likes me to read her chapter books now.

"We can check a copy out from the library." Not today. It's closed on Sundays. "Tomorrow maybe."

Kellum turns his gaze from Mia and the stall to me. "Yeah?"

Chapter 6

He smiles gently, our eyes meet, and my belly flips. Memories flutter to life again. Dancing by the bonfire, his hands sliding from my hips to the small of my back.

"I'd like that," he says.

I swallow, and I shuffle ahead to the next stall. "Come see this fella, Mia. He's got a white star on his nose."

We visit all the stalls, and Mia's curiosity starts to win out against her hesitance. She wanders ahead, and somehow, Kellum knows to let her go. She needs to be brave in new places. I'm not always there.

Besides, she's too reticent to get into any danger. She hangs back, and if the horses show an interest in her, she backs right off.

"We need to get you two some boots."

I startle. Kellum's come up right beside me, his arm brushing mine, and he's checking out my fake Chuck Taylors. "They're cute, and they'll do for today, but you ladies need riding boots."

"I don't think that'll be necessary." I'm pretty sure I don't want to get on a horse.

"Field boots, I think. You don't look like the cowboy boot type."

"What's the cowboy boot type look like?"

He shrugs, "Around here? Belly shirt. Tight jeans."

"Who wears a belly shirt to ride horses?"

"I don't know. Around here, you only see cowboy boots at the bar on Saturday night."

"Oh, yeah. You wear yours to the bar?"

"I don't go to the bar."

Neither do I. Some of the other mothers do. Every weekend. They leave their kids with someone and close down the joint. I hear 'em carrying on as they stumble home at three in the morning, slamming trailer doors and waking the little ones.

I know it's how they get by. We've all got the thing that keeps us going. Drinking has only ever set me back, though.

Like the night we met. I would've never done that sober. Let him lead me into the woods, kiss him, opening my mouth with no coaxing, bending forward when he urged me, his one hand supporting me, pressed over my heart, as his other fumbled with his buckle.

My face blazes. I'm burning up despite the gust of the fans.

Kellum frowns down at me. "Let's get some water. You look flushed." My cheeks flame even hotter.

"Come on, Mia. Let's find some sugar cubes," he says, heading for Mr. Bill's office.

I pause a moment, shaking out my shirt to cool myself, before I follow. I don't need to be thinking about that night. It was a one-off. A moment out of time. We'd both been drinking. That's the only reason it went the way it did.

Kellum leads us to the far end of barn where there are steep stairs—almost a ladder—leading up to a loft. He gestures for me to go ahead. I do, grabbing Mia's hand so she comes up right behind me. I don't want to give him a front row seat to my ass.

He probably wouldn't check it out. He's been a perfect gentleman. Not even the slightest bit like he was that night.

I'm distracted when I emerge in the office, which is why I yelp when I see two men sitting there. I'd thought we were alone.

"Shay?" Kellum calls from behind, worried.

Both men hustle to stand.

"Shay?" Mr. Bill is behind his cluttered desk, and he doesn't look a day older than I remember. He still has a headful of messy white hair, bushy eyebrows, and a stoop that strains the back of his plaid shirt. "Buck Crowder's Shay?" He grins ear-to-ear. "Well, get on in here, girl."

He waves me in, and the young man he was talking to shifts back to make room. Mia and Kellum shuffle in behind me.

"Hi, Mr. Bill," I say.

"Kellum?"

The younger man is gawking at Mia, a question in his eyes. He's bigger than when I knew him, but it's definitely Jesse, the youngest Wall brother. He's close to my age, but he was a sophomore when I went to Stonecut High. We didn't know each other. Everyone knew him, though.

Chapter 6

Jesse Wall looks like an angel someone would paint on the ceiling of a church. Curly, golden hair. Sharp cheekbones and pillowy lips. He's as pretty as a man can get, and he never talks. Painfully shy.

Maybe he's like Mia?

I take a closer look. He's making eye contact. He offers a slight smile in greeting, although there's confusion written all over his face. No, he's not like Mia.

Kellum skirts past us, putting himself between the men and us.

"Jesse. Uh—" He glances back at us. Then he draws a deep breath and grabs my hand. I jump.

What's he doing?

He's grabbed Mia's hand, too, and he draws us to his side. "This is Shay." He raises our clasped hands. "And this is Mia."

She's letting him touch her.

He's touching me. His hand is rough and big and warm.

He's not letting go.

He clears his throat. "They're staying with me. We were gonna ride Orange Blossom."

"Shay Crowder. I can't believe it." Mr. Bill makes his way from behind his desk, clucking his cheek. He moves slow, shuffling. It can't be easy for him to make it up the stairs. "Buck's favorite grandbaby."

I can't help the smile that softens my lips. "How are you doing, Mr. Bill?"

"I could complain, but I don't, right kid?" Mr. Bill elbows Jesse. Jesse's gaze is darting from Mia to me to Kellum. I watch understanding dawn on his face.

"That's right," Jesse says. He and Kellum have locked eyes.

"So, what are you doing back in Stonecut? And staying with Kellum?" Mr. Bill does not seem to see what Jesse does.

What do I say? I lick my dry lips.

"At the moment, we're looking to take Orange Blossom out," Kellum interjects. "She up to some new riders?"

"Always." Mr. Bill goes on, undeterred. "But what brings you back, girlie?"

"You look th-thirsty," Jesse interrupts. It's awkward, but I'm so grateful. "Do you want some water?"

"Yes," Kellum answers. "We came up for water and some sugar cubes, if you can spare them, Bill?"

It's oppressively hot up here. There's a small circular fan mounted in the corner, but it's blowing at Mr. Bill's seat. It does nothing for air circulation.

Sweat trickles down my temple and dribbles down my back. My palm is slick against Kellum's.

"Here you go." Jesse bends and grabs three waters from the mini-fridge behind him. Kellum has to drop our hands so we can take them.

I unscrew Mia's and hand it to her. I press my bottle to my clammy chest. The cold feels amazing, but I feel more nervous now without Kellum's hand.

If Mr. Bill keeps pressing, I don't know what to say. Curiosity is written all over his weathered face. He's not gonna drop it.

"You want help saddling Orange Blossom?" Jesse offers. He clears his throat first, and his voice, while deep, is tentative.

"I'd be much obliged," Kellum answers. "Shall we?"

He edges to the side, so Mia and I can head back down the stairs.

"Hey," Mr. Bill protests. "Shay and I need to catch up."

"We'll have you over. When we're settled in. In the air conditioning." Kellum swipes his forehead. "How can you do any work in this heat?"

"Who said I got any work done?" Mr. Bill cackles, nodding to Jesse. "We'll finish later." His gaze follows us as we leave, eyes hooded with speculation.

My nerves jangle.

Folks are gonna know. They're gonna find out. And then what?

Jesse leads the way to a stall by the back doors, and Mia trails

Chapter 6

contentedly behind him. She's not paying attention to anything but the horses.

My stomach churns.

How am I going to tell her? Is she gonna understand?

What am I going to say to people? I kind of figured I'd keep my head down, and generally, folks are content to whisper about you behind your back.

Mr. Bill's not a busybody, though. Well, he's not *only* a busybody.

How is he gonna look at me when he knows I got myself knocked up from a one-night stand?

I shouldn't care. I don't. I just don't know what to say.

"Hey." Kellum stops, and he grabs my hand. He grazes a finger over my lips, tracing my frown, sending shivers racing across my skin all over again. "You don't worry. I do the worrying."

I shake my head. That's not how it works.

Up ahead, Jesse's swung open the gate on the stall with the O. Blossom plaque. Mia hangs back, but every so often, she inches closer. A big patchwork horse swishes her tail, uninterested in her visitors.

"What am I going to tell her?" I whisper without thinking.

"What—um—what *did* you tell her?" Kellum pitches his voice low, too.

"She never asked. I never said." I shouldn't feel awful about it, but I do.

"She never asked?"

I sigh. "For a long time, she didn't talk at all. Then when she did, it was mostly about animals. Mia talks *to* you, you know? You don't really talk *with* her."

I don't know how to explain it.

Kellum nods. "Like Dina was."

"She's different now?"

Kellum nods, his voice warm with affection. "You can't shut her up now, sometimes."

"How did she—did she go to a special school?"

"No, there's nothing like that in Stonecut County. At least there wasn't back then. She was mostly in regular classes, but she had extra help. Speech for one, I remember that. There was a year that Mom homeschooled her. The teacher was not a good fit. Mom was always up at the school." He shrugs. "It worked out."

Yeah. It worked out. For the girl who lived in a mansion on top of the hill, surrounded by ponies. It all worked out fine for her.

He glances down at me. "How is she doing? At school?"

My stomach sours. *Extra help. Speech. Homeschool. Always up at the school.* I know it's stupid, but the words sting like slaps.

"Best we can," I mumble, hugging my arms to my chest.

Jesse's stroking Orange Blossom's neck, calmly murmuring in her ear. Mia's watching his every move.

"Shay?" Kellum asks.

Maybe it's the heat. It's so damn hot in this barn. My eyes burn from the sweat. Maybe that's why I snap.

"You want a full report? It's been six years, Kellum. It'd take a while." I hike my chin so I can glare at his face. "*We* did the best *we* could."

Pain flashes in his eyes. Goddamn, it doesn't make me feel any better.

"I'm going to wait outside," I say. "It's too hot in here. Mia?"

She doesn't acknowledge me.

"Mia." I raise my voice. She hears me. I see her stance go stubborn.

This is a stupid fight to pick at a stupid time, but it's like I've lost my footing, and I'm scrambling for a handhold. I just need a breeze, a breath of fresh air. My tank top and my underwear are stuck to me with sweat, and even my feet are boiling hot.

"Mia!" I holler.

She balls her fists. She's going to have a meltdown. I'm pushing her to it. She wants to see the horses, like I promised, and I'm being a bad mother, and I'm too damn sweaty and hot to slow my roll.

"Hey, Jesse. Can we saddle her up in the yard?" Kellum asks.

Jesse raises his curly head, oblivious to all of us. "Yeah. Sure. Grab the saddle?"

"I got it. Mia, grab your mama's hand. You two can lead the way. Okay?"

It doesn't get any cooler in the stifling barn, but suddenly, I can breathe again.

"Come on, Mia. We have to move so he can get her out of the stall." I hold out my hand, and this time, she takes it, dragging me across the walkway to make room.

I'm grateful, and I'm embarrassed. My face is burning from the inside now.

Kellum goes to the wall where the saddles hang, hoisting one onto his shoulder. His muscles bunch. He's slick with sweat, too.

I want to be mad. It's preferable to the cracked-open way I feel. But my brain and heart can't seem to settle on a feeling. I'm unsteady, but I feel better with Mia's small hand in mine.

Kellum catches my eyes and flashes me a tentative smile. He probably thinks I'm losing it.

"You've never ridden a horse before, have you? Excited?"

"I'm not riding."

Mia blinks up at me, alarmed.

"You can ride, baby. I'm gonna pass this time."

Despite the sun, the temperature drops as soon as we step outside, and there's a light breeze. I instantly feel a hundred percent better. Jesse follows us with Orange Blossom.

Mia's glaring at me, nose and forehead scrunched in disapproval. It's her "you better think again" face.

"I'm not saying you can't."

Mia narrows her eyes. "You go first, Mommy."

I tuck the words away to take out later. *You go first, Mommy.* I file it next to *prehensile tail.*

"So, you're going first then?" Kellum's lips twitch as he swings the saddle over Orange Blossom's back.

She stands there, placid, utterly unconcerned. She has big brown eyes, and a smooth coat of many colors, not anywhere near as shiny as some of the other horses, but obviously well cared for.

She's also tall. Huge. Massive haunches. Big 'ol hooves.

"I didn't agree to that."

Kellum's eyes dance. Jesse elbows him aside, taking over tightening the straps under her round belly.

"Scared?" Kellum teases.

"Cautious."

"She's very sweet tempered."

"She's very tall."

He chuckles. "Tall?"

"Yes. Tall."

"She's broad, too. Once you're up there, you're not going anywhere."

"How am I even gonna get up there?" Her back is almost level with my head.

"I'll give you a leg up," Kellum offers. He's looking at me too closely. I squirm.

Jesse pats Orange Blossom's side, and she bends over to nibble a weed growing beside a wooden barrel. She's lucky she found it. The yard is mostly packed dirt. It'd hurt like hell if I fell on it.

How do you even get down from an animal that size?

"I can get a mounting block," Jesse offers.

"A what?"

"Like a stool."

"She'd stay still?"

"Orange Blossom isn't moving unless you tell her to. She's a pro." For some reason, I trust Jesse a bit more when it comes to the horses. He seems to get on with them really well.

Mia's tugging my arm so I'll get closer, but neither Kellum nor Jesse is showing signs of impatience. Jesse calmly strokes the horse while Kellum stands beside us, watching his brother's unhurried movements.

It's oddly relaxing. Jesse has a way about him. Quiet and gentle. Completely unlike his brothers. Cash was in my grade. I

Chapter 6

had some classes with him during the few months I went to Stonecut High. He walked around in his camo, loud and brash, as if everything was a joke, and he was above it all.

Kellum has the confidence, but not that arrogance. I'd never call him gentle, though.

He wasn't that night. A tingle zips between my legs. Nope. Not now. Not thinking about that.

Kellum isn't gentle, but he does have a way about him. Waiting for us on the sofa, hat in hand. Crouched across from us in the pantry, waiting for the storm to ease.

Maybe it's patience?

In a way, it reminds me of Mia and her animals. She'll wait for the marsh rabbit to pop his head up again as if she's got nothing else to do. Nothing else is as important as waiting.

That's kind of what it feels like, standing here while I hem and haw.

I sigh. "I don't know what I'm doing."

"I'll be there every step," Kellum assures me.

The words are sweet, but they hurt. Ache.

I tuck some fly aways behind my ears, hike up my jeans, and head over to Orange Blossom.

"All right, then. I'll go first, I guess."

Jesse smiles at me over her swayed back. He has Mia's blue eyes and her bow mouth. It's still weird seeing parts of her in these other folks who are almost strangers.

I stroke the horse's neck. Her hair's bristly and a little damp.

"Is it too hot for her in that saddle?"

Jesse shakes his head. "She's all right. She'll let us know if she's uncomfortable."

"She will?"

"Yup. This girl snuffs. If we hear her snorting, we'll know she's unhappy."

I run my fingertips over her soft nose. She pays me no mind whatsoever.

"She's not snorting."

"Nope. She's fine."

"Ready?" Kellum's come up behind me. He left Mia by the water trough. She's sitting on an overturned barrel, taking it all in.

He's close, his front to my back. By some unspoken communication, Jesse nods, gives the horse one last pat, and heads off to stand by Mia.

"Nope."

"You don't have to if you don't want to."

I huff a sigh. "Yes, I do. Mommy goes first." I reach up to see if I can reach the horn. Barely.

"We could saddle up one of the bigger mares. Ride together."

"I don't want to ride anything bigger than this one right here." My cheeks heat. And I'm not sitting between his legs. He's already too close.

I'm stuck between my trepidation and the nerves he's setting off in my belly.

"Alley-oop?" he says.

"Aw, crap," I mutter, and he chuckles.

Orange Blossom is placid and still except for little jerks as she tries to get at the roots of the weed she's snarfing down.

"On three, okay?" He stoops and threads his fingers together.

"Okay."

I put my foot in his cupped hands.

"One. Two. Three." He lifts at the same time as I pull, and I haul myself up, swinging a leg over.

It's not graceful, but at least I'm quick. And I'm sitting high on this horse. Mia lets out of squeal of delight.

"Mommy goes first!" I say, clutching the horn for dear life. Orange Blossom shifts her weight, and while I know it's nothing, my body tenses like the electric bull is about to go crazy.

I saw my grandfather and the other hands mount up hundreds of times, and they made it look like nothing, but it's heady as hell being six feet taller than you were a second ago.

I straighten my spine, clenching my thighs so I can ease my

death grip on the horn. Orange Blossom lurches forward and stops.

"Want me to lead you around the yard?" Kellum asks.

"Can I do it?"

"Sure." He smiles up at me. "Here. Take the reins."

I do. I've seen this a hundred times, too. I click my cheek and nudge her side gently with my heel. She doesn't move.

"Squeeze a little harder," Kellum says.

I do. Nothing.

"Rock your hips forward." My cheeks blaze. I glance down, but he's got his eyes on Orange Blossom. It's innocent. I'm the one with the dirty mind.

I try that, and she finally takes another step forward. I shriek, giggling, and Kellum's gaze flies up to my face.

"That's it, beautiful girl," he murmurs, turning and keeping pace as the mare lumbers forward.

My insides go crazy. I know he's talking to the horse. But still. Jitters whirl around my belly.

I need to get control of myself. This isn't about me. It's about Mia.

I wave to her, and she gives me a short nod. She approves.

Orange Blossom begins to move on her own in a lazy circle around the yard. Kellum walks at our side. I'm grateful. I feel better with him close, but I sure as hell wouldn't have asked.

When we're on the far side, my heart stops thudding a mile a minute. I'm fine. This old girl is so broad, she'd have to fall over for me to lose my seat, and she seems to know what she's doing.

"Look, baby," I call to Mia. "No hands!" I rise and do jazz hands for a split second before I grab the reins again.

"Brave," Kellum chuckles, low so only I can hear him.

"That's me," I say. "No fear."

"That's what she sees," he agrees quietly. "Look."

Mia's eyes are glued on us, wide and round, her body rigid. She's on tenterhooks.

Jesse's glancing down at her, bemused.

"You've been brave for her a lot, haven't you?" He says it as if it's dawning on him, as if he's fitting a piece of the puzzle together.

He's not wrong.

That's what a good mother does. I've always known that life is a series of disasters waiting to happen. Mama was always desperate or barely hanging on or losing it. I don't see why Mia has to think of things that way. I want her to pick herself up and dust herself off. Get mad instead of scared. I don't want her to see me as pushed around. Powerless.

Of course, Mia was born with her dials pre-set, so my efforts are generally for naught. Still, I do try to put a brave face on.

"Mothers do what they have to do."

"You were seventeen."

His voice is raw with something. Not quite guilt, but close.

"I was old enough."

"No. Not to have to do this all alone."

Orange Blossom clomps along, lazily, sending up puffs of dirt with each step. Kellum keeps pace beside us. It's slow and peaceful on the outside. Inside, my feelings are a riot.

The horse is hot underneath me, the sun's hot on my head and shoulders, and my heart skips and slams. I'm stuck up here. There's no shutting the conversation down, not unless I ignore him.

"We've made it all right."

Some days, it doesn't feel that way. But Mia's never gone hungry. Never not had a bed to sleep in, and she's never been sick where I couldn't get her to the doctor.

"She's amazing."

He's watching her, a fascinated half-smile on his face. The similarities are striking. The stubborn set of their chins. The watchfulness of their gaze.

"I know."

He turns to me. "You are, too."

My belly flips, and I'm about to shrug it off, change the subject,

Chapter 6

but he's looking at me so intensely. It's not a throwaway line. He's sincere.

"Thank you." I don't know what else to say.

He nods, somber, as if we've made a deal. "Do you think she'll want a ride?"

"I don't think you could stop her."

Mia's up on her toes, her wariness gone, impatience rising. Kellum chuckles, and we're quiet—companionable—as Orange Blossom plods the rest of the circuit in her own time.

Kellum helps me dismount, grabbing me firmly by the waist and gently setting me down. I'm shorter than him again. His grip on my hips is strong and certain, and he's economical in the movement. His hands don't linger.

There's no reason for the butterflies or the little stumble as I trade places with Mia.

I'm being ridiculous, as silly as I was at that bonfire, losing my mind 'cause Kellum Wall glanced my way. I should not need a reminder of how it ends when I let myself be that kind of foolish.

Except for that one night, I've never been stupid about a man. I learned my lesson.

I tug down my tank top, even though it doesn't need it. Mia hops down from her barrel and skips over, eyeing the horse as if she's taking measurements, trying to figure out the best footholds to scale her.

Mia means business.

"You ready, baby?" I ask.

She nods.

I'm not ready. Damn, the horse is tall compared to her. One hoof is almost the size of her head.

I gulp and force myself to breathe. I was just up on her. It was fine. It's like a pony ride at the carnival, only the pony is one-third the size.

She'll be okay. Kellum wouldn't let her do it if it was dangerous.

I chew my bottom lip.

"Ready, Mommy," Mia says, impatiently. We're all standing beside the horse—Kellum, Jesse, Mia, and me. I'm blocking the stirrup. I need to move.

It'll be fine. I should lift her into the saddle. She probably won't let Kellum or Jesse touch her.

Okay. I'll do that.

"Mommy?" Mia pushes my hip, tries to get me to budge.

"You know, I have an idea," Kellum says. "How about you ride together? Mommy in back, Mia in front."

Gratitude floods my heart, even though I really don't want to get back up on that horse. "Yeah. That's a good idea."

"All right." Kellum gives me a leg up, and I'm an old pro. I scoot back as far as I can.

I'm not sure how this next part is going to go. Mia doesn't like to be touched, but I'm not sure how she'll feel about an alley-oop.

She cranes her neck, reaching for the straps dangling from the saddle.

"Can I help you up?" Kellum asks.

Mia stops and waits expectantly, staring over his shoulder.

He hesitates.

With Mia, you have to learn to read her. She mostly doesn't make eye contact when she's interacting with people. It's a little different with me, I think, because I can read her looks, and that's how she let me know what she wanted for so long. With other folks, though, she'll gaze right past their ear. It unsettles them. Drives Mama nuts. She's always on her to "look me in the eye."

Mia must get antsy, waiting for him to read her mind, because she raises her arms. His face is carefully mild, but I can see him tense.

I realize this is the first time he's going to hold his child.

Kellum and I are both tense. Jesse's got Orange Blossom by the bridle, stroking her nose. Trying to give us space, I think.

Kellum gently lifts Mia and settles her in front of me. I wrap my arms around her to grab the reins. She's rocking with excitement.

"Ready, baby?"

She nods.

Jesse clicks his cheek, and Orange Blossoms starts, no fuss. He ambles off and takes a seat on the barrel.

Kellum walks beside us as we take a lap around the yard. As Mia gets more comfortable, she swings her legs, careful not to hit Orange Blossom's flanks, her happiness brimming over.

"You're riding a real horse, baby," I whisper in her ear. "What do you think about that?"

Kellum's watching us, lips curved, and it's like we're in it together. As if everything is fine, and it's going to be fine, and whatever happened before was a bad dream because this is real.

A hawk swoops way overhead. The sun shines. Soft tufts of white clouds laze in the middle of all that bright blue, broken only by the dark green mountain rising in the distance.

Perfect.

An engine growls, and there's a crunch of gravel from up by the Lodge.

After I checked when we first came up and saw no cars or people, I've avoided looking over there. It's a gorgeous house, if you can call it that. It's massive. Three stories, steep peaked roofs, huge windows, a wraparound porch so wide it's more like a deck.

It's built to look like a cozy cabin with lots of wood, but with its size, it seems more like a fancy hotel. A haunted one.

An extended cab truck pulls into the drive. A door slams. An older man walks around to open the passenger door, but a gray-haired woman hops out, beating him to it. She's wearing high-waisted jeans, a pink collared shirt, and riding boots. He's a foot taller than she is. His collared shirt's tucked into stiff, dark blue jeans.

They're dressed super-casual, but somehow, they still reek of money.

It's Mr. Wall and his wife.

They're staring down at us.

She gapes. He lays his hand on her shoulder, but she shakes it off, stalking forward.

I tense.

She spits words over her shoulder at him. He grabs her forearm, urges her toward the house. She yanks her arm out of his grasp.

I can't make out what she's saying, but from her tone, she's pissed. They're a bit too far away, and the breeze is just strong enough.

They're too damn close for comfort, though.

I tighten my arm around Mia's chest. Mrs. Wall strides down the hill, shading her eyes with a hand. She's fixed on us. Mr. Wall's still arguing, dogging her heels. He must say something she hears because she stops dead in her tracks.

Yeah. They need to stay right where they are.

"Kellum? We're done." I lightly tap Orange Blossom's side. She does not take the suggestions.

Mia whines. Crap. I know better. In a situation like this, I need to give her a five-minute warning. And then a one-minute warning. And another one-minute warning.

Mia's teacher calls it *transitions*. That's one of the items in the report I'd get from the school at the end of the week. How she did with transitions. She always got all her points, even on days she was at home sick, so I figured the teachers were literally just checking boxes.

Mia's awful with transitions if she's deep into what she's doing.

Mrs. Wall doesn't come any closer, but she doesn't go back to her house, either. What's she gawking at, anyway?

She can turn around and leave like her husband wants. Keep it moving.

"Kellum?"

He nods and grabs Orange Blossom's bridle, quickening his pace. Now the old girl speeds up.

Kellum's face has shut down. That's the only way I can describe it. He looks like he did when he pulled over in his cop car. It's an expression that matches his uniform.

Mia's shaking her head no, a distraught moan low in her throat. She's gonna lose it in the middle of the yard with that woman watching.

My brain races. "We told Patty and Rose we'd give them sugar cubes. And here we've forgotten them."

Mia stills. She's thinking.

I've got a point. She knows it.

"Poor critters. Probably waiting all this time for us to come back." I lay it on thick.

Jesse's risen to his feet. He's taking it in—his parents heading down the hill in fits and starts, Kellum leading us back to the barn.

Jesse's so quiet, I'd almost forgotten about him. It's hard to imagine, pretty as he is, that he can fade into the woodwork, but he does.

He exchanges a long look with Kellum.

"You want me to go?" he asks.

"If you would. Shay, Mia, and I are going to go back to the house. We'll see you later."

"Right." Jesse flashes us a shy smile and lopes off toward the Lodge. His mother has started toward us again.

"Kellum?"

He's helping Mia down. I'm watching the Walls. She's furious, her hands going a mile a minute. Mr. Wall keeps arguing, but he doesn't seem to be getting anywhere.

"Kellum."

"It's all right. It's handled." He offers me a hand.

Jesse's on a path to intercept them. He's raising his hand, waving them back to the Lodge.

What's happening here? Is she coming to run me off? The skank that tried to trap her son? She's clearly livid.

Does she want to check Mia out? Judge for herself if it could possibly be true? Let us know exactly how welcome we aren't?

Anxiety sours my stomach. The heat's finally getting to me. My temples throb.

I don't want this woman near Mia. I don't want any of these people near her. Or me.

I haven't felt like I did that day those men came to send me packing in years. I won't feel that way now. Never again. And no one is ever gonna make Mia feel like that. Not on my watch. Never.

I'm getting us the hell out of here.

Along with my aching head, I've broken into a fresh sweat, and it's burning my eyes. I grab the saddle horn and swing my legs over, lowering myself to the ground.

Kellum's forced to take a step back and give me space.

"Come on, Mia." I grab her hand.

Behind us, Jesse's reached his parents at the bottom of the hill. I can hear their voices better now. I still can't make out the words, but I can hear the high, indignant tones as clear as day.

No worries, lady. We're leaving.

I pull Mia through the barn. She trots to keep up, but she's not complaining. That's my girl. If she's not having one of her moments, she generally lets me have my way.

"Shay!" Kellum follows us, leading the horse.

Mr. Bill's by the stalls. "Take care of Orange Blossom, would you?" Kellum asks him.

"Sure thing."

"Shay!"

We clear the barn doors, and Mia catches sight of Patty and Rose.

She stops, digging in her heels. Kellum catches up. I can't see through the length of the barn to tell whether Mr. and Mrs. Wall are still coming after us.

Sweats drips down my face. It's so freaking *hot*.

How does Kellum look so unwilted? No wet patches under his arms. There's a sheen of perspiration on his face and neck, yes, but no sign that he's suffering this absolute misery that's short circuiting my brain.

Mia glares at me. I glare at him.

He hands me a bottle of water.

"Drink."

I take it, unscrew the lid, and chug. I'm not proud. I'm miserable. I pour a handful and splash my face. It doesn't matter if my top gets wet. It's already soaked with sweat.

"Better?" he asks.

I grimace. We need to go. My anxiety's rising to an unbearable pitch. I can't deal with a confrontation with his parents right now. I will if I have to, if that's what needs to happen, but all my reserves are gone. I'll cry. The only silver lining is that no one would be able to tell with all the sweat.

Mia wanders off to get a closer look at Patty and Rose. She stands well back and to their sides, so I don't call her back.

"Hey." Kellum guides my hand, the one holding the water bottle, back up to my lips. "Jesse's got this. Everything's all right. You don't worry. I'll handle them."

I scoff, but I drink.

"No." He tilts my chin with his thumb until I'm looking at him. "You need to understand. You worry about yourself and our girl. I worry about everyone else. That's how this works."

"You can't just say it, and it's so."

"Yeah, I can." And he smiles. Like he did that night. Wide and lazy and confident as hell.

It does things to me, sets my chest to thumping and thudding, messes up my train of thought. I shove the bottle back at him and fold my arms. My shirt is so damp.

"We'll do things in our own time. When we decide. Anyone wants to get to you two—*anyone*—they go through me."

Then he digs in his pocket and pulls out a handful of sugar cubes. He holds one out to me, eyebrow raised.

"I'm not scared of them," I say.

"I know."

"I just don't want to deal with it right now."

"I don't either."

I huff a sigh and grab the sugar cube. "Why are you so damn agreeable?"

"Literally no woman has ever said that about me before."

We turn in step to walk slowly toward Mia. A breeze whips up, rustling the treetops. It cools my cheeks.

"What do they say, then?" It's out of my mouth before I have time to think about it.

He blinks, and his lip twitches. "Pretty much the opposite."

"You're grumpy?" He doesn't strike me that way.

"No. More like I keep to myself."

I nod. Me, too.

Mia sees what I have, and she tries to pry my fingers open.

"Ask him. This one's mine." I pop the crumbling white cube in my mouth. Sweet as I remember. Grandpa used to sneak me one after we treated the horses.

"Here you go, Little Bit." Kellum drops one in Mia's open palm.

We spoil Patty and Rose, petting them once they've snarfed up the sugar cubes. A cloud drifts over the sun, and with the breeze picking up, the temperature becomes bearable again.

Mia's not talking, but she's smiling and at ease.

Eventually, when Mrs. Wall doesn't come barging through the barn to confront me, I relax, too.

We stroke Patty's side, Mia between us, her flank rising and falling as she chomps at longer grasses by the fence post that the weed whacker missed.

We're so quiet, that when my stomach growls, there's no denying it. Mia snickers. Kellum slides me a glance.

"Hungry?"

"I could eat."

"I've got bacon. And I think I've got a tomato ripe enough to pick. How about BLTs?"

"You grow tomatoes?"

"I have a few plants on the back porch."

That sounds nice. I've always wanted to buy a plant or two

Chapter 6

when I walk past the pallet in front of the grocery back home, but I could never justify the expense.

"A BLT would be nice."

"Want to help me pick a 'mater?" Kellum focuses his effortless, killer smile on Mia.

My belly flips. She completely ignores him.

"Five minutes, Mia," I say. She inches closer to Patty, stroking and murmuring. She completely ignores me, too.

She's in love. I can hardly blame her.

7

KELLUM

I guess I've never felt love before. Not real love, not this kind. It's like some kind of magical being reached into my brain, and rearranged everything. In an instant. Without warning. Mia is now the most important thing in the world, bar none.

And I'm scared shitless.

I have to leave Mia and Shay for a while, and I've already stopped myself twice from calling Ernst down at the station and asking him to park in front of the house while I'm gone.

They're both just so small.

Mia's snuggled up to her mother on the back porch swing, trotting a little plastic goat up and down the arm. Shay's watching the sunset. The glow sets off the red in their hair. Together, they barely take up half the seat.

Shay has her feet tucked under her, flip-flops under the swing. The chain creaks. I need to spray it with some WD-40.

The sound's not unpleasant, though. I lean against the doorway and listen and watch.

Mia's just as pretty as her mother. When I first saw her, it was the resemblance to Dina that struck me. But now I see Shay. Mia has her mother's thick, auburn hair and her stubborn chin.

I dry the salad bowl from dinner, taking my time.

Chapter 7

I need to go up to the Lodge. I'm already later than I said I'd be, and I need to deal with this now. Mom almost messed things up today.

Dad says she didn't know. He never told her. He swears he thought it was all a lie. After they confronted her, Shay left town, and he saw Buck Crowder every day until he had the heart attack, and Buck never said a word about a baby.

I've never mistrusted my father's word before, and I can't bring myself to now. He's an honest man, but he didn't tell me about it, did he?

It sours my guts, so I shove it aside and focus on Mia and her mama swinging.

This morning on the phone, I agreed to go up to the Lodge tonight. It wasn't my idea, but Shay and Mia had come down to the kitchen, and I didn't want them to hear me with my voice raised, so I said I'd come.

I cough—just a tickle in my throat—and they both jump and look at me. I smile, and they settle back down.

They're both skittish as hell. Deservedly. I don't think Shay realizes it, but they cover each other. Shay's a good mom. She watches Mia carefully, hovers enough but doesn't crowd her. She makes sure Mia gets what she needs, but she doesn't push.

And Mia follows Shay's lead. She has absolute trust in her mother.

They make good partners. As deputy, I ride alone, but when I was on the beat, I had both good and bad partners. It's a nice thing when you can work as a unit.

They've been alone in the world for too long. The shit that could have happened—what must have happened. A seventeen-year-old with a premature baby and no money.

How bad was it for her back home that a moldy trailer with no electricity was a step up?

Fuck.

And it's my own goddamn fault.

Rage surges in my veins, and I step back into the kitchen. They don't need to see it on my face.

I lie awake in bed last night, staring at a spider-line crack in the ceiling, rigid with fury. I'm exhausted, and I don't want to leave them. Not even for an hour.

I can't have what almost happened at the barn today happen again, though. Shay's on edge, and she might be young and broke, but she's got backbone. I don't doubt for a minute that she has the ingenuity to disappear if she wants to.

She's nothing like the fractured memories I have. That woman—girl, I guess—she was wild. Hungry. She sucked my tongue and screamed when I slammed into her wet pussy. Later, in the river, she splashed and laughed. Carefree.

Now she's quiet. Watchful. Her smiles are brittle.

If not for Mia, I'd hardly be able to believe it's the same person.

Was she that drunk that night? Was I? Or can six years change a person this much?

I move so I can see her through the window. The sun's last rays are hitting her face, so she tilts her head back and closes her eyes. She's tired. Mia's not.

I want to be here. I want to sit on the porch with them and watch the fireflies come out.

But I keep my word.

I grab a glass from the cabinet and Mia's red lion cup from the drying rack. I pour both of them ice waters. They don't drink enough, especially after a day in this kind of heat.

I give them the water. Shay stirs, offering me a tight smile of thanks.

She doesn't like me. When I get close, she gets stiff and folds herself up.

Does she think I took advantage of her?

Did I?

Acid scores my throat.

I need to go.

"I'm heading out for an hour or two. You gonna be okay?" I

already mentioned that I had an errand earlier at dinner. Shay didn't press for details.

"Yeah."

"Drink all that." I nod to the glass in her hand.

She rolls her eyes.

"Crap. I need to give you my number." I reach for my cell.

She shakes her head. "Don't worry about it. I'm out of minutes."

"Out of minutes?"

"Yeah. I have a pre-paid. I'm out of minutes."

"You don't have a phone?"

I understand what she's saying, but it adds more fuel to the fire burning in my chest. She was alone with a six-year-old in a trailer with a door you could kick open with no effort—and she had no working phone. What if she needed to get a hold of the doctor? Call in a refill on Mia's inhaler?

I'm scowling at her, and I know I need to stop. She's taking it personally, drawing her knees tight to her chest and glaring back at me.

"You can call 9-1-1 on it without minutes," she says.

"I know that."

"Then why are you hassling me?"

"I'm not—" I run a hand through my hair. Mia's eyeing me, scooting closer to her mother.

I exhale. "There's a house phone in the kitchen. And another in my office. I'll leave my number on the fridge."

"Okay."

"We'll get you a phone."

"Fine."

She stares meaningfully behind me at the door.

"Shay—"

I stand there because I can't leave. Because somehow in the past twenty-four hours, God changed it so that if I don't know that these two are okay, I can't think right.

"Don't you have to be somewhere?" She purses her lips. "An

errand, you said?" She puts the emphasis on errand as if she's calling bullshit.

"I'm going up to the Lodge."

"To talk to them?"

I nod.

She was tense before. Now she's as taut as a wire.

"What's going to happen?"

"Nothing you have to worry about."

"What if—" She glances at Mia, and then she chews her lower lip. "Never mind."

"Shay—"

"Drive safe," Shay says, turning her head to stare at the mountain. It's purple against the orange sunset.

Mia looks at her mother, then me.

Goddamn it feels like a test. And I'm failing.

We can't talk it out here and now, even if Shay were willing, and from the tilt of her chin, I'd say she's not.

I sure as hell can't leave things like this, though.

Mia sets her goat on the arm of the swing so he's staring right at me.

I've got an idea.

"Be right back."

I hustle through the kitchen, taking the stairs two at a time. Stacked in the corner of my bedroom, in a leather trunk I've hauled from house to house, is an old tin. It was my grandfather's. It's filled with toy knights. I loved them as a kid. The knights had maces, swords, bows and arrows.

And they had the best horses, completely realistic, captured high-stepping or rearing.

I pop the knights off and stash them back in the tin.

I return to the porch more slowly. It seemed like a good idea, but now? What does a little girl want with some tin horses?

Maybe I just need to go.

I take a minute to jot my number down and stick it to the fridge. Then, I go back to the door. Shay and Mia are communing, almost nose-to-nose. Mia's trotting her goat along Shay's shoulder. It looks like Shay's breathing in Mia's hair. I've noticed that Mia stays close to Shay, but she's not a snuggler. They don't hug. This is the closest I've seen them.

When they see me, Mia crawls off Shay's lap to face me.

"What's that?" Shay asks.

"I, uh—" I hold up a horse. I left the others on the counter.

Mia hops up from the swing.

Shay squints. "What is that horse wearing? A blanket?"

"It's a caparison."

"A comparison?"

"Caparison. It's a covering for a knight's horse."

"So a blanket?" Shay edges forward on her seat. Humor sparkles in her golden-brown eyes.

I straighten under her gaze. My blood quickens.

"Yes. A blanket."

Mia looks to her mother, and Shay nods her permission. I gently hand Mia the horse.

"There are more in the kitchen." Mia darts around me.

Shay rises to her feet. "On the bright side, a whinny's overall less annoying than a bleat."

"She makes noises?"

Shay nods, shyly. "When it's only the two of us, yeah."

I step closer and lower my voice. "You don't have to worry."

She huffs a small sigh. "Sure."

"I'm going to go have a conversation. Then, I'll be back."

She's so spooked, and I don't know how to make it okay. What can I say to reassure her? My folks are good people. I honestly don't understand how they could make a mistake this big.

I don't think Shay realizes it was a horrible mistake. That's what she must be worried about. She's worried that when I come back, I'll want them gone.

Fuck.

She's scared.

It's getting dark, she has a six-year-old, and she's only got two hundred dollars and no minutes left on her phone.

She's terrified.

I don't think. I lean forward and press my forehead to hers. It's instinctual, as if I can transmit my certainty to her.

"There is nothing anyone could say that would keep me from my daughter," I say, low, so there's no way Mia can overhear.

Shay's breath hitches. Her eyes swirl with confusion, and her chin trembles. She smells good. Sweet. I inhale.

What am I doing?

This isn't like that.

I don't have the right.

But she stays perfectly still.

Something roars to life inside me. Something I've only felt once in my life—that night at the bonfire. I want to touch her. The need shocked me then. It terrifies me now.

It's not me. I'm not that kind of man. I'm not Cash. I don't do whatever I feel. And I can't afford a misstep now.

I force myself to back off. "There's ice cream in the freezer. It might have some ice crystals, but you can scrape them off."

"You need to go grocery shopping." She's collecting herself, crossing her arms again.

"We'll go tomorrow on the way back from getting you a new phone."

"That's how it's gonna be?" She's playing tough, but there's still a quiver to her lips.

I want to soothe that trembling. Take her mouth. Wrap her in my arms, stroke her back, hold her until she drops her walls.

I want to touch her, more than I've wanted anything in years, but I also want her to let me—let me touch her, protect her, care for her. For Mia.

I want her to trust me.

"That's how it's gonna be," I say, gently.

And before I turn to go, I let myself touch her lower lip. A slow stroke of my rough thumb against her soft skin. I tug, revealing her even, white teeth. The tip of her tongue. I brace myself for her to turn her head or jerk away.

But she stays still for me. She swallows, and her slender throat bobs.

My blood roars.

Her gaze drops to the porch. I can hear her breath catch.

I summon more strength than I thought I had, and I trip down the back steps and head off before I ask for more.

I want more.

I want everything.

~

I WALK UP to the Lodge. I'd intended to drive since I'm already late, but I need the time to get my head straight. And my cock settled down.

I thought that night at the bonfire had been exaggerated in my mind.

I was drunk. Elizabeth and I had split again—I thought for good that time—and there was a get-together. An unofficial five-year reunion. We were rehashing old times. There was a keg. The mood was wild. Music was blaring from someone's truck; there was hooting and hollering. It had been a hot day, but the night had a chill to it, and the moon was full.

I've never been a heavy drinker, but I'd been keeping up with the guys, beer for beer.

And then she caught my eye. Pretty sequined tank top. Jean shorts. Thin gold hoops in her ears, flashing through strands of thick auburn hair.

She'd been checking me out from under her thick eyelashes. Shy. But when I smiled at her, she smiled back.

I sort of wandered over, no plan in mind. She'd been standing with Pandy Bullard and a few other girls from our class. I knew the girls—our senior class was only two-hundred-some kids—but we didn't run in the same circles. Everyone knows Pandy, though. Pandy introduced us.

I forget just what she said, but I got the idea Shay was from out of town. I sure as shit didn't get the impression she was underage.

I asked her to dance. I didn't know what to do. I never hit on women. I was always taken, or those times I was single, women approached me. I never had a type or preferences, except for easy. Not easy, sex-wise. Just low drama.

I wasn't the guy who put moves on women, so I guess I did what I saw in the movies. It was a slow song; I put my hands on her hips. We talked. I don't remember what we said.

I led her away from the fire into the woods. She came. Uncertain, but smiling. I must've had the intention of doing something. Kiss her, maybe. Talk to her where I could hear and all eyes weren't on us.

I didn't say anything, though. I kissed her. And then it was like a switch flipped in my brain.

It was—I've never been like that before or since. I ripped her panties, tugged up her shirt to bare her beautiful tits. Her hard, dusky brown nipples. I sank to my knees, suckled her, and she was clawing my back, moaning, and I stood, bent her over, propped her against a tree and thrust into her hot, tight pussy. She screamed and bucked, taking me to the hilt. She was wet and hot, and I couldn't have stopped.

But I did. I put a condom on.

She asked.

Shit.

I remember.

She said, "Condom." Tentative and breathless.

I pulled out, and I fumbled in my wallet. Then I sank back inside her, and it felt so fucking good. I didn't last much longer. I strummed her clit until she seized my cock like a vise, and then I came harder than I ever had before.

In my memory, she was as wild for it as I was.

Or was she?

Chapter 7

I didn't realize the condom broke. What else did I miss?

I scrub the back of my neck. The walk to the Lodge isn't long enough. I'm more worked up now than when I left. More twisted up. I stop at the barn, lean against a fence.

I'd felt guilty after for being so rough, but I wanted back in that pussy, too. So damn bad. I wanted to make it last. I took her to the river. We were both sticky with sweat, and the water was cold.

I was going to fuck her again. Slower. Sober.

She got bashful, but she let me hold her hand, lead her out to where the water lapped above our waists. She let me wrap her legs around my hips and kiss her slow.

She was so beautiful. She peered up at me like I was magic. Superman.

And then Gary Ellwood came looking for me, hollering from the back. Steve Scheurman had tried to drive drunk and hit a tree.

I didn't want Gary to see her. I said I'd be there in a minute. I led her out of the river and told her to wait there for me.

I left a naked, seventeen-year-old drunk girl alone by the side of a river.

Steve was fine. His truck needed a new fender, but he walked away without a scrape. When I came back to the river, Shay was gone. And I was grateful 'cause as I sobered up, the shame settled.

That's not how I was raised. To fuck a woman from behind in the dirt. Push her up against a tree not even knowing her full name.

Everyone saw us walk into the woods together. There'd be talk. And my father always impressed on us boys that talk might mean nothing to us, but it can ruin a woman's reputation and make her life hell.

The same father who visited Shay months later and convinced her to leave town.

My grip tightens on the fence slat, splinters biting my palms.

I half-figured I'd find Shay the next morning. Apologize. Someone said Shay had gotten a ride with Pandy. She was fine.

And then when I got home, Elizabeth was on my front porch,

saying she realized she'd made a huge mistake. She wanted me back.

I'd always treated women with respect. I'd never become an animal before, fucking in the dirt, sloppy drunk and out of my mind.

I'd made promises. She said she was so sorry. Could we just talk?

I invited her in. I'd thought it was the right thing to do. A few months later, we were married.

I grind my teeth. The moon has come out, shining above the mountain. Just like that night. All the trees are cast in shadows, but you can still see the path. Every building is outlined. You can say you're in the dark, but you can't say you don't see everything clearly.

I left a girl—not a woman, a girl—my seed in her belly, alone by a river. I put a baby in her, and then the men who raised me chased her away.

There's a hollowness in my chest. It outweighs the rage and the fear.

What kind of man am I?

I don't even fucking know anymore.

I continue on to the Lodge. The lights are shining from the first floor and Dina's turret. I walk around back and let myself in. I shuffle my boots on the mat, steeling myself.

That feeling I always used to get when I walk into this house—that ease that comes from the familiar—it's gone. Truth be told, it's been gone for a while. I haven't been coming to Sunday dinner as much as when I was married. There's always questions now. Dad's always hushing Mom.

It's been easier to trade shifts, to let Ernst spend the evening with his family. I'm lucky he agreed to switch back this weekend with no advance notice.

I square my shoulders and cross through the mudroom into the kitchen. A hush falls.

Chapter 7

My parents are sitting at the kitchen table. There's a bottle of whiskey and two shot glasses in front of my father. Van and Cash are standing at the breakfast bar holding beers.

Guess we're drinking.

"Son." Dad nods at the empty chair across from him. Mom worries the stem of a wine glass, her eyes rimmed with red.

"Kellum—" she starts, rising as if to give me her usual hug.

"Dear, we agreed," Dad interjects. She casts him a scathing look and sinks back into her seat.

"I'm so sorry." Her eyes fill with tears. "I didn't know. If I had known—"

"Dear." Dad lays a hand on her arm. "Let him sit."

I do. Dad pours a shot and slides it across the table to me. I toss it back, relishing the burn in my throat. I knock it against the table. He fills it again.

"Really, John?" Mom says.

Dad ignores her.

I try to gather my thoughts, ask what I have to ask, but the rage is stuck in my throat. This is my family. We're closer than most. Blood binds us, but so does the land. The business. Faith and respect.

But in this moment, I feel surrounded by strangers.

"How the hell did this happen?" I ask, placing my palms on the tabletop so I don't curl my hands into fists. "Just tell me how the *hell* something like this happens?"

"Basic failure of birth control is my guess," Cash quips from behind the counter.

"Not helpful," Dad barks at the same time Mom says, "Cash!"

The only thing bigger than Cash's mouth is his utter lack of concern about getting his ass beat.

"You can shut up," I tell him. "I'm gonna get to you."

Cash raises his palms in the air, but he doesn't say anything else.

"Lay it out for me, Dad."

His gaze is level. He's the one who taught me to meet a man's eye. How it's a sign of respect. It used to drive him nuts that Dina wouldn't make eye contact. Still does, but Mom has browbeat him into leaving it be.

He wipes his nose and drums his fingers on the table. "Cash came to me and your uncle. He said there was a rumor going around that you knocked up a high school girl."

"You didn't think to come to me?" I toss over my shoulder. Cash has the good grace to look uncomfortable.

"I knew it wasn't true," Cash says. "You go off half-cocked and confront her with witnesses? It becomes true. Officer Wall knocked up a minor? That shit's got legs. You know how this town is."

"You didn't think I had a right to know?"

"Man, we all knew it was bullshit."

"Cash!" Mom says. It's a reflex, but I think we're past "put a quarter in the jar."

Cash shrugs.

Dad shifts in his seat. "Do we know for sure? Are you—are we maybe getting ahead of ourselves here?"

Mom sputters and leans forward in her chair, finger pointing. "You saw her, John. Don't act like you didn't see her, too. She wasn't that far away. That child is the spitting image of Dina at that age. *Spitting image.*"

"Don't you think Buck Crowder would have mentioned it?" Dad insists. "Don't you think he would've spoken up."

The room falls silent.

"Why wouldn't Buck have mentioned it, Dad?" I ask. It's a good question.

Dad's gaze falls to the bottle. He seems lost for an explanation.

Van sighs, aggravated. He stops scrolling through his phone. Up to this point, he's been multi-tasking. "Son, we did what we had to do."

"What does that mean?"

He rounds the counter and pulls up a chair, crossing his legs. His pant legs rise to show fancy silk socks. The longer he lives in

Chapter 7 145

the city, the less he looks like the man I remember mudding with when I was young.

Van and Mom were both raised on the farm, but Van went away to college. Horses were the first of many investments for him. Stonecut became his weekend getaway, his summer home. Mom fell in love with a local hand and married him. No matter how prosperous the farm got, how well the trust did, Dad was always the guy in jeans and work boots. Van wears loafers now.

"It means there was a problem, and we solved it," he says. "We gave her a choice."

"What choice?" My blood runs cold.

"What are you talking about, Van?" My dad seems genuinely confused.

"You were there, John. It was understood that if the girl insisted on the story, Buck would lose his job."

My stomach drops. Mom gasps.

"We're supposed to keep a man on payroll if his kid is slandering the family?" Van scoffs.

"It wasn't a *story*." Mom's voice cracks.

"We didn't know that, did we? Which would you have believed, Kelly? That some troubled girl was lying about Kellum fathering her baby—for attention or to make a play for a payout, who knows —or that Kellum actually had sex with a minor?"

Van shakes his head. Shame burns my face.

"To be honest, I felt bad for the girl. I figured she probably got herself knocked up, maybe she didn't know who the daddy was, and she needed a way out. I even went back. Gave her some cash to take care of it."

"Oh, Van." Mom sets down her glass.

I feel like I've been slammed into a wall. My ears ring. Adrenaline courses down my veins. Van tossed her money to get rid of it. My child. Mia.

"You didn't know the girl, Mom," Cash says. "Trailer trash is harsh, but it fits. I mean, she was Buck Crowder's granddaughter."

I turn to scowl at him. "What does that mean?"

"You know what that means." Cash gets his hackles up, and everyone shifts nervously in their seats. Cash is the one with the hair-trigger temper. I'm the even-tempered one. No one thinks I'm going to lose control.

Back then, no one would have believed I was capable of doing this thing.

Oh, God, it's on me. At the end of the day, *all* of it is on me. The weight is crushing.

And there's Cash, smirking. Happy that his perfect older brother has fucked up. Not caring at all that we're talking about people's lives.

"No, Cash, explain what you mean."

Cash snorts. "Did she even have all her teeth?"

I'm out of my chair in an instant, hopping the counter, swinging. My knuckles crunch when they crack Cash's jaw, and I relish the pain as it drives the shame from my mind.

"Boys!" Mom screeches.

Cash is ready; he's always ready. I drive my fist into his face again, and he lands a blow to my gut. We're on the floor, grappling, wrestling, and everyone's shouting.

"John, do something!" Mom hollers.

The pain's not enough. I can still feel the guilt.

Cash elbows my head, knocking it into the wall. I drive a knee into his stomach. A chair falls over with a bang.

We're too evenly matched, and we've been scrapping our whole lives. He'll never stop, and tonight, neither will I.

"John," Mom pleads. "Someone is going to get hurt!"

Then there's a scraping sound, and a blast of hot air. And then a gunshot.

Mom screams.

Dad, who's been stalking us, looking for an opening, lunges, grabbing Cash and wrestling him across the floor. Cash is shocked enough not to swing.

Van uses his chest to push me the other direction.

Chapter 7

Dina's standing at an open window with a smoking gun.

"Where'd she come from?" Cash asks.

"Dina," Mom gasps.

"You are too loud." She engages the safety and tucks her little silver pistol back in the waistband of her jeans. "Too loud," she growls, glaring at Cash, and then she heads back where she came from.

"Sorry, Dina. We'll try and keep it down." Cash grins, his teeth covered in blood.

"I'm trying to work."

"Yes, ma'am." Cash is barely keeping a straight face. Mom's eyes are bugging in horror.

"I'm on a deadline."

"Dina, you cannot fire a gun in the house," Mom admonishes.

"I fired a gun *outside* the house."

"Through a *window*." Mom gestures. The curtains are flapping in the evening breeze.

Dina tugs the window closed, flips the lock, and heads back upstairs. Cash cracks up. He falls out and slumps to a chair, gasping for air.

His face is a mottled mess of bloody cuts and bruises. Mine can't look much better than his.

This is gonna freak Mia out. I hang my head. It's like I'm incapable of making the right decisions anymore. Shit. Could I ever?

The fight drains out of me, leaving a gaping hole. I scrub my chest. My knuckles are swollen, but not bloody.

What am I doing?

"Can we all sit?" Van waves at the table. Mom bends over to pick up a chair. "Cash, maybe you can find somewhere else to be?"

Cash sniffs, wiping blood from his nose. "Yeah. Okay. I'll go down to the barn. Let Jesse know we're not gettin' robbed."

He claps me on the back and laughs on his way out.

The kitchen reeks of whiskey. At some point, we must have knocked the bottle over.

Mom starts wiping down the table. Dad takes a seat. I follow.

My ribs ache, but they're not broken. Probably not even bruised. My left eye socket throbs, and my lip is split, but other than that and some twinges, I'm good. Could have been worse. Cash fights mean.

Maybe I can, too. In the moment, I wasn't going to stop. I wasn't playing, either. I didn't know I could be like that. I've got to collect myself. This needs to be about Mia and Shay. I draw in a breath to speak, but Mom beats me to it.

"I want to meet her," she says. "When can I meet her?"

"Shay doesn't want that."

"You need to explain to her that I didn't have anything to do with what happened." Mom grabs my hand, and my knuckles throb. "You need to know that if I had been aware, this would not have happened."

"I know, Mom. But Shay doesn't want anything to do with the family."

"She doesn't get to make that call," Van interjects. "We need to loop Don Prescott in. Get a name for someone in family law."

Hell, no.

"We're not calling Don Prescott." Don's the lawyer for the trust.

"There are implications you might not have thought through, son. We need to know what our exposure is. This impacts the trust. There are going to be custody and support issues that need to be resolved. And you're going to need to start with a paternity test."

Mom clucks her tongue.

Van cuts her off. "Kelly, all I'm saying is that there's going to need to be legal documentation for the trust."

This is the uncle who took me on my first hunting trip. The guy who let me borrow his Maserati to go to prom. *Exposure. Documentation.* Jesus. When did he become so bloodless?

I shake my head. "Shay calls the shots. If she says she wants a lawyer involved, I'll get her a lawyer."

"You're not thinking clearly." Van casts a look at Dad, an appeal for backup, but Dad's gone silent.

Chapter 7

"You're not hearing me." I point toward the house down the hill. "She's gonna *bolt* if she thinks for a second that her child is in danger. What's she going to think if she hears the word lawyer?"

"You're proving my point. You need to protect your interests here."

"Shay and Mia are my interests."

Van huffs a sigh. "John, you talk to him."

Dad is following the conversations, brow knit, spine straight as always, but his head's bent. He looks tired. Older.

"What does she want?" he asks.

I don't know. "I don't think she wants anything."

Van scoffs. "Ask her for a number. She'll have one for you."

Fifty thousand, she'd said at first. And then she peeled twenties off a stack and tucked them in her bra. "You don't know her."

"Son, I mean no disrespect," Van says. "But you don't either. This is all supposedly a coincidence? You happen to run into her walking by the side of the road?"

"That's how it happened."

"That's not how the world works." He leans back and narrows his eyes, taking in everyone one by one. "You all are starting to believe your own bullshit."

"What does that even mean?" Mom shoots back.

"It means this isn't Mayberry. The folks who move out here have made a nice little playland for themselves. The white picket fences, the cutesy lamp posts on Main Street. Real slice of Americana. But people are still people, Kellum. You've got money. She's got none. She's playing an angle."

I shake my head. "The angle where she raises my child with no support for six years?"

Van shrugs. "Maybe she's not bright. Maybe she didn't figure out she was sitting on a goldmine until recently."

"You don't know what you're talking about."

"And I don't think you know what you're doing. She's got you by the balls already. No lawyer—" He snorts. "*She* calls the shots.

She's gonna drain you dry, and then she's gonna take that kid and disappear again. Mark my words."

"You can't possibly know that."

"I know that she had no problem taking my money back then, and she didn't have a word to say for herself."

"How much?" I ask.

How much did she have to get herself out of town, to buy the cradle, the onesies? When I was married, I got dragged to my fair share of co-ed gender reveals and showers. I know how much *stuff* a baby needs.

Van shrugs. "A hundred. Maybe two."

My stomach lurches. That's nothing.

We're silent for a long minute. The clock ticks on the wall. My big brother, John Junior, made it in woodshop. It's got a mirror with a deer etched on it, and the clock face is camo.

John left Stonecut when he turned eighteen and made himself his own life a few counties over. He was a firefighter for a while, and then when his marriage fell apart, he took up with some bikers. Now he works construction. He reconciled with his wife. They gave Mom the grandbabies she wanted so bad. She's always bitching that she only sees them at holidays.

I never got why John left. Stonecut's a great place to live and raise kids. Crime is almost nonexistent. The air's clear. We don't have traffic or overcrowding, and if you want something we don't have, the city's only a few hours away. You can make a weekend out of it.

John never really said why he pulled up stakes. He's the most decent man I know, though. Did he smell the rot?

White picket fences. Wrought iron lamp posts with hanging baskets. Boutiques and galleries and the 5-star restaurant in the rehabbed mill.

A beautiful lodge with soaring ceilings and the newest appliances.

And down the hill, my daughter was sleeping in a moldy trailer with no electricity because of my family.

Chapter 7

What do you call that besides rot?

I do not doubt these people's love for me. I don't doubt that all of them—Van included—believed they were protecting me.

But I'm not the one that needed protecting. Shay was seventeen-goddamn-years old. I was a police officer. Del shouldn't have gone with my folks over to her place. He should've arrested me. We all fucked up, but it ends here. I push back and stand. Mom has tears in her eyes. Van's pissed. Dad looks resigned.

"I'm heading back. We need some time. Shay doesn't feel comfortable with y'all, and I need you to understand that from here on out, I back her. No lawyers. No bullshit. Mia's the only important thing. I'll call when things settle down."

Mom smothers a sob. Dad reaches across the table to grip her hand. My chest aches. I don't want to hurt her. She's a tough woman, though. She'll come through for me on this.

Dad clears his throat, but Mom speaks before he can. "We understand, Kell. Whatever you need."

Van scowls, glaring at me in disbelief, his opinion clear.

"Before you go—" Mom dashes away the tears and forces a smile. "What's she like? Mia?"

A strange warmth suffuses my chest. What's she like? It's so hard to say. She reminds me of the saying "still waters run deep."

Yeah, she's like Dina with the selective mutism and the meltdowns. But Dina has a busy mind. It's always buzzing. I don't get that sense with Mia. She's soaking it all in. She has a peacefulness about her. A watchfulness.

Now that I think about it, kind of like me.

I can't say all that, though.

"She's perfect." I muster up a tight smile. "I'm sure you'll meet her soon. I'll talk to Shay. In the meantime, give us space. Steer clear. Everyone."

Van shakes his head. His phone's already back out, and he's scrolling. "That's a mistake, letting her call the shots."

Mom hushes him, eyeing me warily. My temper's back in check, though. I walk my shot glass to the sink.

"Wouldn't be my first," I say and head out, ignoring the burst of agitated conversation that breaks out when I'm halfway out the door.

Clouds have covered the moon, and it's nearly pitch black, but my feet know the way.

The night smells crisp, like gathering dew, and even though my body aches, my mind feels sharper than it has in months.

Crickets chirp in the fields, and as I pass the barn, there's a gentle stamping and a whicker or two. That gunshot must've stirred the horses up, but they've clearly settled now.

In a way, everything feels wrong. Home isn't home. Family is not who I believed them to be. I'm not the man I thought I was.

But my feet still hurry, and the closer I get to the farmhouse, the lighter my heart gets. I haven't hurried toward something in years.

Back when I was a kid, I lived to gear up to take the field. That Friday night high. Nothing like it. And then after the academy, putting on the uniform and heading out. For those first few months, I got the same buzz.

But by the time Elizabeth and I finally got married, we were both already carrying the weight of disappointment. I can see that now. I never hurried home. It made me a good officer and a shitty husband.

She'd taken up with the high school football star, the most popular guy in school. She married a man content to be a cop. She never understood my "lack of ambition" as she called it.

I don't know. Maybe it is lack of ambition. When I thought about what I wanted to do, though, I always came back to that night on the Albanstown Road. That couple in the SUV. They were hurt bad and scared shitless. Del said if we waited for backup, the vehicle could slip down further, right into the river.

It was pouring rain, the mud was sliding, and it was darker than it is tonight. We operated by sound: John, Del, and I. We got the woman out first, and then her husband. They were in their seventies. Probably shouldn't have been driving so late considering the conditions.

But that feeling when we got them to safety, standing by the side of the road as the paramedics shut the ambulance door—that was what I wanted. Nothing else appealed.

Elizabeth figured she was marrying a man who'd eventually run the town, a man like her daddy, the banker. She got me instead.

So she found her own ambition, and that worked for a while. The news anchor gig. A seat on all the town committees. But every new social notch required new stuff. She didn't feel the need to keep up with the Joneses; she needed to *be* the Joneses.

I could have kept us going forever, but she was never satisfied. I had this idea that if I cut her off, she'd kind of sober up. Dial it back. Instead, it drove her to ugliness. I cancelled a credit card she'd opened in my name, and she threw a lead crystal vase at my head and cracked my forehead open. It needed five stitches. Bled like a son-of-a-bitch.

I could never understand the rage.

I was a good husband, right? I provided. I didn't cheat. I went to all kinds of shit I had no interest in, and I made polite conversation with every pompous ass in three counties.

But if she could've done me real damage with that vase, she would have. The hate was real.

I never understood why, not until this moment, hustling along the path to the house.

To me, Elizabeth always felt like doing my duty. Being with her was what I was supposed to do.

The daughter of the man who owns the bank and the son of the richest man in town. Prom Queen and Prom King.

I was supposed to ask her out after that kiss, so I did. I was supposed to hang up on Shay and forget about her, so I tried. I was supposed to marry the woman I was with for years. I followed through on my obligations. I didn't consider happiness, only what was right, and I hurt all of us.

There's an awfulness that compounds as I fit the pieces of the past together, arrange them in their place. But as I mount the back steps, there's something else, too. Something I didn't know I was missing.

As the board creaks and I ease open the screen door, I am happy to be home.

It's so undeserved, there's no other word for it than grace.

The lights are out. Shay and Mia must be asleep upstairs.

Gratitude fills my heart, spilling into my empty chest.

I screwed everything up, and damned if I'm not looking forward to what happens next. It's a hell of a thing.

8

SHAY

I kept Mia in her clothes. I changed into a pair of leggings and a clean tank top, and then I packed our bags. Just in case.

If Kellum comes back from his parents with his head filled with nonsense, we're out of here.

Mia fell straight to sleep, the knight's horse in her fist, but I'm too on edge to lie down. I sit in the rocker without rocking and crack a window so I can listen to the night noises. And so I can hear when Kellum comes back.

I can imagine what they're saying to him. Mia's not his. I'm a gold digger. He better call himself a lawyer.

I'm the enemy, right?

I think about that day in Grandpa's trailer more than I should. It took three grown-ass men—one of them the sheriff—to run off a seventeen-year-old girl. I didn't see it for a long time, but eventually it occurred to me that you don't come that hard after a small problem that's easily solved.

I was a threat. I had power. Lord, I wish I had the gumption then that I've found now. I would've left town with more than a hundred bucks, that's for sure.

I can't be too hard on myself. We didn't have people like Kellum's family where I came from. No one had much money.

Helicopters and mansions and folks that'd tip you fifty bucks after squeezing your ass—not a thing I was accustomed to.

The Walls and Prices did what they wanted around town, and I figured they could do what they wanted to me and Grandpa, too. I was likely right.

The kind of money they have is hard to wrap your brain around. The horses. The houses. Not one, but three. This is the humblest, but it's huge, and it creaks mightily as the temperature cools.

What kind of people have all this and stomp around in jeans and muck boots as if they're everyday people? It's weird.

And then there's Kellum. I don't understand him at all. He's not like he was that night at the bonfire. At all.

I push off the floor with the balls of my feet and rock the chair, keeping the motion small and quiet.

That's not entirely true. He still has the same confidence.

He knew what he wanted that night. He went after it, and I lost my damn mind because the football star I'd watched from the stands as a girl was paying attention to me. This full-grown man, a police officer to boot, wanted *me*. And who was I? Nobody.

It was heady stuff. I figured nothing so crazy would ever happen to me again, so I should give in, go with it, take it all in and tuck it away for later when I'm turning down Elton from the service station for the hundredth time, knowing he's probably the best choice I'm going to get.

I let Kellum do what he wanted, but he didn't seem to have any kind of game. He was purely hungry. It did something to me. Turned a key in a lock. Then at some point, I wasn't just going along with it anymore. I was hungry, too.

It was scary.

I hadn't done it with a man before, but I'd touched myself plenty. It hurt at first, but then I got used to it. It still burned, but it also felt good. Really good. I even stopped marveling about how I was with *Kellum Wall* because my body was chasing something,

Chapter 8

and it didn't really matter that he was this big deal 'cause he was making me feel so good. I just wanted him to keep going.

It felt dirty, and wrong, and totally unlike me, and I loved it. I loved swimming in the river with him afterwards. I would've let him do it again if his friend hadn't come for him.

I haven't felt so wild since. I've hung out with a few guys, mostly from work, and I've been kissed and felt up. My mind didn't go there, though. Maybe because I was always worried about Mia and watching the clock. Mama's fine as a babysitter when she's sober, but I have to be careful to get home before the beers add up.

Eventually, I got old enough that I worried more about Mia than about missing out on being young, and I didn't bother with boys anymore at all. Haven't missed them.

Sometimes I wonder if I'm not quite right. If I'm too hard. Mama has always said I'm a cold fish. I've never seen the upside in being warm, though. The one time I was, I got burnt, didn't I?

I shift in the rocker and squint into the blackness. Up on the hill, the Lodge's lights are blazing. It's like a painting you'd buy at the mall. Almost impossibly pretty and perfect.

What if Kellum comes back and says he wants a paternity test? My belly lurches.

Well, then we get a paternity test, I guess. It's his right.

What if he offers me money to get gone and stay gone?

I take it.

Why does that thought make my stomach ache? It would solve all manner of problems.

A picture flashes in my head of Kellum carefully placing a sugar cube in Mia's palm as if it were a diamond. She accepted it with such seriousness, offering it to Patty who slurped it up in a split second. Mia tilted her head up to Kellum, and he nodded his approval.

The wanting tears through my chest, and my eyes burn.

Mia *deserves* that. Not for a day, but forever. Mia's the most important person in the world, and I'm the only one who thinks so, and I want so goddamn bad for there to be another person who knows how miraculous and beautiful she is.

If there were two of us looking out for her, it'd be safer. I've never felt safe, but the longing for the feeling has teeth. It's so strong that I have to wrestle it down.

If Kellum comes back with a cash offer, that's that. The decision is made for me. No more sugar cubes. And money is its own safety, isn't it?

What if he doesn't come back alone? What if his people come with him?

That's unlikely, but the idea sends a jolt of adrenaline through me. I'm not sitting still for them again. That's for damn sure.

My nerves are raw, and I'm lost in thought, so when I hear footsteps on the back porch, my heart lurches out of all proportion to the sound.

I catch a glimpse of the top of Kellum's head in the porchlight. He's alone. I release a breath I didn't know I was holding.

I should close the window and go to bed. If his folks have messed up this peacefulness, I can wait to find out what happened in the morning.

But my nerves won't let me put it off.

I need to know where we stand. The anxiety skitters across my skin like an itch.

There's a light on in the kitchen. Kellum's rummaging around in the freezer.

A late night snack?

I pause in the doorway. His back is to me. He's trying to wrap what looks like a bag of frozen peas in a dish towel, but he's not doing so well. The towel keeps slipping loose. The sink's running, so I guess he doesn't hear me.

I clear my throat.

He turns.

Whoa. He's been brawling.

He's got a black eye and a cut lip. The lip's not too bad, but the eye is a doozy. Puffed almost all the way shut. His neatly trimmed hair is all mussed. He looks broody and stressed and furious and beat down, all at the same time.

"His good eye darts guiltily to the bag of peas.

"Who won?" I ask as I tread closer.

His lip twitches. He seems surprised, I guess 'cause I'm not losing my shit.

He holds up the peas, the towel slipping loose again, chagrined. "My temper."

Some of the nerves that have been plaguing me settle. I give him a once over. His knuckles are busted up, too.

"Went that well, did it?" I take the peas and lay them on the counter, wrapping the towel around them tightly.

"Here. Sit down." I nod at the kitchen table.

He walks over, turns the chair so it faces the room, and eases himself down.

"They got your ribs, too, eh?"

"Yeah." He leans back against the edge of the table. He's obviously hurting, but there's nothing weak about him. The swell of his biceps in his T-shirt sleeves and the ripple where the fabric stretches against his abs both say this man could go another round.

Jitters flit around my insides. I'm not afraid of him, but the feeling's close. He's just bigger than me, that's all. Intimidating, even though he has perfect manners.

I gingerly step between his knees and press the peas gently to his eye.

"I can—" he says, reaching for the compress, his fingers tangling in mine.

I swat them away. "I got it."

I stand between his legs. Denim clings to his muscular thighs. I hold the peas to his face, and tingles dance across my skin, matching the jitters swooping in my belly. It's only nerves. I don't generally get this close to other people.

My worry lifts. With a shiner like this, I suspect things didn't go the way his folks wanted.

"What happened?"

Kellum sighs. "My brother ran off at the mouth. He tends to."

"Cash?"

"Yeah."

"He was a dick in school."

"He mess with you?" Kellum leans forward, and then hisses when I don't budge and he ends up putting too much pressure on his eye socket. I draw back, but he snatches my wrist, guiding the peas back to his face.

"Not really. I wasn't on his radar."

"What do you mean *not really*?" he presses, tensing.

"I mean, he ran his mouth all the time. I sat with Glenna Dobbs at lunch. He always had to say something when he walked past us, but it wasn't usually directed at me."

"Was it ever? Directed at you?"

His muscles are bunched even tighter now, and he's straightening in the chair.

"What? You gonna go back up the hill and let him shut your other eye for you 'cause he called me 'the dregs' back in high school?"

He skewers me with one bright blue eye. "Yes."

The giggle flies out of me and ends with a snort.

"You don't think I would?" he asks.

"If you did, it'd have nothing to do with me."

"What do you mean?" His expression goes mulish, as if I've insulted him.

"I mean obviously he knows how to get under your skin the same as everyone else's."

His brow furrows, and he's quiet for a moment as if he's mulling something over. "He was pulling his punches."

"Really?" I raise an eyebrow. Can't tell from where I stand.

"Yeah. He was careful of my ribs."

"You broke them when you saved that baby, didn't you?"

He blinks. "You know about that?"

"Everyone knows about that."

Chapter 8

"It wasn't a big deal."

"I saw you on that morning talk show."

He glances down and readjusts himself in the wooden chair. "Del thought it'd be good for the department if I went on in my uniform. We'd had some bad press before that."

The rescue was pretty much the first thing Pandy told me about when I got back to town. She showed me the clip from the TV show. I watched it more than I'd care to admit, late at night, the sound down real low so it wouldn't wake Mia.

He was so awkward. Impeccably groomed and movie-star handsome in his uniform, but the lady interviewing him could hardly pry anything out of him.

What did you think when you saw Mr. McAllister on the bridge?

Better call it in.

Your heart must have been in your throat. And Stonecut is a small town, right? You knew Mr. McAllister?

Yes, ma'am.

Did you have any idea, any indication at all, that he was going to do this unthinkable thing?

No, ma'am.

What was going on in your mind when he—well, and here is why we warned sensitive viewers and viewers with young children that they might want to mute—what was going on in your mind when Mr. McAllister threw his two-month-old infant daughter from the bridge? The river was several stories below. We're told it's twenty-feet deep at that point. What was going on in your mind in that moment, Officer Wall?

Better catch her.

Kellum shifts again in his seat. His thigh bumps my knee. I lift the peas and take a peek. The eye doesn't look any better.

"What did you think? Of the interview?" He picks at an invisible spot on his jeans.

"You didn't embarrass yourself."

"Not too much," he says.

"Not too much." I agree and reapply the peas.

"If you want me to pop Cash next time I see him for being an asshole in high school, I'm willing to do that. For you."

"I'd be much obliged. He was way worse to Glenna Dobbs."

He relaxes again. "Yeah. He's always had it out for Glenna. I have no idea why."

"What is it that he said about me?"

Kellum presses his lips together. "Nothing worth repeating."

And just like that, the moment cracks. It had been—friendly. I'd gotten distracted from the worry and the butterflies and that feeling I've had since Kellum found us on the road that I'm hardly balancing and the floor keeps tilting.

Now it's like it was. Tense. Fraught.

"Right." I grab his hand to have him take the compress, but instead, somehow, his fingers wind through mine. He doesn't let go.

I glance down. His large hand fairly swallows mine, his knuckles red and swollen. It must hurt to hold on with such a firm grip.

What is he doing?

If I tugged, he'd let go, wouldn't he?

I'm staring at our clasped hands, my mind spinning, and he's calm and collected.

"Everything is okay," he says. "I worry about my family. You worry about ours."

"Ours?" My heart thuds. If he didn't have my hand so tight, I'd back up. He's talking crazy.

"Yes. Ours."

"This is only for a little while." I can't retreat, so I keep holding the peas to his face. I stop staring at our hands. Try to ignore them. He squeezes me with his legs, and the insides of his thighs press against the outsides of mine.

"This is for as long as you'll stay."

"What did they say?" I change the subject because my face is flaming, and I don't know what's happening here.

"Bullshit, mostly. I don't want to repeat it, but I figure the way it's gotta work between us is, if you want to know something, I'm going to tell you."

"I want to know."

He extends his legs, and now, even though I haven't moved, I feel closer to him. He cups the back of my left knee. It's a light touch, but it's steady, designed to keep me where I am.

Why's he doing that?

"I asked how it could happen," he says. "It seems like Dad and Cash genuinely thought it was gossip. They thought they were protecting me."

I tense. Kellum squeezes my knee.

"Van says he figured you were pregnant, but it was another man's child. He's focused on the money."

"What money? Back support?"

Kellum jaw flexes. "I will be squaring up with you. Also, you need to know that Mia's provided for in the trust my grandparents created. She has an ownership stake in the farm. Like my brother John's kids. It's not just the farm. There are other investments. She's going to be taken care of. For life. No matter what happens here."

It's good news. It just doesn't register as real. It's *too* good.

"That all you talked about? Money?"

He shakes his head. "My mother really wants to meet Mia. She says she didn't know what was going on."

I remember that woman stalking down the hill. She seems the type used to getting her way.

"What did you say?"

"I said that you call the shots."

I raise an eyebrow. "I call the shots?"

He takes our intertwined hands and rests them on his rock-solid thigh. It's so strange. He's touching me, and it's not casual, but it's not sexual either. It's...I don't know. I have no frame of reference.

The hand cupping the back of my knee has slipped up an inch and now rests on the back of my thigh, not high enough to be indecent, but still—I've never been touched there. It's not a place a man touches a woman when he's trying to get her pants down.

"With Mia, yes. One hundred percent."

"But not with other things?"

He's staring at me intently with the one eye. The bag of peas doesn't take him down a peg at all. His confidence is unshaken.

"With other things, it depends."

"On what?"

"On what's right."

"And you decide what's right?"

"We decide together."

I can't imagine this man conceding anything, to me or anyone. He'd be a gentleman about it—of course, he would—but he'd end up getting his way. Mia and I are in his house, aren't we?

"Yeah, right. How would that go?"

"Like this." His lips curve, and a spark flashes in his eye. Mischief. That's new. I shuffle, curling my toes into the plastic on my flip-flops. "I want to kiss you."

My face flushes, heat unfurling in my belly, a chain reaction that steals my breath. I step back on instinct, but he has my hand, and his palm is bracing the back of my thigh.

"Is that a no?" he asks, calm, no pressure implied. A simple question.

My stomach swirls. Where did this come from? Is he high off his fight? He wants to screw around, take the edge off?

My gaze flits down to his mouth. It's swollen and there's a cut on the corner. "Your lip's busted."

He grins, flashing those bright, perfectly even teeth. "That's not a no."

Why didn't I say no?

Because my heart's thudding faster and faster, and the jitters have been joined with a tingling between my legs. It's so strange. I don't ever feel this way. Not with a man. Alone in the shower with my thoughts, sometimes. But this? I shift in my flip-flops, digging my heels into the rubber.

Chapter 8

It's quiet, and the only lights on are the one above the stove and the bottom of an antique hurricane lamp on the china cabinet. The room's dim and shadowy. We're alone. Mia's asleep. No one knows what we're doing. It's a secret.

"You can kiss me here." He touches the unhurt corner of his mouth with the tip of a finger. Before my skin registers the absence, his hand is back on my upper thigh, stroking down to my knee and back up again. My belly quivers.

"Why don't *you* kiss *me*?" I whisper.

I shouldn't be doing this. I should drop the peas in his lap and go back upstairs. What good can come of this?

"I want *you* to kiss *me*," he insists.

"You always get what you want?"

"Never." He pauses, and his eyes turn a deeper scorching blue. "Only once."

"Yeah? When was that?"

"You know."

"No," I say, but I do. He's talking about that night. The tingles between my legs have turned into an ache. I'm swollen there. And wet.

"You don't remember?" he asks.

"Not much," I lie.

"I do." His gaze skims my hair, my breasts. My nipples contract into hard, achy points. Can he see? My tank top's dark gray, but he's so close. I bet he can tell. "You were so beautiful."

My cheeks burn. I dab absently at his cheek with the peas for something to do.

"I couldn't figure out what color your hair was. In the firelight, it looked red, but in the moonlight, it looked brown."

"It's auburn." Instantly, I feel stupid. He knows what color my hair is now.

He draws our entwined hands to his chest, rests them above his heart. I can feel a dull thud through the cotton.

"It's beautiful. I'm so happy Mia has your auburn hair."

An ache slips through the swirling in my insides.

"I've never felt so lucky as when you let me touch you. Do you remember?" His voice is low, confidential.

I shake my head, but it's a lie. I remember feeling grateful. Mind blown. Kellum Wall was talking to me. Kellum Wall asked me if I wanted to dance. Kellum Wall was kissing me.

"We were alone, in the woods, and you were looking up at the moon, and I was behind you," he recalls.

I remember. Of course, I do. The moon was so impossibly big. No matter that I was alone with Kellum Wall. I couldn't help but stare. It was the kind of moon you think people in skyscrapers must be looking down on.

"I was jealous. You were so into the moon, you forgot I was there."

"No, I didn't." I exhale. I could never have forgotten.

"I wrapped you in my arms and slid a hand under your shirt. Your skin was so soft." He moves the hand cupping the back of my leg, skims lightly across my thigh and nudges up my tank top. Then he strokes the bare skin right above my waistband.

Tingles zip from where his fingers graze my belly. My breath catches.

"I asked if it was okay." He rests his hand flat above my belly button. It's so huge, his pinky grazes the underside of my breasts. "Is this okay?"

I don't know. This doesn't make sense.

I feel like I do when I'm swimming. I know how to doggie paddle, but that's it. If I'm trying to go very far, I have to stop, float, and then I keep flailing until I get where I want to be. I'm told it looks a lot like drowning.

It feels like it, too. It feels exactly like this.

I'm scared.

I shake my head no. He removes his hand from my belly, but other than that, he doesn't move.

His body is tense; he's holding himself so still.

Why does he want to touch me?

Why do I want him to? I'd call it curiosity, but it's stronger than that. Way stronger.

What would happen if I kissed him?

Would it be like before? Would we end up on the floor or with me bent over the table? My pussy clenches, but my chest aches. That's not what I want.

He waits, patient. The towel is growing damp as the peas defrost. The cold is numbing my fingertips.

I reach past him and set it on the kitchen table. My hair falls in his face.

He sucks in a ragged breath.

I half-straighten, and then, almost on a whim, I brush my lips across the corner of his mouth. He exhales, winding his arms around my waist.

Blood surges through my veins. Is he going to take what he wants now?

"Again," he says, smiling.

"Again?" I search his eyes. They're on fire, but his control is obvious. It's in the rigidity of his shoulders, the pressure in his embrace. His muscles are rock hard, but his grasp is gentle. There's room to move, if I want to pull loose.

"Please," he says.

I lean forward and taste him again. A hint of whiskey. Soft and firm lips. The swirls in my belly dance and writhe. He kisses back, careful but sure.

When I withdraw, he lets me.

"Why do you want to kiss me?" It's a stupid question, but my brain's glitching. Foggy.

"I want to do more than kiss you."

"Why?"

"It feels good. Better than good."

"How so?" I demand.

He chuckles and tucks a strand of hair behind my ear. Shivers dart down my neck. "Sweet. Perfect. Made for me."

"You can't say things like that," I whisper.

"Guess I shouldn't then."

"It's just about sex."

His jaw tightens. "Just sex," he repeats. His eyes darken, but his hold on me doesn't change. "Have you been with a lot of men? Since—?"

I squirm. I should end this. That's not his business. This whole conversation is crazy. He's Mia's biological father. That's all.

But there's a tic in his temple. He really wants to know if I've been with other people? Why?

"Shay?" he prompts.

"Have you?"

"No one since my ex and I split."

Something thaws inside my chest, which is foolish. It's no concern of mine if he's seeing someone.

Still, I can't help asking, "Are you, uh, dating anyone?"

Amusement flashes across his face. "No. You?"

I shake my head. "I don't have time."

The truth is, even if I did, I wouldn't. The times I've hung out with a guy—it wasn't what I wanted it to be.

He relaxes back in his chair. The playful twinkle in his eye is back. "Kiss me again."

The jitters dance and whirl, and it's like my body's spinning wool in my mind. All my walls, all my lines, everything gets hazy.

Besides the faint whiff of whiskey, Kellum smells of clean sweat and cotton. Even sitting, he's so much bigger than me, twice as broad. I'm an average-sized woman, but I feel surrounded. He's a lot.

My heart pounds. My breasts are tender, full and heavy. The stiff fabric of my tank top brushes my nipples and makes them ache. I took my bra off hours ago when I changed for bed. It's hanging from the knob on the back of the rocker.

Does Kellum know I'm not wearing a bra? He must. His finger brushed the underside of my breasts when he rested his hand on my belly.

I liked that.

Chapter 8

I like this.

I never get to have what I like.

The bills are the boss. And Mia's needs. And Mama's constant, ever-changing dictates of "how things are gonna be from here on out." What *I* like is only a consideration when I treat Mia to a donut after she's good for the doctor or dentist.

I get chocolate glazed.

My mouth waters. Kellum's lips are firm. Very lightly chapped. Why is he waiting, so still and patient?

I swear, the devil gets into me.

"You kiss me this time," I say. It's out before I realize what I'm saying.

He smiles, wolfish, letting go of my hand and sinking his fingers into my hair, cradling the back of my head, drawing me closer, taking my lips, sipping, tugging, urging me to part for him.

The jitters disappear, swamped by a wave of wanting, a rising heat.

I open for him, and he slips past my lips, his tongue slicking against mine, stroking. He's in my mouth. There's a memory, but it's flickering, and then it's drowned out by now, this moment. His taste. His breath and mine.

He doesn't ease up, not for a second. He demands more, tangles us together, then he sips at my lips again, gentle, until I part to coax him back because I want more.

I'm hot, panting, and my legs are wobbling. I brace myself against his shoulders. They're so solid. I test the strength, curling my fingertips into the muscle, and I can hardly make a dent.

"Okay, okay," he gasps between kisses, and I don't know what he means. He seems to be talking to himself.

He lets go of my hair, stroking his hands down my back, and my knees give out. I sway and cry out against his tongue, and he immediately lifts me, resettling me so I'm in his lap, straddling his thighs. I let him rearrange me like a rag doll 'cause I don't want to break the kiss that goes on and on.

I need it. It's everything.

He's as stiff as a soldier underneath me, but his mouth is hot and insistent.

"Okay," he breathes again and wraps his arms around my ass, drawing me closer until a hardness notches between my legs.

It feels good. There's denim and cotton between us, so the only sensation is pressure, but it's such a good pressure. My pussy's throbbing, and I can't help but grind. He guides my hips, urging me to rock, to chase the coiling need that's winding tighter and tighter.

He stops kissing me. I whimper.

He grips my hip with one hand, digging his fingers into my soft flesh, keeping me right where I am as he takes his other hand, grabs the neck of his shirt and drags it over his head, mussing up his hair even more.

I touch. I can't stop myself. His chest is hot and a little clammy. There's a dusting of hair on his pecs and a trail down his taut belly leading into the waistband of his jeans.

I swallow hard. There's the bulge, pressing against his zipper, grinding against my swollen pussy.

I stroke lightly down his chest. Except for the crinkly hair, his skin is smooth. His hard muscles ripple the tiniest bit under my touch.

He's breathing hard, staring down in fascination at my hand on his chest. I've gotten distracted from my rocking, but he's picked up the rhythm, rolling his hips. I'm gasping, too.

He grabs the sides of my tank top.

"Arms up," he orders.

I raise them, and he eases my shirt over my head, dropping it on the table behind him. He sucks in a breath.

My breasts bob gently as I ride him, and I guess I should be embarrassed, but I'm lost in the growing tension, the amazingly *good* feeling that has an edge now, a hunger.

He brushes a kiss on my straining nipple, and my belly clenches. I arch my back on instinct, and he takes the nipple in his mouth, suckling, and I can't help but writhe, my body bearing

Chapter 8

down, demanding more and more. He grazes my nipple with his teeth, and I moan.

He can't stop. I'm floating down a river of sensations, and I've only been here once before, and it was like a dream then, and it's a dream now, but not a foggy, vague one. It's a dream where you're running. You're being chased. Your heart's pounding. It's a dream where it can't possibly be happening, but it is, and I'll die if he stops touching me.

I'm slip-sliding against my panties, my pussy lips teasing my clit, and I'm so wet. My pants are soaked. Am I soaking his jeans?

My pussy spasms. I'm not coming yet, but I'm so close.

He strokes down my spine, cupping my shoulder blades. I love his rough fingers on my bare skin. I love it, and it isn't enough.

I mewl, a demanding whine in the back of my throat.

"Okay," he pants. "Okay." He snakes a hand between us, tilts me back, and he slips his fingers past my waistband, into my panties.

Yes, yes. I want him to feel how wet I am. I can't really spread my legs anymore, but I scooch back, make room.

His rough hand cups my pussy. He presses his forehead to mine.

"Okay, beautiful," he pants. "You're gonna cum for me now."

He delves between my slippery folds, two fingers plunging in, and his thumb finds my clit, circling. I'm moaning now, a low constant keen as he drives me closer and closer, and the pressure builds and builds, and every inch of my skin is on fire, and he's the only one who can make me feel all better.

He drops gentle kisses all over my face, and in between, he murmurs against my mouth. "You are so beautiful like this. You feel so good. I need you to cum, baby. Cum all over my hand."

He flicks my clit faster, using his other hand to squeeze my breast and tease the nipple.

He's flushed, brighter than me, and I'm grinding in his lap, riding his fingers.

"Baby, I can't—" He stops mid-sentence, gritting his teeth,

tensing his whole body. He sucks down a ragged breath. "Okay. I'm okay."

"Why do you keep saying that?" I pant, and he kisses me, easing another finger inside me, stretching me, and now I'm tumbling, crashing, the swirls finally bursting, flooding my limbs to my fingers and toes, and my vision goes black for a second as I cry out against his sweat-slicked shoulder.

"There it is," he says, his voice a deep, self-satisfied growl. He keeps his fingers inside me for a few more moments. I can feel my walls flutter, aftershocks of my orgasm. Can he feel it?

He withdraws, slowly, but I don't move. I can't. I'm a limp noodle, plastered to his chest. He wraps his arms around me. Between my legs, he's still hard as a rock.

"You didn't cum." I make a half-hearted effort to start rocking again, but I can hardly keep my eyes open. I'm a jellyfish.

He hushes me and trips his fingers lightly up and down my spine.

"Next time," he says.

Next time? The thought is followed quickly by another.

"Why did you keep saying 'okay'?" I mumble.

"Shit. Uh—" He brushes my hair behind my ears, nuzzling my temple with his nose, a long, raspy moan reverberating from low in his throat. "I didn't want to, uh, you know, lose control again. With you."

"Lose control?"

There's a pause. "Yeah. Like that night."

"You lost control? By the bonfire?"

The languorous, cat-on-a-windowsill-on-a-sunny-afternoon feeling seeps right out of me like water down the drain. I struggle upright, forcing my wrung-out muscles to bear weight.

He nods, somber. "Yes. And I regret it. Deeply."

He meets my eye, guilt and disgust shining through. "I should have never lost control with you that night. It was wrong. I'm not the kind of man that does that type of thing. I'm better than that. I was raised better."

He's so damn sincere.

It's like a bucket of ice water is dumped directly into my brain. The fog disappears. Suddenly, I have no problem drawing myself away.

That's something about humiliation. It cuts right through the bullshit. Really clears the sinuses.

I climb off his lap, wobbling, barely finding my footing. His good eye widens in surprise, but he doesn't try to stop me. If he did, I swear, I'd make his right match his left.

"Shay, I mean it."

"I heard you."

"What did I say?" His brow furrows.

"You heard you, too."

I snag my tank top and yank it back on.

"Shay." He stands, bulge still popping his zipper, but he's frowning at me, as if he has the audacity to be hurt and bewildered.

I am not one to pin all human shortcomings on half the species, but damn. Sometimes? Men. Holy hell.

"I regret fucking you, too, back in the day. It was also a sad personal failing for me. I have no excuse for lowering myself so much as to fuck you, but rest assured, I was raised with higher standards." I lift a shoulder. "So sorry. I just want you to know that I would never have touched you with a ten-foot pole had I been in my right mind."

I nod. Think that about covers it. I turn on my heel, but before I leave the kitchen, another thought occurs to me.

"Oh, and go fuck yourself."

I stomp back up the creaky stairs, as best I can in flip-flops, and I don't look back.

I never throw tantrums. Not ever. But I have to say, there's a righteous energy to it. I don't want to lie down and go to sleep. I want to tip over all this fancy antique furniture and make it go boom.

I want to go back downstairs and tell him that I was raised

better, too. I was taught to steer clear of entitled, holier-than-thou, my-shit-don't-stink douchebags, and the only reason I gave him the time of day was because I was drunk.

He thinks I'm a slut.

The realization slams into me. He deeply regrets a quickie with a slut who ended up getting herself knocked up.

That's what he was raised not to do. Be with a woman who would do what I did.

Was that what he was thinking when he fingered me? That I'm a slut?

My nails bite into my palms, and my stomach lurches. So what if he does?

First, I don't care what he thinks. Second, there's nothing wrong with being with men if it makes you happy. If Mama only took them out for a drive and didn't keep bringing 'em home, she'd probably be a happier woman.

I've known women who are with a new man each week and have their shit on lock, and I know women who've been with the same loser since high school and cry their eyes out in the ladies' room at work on the regular.

If I wanted to be a slut, I would. I stand by my previous statement. Kellum Wall can go fuck himself.

It's not until much later, when I calm down enough to tuck myself under the quilt next to Mia, that the anger finally wears off and a lonely ache takes its place.

The house is silent except for the whirr of the air conditioning. I heard Kellum's footsteps in the hall heading toward his bedroom an hour or so ago. The moon shines in the window, turning all the old furniture a deep velvet blue.

I'm able to sort through things well enough to figure out I'm mad at myself, too. Maybe more than I am at Kellum.

I shouldn't have gone anywhere near him.

I know better, but damn if everything isn't topsy-turvy. This big ol' house instead of a stinky trailer. Peace and quiet instead of the constant blare of Mama's TV and the neighbors' shouting. I can be

Chapter 8

forgiven that, for a moment, I let myself get confused about which way is up.

It's an impossibility, but it's the story we're told, over and over, isn't it? The prince finally rescues the princess. It was all a terrible mistake, but her troubles are over now. He's been looking for her all along. Pining for her. And now that everything has been put to rights, it'll be happily ever after for everyone.

I haven't ever believed in fairy tales, and still, the dumb part of my brain that is impervious to experience and common sense lit up like a Christmas tree after a few kisses, didn't it?

It was a terrible mistake all right.

Kellum said so.

I was the mistake.

He hasn't been pining after me. He's been married to another woman.

And nothing is put to rights. I've got some vague promises that Mia has money coming to her, but in cold, hard reality? I've got two hundred dollars cash, and the man making me promises got into a fistfight tonight.

What if this were Mama? If she told me a man said he'd take care of us, but he's living in his grandparents' old house, and he settles things with his fists? I'd start making plans for finding Mia and I another place to stay.

I'm never this foolish.

Tomorrow, I need to find out how to make the cash coming to Mia more of a sure thing. A lawyer would help, but I don't have that kind of money.

When Mary Joy Engle sued General Goods after that shelf fell on her, she got a guy to represent her for a cut of the settlement. It ended up being almost fifty-fifty, but as Mary Joy pointed out, fifty percent is a hundred times more than zero.

She's about as good at math as she is at stacking boxes, but the point's valid.

Tomorrow, I'll go see about a lawyer, and I'll go by the school to get Mia registered. I don't see us staying in this house much longer, but we're gonna have to make a go of it here in Stonecut. Classes start soon.

I'm going to have to shove this all down, shut the door, go on as if I didn't lose my good sense for a hot minute.

I'm going to have to remember what I am, and what Kellum Wall is, and how the story plays out in real life. The poor girl gets screwed. The rich man carries on and everything works out just fine. For him.

I need to remember what people like him are capable of.

And I'm going to need a ride into town.

9

KELLUM

I fucked up. I stand in the kitchen for a while, trying to piece together what happened, waiting, thinking maybe Shay'll come back. Elizabeth would do that. She'd stomp off in a huff, get halfway to her car or wherever, and then she'd come back to finish giving me hell.

I stand there a long time before I give up.

When I go upstairs, her door is closed. There's no light, no sound. I can't knock. I'd wake up Mia.

Besides, my cock is still hard, and I don't know what to say.

I take a shower, cum in my hand before I wash off the scent of Shay's pussy on my fingers, and eventually, my head clears enough to think it through.

I replay what I said. How she responded. Maybe I didn't phrase it quite right.

When it hits me fully what she must think I meant, my gut cramps. She thinks I regret sleeping with her because I'm better than her. Like I was raised better than to be with someone like her.

This is why I don't talk. I'm as bad as Cash when I open my mouth.

I lie down, but I don't get much sleep, just fits and starts. I'm scared shitless that I'm gonna hear their soft footsteps in the hall as they sneak out. Shay's got to be considering it. She was pissed, and she had a right to be.

The way I treated her was wrong. Not because I'm better than her, but because she should never be treated like that. Not by me or anyone.

And back then, I let so many people's voices in my head, my own notions got drowned out.

Somehow, Elizabeth knew I'd been with someone else that night. I'm guessing someone at the bonfire texted her. That's why she was on my porch when I got home. Later, when Shay called, Elizabeth was sitting next to me on the couch. After I hung up, she said it'd be cruel not to block her. The kindest "no" is a firm one.

As if Shay were a dog.

But Shay only ever called that once, and it'd been so long since that night at the bonfire. Why wasn't I curious about what she wanted?

I didn't question it because everyone in my life treated me like I was special. Girls chased after me because I was hot shit. Of course, Shay was calling 'cause she wanted me. Everyone wanted me.

And that voice is still in my head, isn't it?

Telling me I should regret that night because it was beneath me.

But Shay's not less than. She's beautiful and tough and delicate and clever. She let me in, and that was a gift, and I let myself be convinced it wasn't.

Damn, but she was the sweetest thing I ever tasted then, and she tastes the exact same now. Kissing her is like biting into a peach, the softness, and then the sweetness.

I groan and roll onto my side. The sun's peeking out, and even though I was only asleep for an hour at most, my fitted sheet has come loose, and my flat sheet is tangled in my legs.

Instantly, the memory of last night rolls over me again. It was amazing.

Chapter 9

As in I was fucking *amazed*.

Shay's so wary and guarded, but the second she drops those walls, she's pure appetite. God, she wanted it. She wanted me. She was begging for it, clinging to me, her whole body writhing, her pupils blown as if I was her drug.

So demanding. So vulnerable. My cock throbs, and I stroke it slowly.

I've had plenty of sex. I know how to warm a woman up, how to make her cum. But I have no idea how to make a woman respond like Shay. As if I'm everything she needs, and she's lost her mind.

She made me feel like a king.

I made her feel less than.

I'm an asshole.

I drop my dick, swing my legs over the side of the bed, scrub the sleep from my eyes, and drop to do my morning pushups. I add a few reps of crunches and a set of burpees, too. It doesn't ease the unsettled feeling in my gut, but it wakes me up.

I have work today. I should call in. Del will understand. Family comes first.

But I doubt Shay wants me underfoot. She might be more likely to stay if she doesn't have to look at my face. I can take the day to figure out how to fix this.

I shower and shave, which clears more of the cobwebs. Coffee will finish the job.

I'm shirtless and tugging up my pants when my bedroom door creaks open. My heart jumps. Shay? Is she coming to tell me she's out of here?

A very small hand wraps around the door, followed by a very elf-like nose. I exhale.

Mia.

She pushes the door wider. She's already dressed for the day in fuzzy pink shorts and a tank top with bright cartoon fish.

"Hi, honey." I grab my undershirt and quickly tug it on. "Good morning."

She lingers in the doorway.

"Where's your mommy?" She shoots a glance down the hall to the guest room. Now, with the door open, I can hear the faint sounds of a shower.

"You hungry?"

She blinks.

Damn, but she has my eyes. There's a tightening in my chest. I clear my throat.

"What you got there?" I nod to her balled fist.

She seems to consider, curling her toes in her flip-flops. I've seen Shay do that, too. It's a nervous habit. Her wary gaze shifts between the floor and my face.

Finally, she holds up my old knight's horse.

My eyes prickle, and that's when I put two-and-two together and realize that she's sneaking peeks at my bruised face. Shit.

It throbbed this morning when I woke up, but after the months recovering from my leap into the river, I've learned to ignore aches and pains. And my mind was on something else.

"I, uh, I made a bad decision. It's all right, though. Everything's okay."

Her face is blank. Not her default, watchful calm, but a careful blank. It's so eerily similar to how Dina looks when she's uncertain.

"It won't happen again," I say, my cheeks burning. I focus on the task at hand, grabbing my uniform shirt from its hanger to shrug it on, button it up, and tuck it in.

Mia tightens her fingers around her knight.

"When I get dressed, I'll make breakfast, okay? How about eggs? Do you like eggs?"

I usually only have a cup of coffee in the mornings, but neither Shay nor Mia need to be skipping meals. Mia's all elbows and knees. Shay has those tits and that ass which make you think she's eating just fine, but when she raises her arms over her head, you can count her ribs.

Chapter 9

I push down an uncomfortable surge of arousal and concern. Not helpful in this moment.

Mia hasn't answered, but she has taken a few steps into my room. She's checking it out. This was Van's room when I was growing up. Mom's room was the guest room. My grandparents took the small room I use for gym equipment and storage. That's who they were. They put their kids above everything else. And the son above the daughter.

Mia examines the bric-a-brac on my dresser, and she peeks at herself in the mirror.

I pin on my gold star over my right pocket and the ridiculous gold name tag over my left. Del gave everyone in the office the name tags for Christmas two years back. The number of times people I've known my whole life have squinted to read the name, and then sounded it out, just to bust my chops—well, it's a gift that keeps on giving.

Mia comes over and sits on the edge of my unmade bed, her flip-flops dangling from her tiny toes. Do she and Shay have any real shoes? Shit. There's a lot that needs to be seen to. Maybe I should call in to work.

But if I start today with asking whether Mia needs shoes, that's gonna come off as me not thinking Shay can care for her. I don't need to add fuel to the fire I started with my dumb mouth.

I go to the safe I use as a night table. I keep my duty weapon, handcuffs, pepper spray, and all the crap that goes on my belt there instead of at the office. We're such a small department and office quarters are so cramped that it doesn't make sense to have a locker room.

Mia watches my every move, swinging her thin legs. Dina had a lot more meat on her bones at that age, even if she was picky as hell about what she ate.

"You liked those pancakes. What if I make some waffles this morning?"

I think my grandmother's old waffle iron is in the drawer under the stove. I never go in there, but I seem to recall from when I first moved in.

Mia stares past me, to the door. I follow her gaze, and my heart skips.

Shay.

Her hair is wet, her arms are crossed tight, and she's wearing a sundress. It's simple. Solid green. Hits mid-thigh with a modest neckline. It honestly looks like something my mom would wear to church.

But she's fucking stunning. The green teases out the gold in her eyes, and the straight cut strains across her tits and hips.

I swallow. My mouth is dry.

She's mad as hell.

"Good morning," I say. My voice comes out lower than usual.

She jerks her chin and holds out her hand. "Come on, Mia. We don't want to bother him while he's getting dressed."

"It's no bother."

Shay keeps her arm straight and hand open. Mia hops down immediately and goes to her.

"She's fine." My stomach doesn't feel right. I finish buckling my belt. I don't like how easy it is for her to call Mia away from me.

I'm assuaged somewhat when Shay doesn't move immediately to go.

"You're going to work?" she asks.

"Yeah. I'll be back at five."

"I need a ride into town."

What? My adrenaline spikes. Like hell she does. I force myself to breathe. I did not handle last night with any finesse. I need to take a moment. Be calm.

"What do you need in town?"

She shifts guiltily, and her stare slides off past my ear. "I need to register Mia for school."

Yeah, that does need to happen. We probably have about three weeks before school starts.

But what's the guilt about?

"That's all? I can take a long lunch. We can do it then."

"I have errands, too."

"Is your plan to try and get the power turned back on in the trailer?" I'm squared off, facing her now. I recognize I sound like a cop. Hell, I am a cop.

"No."

"I can take a half day. We can go up to the school around lunchtime and do your errands after."

She bristles, drawing herself up to full height. Fierce little critter.

"I didn't ask for that. I asked for a ride to town."

I try to reason instead of putting my foot down, which I'm itching to do, and which would most certainly blow up in my face. "How do you plan to get back once your errands are done?"

She shrugs. "We'll walk."

"It's almost four miles."

"What do you think we were doing when you ran into us? We walk to and from town all the time."

"But you don't have to. I'll give you a ride."

She huffs and rolls her eyes. "Don't see why you couldn't have said that in the first place. I'll call you when we're done."

I blink. What just happened?

I'm not a hundred percent sure, but Shay agreed that I'm bringing them back home after their errands, so I can breathe again.

"Come on, Mia. He's got eggs." Shay leads a willing Mia off downstairs, and I'm left alone, befuddled, to trail after if I'm so inclined.

I am, so I do.

I sit at the kitchen table and nurse a coffee while Shay scrambles Mia an egg. She tucks a dishcloth into her neckline as a makeshift apron, and she's done the same for Mia as a bib.

At first, I get the silent treatment. Shay's jaw is set, and she won't look anywhere near where I'm sitting. I picked a different chair from last night. She's blushing like crazy every time she catches sight of that chair, though.

I like it.

She sets a steaming plate of eggs in front of Mia. Mia stares at it, making no move to pick up her fork.

Shay puts her hands on her hips and huffs a sigh. Mia nudges the plate a millimeter away with the very tip of her index finger.

"Seriously?" Shay says.

Mia is impassive. She looks so much like Shay in this moment. I school my face so my lips don't curve.

"There're three eggs on that plate getting cold."

Mia is unmoved.

"Kellum is gonna think you're spoiled."

I don't, but I'm not foolish enough to get in the middle of this.

"Glory day, Mia." She throws her hands up and goes rummaging in the cabinets in between tending to the eggs she has cooking in the pan.

"What are you looking for?" I ask, careful to keep my tone helpful.

"Do you have hot sauce?"

"No, I don't think so. We can get some."

"Ketchup?"

"In the fridge."

"You keep ketchup in the fridge?"

"Where do you keep your ketchup?"

"In a cabinet. You like cold ketchup?"

I hadn't ever really thought about it. "Not particularly. I guess it's a force of habit. That's where my mom kept the ketchup."

Shay's found the bottle, and now she's thumping the bottom over Mia's eggs.

"You put ketchup on eggs?" I mean, I've heard of it. I've never seen it done in real life, though. It's not pretty.

"We prefer hot sauce, but you don't have any."

"We'll put it on the list."

Chapter 9

She casts me a sidelong glance as she goes back to the stove. There's mistrust. A smidge of bashfulness. And a hint of softening. My breath quickens. She's not angry anymore. I know what an angry woman looks like.

I haven't completely blown it.

"Put eggs on your list, too," she says, dumping the empty carton in the trash. She stares at the plate she's set out on the counter and frowns.

After a long minute, she huffs and takes another plate from the cabinet. She divides the eggs evenly, and brings them over to the table, sliding a plate in front of me.

I hate scrambled eggs.

"Thank you."

She shrugs.

I shovel the eggs down. As a kid, I figured out that you don't taste them so much if you don't chew.

"You were hungry," Shay observes, eating hers like a lady, terry cloth hand towel with a turkey wearing a Pilgrim's hat covering her chest. She needs a decent apron. That goes on the list, too.

"Guess I was."

She squints at me. The sun's higher now, and the lacy kitchen curtains aren't blocking any of it. "Your face looks the same."

"Handsome?"

I know I shouldn't tease—not when things are so fraught and unsettled—but when roses show up on her cheeks, I'm not sorry.

"Less so today than usual."

"But I'm usually handsome, then?" I grin tentatively. If she bristles, I'll stop. But if she keeps blushing like that, I'm going to keep pushing. I think Shay needs to be pushed. Gently.

"If it suits you to think so."

"It would suit me if *you* think so."

She sucks in her cheeks, but she can't quite stop her lips from twitching. "You're full of it."

"Full of delicious scrambled eggs." I rub my belly and nod to Mia. "Right?"

"Your face didn't say 'delicious,'" Shay smirks. "Your face said 'I hate eggs.'"

"You mean my usually handsome face?"

"It was basically green a minute ago."

"I bet the color looked good on me." I risk another grin.

Shay's lips contort. She's trying not to smile back, but she's losing big time.

"Green was an improvement."

"See? I look better than yesterday. You can admit it. It's only true."

She rolls her eyes and stands to clear the table.

"I can get that." I grab my plate at the same time she reaches for it. Our hands graze. She snatches hers back like it burns.

My mood drops like a stone. I don't want her to recoil from my touch. It has a wrongness to it, as much as last night had a rightness.

And not a thin kind of rightness like opening my checkbook at a charity events or putting on the uniform.

A sterner rightness. One that can stand on its own, that doesn't need me to put on a tie and mind my language. Like the rainy night at the ravine. Folks were hurt and in danger of being hurt worse, and the right thing to do was so clear we leapt without looking.

I kissed Shay last night because she needs to be in my arms. She and Mia need to stay in this house where I can take care of them, and it's not about guilt, although I feel it in spades. It's not even about doing the right thing by them.

It's because Shay in my arms and Mia safe and content has the rightest feeling I've ever brushed against. I don't know if we have anything in common. Maybe I've gone crazy from living alone in this house with only the bat in the attic for so long now. Doesn't matter.

I need to fix it so Shay never snatches her hand away from mine ever again. And I'm in trouble, 'cause words are not my strong suit.

Chapter 9

She's washing the dishes by hand in the sink.

"The dishwasher's under the counter there," I point out.

She glances down and grunts. "Oh. I'm almost done."

I shove my hands in my pockets. Mia has her critters out and lined up all nice and straight. She has the knight's horse, an ostrich, a giraffe, and a donkey.

"Your Mama's gonna get you signed up for school today, eh?"

Mia ignores me, and her face is impassive as she pushes the donkey over onto his side with the tip of one finger. Then goes the giraffe and ostrich. Finally, she glances up in the direction of my face as she slowly and deliberately knocks over the horse.

"That excited, eh?"

"I'm ready," Shay says from the back door. She's slung a small backpack-style purse over her shoulders, and she's slipped on a pair of shoes. Not flip-flops. A stiff pair of black flats that look like the kind that hang from racks, the kind meant to be accessorized with an outfit, not for every day. Elizabeth had dozens of pairs, some still on the plastic hangers.

Shay can't walk around town on errands in those shoes.

She's not a vain woman. At least, not that I've noticed. These must be the best option.

Goddamn it. Shoes go on the list.

Maybe I should call in. Drive down to the outlets in Shady Gap. It's only a little over an hour away. We could get Shay and Mia all kitted out.

Mia's collected her critters, and her terry cloth pockets are bulging. She's waiting beside her Mama now.

I barely won the argument about driving them to and from town. I'm not sure how Shay will take a shopping trip, and right now, giving her the reins seems the wiser choice.

I snag my hat from the peg by the back door and down the rest of my coffee, trying to get that egg taste out of my mouth.

"After you, ladies."

They're both silent on the drive into town. I spend most of the time thinking about how I can get a car seat before it's time to take them home.

Shay stares deliberately out the windshield, and after we pass the horses, Mia busies herself with a duck that found his way into her crowded pocket.

I get the squad car detailed frequently. Drunks and puke are the perpetual bane of small-town law enforcement. Consequently, the cab smells strongly of chemical cleaner. Yet, somehow, Shay fills my senses. There's soap and shampoo of no particular scent that I could name, but stronger than that, there's Shay. Earthy. Warm. Real.

My cock twitches. I didn't get nearly enough last night. I want to lay her out on my bed, take my time, bury my head between those tight-pressed thighs and inhale. Lick until I turn that heady scent even muskier.

Hell.

Even though the AC's blasting, I roll down my window. Thank the Lord she's staring straight ahead. My cock is entirely indecent.

I force my mind to the tasks for the day. I need to process the paperwork for harvest day. I need to touch base with Del and see what he's dumping on my plate this week. Figure out what days I'm going to take off. I need time with Shay and Mia. Del's troubles are going to need to go on the back burner for a spell.

I also need to talk to him more in depth about Rory Evans. I understand that he followed up, and the girl isn't missing, but Sarah and Ed landed in my office, and with something like this, I'm going to dot the I's and cross the T's.

I'm aware of Del's attitude toward the folks he calls river rats, the people who live past the railroad tracks down where the banks of the Luckahannock get weed-choked and the water runs shallow. I'm sure he did all the things he was supposed to do to close the report, but another pair of eyes can't hurt. When I call Sarah Evans back to reassure her, I want to speak from full confidence.

By the time we hit the town limits, I've got my mind on business.

Chapter 9 189

"You want me to drop you at the school?" I ask. "I could come in with you."

Shay shakes her head. "The lady said not to come until closer to noon. Just drop us anywhere."

"If you tell me your errands, I'll drop you there."

Shay slides her gaze out the window. "Drop us in the square."

"There's nothing in the square."

It's a rehabbed fountain from the fifties, a gazebo, and benches. There's a view of the river and town hall. Shay can't have business at Town Hall. It's all municipal office space. Any paperwork a person needs gets handled at the courthouse annex.

"You gonna drop us off or not?" There go her arms. She's folding them tight. She had been picking at the hem of her dress.

"Yes, ma'am. Where and when am I picking you up?"

"We'll come by your office when we're done."

Not good enough. I'll have no way of getting a hold of them or knowing where they are. My hands tighten on the steering wheel until my sore knuckles burn. How am I going to let them out of the car?

Panic like I've never known floods my chest.

They could walk away, and I'd never see them again.

I want to keep driving, but I'm at the square, and I'm not being reasonable. Shay's bags are at the house. She's a sensible woman. She wouldn't leave without her stuff.

I pull over. Shay reaches for the door handle. I put a hand on her thigh.

She freezes.

I lick my suddenly dry lips. I need to say something. This overpowering force inside me won't let Mia and her leave my sight with things as they are. Unsaid. Unsettled.

But Mia's in the back seat. She's got herself unbuckled, and she's struggling to jam all those critters back into her pockets.

I take a deep breath.

"Shay," I speak low, and keep my voice neutral. "I know you don't want to tell me what you're doing today. Probably because you're making plans. You don't trust me. Maybe you don't like me very much either."

I pause, but she doesn't reply. She's listening, though. Her eyes flit to mine every so often.

"But I need you to understand that, right now, you two are the most important people in my life. I'm going to let you out now because I have to, not because I want to, and I'm going to wait for you to come by all day, scared shitless that you won't."

Her gaze shifts down, guiltily.

"Here." I take out my cell and tap a few buttons. "Just press one and you'll get dispatch. They'll radio me with your location, and I'll come get you. Whenever."

I hand her my phone. Every second she waits to take it, my muscles bunch tighter and tighter. Finally, she grabs it and slips it into her miniature backpack.

"Come on, Mia," she says, not waiting for me to open her door. I open Mia's instead, and I stand beside her as Shay rounds the car to fetch her. The day's already a scorcher. Neither of them have water bottles.

I reach for my wallet and pull out a fifty.

Shay draws herself taller when she sees what I'm doing. She damn well better not be too proud to take money for our daughter.

"For waters and lunch," I say, holding it out. She purses her lips, but she takes the bill.

"Thank you." It's begrudging as hell, but for some reason, my lip twitches. "I, um—I'll call when we're done."

She grabs Mia's hand and sails off up the hill toward Town Hall. The school is the other direction, due east. The shops on Main Street are due west. There's nothing on Bell Street but the rehabbed Victorians that relocating city folk have been snapping up.

The view is killer with the river at the foot of the hill, Stonecut Farm and the mountain rising in the distance.

Does she not know how to get where she's going? She must. It's a small town. It doesn't take a month to get familiar with every street, and she's been around longer than that.

I'm wracking my brain, staring after them, when I realize where they're going.

Some folks have put out a shingle on their gracious front porches. Bob and Sue Acheson have a bed and breakfast. Tate Alford started doing taxes from home when she inherited from her parents. And Don Prescott lives at the top of the hill. He has a sign that reads D. Prescott, Attorney at Law.

Shay's trying to get herself a lawyer.

I start after them, driven by a wave of rage and panic so strong, it roars in my head.

The fuck she will.

An old lady walking toward me with her dog jerks his leash and swerves down another path.

I'm halfway across the street by the time my good sense has the chance to shout loud enough to be heard above the pounding in my ears.

Don Prescott will send her packing. Conflict of interest. There are only two other lawyers in town. Pam Bosko does criminal defense, and Wayne Daly is semi-retired. All he does these days are wills and the like. I'm sure Don's farmed out some of our work to him.

She's not going to get anywhere. Not today.

And even though I'm furious, I recognize the part I played in putting this idea in her head.

I shouldn't have touched her. I should have stood back and let her get comfortable and made her and Mia feel safe.

And I sure as shit should have kept my damn mouth shut.

Lesson learned.

I need to go back to square one. Drag myself back to my vehicle and get to work.

It's damn hard. Turning. Walking away from those two small figures hiking up the hill. Shay's patient pace slows to match Mia's short legs.

I linger in the middle of the road, hands fisted, torn.

The sun is burning away the last of the morning fog, and bullfrogs honk down on the riverbank. It's going to be another scorcher.

A car slaloms around me.

"Hey!" I call out before Shay's too far to hear.

She looks over her shoulders, surprised.

Shit. What do I say?

"If you get into trouble, call dispatch. Okay?"

She rolls her eyes, turns, and picks up her pace.

I go back to my car to start my day as if this is okay, as if it doesn't feel like my heart has somehow wrenched itself loose from my chest, and I have no choice but to watch it walk away.

10

SHAY

In high school, when I worked at the diner on First Street, I'd go for a walk on my break. If you hung around, the owner would try and get in your pants. I got groped more times in the Over Easy Diner in six months than I did in my entire life before or since. It was like the name was wishful thinking, not a pun.

So I'd clock out and wander up Main Street past the fire house and the huge urns overflowing with flowers in front of Stonecut Drug, and I'd window shop the art galleries and women's wear boutiques. Then I'd cut across past Town Hall and head down Bell Street.

Bell Street is mostly big ol' houses with gingerbread trim and turrets with steep, pointy roofs. I'd always crane my neck to peek in the high windows and see if I could spot a ghost. Those kinds of houses.

Anyway, it's mostly residences, but some people have businesses, and they have fancy signs hanging from the porch. Like D. Prescott, Attorney at Law. It's been a few years, so the whole way, I'm hoping he's still there. I don't have a plan B.

I guess now that I have Kellum's phone, I could do a search. I tug the straps of my purse so it's snugger against my bag. I brought the hundred dollars just in case. Along with the fifty and the phone, I'm feeling rather flush.

And confused.

Really confused.

I'm the type who can't stay mad or hurt overnight. I go to sleep, and whatever got me bent out of shape just vanishes as if my brain can't hold it while conked out. I don't forgive or forget. I don't make a habit of deluding myself. But the feeling itself is gone.

So when I found Mia on Kellum's bed, no more than two feet from him, happy as a clam, there was room in my heart to be floored.

She's not that way with people. For her, it's not fear so much as wariness, and when that wears off, it's lack of interest. People just don't do it for her. She likes animals.

But she does like Kellum. As much as I've ever seen her take to a person. Maybe it's a case of like calls to like.

There's a niggling at my heart. I ignore it and plow ahead. This dress itches like crazy. My feet hurt, and they're already sweating, so I'm slipping around in the soles, giving myself blisters. My forehead aches like I tied my ponytail too tight.

It doesn't matter that Mia's taken to Kellum. That's fine. It's good even. I'm not taking her away; I'm just looking for help so I don't need to rely on him.

He might be fine for her, but he's not for me. I'm the teenaged slut who lured him into temptation. That's not firm ground for a person to be on. I paid attention in English class. There's nothing but trouble for that girl.

Anyone in my position would get a lawyer. Mama would have already speed-dialed those men from TV. Gillespie and Fox: *If You Have a Case, You Have an Attorney.*

Close to the top of the hill, I stop in front of a dusky blue Victorian with red shutters. My chest loosens as I catch my breath. The sign's still there.

I take a minute and wipe the sweat from my forehead. Damn, but it's as hot and muggy up north as it is back home.

Chapter 10

I squeeze Mia's hand. "This won't take long. Promise."

She's taking it all in. The flower beds with begonias and dahlias and snapdragons of every color of the rainbow. The weathervane on the roof with the rooster.

"Big house, eh?"

I square my shoulders and make sure my bra straps aren't showing.

"Let's do this."

I lead Mia up the steep steps to the wide porch. The shade is a relief.

There's a sign that says "Ring for Entry" next to a button. I do. I can hear the buzz through the storm door. They've got the other door open, so I can see into a hallway with a fancy, gold-framed mirror and marble table at the end, and I can see an older woman emerge from a room and shuffle over to let us in.

She's Mama's age, but she's wearing an expensive-looking mauve suit with a pencil skirt and jacket with shoulder pads. Her hair is dyed blonde. Her roots are showing gray.

She cracks the door.

"No solicitation."

Well, crap. That's how this is going to go.

"Ma'am, I'd like to talk to Mr. Prescott. The lawyer."

She scans me head-to-feet as if she hasn't already taken a long gander on her way to the door.

"You don't have an appointment."

"No, ma'am. But I would like to set one up. Is he here?"

"What is this in regards to, please?"

"It's a personal matter. Should I call to set up an appointment?"

"That would probably be best, Ms.—?" She's looking down her nose so hard her eyes are nearly crossed.

"Shay Crowder."

Her brow furrows. You can see the wheels turning in her brain. "Are you related to Buck Crowder?"

"Yes, ma'am. He was my grandfather."

The hostility falls from her face like a curtain. It's not replaced by friendliness, exactly, but she can place me now.

"My condolences. Buck went to my church."

"Stonecut Methodist," I supply. I went with him on occasion. I don't remember her, but I never paid much attention during services.

She nods, and her gaze lowers to Mia. She flashes a fake smile. "And who is this? Buck's great-grandbaby?"

"Yes, ma'am. This is Mia."

"Hello, Mia!"

Mia studies at her feet in silence.

The woman glances at me expectantly. I know I'm supposed to force Mia to use her good manners and respond, but first off, Mia just won't, and secondly, the lady didn't bother to use her good manners when she answered the door, so now we're even.

The woman's lips thin. She seems to consider for a moment before she opens the door wide.

"Mr. Prescott happens to have a light morning. Come on in. I'll see if he can squeeze you in."

A blast of air conditioning hits me in the face. Sweet relief. I follow with alacrity, basking in the cool. The place smells like old things, but you can tell they've got help cleaning. Every surface shines. They've put money into the place. While the lighting fixtures and molding look antique, the carpet is unworn and the paint is fresh.

This is a very Stonecut place. It looks quaint and homey, but it's a front. Like the cozy lodge that's bigger than the Holiday Inn back home.

"You can wait in here." The lady gestures to a converted parlor that overlooks the porch. "I'll see if Mr. Prescott can see you."

The couch is fancy leather with wood arms and feet. Mia and I take a seat. It's slippery. Mia manages to slide onto the floor a few times for fun before I give her a look.

Based on the lady's general snobbishness, I figure we'll be waiting a long time, and I'm not optimistic that we won't be sent on our way in the end. Yet, no more than a minute later, an older man strides into the room, arm extended.

"Miss Crowder!" I stand and take his hand. His grip is like a vise.

"And this must be little Mia!" He smiles at her, but it's perfunctory. His focus is right back on me.

He's a man in his sixties who's holding on to his handsome. He still has thick hair, silver and styled. He's tall, fit, and dressed to the nines. Gray suit and shiny black shoes. He doesn't look small town. He looks like a TV lawyer.

"I knew your grandfather for many years. My deepest sympathies. Stonecut lost a good man."

I nod, ignoring the tightening in my throat. Grandpa *was* a good man. The best.

"If it's all right by you, Linda's grabbing some coloring books from upstairs. We have quite the collection for the grandkids, you know. She can keep an eye on Mia here while we chat, if you're okay with that?"

He smiles wide. He has veneers.

Mia has plopped herself on the floor, and she's lining up her critters on the coffee table.

"Here she is now," he booms as Linda bustles back in, arms loaded with books and toys. "Find what you were looking for?"

Linda's attitude is entirely changed; she's transformed from a battleax to Mrs. Claus in five minutes.

"Yes, sir. It was all where you said. We've got some fun toys here to keep us occupied, right, Mia?" Her voice is bright and phony.

Mia turns her pockets inside out to make sure she's got all the critters.

The cords in Linda's neck strain.

"Ma'am, Mia doesn't talk to strangers," I try to explain. "Sometimes folks get it. Sometimes they don't."

"I see," she sniffs and sets down the toys.

"She'll be fine with her animals."

"I'll just sit here then." Linda lowers herself into an overstuffed leather chair, back ramrod straight.

"She does better if left to her own devices," I say, but Linda's already decided to take offense.

Maybe I should bring Mia with me. She doesn't need to hear this, though. She's an iceberg. She understands ninety percent more than you'd think she does.

"Linda will take great care of her, won't you, dear?"

Linda perks up at that. "Of course."

"Shall we?" Mr. Prescott gestures to the door. His office is directly across the hall. If he leaves the door open, I'll be able to watch Mia.

I go ahead, and thankfully, he leaves the door ajar.

"Please, have a seat. Would you like coffee? Bottled water?" He unbuttons his jacket and settles himself behind his massive wooden desk in an oversized, leather swivel chair.

"No, thank you, sir." I sit across from him in another big chair. I brace my feet flat on the floor so my ass doesn't slide down this slippery leather.

The wall behind him is entirely covered with shelves filled with books that look like they've never been cracked open. He has a sleek white laptop on his otherwise clear desk, and there's a globe on a stand by the window. Paintings of horses in pastures hang on the walls in thick, carved frames with little lights attached above.

Folks in this town sure do love their horse paintings. There's as many horses hanging here as there are paintings of Jesus back home.

Mr. Prescott clears his throat and offers an encouraging smile. "So, Miss Crowder, what brings you here today?"

I clutch the purse I've set in my lap. "I need a lawyer."

"And why is that?" He clicks a silver pen. There's no paper. Must be a habit.

"I—"

Crap.

Chapter 10

I've never really talked to anyone about this before. Not since I told Pandy I was knocked up seven years ago. Mama assumed what she assumed, and I never elaborated much.

I didn't expect it'd be hard to talk about. It is what it is. I'm not the first single mother in the world. I'm not ashamed. Exactly.

"I need help with Mia's father." I swallow past a lump in my throat.

Mr. Prescott waits patiently, his calm expression inviting me to continue when I'm ready.

"See, we aren't married. We weren't ever together, and I left town when I was expecting Mia. He never knew about her. But he does now, and I need a lawyer to help make it all legal."

That came out wrong.

"I mean, to help set up visitation and child support and all that."

Mr. Prescott leans back and steeples his fingers. His chair creaks.

There's a knot in my stomach. I peek at Mia. She's still at the coffee table, arranging her critters.

"What are you planning to do?" he finally asks.

I don't entirely understand the question.

"I, um, I don't know? Stay here for now, I guess. Get Mia enrolled in school."

He swivels ever so slowly in his chair, waiting for me to say more, his face carefully bland. The back of my neck prickles.

"What is it that you want from the father?"

I shrug. "Whatever's fair. There's a calculation, right? For child support?"

There is in South Carolina. There's an online calculator for it and everything. It's a frequent topic of conversation in the break room at work. Back support, garnishment, withholding, contempt.

"And what would you consider fair?" he asks.

I don't know. What the calculator says. My temper flares, but I'm careful not to let it show. I'm trying to get this man to do me a favor. I don't need to get salty because he asks me questions I haven't thought through.

"I'm not sure, sir."

"You must have a number in your head. Ballpark it for me."

I really don't. Besides, this feels like we're getting ahead of ourselves.

"Do you think you can help me?" I ask. "I can't pay out of pocket, but I know that sometimes lawyers make out a deal where they take part of the settlement."

A look almost of victory breaks across his face. His eyes harden to beads, and he smiles. For real this time. Back teeth and everything.

"Settlement?"

I shrug. I don't know the exact words. I clutch my purse to my chest. This doesn't feel right.

Mr. Prescott pushes back from his desk and crosses one lanky leg over the other. "I'm sorry, Miss Crowder, but I'm not able to take you on as a client."

The knot in my stomach grows.

"It would be a conflict of interest, I'm afraid. I'm council of record for the Price Trust."

Price as in Van Price, Kellum's uncle?

"The Prices and the Walls are longstanding clients. But I can give you the name of a colleague up in Anvil who does family law."

Well, crap.

"I'd appreciate that."

There's a murmur from the other room. Linda's trying to talk to Mia in a high singsong voice. I strain to hear what she's saying, but my brain's cranking, flipping around like the wheel on that game show. Tick, tick, tick. I can't focus.

And then it clicks in place.

This goddamn weasel.

I never told Don Prescott that Kellum is Mia's father. The only way he knows he's got a conflict of interest is if he knows that already.

He knows who I am.

He was pumping me for information.

Asshole.

"Right then." I stand and swing my little backpack on. Should have known. The Walls and Prices own the town.

"Miss Crowder. Please." He gestures to my chair. "I can't take you on as a client, but I can make you an offer. It might solve your problems. No lawyer needed."

He bares his teeth, his eyes glittering and hard.

I string my thumbs through my backpack straps and wait. Men like these don't need permission to go on.

"Ten thousand dollars," he says with a pause between each word like he's announcing the grand prize.

My heart rate kicks up a notch.

"For what?"

"A fresh start. Take your beautiful daughter. Go back down south or maybe start over somewhere new. Florida. California."

Ten thousand dollars is a lot of money, but it'll last you maybe half a year in South Carolina if you stretch it and make the pennies squeak. I watch storage auctions on TV; I've seen what those folks pay for things. I don't think ten thousand would last three months in California.

And why is history repeating itself, anyway?

Back when I was pregnant, Kellum's folks wanted to save his reputation. Hide the evidence. Are they seriously still worried about what folks will say? Nobody's gonna care if a divorced man has a kid.

Is it themselves they're worried about? They don't want the scandal? It's not the fifties. It's hard to believe anyone worries so much about a baby born out of wedlock these days. Even in this old-fashioned town.

"Why?" I ask.

"Why?" he repeats.

"Why do the Walls want Mia and me gone so bad? If they don't want anything to do with us, they can steer clear."

He flat out ignores the question. "Think about it Miss Crowder. No paternity test. No court dates. No ugliness."

Do they still think she's not Kellum's? And hold up—court?

"Why'd there be court dates?"

"Miss Crowder," he sighs. "I'm sure Kellum is reeling right now, discovering you've withheld his alleged daughter from him for six long years—"

My cheeks burst into flames. "I—"

He whips up his hand and speaks right over me. "But I can guarantee you that after the shock fades, and he understands what you did by hiding the child from him, robbing him of the chance to be a father, he will make sure his interests are protected."

He pauses, letting that sink in. And then he asks, all sly, "How confident are you of a paternity test, Miss Crowder? And how do you like your odds in court in Stonecut County."

My heart thuds, and my gaze flies to Mia. She's okay. It's quiet again in the other room. My throat is tight with panic, but I can hold it together because Mia is fine.

"What does that mean?"

He leans forward. "There's not a judge in three counties who doesn't golf with Van Price. That's a fact. Of course, our judges are impartial. Same as you're the innocent victim of a big, bad man who took advantage of you. Such a dedicated mother, done so wrong, you didn't seek out support from the child's alleged father for six years." He sneers. "That's your story, isn't it?"

My gut churns. I'm gonna puke. "I don't have a story."

"Sure you do. And I bet it's an interesting one." He slides me a long glance, thin, gray eyebrows raised. "What have you been doing the past few years, Miss Crowder, eh?"

Working at the damn Food Fiesta, stocking shelves. What the hell does he think?

I force myself to breathe. I'm twenty-three years old. I'm not a kid anymore. I'm not gonna go curl up in a ball on a bathroom floor.

This man figures I'm some sort of grifter. He can't seem to get it straight in his head, though.

Am I passing off another man's child as Kellum's? Or am I trying to shake his people down through a custody battle? And then there's the ten thousand dollars, which seems to say they don't care which it is, they just want the garbage to take itself out.

The knot in my stomach sits there, gross and heavy as lead, while my breakfast churns. Eggs on a hot day. I knew it was a bad idea.

I bet this comes down to the fact I belong to the help. I'm not a decent person like them.

That's how they all see me, isn't it? I'm trash. Cheap slut. Liar, conniver, whatever. But above all, cheap.

That's how they see me, and that's how they'll see Mia.

My heart sinks, but my brain keeps plugging along, impervious.

Ten thousand dollars is a lot of money for cheap.

I curl my toes in my flats. They gape at the sides. At least my dress itches less now that it's damp from sweat. It was a flea market find. So was the cute little backpack purse. I know it's a young look for me, but I always wanted one in school, and I never had one.

From where Mr. Prescott sits, I must look like I'm not worth much.

But I'm not seventeen anymore, and math was never my weak subject. If Kellum makes a hundred thousand a year, child support has to be at least five hundred a month. At least. So they're offering me a year and a half of support to get lost forever?

They think I'm stupid. And greedy. Probably desperate, too. I'm not any of those things, and except for desperate, never was.

"You give me ten thousand dollars, and Mia and I just leave?"

"There'd be some paperwork. Assurances on both sides. But yes, in essence."

"And Kellum's okay with this?"

Mr. Prescott's expression gets cagey. "As the attorney for the Price trust, I act in the best interest of all beneficiaries of which Kellum is one."

Well, that's a sentence where the words came out in the most backwards possible order.

"Kellum knows about this offer?"

"Miss Crowder, it's really quite simple. You could use this generous settlement to make a new start. Or you could persist on your present path which will end up in front of a judge, and not one inclined towards a woman who kidnapped a child and kept that child from her father." He clicks his pen. "I can guarantee that will not end well for you. Are you willing to risk that? Risk your custody of that sweet little girl?"

Fear floods my chest.

There's a time I would have folded under a threat like that. The day Kellum's folks paid me that visit. And when Mrs. Rice took me aside and told me if I was going to miss so many school days, it'd be better to drop out and get my G.E.D. Easier on everyone. Spare myself all the loose talk. And heavens forbid if my water were to break right there in class. Would I ever live that down?

There was a time I assumed other people knew better than me. They don't.

And we might be poor, but we're not cheap, and we're not trash. And I'm sure as hell not stupid.

Mr. Prescott did not answer my question about whether Kellum knows about the offer. I'm gonna guess he doesn't.

I wonder how high this cheap girl can get this fancy lawyer to go.

I almost say a hundred thousand, but I remember the stacks in Kellum's safe. These folks don't operate on a ten times scale. They're a thousand times better off than people like me.

"Five hundred thousand dollars."

I expect incredulity, but instead, Mr. Prescott's beady eyes narrow. "Three hundred."

Oh, the asshole is lowballing me. If he started at ten thousand,

and he would go as high as three hundred, he's lowballing the hell out of me.

"Eight hundred."

He chuckles, pure condescension. "That's not how a counteroffer works, Miss Crowder."

I press my lips so I don't smirk. This is fun, in a barf-inducing, awful, rickety-carnival-roller-coaster way.

"I know, Mr. Prescott. But I figured if you'd leap up from ten thousand to three hundred without batting an eye, maybe your pockets go pretty deep."

Oh, that pisses him off. He hikes his chin in the air so he can look down his nose at me better.

"I'm happy we've dropped the pretense. Three hundred fifty is as high as I'm authorized to go."

Authorized? So he sat down with Kellum's people and a calculator and they worked out how much it'd be worth to get rid of us?

I grit my back teeth. Screw them.

But damn, that's a lot of money.

I glance across the hall. Mia's on her knees, folded in half over the coffee table, Kellum's horse in her hand. Her hair's falling in her face, but I can make out her lips moving. She does that when she's deep into her play. There's no sound, but she's forming words.

That's how I knew the school psychologist's tests were crap. If you watch her closely, you can read her lips.

With three hundred fifty thousand dollars, I could find a place in a good school district. I could send Mia to private school, even. I bet they don't let children hit each other when the parents are writing checks.

I could get a job where I'd be there when Mia got home every day. An apartment where we both have a room to ourselves. I could get off SNAP. No more nasty looks in the checkout line.

Three hundred fifty thousand dollars would make us safe.

I need to face facts. Mia and I are crashing in someone else's house, I have less than two hundred bucks to my name, I haven't got any family nearby, no job, and rich, powerful people want us gone. Badly.

I never knew my father. I never missed him. Mia doesn't know who Kellum is to her. She'll have nice memories of a visit to a farm. A man who was kind.

It's more than I have.

But if we leave...

No more horseback rides. No more sugar cubes.

My eyes burn. I blink.

I can't think around Kellum like he's not part of the calculation. My brain's been ducking thoughts of him all day 'cause I'm a coward, but even if I put last night away in a little box and shove it deep down, I can't ignore the rest.

He's pushy, and he's got an ornery streak as wide as mine, but he's been nothing but good to Mia.

Does he know how badly his folks want us gone?

Is that what the black eye was about?

If push comes to shove, would he pick us over them? Even if he did, if they really want us gone, can he stop them? I've seen *In the Arms of Love*. It's a soap, but in my experience it's not total fiction—people with money have the audacity to try things that'd never occur to normal folks.

Mr. Prescott clicks his silver pen, rapidly, three times. He's getting antsy.

He can wait another minute. I've never turned down three hundred and fifty thousand dollars before. I have to collect myself.

All these *what ifs* are buzzing in my head, but my eyes are on Mia. She's had Kellum's horse in her grubby paws since he gave it to her. Right now, she's galumphing him across the coffee table.

I don't ever listen to my heart over my head, but in this moment, my heart has finally decided it's taking charge.

I'm not taking Mia away from her father. Not until he shows himself to be cut from these people's mold.

Should I just tell Mr. Prescott, attorney at law, to let his clients know they can fuck themselves?

Chapter 10

It feels like a moment that requires a snappy comeback, but I've got nothing.

"Well, Miss Crowder?" Mr. Prescott taps the pen on the desk.

I'm going to live to regret this.

"No, thank you," I say, and sail from the room, head held as high as I can.

Mr. Prescott rises, but I'm quick, and Mia's been keeping an eye on me this whole time, too. She's already shoving her critters in her pockets.

I walk to the hallway and stick out my arm. She's there in a split second, grabbing my hand.

"Miss Crowder!" Mr. Prescott says, indignant.

But we're down the hall and out the door where the heat slams into my face with the force of a collision, and the sunshine's blinding. I teeter at the edge of the porch before the first steep stair, blinking until my eyes adjust.

My body is as weak and wobbly as if I've had a scare.

Did I do the right thing?

Please, Lord, don't let that man follow me out of the house. I can't do the right thing twice.

I squint in the glaring sunlight and shade my eyes.

And I see him.

Kellum.

Across the street, leaning against his cruiser, arms tightly crossed, tanned biceps bulging, tinted sunglasses, hat tilted forward.

Pissed as hell.

A shiver zips up my spine.

The door bangs open behind me. "Miss Crowder!"

I tighten my grip on Mia's hand and start down the stairs. Better the devil you know.

Kellum starts for us, traversing the empty street in two long strides, arms straight at his sides, shoulders squared. So help me, with those sunglasses, he looks like the evil police robot from that 90s action movie. The time-traveling one.

I brace, unsure. The veins in his neck are popping, the pulse in his temple throbs.

Is he gonna yell at me in the street?

Mia and I hit the sidewalk at the same time he reaches us. He grabs my shoulders in a punishing grip and hustles me behind him, Mia trailing along because I've got her hand. He widens his stance so he's blocking us from Mr. Prescott.

He props his hands on his hips and puffs his chest.

Jitters swarm my belly.

I stay where he put me, but I lean to the side to peer around him.

"You can stay there, Don," he orders, cool and even. "Seems Miss Crowder is done with you."

Mia's gawking, too, but she's curious, not upset. I'm a little gobsmacked. It feels like Kellum's protecting us, but that doesn't quite line up with the fury rolling off him in waves. And besides, Mr. Prescott's coming after me to offer me more money, I'm pretty sure, not to hurt us.

Still, everything about Kellum screams that he's seconds away from laying a beating on that man if he doesn't back away from us.

I should be more alarmed than I am, but I'm still riding the high of turning down a fortune.

"Kellum," Mr. Prescott says, cautious and obnoxiously civil. He's stopped in his tracks on the porch. Linda is on his heels, panting to catch her breath, casting me scathing looks.

Mr. Prescott takes a second to button his suit jacket. Then, he makes a show of scanning the sky. "Hot one, eh?"

Kellum inclines his head ever so slightly.

The air between them crackles.

"I think we're in for some rain later," Mr. Prescott observes.

Kellum doesn't respond. They seem to be taking each other's measure, waiting for the other to blink. Linda glances nervously from one man to the other.

Yeah, Kellum's furious, but maybe not at me. Or not just me. I think he wants to deck Mr. Prescott, Attorney at Law.

How long are we going to stand here in the middle of the sidewalk?

Mia must read my mind. She reaches out and tugs the stripe that goes down Kellum's pant leg. His gaze darts down.

"Oh. Hi, pretty girl."

It's like he's rousing himself from a dream. He shakes himself, and then he flashes her his most gentle smile. "I bet you're getting bored, aren't you?"

Mia keeps her grip on the seam of his slacks.

"If your Mama agrees, we could go over to the playground for a little while before lunch. How about that?"

Mia tugs his pants back and forth. She wants to leave. I do, too.

"Okay," I say.

"I will speak to you later," Kellum bites out, sending Mr. Prescott one last, hard look. It's an unmistakable threat. Mr. Prescott bends his head and takes an unintentional step back.

Tingles skitter along my skin.

Kellum is so different than any man I've ever known before. He exudes authority, even without his uniform and badge. Maybe it's his height or the muscles. He's a man of few words, and that might have something to do with it, too. That and the unshakable confidence.

He's in charge, but he's always letting me lead. Like now. He ushers us past him in the direction of the municipal park.

I don't really think about it; I head off where he sends us. He doesn't follow right away. I can hear his parting shot, low and laced with the threat of violence, "You talk to her again, and we have issues, Don. You understand?"

I don't hear what Don says before we turn down Magnolia Street.

We walk a few blocks in silence, Mia and I a few steps ahead. The sidewalks are too narrow to walk three abreast.

It's raising the hackles on my neck, though, that Kellum is behind me where I can't see him. Probably stewing.

One pang of guilt is followed by another.

I have nothing to feel guilty about. I didn't lie to him. I don't believe in lies of omission. I believe in people thinking they're owed information that is none of their business.

I firm my chin.

He can glower back there all he wants. It's only smart to try and get a lawyer.

He and his family have a lawyer. Obviously.

I'm working myself up so much that when we reach the playground and Mia races off, I whirl on him, ready to have it out.

But he doesn't look like I was imagining.

He's taken his sunglasses off and hung them from the collar of his shirt. His hat is in his hands. His hair's all mussed and damp from sweat, and his eyes have gone a deep blue.

The playground's surrounded by tall shade trees and benches. It's a respite from the unrelenting sun, but it's not enough shade to explain the change in the color of his eyes.

His face is hard, and he's stiff, as if he's bracing for a blow.

I pull the straps and tighten my backpack purse against my shoulder blades.

He stands there, silent, maybe two feet away, facing me, uneasy and waiting.

I glance over at the equipment. Mia's found some shade under a swinging bridge, and she has her critters out.

Kellum swallows. There's light stubble on his chin and neck. His beard must grow fast if he has eleven o'clock in the morning shadow.

I huff a sigh. "Are you gonna say something?"

"I was waiting for you." His voice is pitched a half octave deeper. He's definitely mad.

"I didn't know he was your lawyer."

"He's not. Exactly. He's the lawyer for the trust."

"Of which you are a beneficiary." I remember.

A crease appears between his eyes. "Yes. I am. And Mia is, too."

I raise my eyebrows. "You might want to check on that."

Chapter 10

He draws in a deep, very intentional breath. "What do you mean?"

Well, shit.

I just set myself up.

What do I do now?

This whole walk here, I could have been thinking it all through, but instead, I'm worrying about him.

If I tell Kellum about the offer, I doubt it'll stay on the table. I said no, but circumstances change. Backup plans are good.

And am I a hundred percent sure Kellum doesn't know about the offer? Maybe he's playing a role, doing what he thinks he's supposed to so that when I take the money and skip town, he doesn't have to feel guilty. He wasn't a deadbeat. I was a gold digger.

He's standing there, and nothing about his stance or expression says patience, but he's still waiting. Giving me time.

Way overhead, leaves rustle ever so slightly. There's no breeze down here on the ground, though.

Kellum has to be miserable in his uniform and that heavy belt.

"I thought you were going to work?" I ask.

He doesn't miss a beat. "I called in. Said I'd be late. I'm scheduled for the office today. Not patrol."

"Why did you call in?"

"What were you doing in Don Prescott's office?"

This conversation feels like a betting game, and we both keep raising, and neither of us has any inclination to show our cards.

I fold my arms.

He rests his hands on his duty belt.

Mia's making little mounds of wood chips as homes for her critters. She's getting a bath as soon as we get home.

Home.

Out of nowhere, my lower lip wobbles. I press my lips together hard.

"Goddamn it," Kellum huffs in exaggeration, and grabs my upper arm. "Come on."

He leads me to the closest bench, and says, "Sit."

I do. The wrought iron is warm, but not unbearably so. He sits beside me, legs wide, his thigh brushing mine.

"You are a stubborn woman."

I wasn't always, but yes, I am now.

"Prickly, too," he says.

"If we're trading compliments, you're overbearing."

He snorts.

"That's funny?"

"Kind of. Yeah. That's not really something I've ever been accused of before." His lips curve, and some of that tension eases from his shoulders. I shrug off my backpack purse and set it beside me.

"What do you get accused of?"

His eyes are fading back to a lighter blue. "Too quiet. Standoffish. No fun. Antisocial."

"Sounds like folks would prefer you to be other than you are."

His brow wrinkles a little, and then he eases back, extending his long legs. "Yup. That's about the shape of it."

He stretches his arm, resting it on the back of the bench. He's not touching me, but he's there behind me. Close.

My belly flutters. The feeling comes on again, the one from last night, and if I remember right, the same one from the bonfire.

As if we're the only two people in the world.

No, it's more like we've found a spot of our own, away from everyone else. Me and Kellum Wall and also Mia, playing contentedly in the shade, checking on us every so often from the corner of her eye.

It's a nice feeling. Private. Peaceful. And scary, too.

"Why'd you go to Don Prescott's office?" he asks.

"I thought I should get a lawyer."

"Why?" His tone is careful.

"In case."

"In case?"

I sigh. I'm not used to explaining myself. At work, I do what I'm asked. At home, Mama sees things her way, and there's no sense in arguing. I don't really have friends. There are people at work and on our street in Blazing Trails that I'll have a conversation with, but other than that, I focus on Mia.

I used to talk to Grandpa, but that's a long time ago, now. After I left and had Mia, it was never the same. He'd call sometimes, but he'd keep it short.

I feel a light tug on my scalp. I glance over my shoulder. Kellum's got my ponytail. He's idly fiddling with the ends.

The flutters swoop, and I swing my feet. It's a deep bench. My shoes only just skim the ground.

"In case this goes bad," I say. "I don't want to take your money, but if it gets ugly, I don't want to have nothing."

It's the best I can put it, with him playing with my hair.

"You said something about Mia and the trust?"

I sigh. "I don't really understand what that is, but Mia's not a part of it."

"Why do you say that?"

"Mr. Prescott said he's the lawyer for the trust, right?"

"Yes."

"And you're in the trust, so he's your lawyer, so he couldn't take me on."

Kellum's nodding.

"And then he offered me three hundred fifty thousand dollars to take Mia and go. So, see? Mia's not in the trust. He's not working for Mia."

It's like he gets zapped. Kellum's whole body tenses. He draws his legs in, drops my hair. He's vibrating with tension.

I edge away, putting my hand on my purse.

"He offered you money to leave?" He rises to his feet, paces a few steps, stops.

Over in the playground, Mia sits back on her haunches and stares at him.

I stay put.

"Yeah."

There's a storm warring on his face. All kinds of ugliness, at first. Rage, definitely. Something else, too. Betrayal?

And then his gaze catches mine. The storm clears, and something else dawns.

"You turned it down."

"Yeah."

"Why?"

Temporary insanity. That old saying about if something's too good to be true, it probably is. I don't know.

But I do, don't I?

I'm just too scared to say it. To put it out there in the universe for it to get torn apart.

Mia's risen to her feet and collected her animals. They're overflowing her tiny fists. She thinks it's time to leave.

Oh, God. I can't trust anyone, but I *have* to trust this man.

"Mia needs a father."

We are quiet with each other for a moment. It's on his face—he understands how big this is.

"Will you sit back down?" I say. "You're making her nervous."

He checks Mia—she's squinting, intent on him, thin shoulders rigid—and for a moment, he seems utterly at a loss.

I scoot over and make more room. He takes a seat. After a minute, Mia goes back to playing.

"I'm in this, Shay," he rasps. "You never have to worry about money or anything. You both are taken care of. I swear it."

"Okay." It's becoming clear in my head exactly what I gambled back there in Don Prescott's office. Three hundred thousand fifty thousand dollars for the chance for Mia to have a father who will love her one day.

My stomach turns. If I bet wrong, I lost us a chance at a good life.

I clear my throat. "If you decide you're not, if you change your mind, I'll need help."

I don't think I've ever asked for help straight out before. Here

Chapter 10

on the bench, under the oak, with Kellum, it's not so bad as I thought it'd be.

"I'm not going to change my mind." He braces his forearms on his thighs, watching Mia as she climbs up a ladder one-armed, critters clutched in her free hand. "But if you want a place of your own, I'll make it happen. I prefer you under my roof, but I was serious, Shay. You make the calls."

He swallows, his throat bobbing. "And just so you've got it straight, I don't regret last night, and I don't regret when we were together the first time."

My face grows impossibly hotter, and I tug at the hem of my dress.

"I regret I didn't do it right when we were together the first time, but I'd do it again."

He stops, and I think he's done, but then he grins wickedly at me. "I have every intention of doing it again."

He stands and holds a hand out. I take it, and he pulls me to my feet. "Come on. Let's go get something to eat and head up to the school."

"You're not gonna get in trouble for calling out of work?" I ask 'cause I'm blushing too hard not to change the subject.

"I'm the deputy."

"You make the rules?"

"Nope. I just enforce 'em," he drawls, sliding on his hat like a cowboy, smiling wide and lazy, keeping a tight hold of my hand.

"That line is cheesy as hell."

"Dad joke," he says. "I guess I can make them now if I want."

A look of genuine satisfaction flashes across his face, followed instantly by a frown. "I want to tell her, Shay. Soon. I get that with my folks being how they are, you might not be comfortable with that yet, but—I will make it right. My folks will accept you and Mia. I promise you that."

His gaze doesn't waver. He really believes it.

"They don't need to accept us. If they stay up the hill, Mia and I are fine."

That's not good enough for him, I can tell, but Mia's trotting over. She slips her hand in his empty one.

"Hungry," she says.

"Me, too." Kellum smiles so wide, I don't think I've ever seen a man so happy.

We head back toward Kellum's car, the three of us in step, and a weight lifts, making my steps light.

I made the right choice.

∼

WE HAVE lunch at the Over Easy. Carl is still the cook, but except for surly Miss Denise, none of the waitstaff is the same from when I worked there. The customers haven't changed. Almost seven years later, and they're still sitting in the same booths.

Carl and Denise drop by our table to say hi and offer belated condolences for Grandpa—and gawk at Mia and Kellum. Once they come over, the dam bursts, and by the time Kellum pays the check, almost everyone in the place has come over to be introduced.

A lot of folks knew Grandpa, and they have nice things to say. I get a little choked up. Mia has no memories of him. I like that she's hearing nice things about him.

After lunch, the temperature climbs even higher, so even though the school is walking distance, Kellum drives us in the back of his cruiser. There's something going on—folding tables and lots of kids in the soccer field, and there's no parking in the front lot.

Kellum drops us off and says he'll find a space and meet us inside.

I wish he'd ignore the color of the curb and park right in front. It's a police cruiser. No one would blink an eye.

I don't want to walk in alone.

I smooth my ponytail. Hairs have sprung loose, but it's not too

Chapter 10

bad. I ducked into the bathroom and checked before we left the diner.

I straighten my spine, take Mia's hand, and head on in. This is going to be different. Stonecut Elementary is not Back River.

Back River was one story, the kind of school with painted cinder block walls and dusty tile floors.

Stonecut Elementary looks like what you picture when someone says school: two story, red brick, big windows, stairs leading up to double doors, and a tall flagpole out front in a bed of red, white, and blue petunias.

You do have to buzz and state your business before they let you in. Other than that, it feels like the 1950s.

Inside, everything is perfect. It's clean, cool, and smells like crayons.

Mia takes it all in. There's a bulletin board with a bunch of horses for decoration. Mia tugs my hand.

"I see it."

Even though it's still summer, the floors are waxed to a shine.

I go into the office, and I get instant déjà vu. It's set up exactly like the office in the high school I went to for those few months, down to the polished wood counter and wall of teacher mailboxes.

A large woman in mint green slacks is at her desk, squinting at her computer monitor.

I stand and wait. There's a shiny silver bell for you to ring, but it seems rude to ring it, since the lady is no more than five feet away. Mia is not letting go of her death grip on my hand, and she can't see over the top, so she digs into her pocket for a critter.

There's a big school clock on the wall, and apples and rulers on the curtains. I can hear women chatting and laughing in the back offices.

I clear my throat in case the woman doesn't realize we're here even though she buzzed us in.

She raises a finger and keeps squinting.

Then the phone rings. She answers right away. "Stonecut Elementary. What can I do for you?"

I start to feel stupid. Maybe we should sit?

Kellum has got to be here soon. There were open spots in the back of the side lot.

Maybe we should go wait for him by the front doors.

Finally, the woman hangs up and shuffles over to the counter.

"Yes, ma'am," she says.

"I—uh—I'm here to register my daughter for first grade."

The woman scans the office, frowning.

"She's—uh—down here."

The woman makes a halfhearted effort to see Mia over the counter, but it's too wide, and she gives up. "All right. Who did you make an appointment with?"

"I didn't make an appointment. The lady I spoke to on the phone just said come by. She didn't take my name or—"

The woman's not listening. She bends over and rummages under the counter. She emerges with a clipboard and plops it in front of me.

"Did you bring your paperwork?"

"I'm sorry. What paperwork?"

The woman purses her lips. "When you call to make an appointment, we let you know about the paperwork. You need a birth certificate, her records if she was previously enrolled in another system, immunization, proof of residency."

She's ticking these off on her fingers. My gut clenches. I have her birth certificate, but the other things—Crap. I should have called to make an appointment.

I dig in my purse for a pen and my little notebook. I have to write all this down.

"What do you need for proof of residency?" That's gonna be tricky.

"A mortgage bill or rental agreement and two pieces of mail addressed to you at your current address. You live in Stonecut, don't you?"

The woman raises her pencil thin eyebrows.

"Yes." I have no proof, but, yes. "When do you need all this by?"

"The sooner the better. You're leaving this a little late. School starts the day after Labor Day." The woman pushes the clipboard toward me. "You can fill this out so I can start a file. If you don't have her records, I'll need the name and address of her previous school so I can get them forwarded."

"What if I can't get all this by then?"

The odds of the clinic getting me her vaccination records in time is slim to none. I needed a refill on her inhaler prescription, and it took three phone calls and seven days.

The woman stares at me.

"What happens if I can't get some of this paperwork? Can she start while I'm getting it?"

The woman has the same expression she would if I'd asked to take a dump on the floor.

"All paperwork must be completed before a student is enrolled."

"But can she start, like, on a temporary basis while I'm getting the papers?"

"There's no temporary basis."

"Can you make an exception?"

"An exception?"

I bite my tongue and school my face.

"I don't know what you mean?" she says, brow furrowed, truly confounded.

Then, thankfully, another woman emerges from the back. She's blonde and tall, what my Grandpa would have called statuesque. She's wearing a crisp black suit, heels, and a neat bun.

"Ms. Averly!" the secretary calls, relieved. "Do you have a minute for a question?"

I guess I'm being passed off to the manager.

"Of course, Gail."

Ms. Averly smiles down at Mia. From her height, she can see her behind the counter. "Who have we here?"

"This is—" Gail starts. You can see the moment it dawns on Gail that she didn't ask our names.

"Shay Crowder," I supply. "And this is Mia. She's going into first grade."

"First grade!" Ms. Averly says. "How exciting!"

Mia stares at her feet.

"And are you excited for first grade, Mia? I bet you're *so excited* to start *first grade!*"

Mia shrinks in on herself, hunching her shoulders.

"You're excited, aren't you, Mia?"

"She's shy," I say. "She's excited, though."

It's a bold-faced lie, but if that's what Ms. Averly needs to hear, I'm not too proud.

"So what can I help you with?" She turns that intensity on me, and I have the urge to curl in on myself, too.

Gail answers for me. "She wants to know if we can make an exception for her with the enrollment paperwork."

That's not what I said, but Ms. Averly's already shaking her head.

"I'm afraid that's not possible. It's the law. We have to have proof of immunization and residency."

"I can get it. I just might not get it in time."

"Well, when you get it, bring it on in, and we'll get Mimi registered."

"Mia."

Ms. Averly nods, a vague smile on her face. She's eyeing the door like she's got someplace else to be. I don't think it registers that she misspoke. How is it that this school is hundreds of miles from home, and the people are exactly the same? There must be a type.

This might get heated. I nudge Mia in the direction of the chairs. She takes the hint and grabs herself a seat.

I take a breath and start over. "I might not be able to get all the paperwork before school starts. I'm asking if there's a way Mia could start, and I could bring in the paperwork as soon as I get it."

"No. I'm sorry. That's not possible." Ms. Averly smiles as she says it.

I wring my hands behind the counter. I don't want Mia starting late after everyone else. She'll miss the part where the teacher explains everything. Change always throws her, and she'll have an even harder time settling in.

Well, change usually throws her. She's rolling fine with this whole thing with Kellum. Except for the night of the storm, she's been calm, cool, and collected.

Still. School's a different story. I'm not there, and there are lots of people and noise, her least favorite things.

"Are you sure?" I ask.

Ms. Averly puts on a sad face as fake as her happy one. She's about to turn me down when the bell on the office door jingles and Kellum strides through, hat in hand.

He's a hundred percent Deputy Wall with the swagger, the height, the presence. My dumb heart flips.

"Kell!" Ms. Averly says, her face lighting up for real.

"Hey, Soph."

Soph? Ugh.

"You didn't buzz."

"Len let me in."

"Was he taking a smoke break out front again? You can tell me."

"I never would." Kellum smiles. It's not his real one. It's too charming. His real smile's shy, or if it's big, it bursts onto his face as if out of nowhere.

My shoulders relax. Because he's here and maybe he can sort this out. No other reason.

"What brings you out here? Did someone call to complain that a car is blocking their driveway? Rec camp is only a week, but I swear—the grief!"

She shakes her head, and then she makes a point of smoothing her perfect hair.

"No, I'm here with Shay. To register Mia."

The surprise on Ms. Averly's face is almost comedic. She's

totally confused, but Gail's gaze is flicking back and forth between Kellum and Mia. You can see the gears turning.

"Oh." Ms. Averly's momentarily speechless. "You, uh, know—?" Ms. Averly's brain breaks. She cannot understand how someone like Kellum knows someone like me.

Kellum sets his hat on the counter and moves to stand close beside me. "Shay and Mia are living with me. So tell me what we need to do to get our girl enrolled in Stonecut Elementary."

Our girl. He's not saying it any sort of way, but still, there's a pang in my chest.

"I need proof of residency, and I need Mia's immunization records."

"Okay." The corners of his eyes crease as he studies me. I think he's clueing in to the fact that I'm stressed. "Proof of residency is no problem. You can take my word on that, can't you, Soph?"

She's thrown for a second, but not much longer. "Of course, Kell."

"I'm guessing it'll take a while to get the immunization records?" he asks me.

"It might."

"You're worried we won't get them in time for the first day?"

I squirm. It's strange, having so much attention on me. "I'm pretty sure it'd take them a while to mail them."

"As long as you have them by the first day, Mia's good to go, though, right?" Kellum asks Ms. Averly.

She straightens her shoulders under his gaze. Makes her boobs nice and high. "That's right."

"We'll have them by then."

"Kellum—" He doesn't know about how long the clinic takes. He can't just say it and make it so. Not everything, he can't.

"I'll take care of it, Shay. Do we need to fill this out?" He asks Gail, looking at the clipboard.

"Yes, sir," Gail chirps. She's dropped the bitchy attitude, and now she's smirking like the cat that caught the canary. She thinks she's figured something out. She probably has. "Y'all can have a seat and do it now or take it with you."

"So, uh—" Ms. Averly interjects. "How is it that I haven't met you before, Shay?" She trills a laugh. "I mean, Kell, I was a bridesmaid in your wedding. I could have sworn I met all your folks."

Ms. Gail makes herself real busy rearranging some brochures a little further down the counter.

My chest constricts.

"I knew Shay before I got married," Kellum says, grabbing the clipboard, ushering me over to Mia with a hand on my lower back. "Come on. We can knock this out now."

Ms. Averly obviously has more questions, but she's left standing there, posed to what she must believe is the best effect, gaping like a fish.

It's beneath me, but it's a smidge satisfying.

We sit, and Kellum's pen starts scratching against the paper.

"Do you know what you're putting down?"

"Some."

I peer into his lap. "Her middle name is Adelaide."

His pen stops, and he glances over at Mia. She's swinging her legs and taking a gander at a Student of the Month bulletin board.

"That's real pretty."

My cheeks heat. "It was my Grandma's name."

"How do you spell it?"

"I can fill that out, you know."

"I know." His voice drops. "Let me?"

I swallow. Damn lump. Don't know where it came from.

"A-d-e-l-a-i-d-e." A thought occurs to me. "What's yours?"

"Michael."

Now I know.

"You don't have anything to say?" he teases, continuing on with the address. Good thing, too. I don't know it.

"It's real pretty."

He chuckles, and Ms. Averly and Gail glance over from where they're hanging out by the copy machine.

"Thank you, kindly." He hits the part of the form where they want her old school information. "Here." He passes me the clipboard and pen.

"Mia Adelaide," he repeats quietly. Mia shoots him a glance. He smiles at her. "So, what's your middle name, Shay?"

"I don't have one."

"You don't?" He sounds surprised.

"Plenty of people don't."

"That's true." He sinks back in his chair. "Cash's middle name is Aloysius."

I snort. "That's awful. Where'd they come up with that?"

"Some college named after a saint. My mom went there for a semester before my dad convinced her to come home and marry him."

"She dropped out of college for him?" Turned out well for her, it looks like, but I can't even imagine.

"They were in love."

"Why didn't your dad just wait?"

Kellum's eyebrows knit. "She got pregnant with my older brother John."

"She never went back?"

I didn't either after I dropped out. I started night school a few times, but Mia would get sick, or they'd need me at work, and it'd all get to be too much. You can take the test without classes, but I could never justify paying the hundred fifty bucks when I'd never pass the social studies and language arts. Not when rent needed to be paid.

"She didn't." Kellum gets a far-off look. "My grandparents wanted her home. They told my dad if he convinced her to come back and stay in Stonecut, they'd make him barn manager. It's always been kind of a family joke." His eyes go darker blue. He's thinking some deep thought.

"They made him barn manager?"

"They made him a partner."

"Everybody won, I guess."

Chapter 10

He nods slowly. "I guess." He sniffs, shaking off whatever's come over him. "You're almost done?"

"Yup." I sign and date the form.

"All right, then." He goes to stand, but I put my hand on his thigh.

"Kellum, I'm not gonna get the immunization records in time. You don't understand. It's not gonna happen. With the clinic, everything always takes forever."

Ms. Averly and Gail are making their way back to the counter.

"I'll call Doc Wright. He'll get the records." Kellum stands, hoisting his belt.

He says it with absolute confidence. I bet that's how things work for him. Make a call. Get what you want.

A churlish feeling rises inside me. "What if he can't?" I glare up.

"I'll drive down there and get them myself. Mia will start school on the first day."

Mia's eyes are on him now, round and serious.

"You'll drive all the way to South Carolina?"

"I'll drive to the moon if I have to," he says, giving Mia a wink.

She's frowning at him, calculating. Finally, her lip quirks. "You can't drive to the moon," she says. "You're being silly."

Did they hear?

Ms. Averly and Gail are back at the counter, gawking, but did they hear? Mia spoke so softly, and Kellum's blocking her, but there's no way they missed that, right?

My heart races. I want to shout at them. You heard that. She can speak just fine. Write that down in the file. *You can't drive to the moon.*

Kellum chuckles. "Don't doubt me, woman." He reaches out, and Mia takes his hand. "Ready?"

I stand and follow, disoriented.

This whole thing started in a way I understood. People in charge staring down their noses at me. Paperwork problems. Rules working against me.

But somehow, this has spun into something totally different. Kellum has the clipboard, and the people behind the counter are tripping over themselves to help.

"Is there an orientation?"

"There's a parent night. Let me get you the flyer." Gail searches through her perfectly squared brochures.

"Get them a supply list, too." Ms. Averly adds.

"If you go to Bob's Variety, he'll give you ten percent off." Gail finds the flyer and hands it to Kellum. "The coupon is in the back of the Gazette, but if you just mention it, he'll give you the discount."

"She'll probably have Mrs. Fox. Schedules aren't finalized, but I'll make sure she has Mrs. Fox." Ms. Averly leans closer and drops her voice as if this is on the sly.

Mia cranes her neck to catch my eye. I smile to show I heard it, too. *Fox.* Mia's gonna like that.

Ms. Averly and Gail keep gushing, friendly and helpful, and if I met them now, in this moment, I'd think they were two of the nicest women I've ever met.

I'm almost about to revise my first impression when Ms. Averly finally tears her eyes away from Kellum to address me.

"So, are you related to Kellum on his mom's or dad's side?"

"Those blue eyes come from the Wall side," Gail remarks.

"We're not related."

Ms. Averly brow furrows. This does not compute. "So, I, um—How is it that you, uh—?" She's waiting for me to tell her my business. She's gonna be waiting a while.

I hike my backpack purse high on my shoulders.

"I mean," she spouts a nervous laugh. "Kell, Elizabeth never mentioned you had a, um—"

Gail's starting to look uncomfortable. "I'll just go make a copy of this for y'all." She shuffles off.

I steel myself for a few minutes of awkward silence while we wait. I stare past everything out of the window with the apple curtains.

Chapter 10

When Kellum speaks, it comes as a surprise. "Shay and Mia are very important to me. I haven't had the chance to introduce everyone, yet, but I will. We're really excited about Mia starting school on time, and if there are any problems with the paperwork, I want you to call me directly, okay, Soph?"

It might be the most I've heard out of his mouth at one time. A whole speech almost.

I tilt my chin up a touch.

Ms. Averly draws back. "Of course."

Shay and Mia are very important to me.

I repeat it to myself just once before I tuck it away.

He didn't mean anything serious by it. He was making a point with Ms. Averly.

Gail comes back with our copy, Kellum puts his hat on, and we go. Kellum leads the way, taking us through the building to the back exit.

"That's my first-grade classroom. I had Miss Vernon."

Mia's hanging on every word.

"There's the cafetorium. Half cafeteria. Half auditorium. Smelled like sour milk and sweaty feet."

Mia giggles.

"There's the gym." He pulls up down a hall. "I wonder if they still have the ropes."

My stomach tightens. They aren't going to like us wandering around the place.

"There." He's led us to an old-fashioned gymnasium with shiny wood floors and high windows. There are knotted ropes hanging from the rafters. "I beat everyone at rope climbing. Even the older kids."

He grins at me and my heart skips.

He's so damn handsome. You can ignore his looks when he's striding around like the cock of the walk, but when he lets his guard down, and he's all earnest like this? It kind of makes you stupid.

I lick my dry lips.

His grins wider. "Want to race me to the top?"

"No."

"Why not?"

"I'm wearing a dress." And I've never climbed a rope in my life. We didn't have one at my school.

"I'll give you a head start."

"Can you give me pants?"

"I won't look. I'll be above you. Even if I looked, I wouldn't be able to see up your skirt."

"I don't see why you want to race someone you know you'll beat."

"Come on, Shay." He hustles over and tests the rope, hauling himself up arm-over-arm and dropping before he's too high. His biceps strain. I have no doubt he can get to the top.

"You can't climb a rope with all that on your belt. You'll fall off and shoot your eye out."

"I never fall." He pulls himself up a few feet and drops again.

Mia's fascinated. I've never seen anyone that strong either. I can see how he managed to catch that baby on the bridge.

A bead of sweat trickles down my temple. They don't have the fans turned on in here, and the air conditioning from the hall doesn't reach much past the door.

"It's hot in here."

"Yeah, it is." He grins and grabs his buckle. "I'm going to take this off. You watch it."

"You're really doing this?"

He jogs past us and puts his utility belt carefully on the bottom step of the bleacher. Then he comes over and kneels in front of Mia. "See that over there?"

She nods, waiting for him to go on.

"That's my duty belt. There is a gun and a knife and other dangerous things. It's very important that you never touch anything on that belt. I can trust you with that, can't I, Mia?"

She nods solemnly.

"I know I can."

He slaps his knee and hops up. "Time me. Say 'go' when the second hand is at zero."

There's a huge clock on the wall with a wire guard protecting the face.

"You're gonna fall and break a leg," I call after him.

"Don't doubt me, woman. Say 'go.'"

"Go." I don't look at the clock at all; I'm hung up on watching him. He's quick. Hand-over-hand, eyes on the rafters. He's not even using his legs.

He slips at one point—his hands must be slick. I know sweat is trickling down my back. He grips the rope with his thighs, arrests the fall, and keeps going.

It's so hot in here. I fan myself with my hand, but it doesn't do much good.

It is amazing how much upper body strength he has. I heard him grunting in his room this morning, and the floor shook, so he must have some kind of routine, but I don't see how a few jumping jacks make a body like that. He must live at the gym.

I can't picture that, though. I don't think he'd want to be around so many people if he didn't have to be.

When he gets to the top, he slaps the rafter.

"Time?" he calls down.

Oh, crap.

I finally check the clock.

"Half past one," I holler up.

He busts out laughing, and after a moment of confusion, Mia decides to join in, too, so we're all still chuckling when he jogs past me to get his stuff. He stops for a second and drops a kiss on my lips.

It's so fast, so light, but my toes curl in my flats. My fingers fly to my lips on instinct.

"You can't do that," I mumble at his back.

He grins over his shoulder as he buckles his belt. "Well, I did."

Mia saw that. What is she gonna think?

I glance down, but she's sizing up that dangling rope. Oh, no.

I clear my throat. "We need to get out of here before I melt."

"Yeah, we do," he says, and he winks, exaggerated, playful, and cocky as hell.

My heart's pounding, I'm sweating buckets, and now my cheeks are on fire.

"Impressed?" He saunters over, not stopping until the tips of our shoes almost touch.

"It was all right."

"All right? You've never seen anything like it."

"That's true. I have never seen a grown man in his work clothes climb a rope in an elementary school gym before."

"And you're impressed." He teases as he leads us back out to the hall.

"I wouldn't say that."

"I'll do it one-handed next time."

"You can't climb a rope with one hand," I scoff.

"What is it I say?" he quizzes Mia. She's turned her attention to him. I expect her usual silence, but it doesn't make me anxious. Kellum's not thrown when she doesn't respond.

I'm absolutely flabbergasted when Mia says, in a growly, squeaky impersonation of Kellum's manly drawl, "Don't doubt me, woman."

I keep a straight face, but it's a hard, hard thing.

~

KELLUM DRIVES US HOME, and I take Mia upstairs to give her a bath in the big clawfoot tub. Mia's fascinated by it. The feet are cast iron, molded into three toes like an ostrich or griffin or something. Once she's all clean, I hop in the shower myself.

Back downstairs, I spy on Kellum as I make Mia a snack and try to get her rehydrated. He must've taken a shower, too. His hair is wet, and he's in fresh clothes.

He paces the path that runs along the fence line, snarling into his phone. He's out there a long time. Eventually, he tucks his phone into his jean pocket and leans against a slat, head bowed. He stays like that a while, even though the sun's beating down on him, not a cloud in sight.

I think about taking him a lemonade, but then I figure I should let him be. I wouldn't know what to say. His family is so different than mine. He's got all these people in his business.

Mama never showed much interest in me. She kept me fed and clothed with a roof over our heads. She met her obligations, and she made it clear that when I was old enough, I'd be expected to meet mine.

Mia's playing at the kitchen table. She's keeping an eye on Kellum, too.

I never thought Mama was cold—I thought that's how mothers were—until I had Mia.

I couldn't hold her at first because she was in one of those incubators. When I was on the recovery floor, there was this bossy nurse, and all she cared about was getting me to pump. I was messed up from the preeclampsia meds and my incision hurt like hell, and she's shoving my tit into this plastic cup, cursing under her breath because I wasn't cooperating.

All I wanted was to hold my baby and sleep. Finally, the woman got so irritated with me, she grabbed my chin and she said, "It doesn't matter what you want. That baby needs milk. You're a mother now. Act like it."

Until that second, my brain hadn't really registered the fact that I was a mother. Mia's mother. And I had a moment of pure panic when I realized I had no idea what to do.

Make sure there's food in the cabinets and the electric is paid. That's what a mother does.

And that was no help whatsoever with a baby in the NICU, and my milk wasn't coming in and it was day four, and however I was supposed to shove my tit in the machine, I was doing it wrong.

When the nurse left, I hobbled over to the bench by the window that doubled as a cot. For the dads.

I stared out at the fields across from the hospital, and I thought, "I'm a mother now."

When the nurse came back, I told her I didn't need her, and she could leave.

I figured out how to work the pump, and I hooked myself up every hour until I was red and raw. I set a timer on my cell phone. And after a few weeks, when my milk still didn't come in, and Mia got stronger and lost that yellow color drinking nothing but formula, I figured formula was fine.

I did know what to do. I did whatever I had to do to make sure Mia got what she needed.

Sometimes it was hard, but in a way, it was always easy. Diapers, onesies, someone reliable to watch her while I was at work, shots, her inhaler. It might take some doing, and there were many times I had to settle, but I always got her what she needed.

She could have used a father, but I didn't fight to get Kellum in her life. I didn't understand that maybe she needed one.

Out by the fence, Kellum's the picture of a man alone, but he's surrounded by ties that bind. His people are wrongheaded, but they're fighting for him, in their way.

Mia has only ever had me.

What if she could have had a father all along?

A man to stroll in and make everything right. To make her giggle and somehow—like magic—make the world safe and easy?

A hole opens in my chest.

I suck down a breath and throw open a cabinet.

I can't think about that. It's too much.

I stare at the shelves for a solid minute before I register what I'm seeing. There isn't much. Looks like pasta with butter for dinner.

If Mia and I are going to be here a little while, we need to go to the grocery store soon. The man has a freezer full of hand-wrapped meat—venison it looks like—but nothing in the way of fresh fruit or crackers. Mia's always been underweight. At least I need to get her peanuts and granola bars.

Chapter 10

I wander into the pantry, hoping there might be pasta sauce among the mason jars. I'm rooting through canned pickles when the back door slams.

I tense.

"Your Mama get you a snack?" Kellum rumbles.

There are footsteps and the faucet runs. "Here. Drink this, and I'll get you more." He must have refilled her red lion cup.

"Where'd Mama get to?"

Mia must have pointed to the pantry because the tread of boots heads my way.

I tuck my hair behind my ears. It's still damp. I can't bear to blow dry my hair when it's this hot.

"Shay?"

He ducks through the doorway. I spin to face him.

Why am I so nervous?

His gaze rakes down my front. I squirm. I'm in an old blue T-shirt with a local radio station logo and khaki shorts. Nothing to look at, but he keeps staring.

"What are you looking for?" His voice stokes the jitters in my belly, sets them to swooping.

"Pasta sauce," I manage, my nipples hardening. I hope he can't tell. The T-shirt is thin. My stupid body. It has a mind of its own these days.

Kellum frowns. "I don't think I have any. Were you thinking about dinner?"

I nod.

"I figured I could make grilled cheese."

"You don't have any cheese."

"Oh." He flashes a wry smile, but there's worry etched on his face.

I can't help but ask. "Your phone call not go well?"

He edges further into the pantry, and my heart rate kicks up another notch. "I'm handling it."

I don't know what to say, so I grab a jar and hold it up. "We can always have more peaches."

Kellum steps closer. "You trust me, don't you?"

I grab another jar. "Or pickles?" I make a show of reading the label, but all it says is *Canned by Kelly* in a cutesy font.

His brows spear down. "Shay—"

"Shay, what?"

"Everything is going to be okay," he declares as if that's the final word.

"If you say so."

He exhales in exasperation. "It is."

"Okay."

His jaw tics, and then he stalks forward, grabbing the cans of peach and pickles from my hands and putting them on the shelf behind me. We're chest to chest, our breath coming quick.

I glance over his shoulder to the open door. Mia can't see in.

"Shay—" he prompts and waits, gaze flicking to my lips. My breasts rise and fall like crazy, and now his eyes are there, darkening. Blazing.

"What do you want me to say?"

His lips part, but he doesn't have an answer. And then he has my wrists, and he's raising them, pinning them to the shelf on either side of my head, and I can feel him against me, hard and taut as a wire about to break.

"Don't doubt me," he growls, and he dips his head, but I'm already up on my toes, meeting him more than halfway. I kiss him, feverish, hungry, and if he weren't holding me back, strong fingers gently circling my wrists, I'd ravage him.

I need his tongue, need to breathe him in, sweat and spice, need everything, to touch him everywhere, rough, not gentle. I don't want him to be in control. I want him to be weak and needy like me.

I whine in the back of my throat.

It feels good—he feels good—and I want more. I want everything. I'm not like this, but I am now, in this moment. I take what I want, his mouth, his taste, marveling as my body comes alive, zipping and zinging. I strain against his grip.

More. I welcome his tongue, slick it with my own, nip at him when he teases.

He groans, a harsh, beautiful sound.

And then he jerks himself back, gasping ragged breaths of air.

"Hush," he purrs, resting his forehead against mine, our chests heaving.

If he didn't have my wrists, I'd snatch him back, and he'd come—I know it down to my toes—and my breasts and pussy ache for knowing how bad he wants this, how much strength it's taking for him to hold himself still. You can tell in every rigid line in his body and the massive tent in his jeans he can't help but rock toward me.

The power is heady and my brain's foggy, so when he starts murmuring low, I don't follow right away.

"I'm not doing this. I'm not stealing kisses from you in a pantry, Shay Crowder."

My heart drops. I wish he'd shut up, but he keeps right on going.

"I'm not doing this in the dark. I'm going to take you out to dinner. You're gonna get all dressed up, and I'm going to take you dancing at The Allemande, if you want."

"What's The Allemande?"

"It's a bar. They have a dance floor."

"I don't dance."

He ignores me. "I'm gonna take Mia and you to the Fireman's Carnival, and I'm going to win you a huge stuffed bear. After we get home and put Mia to bed, I'm going to take you upstairs and make you cum on my cock so hard we break the bed and shake the windows."

My jaw drops. His grip tightens on my wrists. His breath tickles my ear.

"All that?" I say, breathless.

"All that. And I'm gonna buy you flowers and chocolates and a decent pair of shoes. Whatever you want."

"Shoes?"

"Whatever you want."

I'm gawping, and all I want is for him to kiss me, or turn his face so I can taste his lips and get swept away again by pure, goddamn real-life magic, but he's serious, and he won't shut up.

"I'm going to take you to church on Sunday and to the Pancake Barn afterwards and then we'll go swimming in the river until the sun goes down."

"Mia and I only go to church on Christmas and Easter."

"Me, too, but we should probably start going on Sundays."

I giggle, incredulous. "Have you lost your mind? Who were you talking to on that phone?"

He draws himself up, and I have to crane my neck to keep my eyes on his. He's sober as a judge now.

"I am going to show Mia how she should expect to be treated, so she has no doubt. And then I'm going to show you."

My face is flaming, and my insides are zooming around out of control, and I don't know what to say.

"Show me what?"

"How a man treats his woman."

I swallow. "You shouldn't say things like that," I whisper.

"Why not?"

"It's—" Too big. Too dangerous. Too impossible. I suck down a shaky breath. "You can't win me a bear and not Mia. She'd be mad as hell."

He blinks, but then he smiles, lowering my arms to my side and brushing a soft kiss across my lips. "Can't have that. I'll win two bears."

I roll my eyes.

"What have I been sayin'?" he teases, backing off, defusing the moment, letting the magic dissipate as he puts distance between us.

Makes me cranky.

"Your confidence borders on delusion sometimes. You know that, right?"

"Tell me that when you've got two, huge stuffed bears crowding you out of your bed."

"Not going to happen."

"You're right," he says, gesturing me toward the door. "You'll be in my bed. Plenty of room."

He winks, cheesy and awkward and the complete opposite of smooth, and my lips twitch.

"Keep dreaming, buddy," I say, but I swish my hips when I pass him to go back to the kitchen, and I'm sure that tonight, when I'm alone with Mia, I'll be replaying his words. They're already unspooling on a loop.

Pretty, wonderful, impossible words.

They can't possibly be true.

But damn if my foolish heart doesn't want them to be.

11

KELLUM

I only sleep in fits and starts. I keep waking up with my cock hard and throbbing or with my heart pounding. The second Mia and Shay go up to bed, whatever miracle was keeping me steady disappears.

I spent an hour in the basement with the punching bag, but it did nothing. When I drag my ass out of bed in the morning, the rage has only grown.

Fucking Van.

He wouldn't take my calls yesterday. He had Dad ring me up and tell me we'd talk it out when he brings Branch and West up to go coyote hunting.

If he thinks I'm going to hold back because my cousins are around, that's not going to happen. Elizabeth showed me their social media. They might be sixteen and seventeen, but with what they get up to, they can hear some plain speaking.

On the phone, Dad said he didn't know about the offer. He swore he'd get to the bottom of it. Van can't act unilaterally. Don didn't run it past him; he didn't have a clue.

What's worse? That the man I've admired the most my whole life is a liar? Or that he's a dupe?

The only thing that keeps me from driving four hours to the

city and settling this with Van now is that I'd have to leave Shay and Mia. I'm not doing that.

Shay turned down the money, but how close was it?

I saw the guilt on her face when she came out of Prescott's office and saw me there. Makes my gut sour every time my brain dregs it up.

If she took the cash, she could lie low for years, and I'd lose them. She's smart as a whip. If Shay wanted to disappear, she would.

The worst part is that I don't rightly know why she turned Don down. She said Mia needs a father, and I believe that, but does Shay? Really? She's practical as hell. She's made it this far on her own, and she's not the least bit sentimental.

Either she's holding out for a bigger payday, or by the grace of God, she somehow figures I'm a better bet than money in the bank. And that scares the ever-loving shit out of me.

I have no idea what I'm doing.

I know what I *want* to do. What I plan to do. But honestly? After high school, that dumb luck I thought was natural superiority has been wearing off like a shitty paint job.

I got promoted to deputy sheriff, and I figured it's based on merit, right? I get the job done. Resolve most issues without using a heavy hand. I handle what cannot be solved peacefully with force only when needed. Yeah, the sheriff is my godfather, but it's a small town. I'm the best man for the job. Everyone says so.

And then the men in suits roll in.

If I'm good at my job, how did I not see a federal investigation coming from a mile away?

An outside hire might've asked questions, but I left Del to his business. A good officer might have caught a clue before Glenna Dobbs, for Christ's sake—the girl who covers the high school sports and church news beats—broke the story and laid out a federal case on the front page of the Stonecut Gazette.

I'm not saying I believe that Del did what he's accused of. If there is equipment missing, it's vastly more likely that Del screwed up the inventory than he's selling military surplus on the black market. But I found out about it in the paper like everyone else.

And then there's my marriage. I figured I'd do the work, and it'd work out, but it went bad, and then worse, and I couldn't stop it from imploding.

Even that day on the bridge. I'm the hero 'cause I caught that baby, right? But how about all those minutes I had to talk him down?

If I were a hero, Billy McAllister would be heading for treatment after sentencing instead of wasting away in SCI Greene for the next three decades. His little girl would have a shot at a sober, sane daddy one day. Maybe not. Probably not.

But I choked. I didn't save that child; I salvaged a royal fuck up.

And I cannot fuck this up.

I'm aware that good advice would be to back off with Shay. Focus on—what do they call it? Co-parenting? I should keep things civil. Learn to work together for Mia's sake.

But I don't want to do that, either.

Beyond the shock, the searing regret, the mind fuck as everything falls apart around me, and nothing and no one is what I thought, is the bone-deep certainty that they are both mine.

Mia *and* Shay.

In my mind, there isn't one without the other.

If it's selfish, I don't care. They both belong to me, and there's no imperative stronger than making it so. Shay belongs in my bed. They both belong around my table, in my house, close by, within easy reach.

It's a physical knowing. As instinctual as catching a ball. As real as anything has ever been to me.

I know without a doubt where they are supposed to be. Under my roof.

And it doesn't make total sense, and if I try to make it logical, my head pounds.

I know I'm not thinking straight. I'm working on not much

Chapter 11

sleep, and I haven't been eating right. Turns out I did have cheese, but sandwiches for dinner doesn't do it for me.

I should stay home today. My body almost demands that I do. Del will give me the time if I ask, but with him distracted, shit will fall through the cracks. I need to follow up on Rory Evans and give Ed Houser some peace.

All of that is secondary to Mia and Shay, but I also think I need some space.

I have to play this right. Not only for the reasons I told Shay but because I can't live with myself if I don't. And if Shay is there, casting me those sidelong glances, half suspicion, half naked hunger, I won't be able to do it right.

I've got to pull myself together. So I buck up and run through my morning routine with the usual number of reps, and then I shower and put my uniform on. This morning, there's no sound of stirring from the guest room.

I head downstairs, make a pot of coffee, and scroll through the news on my phone. Usually, I fill up a travel mug and head out, but my feet are dragging this morning.

I don't want to leave Shay a note. I want to talk to her before I go. I want to see Mia. I need to know Shay's not spooked. I need a hit of that faint blush she gets on her high cheekbones when I get too close.

I want to get a smile out of Mia. Just one before I go.

I pour myself a second cup and wash out the pot. Then I empty the dishwasher. I take out the trash although the bag's nowhere near full. With nothing else to do, I write a note.

And then I stand in the foyer, screwing around with my duty belt. I check my face in the mirror. I didn't shave this morning. Didn't have the patience.

If I'm going, I should go. I'm already late enough that Bev and Nancy are going to give me shit.

There's a creak in the hall upstairs.

I straighten my shoulders.

Then there's a soft padding of feet toward my bedroom. Mia.

I clear my throat. Her footsteps turn, and she appears at the top of the stairs.

A wave crests in my chest, warm and aching.

Her hair is all tangled, and she's barefoot. She's wearing a wrinkled pink sundress and has a stuffed rabbit shoved under one armpit.

She yawns, scrubs her eyes, and peers down at me.

"Good morning, princess."

She comes down, taking each step deliberately, tiny hand gripping the bannister. She stops at the bottom and eyes me up.

"I have to go to work."

She glances toward the kitchen.

"Are you hungry?"

She sniffs and pads off down the hall. Guess she could eat.

I hang my hat back up on its peg and follow her.

She climbs into the same chair she sat in for dinner last night. And breakfast.

Her chair.

I scrub my chest.

She sets her bunny on the table and peers out the window at the horses in the distance.

I dig into the cabinets. I've got three different kinds of protein shake mix. No cereal. No oatmeal. I check the fridge. We're out of milk. That means no pancakes.

Oh, lord. Looks like we're gonna have eggs again.

"Do you like fried eggs?" I grab the butter and some bread for toast.

Mia glances at me. She doesn't seem turned off by the suggestion.

"They're gonna be over medium." I can't stand runny whites.

I'm definitely heading to the grocery store after work. I'll swing by and pick-up Shay and Mia so we can stock up on what they like.

I heat the pan and watch Mia pet her bunny as she tracks the horses. Her eyes are lively and bright, flickering back and forth.

You can tell all sorts of things are going on inside that brain. So much like Dina.

"Your—" I stop myself and clear my throat. "My sister Dina used to love watching the horses. She had a treehouse on the edge of the woods, and she'd climb up and watch them for hours."

Dad, John, and I built the treehouse one summer when Grandpa Price was still alive. He sat in a folding chair bossing us around while we did all the work. Pissed John off no end, but it's always been a good memory. John's so much older, he didn't spend much time with Cash and I before he struck out on his own.

Mia scoots up 'til she's kneeling in her chair and bends over the table to get a better look out the window. She's looking for the treehouse.

"It's on the far side of the Lodge. I'll take you up there after work if your Mama says it's okay."

The ground staff has been keeping it in repair. Mom wants it to be ready when John's kids are old enough to use it.

For all I know, Dina might still spend time up there. She marches to her own drum. She's a night owl and a homebody, so I don't see her much, but she's happy. I think.

"There's a swing hanging from it. And a trap door."

Mia's face lights up. Maybe I can draw Shay a map, and she can take her up there today.

"You have to be careful, though. It's really high up."

Mia starts to wriggle with excitement. Her little nose twitches. I can't help but chuckle. She's like a rabbit that's caught sight of the garden.

I flick water in the pan, and it sizzles, so I crack four eggs.

"I can't wait for you to meet Dina."

Mia turns her attention to me—to the eggs, actually—but I'll take it. "You have the exact same eyes and nose and chin. She could be your twin."

Her ears perk up.

"Dina's the smartest person I know. She doesn't talk much. She never talked at all when she was little—"

Mia cocks her head. I grin. Dina does that, too. It's her "go on" look.

"She's younger, so she was our responsibility, my brother Cash and I. But she's stubborn. You can't tell her anything. And she's fierce. If she thinks something's not right, she'll fight like h—She fights hard."

I'm not sure where I'm going, but with Mia so intent, I'm not going to stop. I flip the eggs.

"She's also short. The men in the family are tall, but the women favor my grandma, who was maybe five feet tall. Anyway, Dina got Cash and I into a lot of fights."

Mia leans forward.

I grab two plates from the cabinet.

"Well, we had to back up our little sister. She'd rush in, so we had to follow, you know?"

I remember one time when we were on the bus home. I was in middle school. We'd just picked up the little kids from the elementary school. A fifth grader pushed a kindergartener in Dina's class down the aisle. Dina went after him. Cash and I had to pile on. There was a scrum. The bus driver had to pull over and yank kids off each other. I got a bloody nose.

Cash and I both had to go cut a switch from the willow tree for that one. Cash had to threaten to drop Dina's computer out the window to keep her from talking.

I'm lost in the memory, so I almost miss Mia's soft voice. "Does she like all animals?"

My chest tightens. I plate our eggs and bring them over to the table. "Yes. She particularly likes dogs and horses, but I think she likes all animals. She's really into computers and music."

Mia ignores her food. She wants to hear more.

"She actually doesn't eat animals. She's a vegetarian."

"Does she eat eggs?"

"Last time I noticed, yes." She goes between vegan and vegetarian, and I can't keep up.

Mia grabs her fork.

Chapter 11

"You want ketchup?"

She shakes her head and digs in.

We eat in silence. The air conditioner hums, and the clock ticks on the wall. When we're almost finished, I hear Shay on the stairs. My heartbeat picks up.

A moment later she appears in the doorway, her hair tangled, her feet bare. She's in a wrinkled white T-shirt and yesterday's shorts. Her bra's pink. It shows through the thin fabric.

Blood rushes to my cock.

She yawns and arches her back, and I grin.

"What's funny?" she grumbles.

"You're doing the exact same thing that Mia did when she woke up."

She rubs her eyes, sniffs, and shuffles over to the table. "You made eggs?"

"Yup."

"You gonna make me eggs, too?"

My grin widens. "Yup."

I think she's genuinely surprised when I get up and turn the stove back on. Her face softens.

She's gonna learn. I don't mind spoiling her grumpy ass. Matter of fact, it's swiftly becoming one of my favorite things.

I crack two more eggs and pop some more bread in the toaster. "I have to go to work. I'll come back at lunch. I can take you into town if you want to go then. We can go grocery shopping after my shift."

"Okay." Shay tries to run her fingers through Mia's hair to work out the tangles, but Mia ducks her head.

"I told Mia about a treehouse up by the Lodge. If you want, I can draw you a map. You can go exploring."

Shay's eyes narrow. "I think we'll stay down here."

I nod. "There's cable. I have some DVDs—"

"We'll manage," Shay interrupts. "We'll be here when you get back."

She's meeting my gaze. A crackle of energy zips between us,

and my cock jerks against my zipper. A picture flashes in my mind. Her in the woods, the moonlight on her bare breasts, high and firm, writhing against me, seeking me with her hips, head tossed back and eyelids closed.

My throat grows dry, and I turn to face the stove.

As I force myself to inhale, trying to get my head straight, she's fussing at Mia to let her untangle her hair.

"If you don't let me fix it, we'll have to get the wide-tooth comb."

Mia whines.

"Well, then stay still, and I'll get this knot out, and we can use the brush."

There's a yelp.

"Stay still."

By the time I turn around, Mia's in Shay's lap, and she's combing her fingers through the snarls. Mia's wearing a mutinous expression, and she has a death grip on her stuffed rabbit.

It hits me all at once, and I sag against the counter.

I missed so damn much.

What did Mia look like as a baby? What did Shay look like with her belly round and sticking out? First words, first steps, first tooth. All lost. The immensity of it—it's as cold and deep as grief.

"I like them with the yolks runny," Shay says, casting me a funny look.

I shake myself off and flip her eggs. They're a little brown and crispy.

"I can finish them up if you're late for work," she says.

"Nah. I've got it." I clear my throat and butter her toast. "What about if you and Mia came with me?"

"To the sheriff's office?" She raises an eyebrow.

"You could go shopping downtown. I'll give you some money. Mia needs new back to school clothes, right?"

"You mean shop at those little boutiques on Main Street?" She's turning up her nose.

"You should both get riding boots, too." Sneakers were fine for

Chapter 11

the other day, but they need decent footwear if I'm going to take them out on the trails.

"Those shops are really pricey."

"We can meet up for lunch. Go to the playground again." Yeah, this is a better plan than leaving them alone in the house.

"How are we gonna spend all day shopping?"

Seriously? I never needed to convince Elizabeth to spend money. I don't seem to be getting anywhere with Shay, though. I shut up and slide the eggs onto a plate.

What are the magic words here?

How the hell does this woman's mind work?

Mia's head is thrown back and resting in the crook of Shay's neck. They both stare at me, round-eyed.

Fuck it. How about the truth?

"I want you both close. That's all."

Shay winds her arms around Mia's middle. My fingers twitch. A feeling like jealousy burns in my throat.

Feelings I can't begin to make out war across Shay's face. Finally, she says, "Okay. I've been meaning to take Mia to the library." She glances down at herself. "Do I have time to get a shower?"

"You have all the time you need."

She offers me a small smile. I give her one back. A weight lifts from my chest.

I better call Bev and Nancy. Have them tell Del I'll be late. My girls have to get themselves together.

Shay quickly eats her breakfast while I do the dishes, and then she showers. I dry the plates and return Mia's red lion cup to the cabinet above the sink.

How many meals has it been?

Three breakfasts. Two dinners. But Mia's cup has a place now, and she has a chair. So does her mother. Both of their pairs of flip-flops are under the bench in the foyer.

It feels like family. Overnight. Sudden and strange and new and impossible.

And it feels so fragile, and so completely right.

∽

Shay gets really prickly when we get into town, and I hand her my credit card. After her shower, she changed into a red gingham skirt that clings too tightly to her ass and gapes at the waist. She's wearing a white shell. I can see her bra through it, and in the car with the A/C blasting, I can her see her nipples.

Hard little points. Mouthwateringly perfect.

I want to give her a jacket, but it's in the nineties again.

And why do all her clothes not fit? She's an average-sized woman.

I park in the lot behind the fire department. This time I made sure Shay put two bottled waters in her purse. The plan is that we'll meet in front of the diner at noon.

I thought we'd agreed that Shay was going to be doing some shopping this morning, but she's got her arms crossed, and she's staring at my Amex like it's a snake.

"I can't use your credit card."

"Why not?"

"It doesn't have my name on it."

"What does that matter? They just run it through the machine."

"They ask for ID."

"What?" I don't think I've ever been asked for ID when I use a credit card. Certainly not in Stonecut. "No one's going to ask for ID."

"Yes, they are." She hikes up that chin. "And then when I don't have any, they're gonna call the police, but I guess that'll be convenient. They can drop us off at the sheriff's office."

"Shay. That's not how it works in Stonecut."

Her eyes almost roll out of her head. "Kellum. That's exactly how it works in Stonecut."

Chapter 11

She's wrong, but she's not budging. "Well, I don't have much cash. Maybe sixty bucks."

"We'll go to the library."

"You can't spend all morning at the library."

"Sure, we can." And I swear, both Shay and Mia's faces light up at the same instant. Are my girls bookworms?

"Yeah?" I can't help but grin at their matching looks of pure, sneaky delight. "What are you going to do for four hours at the library?"

"Uh, *read*." Shay blows a loose strand of hair off of her forehead.

"Horse books, Mama." Mia smiles up at Shay, filled with glee.

Shay nods, completely serious. "As I recall, they have a lot of books on animals."

"What do you like to read?" I'm charmed by the picture. Shay and Mia, snuggling in a window seat, noses in books. It's hard to imagine, but there's a rightness to it, too.

"Recipes," Mia answers for her.

"I didn't know you liked to cook?"

Shay shrugs, her eyes cast down. Bashful.

"I don't ever have much of a chance. But I like recipe books. And the craft books. That section."

Now I can imagine it clearly. The end of a long day. Mia finally in bed. Shay in the lamplight, flipping through glossy pages. Like I skim through Cash's hunting magazines when I'm at his place. Thinking if I only had the time. The energy. The money to spare.

I clear my throat. "Okay. Then we'll meet at the diner? I'll try to knock everything out so I can take the afternoon."

"You don't have to."

"I want to." I grab her hand. Her eyes widen. I don't know what I'm doing. I squeeze. "Make a list? With what you want from the grocery store?"

She considers our hands. And then she squeezes back. Briefly. My heart soars.

"Okay."

"Take care of your Mama, Little Bit," I say, and chuck Mia under the chin.

I linger in the parking lot as they head up Main Street, the sun catching the red glints in their hair. It's easier to let them go than yesterday, but it's still one of the harder things I've done.

When they disappear around the corner, I head inside.

The office is the same as usual. Bev and Nancy are at their desks. Del's door is cracked, and he's bellowing at someone on the phone. There's no one waiting.

Nothing's different, but it *feels* different.

"Oversleep?" Bev greets me.

Her eyes bug when she catches my shiner, but she ignores it politely. She's had practice. Lord knows that Del comes in with souvenirs from his late nights at Birdy's more than he ought.

"I'm here now," I say. "Any messages?"

"Nope."

"Sarah Evans didn't call? Or Ed Houser?"

"Haven't heard from 'em."

I hear Del bark, "You need to fix it. Understood?" And then it's quiet in his office.

It'd probably be better to give him time, but I'm not putting this conversation off. He owes me answers, too. And with Del these days, there is no such thing as a good time.

I knock on his door and let myself in. "Del?"

"Kell," he waves me in. He's rooting through files on his desk. "Come in. Sit."

His face has a gray pall, and the crow's feet in the corner of his eyes have deepened into creases. He hasn't been trimming his mustache. I can smell the stale whiskey from here.

The words I need to say start to feel like piling on.

He finally gives up shuffling his papers. "What's going on, Kell? I've got messages from Van and your dad. Everyone's being vague as hell. Then, you call out yesterday. Son, whatever it is, now is not the time."

His eye catches a folder. "There it is. I need you to follow up on

Chapter 11

this. It's a permit. The mayor's up my ass about it." He passes it over the desk.

I flip it open. It was filed back in May.

"I'll handle it today."

"Obliged. I know you're taking a lot on. I appreciate it. I do. I can't have you disappearing on me. It ain't like you, son."

His gaze flits between his computer screen and me. He must be expecting an email.

"We need to talk."

"Shit, son. Talk." He leans back and props a foot on his knee. He hasn't got his duty belt on. No tie. No star.

Under the scent of liquor there's a reek of stale sweat. He's losing his grip.

This is the man who gave me my first BB gun on my sixth birthday. I was the happiest kid on earth before my mom snatched it out of my mitts. Del tossed the ball with Cash and I every Sunday when he'd come over for the game. He did a reading at my wedding.

He was the only one in the family who never said "Are you sure that's what you want?" when I said I wanted to be a cop.

It's been several years now since we last threw a ball.

He sniffs and checks his email.

I plunge in, no preamble. "Do you remember Shay Crowder?"

It takes a long damn time. At first, there's no sign of recognition on his face, but I can see the moment he remembers. I see the pieces fall together, ponderous and slow. There's no shame on his face. Not a hint. Only vague irritation.

"Shit. She's back in town?"

"With my daughter."

"Goddamn." He scrubs his face. "That's why Van's blowing up my phone?"

"I'd imagine so."

"Son," he sighs. "We figured she was lying."

"That's what Dad says."

"We asked if she was pregnant. She denied it."

My adrenaline surges. "You interrogated her. She was seventeen. She told you what you wanted to hear."

He has no excuse. He's had the training.

"The kid is yours? You're sure?"

"Positive."

"You took a test?"

"I'm sure."

He shakes his head. "Well, shit. I would've never put money on that. You weren't that kind of kid, Kell."

"I wasn't a kid." I'd been wearing a uniform for two years at that point.

He looks up to the ceiling for patience. "You know what I mean."

"No. What do you mean, that kind of kid?"

"I don't know, Kell. The kind who knocks up jailbait from the trailer park. Jesus. You can stop sitting there all high and mighty."

My fingers dig into the arms of the chair. "I'll thank you to never let shit like that out of your mouth again."

He barks a cynical laugh. He doesn't sound like the guy I grew up with, but it sure fits the man he's become since the accusations.

"Sure, Kell. Always the Boy Scout, ain't you?"

"What the fuck is that supposed to mean?"

He stays in his seat, but he puffs his chest. "It means the act is tired."

"What act?"

"This—choirboy shit." He waves his hand at me. "You know, Van says you honestly are a goddamn hall monitor. I always thought it was bullshit, that you just knew how to keep your mouth shut." He glances at a tall stack of files in front of him. "But Van's right, isn't he?"

Del's clearly not himself. The pressure's gotten to him. And the smell of whiskey isn't just coming off his clammy skin, it's coming from his coffee mug, too.

"I've made mistakes," I allow, trying to defuse the conversation.

He scoffs. "Mistakes. Right. You raw dog some skank at a

kegger, and you want to walk into this office, tell me to watch my mouth. Get the fuck outta here with that, Kell."

If I were Cash, my fist would be buried in his face. But I'm in uniform in the sheriff's office. I walked in here. I grip the arms of the chair harder until my knuckles blanch white.

"I just want to understand."

He comically widens his red eyes. "Oh, yeah? Do you?"

"Yes, Del, I do."

"'Cause from where I'm sitting, you're pretty damn happy strolling around town like Andy-fuckin'-Griffith. I wouldn't want to tell you Santa Claus ain't real."

"Say what you're gonna say, Del."

He clasps his hands and rests them on his paunch. The extra weight's a relatively new development, too. Probably the booze. He smirks.

"You never could see what's in front of your face. You always bought the bullshit. That SUV we pulled out of the ravine off the Albanstown Road? You remember?"

"Of course, I remember."

"Yeah. That's why you said you wanted to be a cop. Made your Ma's eyes mist up every time you'd tell the story. You realize they were both drunk as hell, right?"

I had no idea. I remember the torrential rain. The flashlights barely cutting through the blackness. The blood.

"They were fighting. Again. Mike swatted Patty, and she grabbed the wheel and yanked. Almost killed them both."

"I never heard that."

"Then you weren't listening. Let me ask you something. Did you know her? Buck Crowder's girl? Before, you, uh, met her."

I keep my gaze straight. "No."

"No." He sips from his mug. "Well, we did. She's Rayanne Crowder's girl. Rayanne would fuck any guy who'd buy her a ticket to the movies, and if she didn't like it when he moved on, she'd have something to say about him."

"That's her mother. Not her."

"Sure, sure. I remember when Rayanne turned up pregnant, spinning nasty stories about Jim Ellwood. She left town, too. Went to live with relatives in one of the Carolinas. Lot less drama after she was gone."

"Shay's not her mother."

"Bullshit. You're John Wall's kid, ain't you? Ain't I Frank Willis' son? You've done this job long enough. How far does the acorn tend to fall from the tree?"

"You should have brought it to me."

Del shakes his head. "You would've blown your whole damn life up. Over what was probably idle talk."

"It was my call, Del." My voice rises. Out in reception, Bev and Nancy's chatter falls silent.

"Let me ask you something. She's back now?"

I drop a curt nod.

"After what, seven or eight years?"

I shrug a shoulder.

"Where has she been all this time?"

"South Carolina."

"Not what I'm asking. I'm asking what she's been doin'. If you're the kid's dad, and you're the damn deputy sheriff, and your family's rich as Croesus—ya'll don't show it off, but there's not a man in the tri-state area who don't know about the Walls of Stonecut County."

He waits. I nod. It's true.

"What's she doing in South Carolina, Kell? If she's got this kind of payday waiting for her here, what game is she running down there?"

"You don't know what you're talking about."

"You've got a child's conception of the world, Kell. Not a man's. Elizabeth played you for years. She did whatever the hell she wanted with whoever, and when she was done playing the field and decided she wanted a ring, she asked for one, and you gave it to her. And she knew you would because you're a Wall."

"What does that mean?"

"Sometimes? I agree with Van. Means you're thick in the head." I spit through clenched teeth. "Mia is mine, Del. That's the key fact here. And I had the right to know I was a father."

"Have you done a test, Kell?"

"There's no doubt in my mind."

"No," Del shakes his head and chuckles bitterly. "There never is."

He sighs and glances at his monitor. "Listen. As far as it goes, I'm sorry we didn't come to you with it. We thought we were doing the right thing. Accusations can cause a stink that doesn't wash away, even when they aren't true. We were trying to spare you that."

Del flips his thumb through his stack of files, and flashes me a sorry smile. "I know that better than most."

His combativeness drops, and he's not the sheriff, and he's not the cocky man who's been like an uncle to me since before I can remember. He's old. Worn out. Holding on by a thread.

"How's Aunt Lil?" I ask.

"She's holding her own."

"She's bouncing back from the treatments?"

"She gets exhausted quicker, but she's getting better every day. Doc Wright says it's a waiting game now. She'd like to see you. If you have time."

"I'll make time."

We sit in grim silence for a few moments. The storm has passed. There's no resolution. Only more ugliness and cause for regret.

"Shay and Mia are going to be family. They are family. All this shit—we have to get past it." I don't know if I'm telling him or reminding myself.

"Whatever you need, Kell. You know that."

I move to stand. Del exhales.

"Before I go, Rory Evans?"

Del groans. "Thank you for taking Sarah and Ed. I get why Ed's worried. Sarah—she needs to worry about her own self."

"You spoke to Rory, though."

"I did. She's in the city. Brooklyn."

"She just left town?"

Del finishes off whatever's in his mug and grimaces. "I don't know. There was something with a man. There always is. She was being vague, but she's good. Waiting tables. She asked me to say goodbye to Dina for her. I didn't know they were tight."

"Yeah. They've been friends awhile."

"Didn't know Dina had friends."

I shrug. "Generally, she doesn't."

"Well, you can let Ed and Sarah know she's fine. Maybe Sarah will take it from you. Probably not. She'll drop it when she falls off the wagon, though. She's about due."

There's a casualness in his tone that sticks in my craw. It's not different than his usual manner. I always write it off. That's Del. He talks tough, but he's a good man. He'd give you the shirt from his back.

Well, he'd give *me* the shirt from his back.

"I'll call today." I slap invisible wrinkles from my pants.

"Thanks, Kell. I know you're picking up a lot of slack. And I hate to ask but—"

I brace myself. "Yeah?"

"I'm gonna need you to call Elizabeth back. She's blowing up my phone now. The Harvest Day Parade. I'm gonna need you to do that."

"Are you serious?"

"You sit in the back of a convertible in your uniform and wave."

"Del, no."

"It's two months away."

"It's not my thing."

"Jesus, Kell." He bends over and rummages under his desk. I want to leave before I have to watch him pull out the whiskey bottle. He has his hand in the drawer when he slumps over and plops in his head in his other hand.

"You all right?"

Chapter 11

He closes his bloodshot eyes. "To speak the truth? I don't know, Kell. You sit in this chair long enough, you make enemies."

Six months ago, he had his boots propped up on the desk and was flirting with Nancy. Now his wife has a cancer diagnosis, and the Feds are up his ass. I can't hold onto any anger at this man. Anger doesn't hold in the face of so much loss.

"What can I do?"

"Call Elizabeth back."

I exhale. "Shit."

"Is that a yes?"

"Close as you're getting."

He summons up a wry smile. "Maybe you'll get lucky, and it'll rain."

"Maybe."

"Close the door when you go?"

"Sure thing."

I head out, and it isn't until I'm at my desk, getting ready to call Sarah Evans, that I recognize the uncomfortable feeling lodged in my chest.

I've spent my time in court. Testified in many cases. Most are straightforward. A few times, and in my experience, it's always been vehicle-related or slip and falls, I've been called up in a high stakes jury trial. More often than not, Wayne Daly has represented the party with deeper pockets. He's an old dog, but he still has a way with witnesses.

For lack of another way to put it, he triggers them right out of the gate. Raises the temperature. Disconnects their brains by pissing them off. Then he dials it back, and hits them with the *how abouts*. He casts suspicion and doubt, and he's not particular about the direction or consistency. And then when he's got the witness contemplating all manner of bullshit, he'll trip on the carpet.

If he's in a room in the old county courthouse, he'll trip on the hardwood. I've seen him do it a dozen times.

He gets this chagrined look, and he shrugs, as if to say, "Look at us. Two fools. We're both just human after all, and this is nothing but sound and fury."

He changes the direction of his questions and his tone, and the witness obligingly follows wherever he leads. Without fail. I've watched plaintiffs tank their own cases and defendants tell on themselves.

I always attributed it to pure stupidity.

Sitting here, phone in hand and a stone in my gut, it occurs to me that it's simple human weakness, too.

We want to reconcile. We don't want there to be bad guys in real life. Especially bad guys who look like us. Like what we'll become one day.

An old man tripping over carpet.

A good cop with a string of bad luck.

Del, Van, and Dad made a terrible mistake. But it was an understandable one, wasn't it? Shay's mother was a liar and a slut, after all, and do I even know that Mia is mine? And if she is, why didn't Shay come collect her payday? She must have been running a game on someone else.

They can't be held responsible. They're the good guys.

I *know* these men.

One day, I'll *be* them. I'll be sitting behind the desk in the big office.

Isn't it easier if Del and I are just two men who have made the wrong call? Forgivable. Understandable. Regrettable, maybe.

But human. I've watched Wayne Daly stumble a dozen times, and I've smiled to myself. And didn't I just walk out of Del's office, pitying the man, with marching orders to call my ex?

An uneasiness settles on my shoulders.

It would be easier if this was all an honest mistake.

But do I believe that?

At the end of the day, I'm a decent cop with decent instincts.

What's my gut saying? If I put aside everything I know about these men, does the story jive?

Did they do what any man would in their place?

Chapter 11

Or did they casually use their power to make a seventeen-year-old girl disappear when she became inconvenient?

Like I did when I hung up that phone?

~

I leave a little early for lunch and run home for cash so Shay can buy back-to-school clothes. We meet for sandwiches at the Over Easy. Mia and Shay both show up with armfuls of books. After we eat, I stow them in my truck, and the ladies head off to shop. At five o'clock when we meet at my cruiser, Shay's weighed down with bright yellow bags from the Family Discount out on Route 7. Almost a mile and a half outside of town.

Shay and Mia are both tomato red, dripping with sweat, and grinning ear-to-ear.

Shay holds the bags up. "There was a sale!"

I was expecting her to walk up with two or three nice paper bags with ribbons for handles, a couple items, as Elizabeth would say. That's what she'd come back with after spending a few hundred in the boutiques on Main Street.

Shay's hauling the mother lode.

And she made a three-mile round-trip trek in ninety-plus heat. And there's no sidewalk on Route 7. Goddamn it. My teeth clench.

She lowers the bags and her smile fades.

I cannot have her and Mia traipsing along the highway. A woman and girl alone. This is a safe community—we work like hell to keep it that way—but I don't delude myself. Bad shit can happen anywhere.

It's on my lips to say so. Ask her what she was thinking.

But her shoulders are as rigid as a coat hanger now, and damn, now that I think about it, Mia must need more than "a couple items."

I pop the trunk and take the bags from her, hefting them in my hands.

"You two made out like bandits." I venture a smile at Mia,

standing at her Mama's side, mimicking her Mama's defensive stance. "You're all set, now, aren't you?"

Shay's shoulders slowly relax. "She still needs a coat. They don't have the real winter clothes in yet."

"We'll put that on the list."

I open the back door, and Mia crawls in. Then, I open the passenger door for Shay. She eases past me and gracefully seats herself, wary, aware, casting quick glances at me from the corner of her eyes as she slips off her shoes and stretches her feet. There are angry red marks where the plastic rubs her skin.

"Did you get anything for yourself?" I know she didn't, even before she shakes her head.

As soon as I turn on the car, I blast the A/C, and she moans, a satisfied mewl that goes straight to my dick. I crack the windows to let out the heat.

"You still up for grocery shopping before we head home?" She looks beat, but if we don't go now, we'll have to stop for dinner. The cupboards are bare.

"That's fine." She leans back and closes her eyes, letting the air conditioning blow in her face. The wisps of hair framing her face go flying. She has the look of a pleased woman. Like the other night in the kitchen.

A jolt of desire courses through my veins. I'm getting us back there, and it's not going to blow up on me this time. She's going to curl into me with that satisfied expression, and I'm going to keep it there.

Somehow.

In the back seat, Mia stares out the window, taking in the scenery. We drive in silence for a while, down Main Street to the river, past the square and the school.

A heaviness in my chest lifts. Life is simple in this moment. The pieces fit. This is how it's going to be. The three of us.

Shay wriggles straighter in her seat and slides her shoes back on. "The kid's store downtown wanted thirty dollars for a shirt."

She says this like it's an affront to all that's right and decent. I pop a button to loosen my collar. I guess Shay hasn't been admiring the view. She's stewing on this.

"I got Mia four outfits for what they wanted for one shirt," she adds, glaring out the windshield. I'm not entirely sure where this is coming from, so I nod.

"I didn't *want* to walk all the way out to Route 7."

I didn't say anything back at the office. But I guess my face did. I exhale.

"Mia's outgrown most of her long sleeves. You wouldn't believe it to look at her, but she's grown almost three inches since winter. She can wear last year's tops, but the pants are gonna be high waters."

Shay's got those arms crossed.

Do I come across that judgmental? That I'd make her this defensive with a look?

Shit, I'm sure I do.

I want her to know she can spend thirty dollars on a shirt and buy as many of them as Mia wants. That I'm going to be getting her a car, a safe one, as soon as I can. I will see to it that she has money to spare for herself. She will have as much as she needs.

I just don't see how saying all that will convince her to unfold those arms. She doesn't operate like other women I've known. When Elizabeth wanted to spend over the budget, she'd come at me coy and sexy. Or pouty. When Mom wants something, she gets it, and tells Dad after.

I swear giving money to Shay feels like handing her a bomb.

We're going to have to work it out. And she's not walking down Route 7 again. But now's not the time, not with Mia in the back.

I reach over and turn on the radio to the oldies station. Upbeat Motown fills the cab. Shay's eyes narrow.

"So what are you going to make us for dinner tonight, woman?"

Her eyebrows rise to her hairline. "What am *I* going to make?"

"I made dinner last night."

"Grilled cheese."

"You say that as if you weren't impressed."

She snorts.

"I didn't hear you complaining when you ate it."

A few sparks burst to life in her brown eyes. "I don't talk with my mouth full."

"Well, if you can do better, woman, let's have it."

"You sound like a caveman when you say 'woman.'"

"I sound rugged and manly."

She giggles. It's a sweet sound, so unexpected. I want to hear it again.

Mia's watching us now.

"No one says 'woman' anymore," Shay says. "It's backwards."

I incline my head, feign seriousness. "You may have a point, beautiful."

Pink circles bloom on her cheeks. She fidgets with her backpack straps and glances out her window.

"So, beautiful, what are you making for dinner?"

As she shifts and blushes all down her neck, my body tightens. Blood rushes to my cock, and my shoulders tense.

Damn, but my mouth waters for her. She *is* beautiful. Not in an obvious, blonde movie star way, but like a bird in flight. Like a doe in a clearing. She was just made by a skilled hand.

"Pork chops," she says. "If you stop calling me that."

I hum in appreciation. "I do love pork chops."

She lifts her chin, self-satisfied.

"All right, angel, it's a deal. Pork chops it is."

She huffs, and in the back, Mia's tracking us as if we're as fascinating as the horses.

When we get to the grocery store, the red is gone from Shay's face, and she's collected herself again. Good. I don't want other men to see her off-kilter. The thought sets me on edge.

We get a cart. At first, I push, but when I see that Shay's reluctant to take things off the shelf, I have her take over. It's still a process not unlike pulling teeth.

Chapter 11

"Does Mia like these?" I hold up a box of crackers shaped like fish.

"We don't get those."

"Why not?"

She shrugs. I'm catching on. That means because it's too expensive.

I shake the box. "Mia? You think you'd like these?"

Mia looks to her mother. I groan and throw the box in the cart. We're in aisle three. There are twelve damn aisles, and my stomach's growling.

The produce section was easy. Shay said yes to everything I suggested right quick, as if she was trying to nail me down before I changed my mind.

As soon as we hit the packaged goods, the tooth extraction began.

"Which cereal do you guys like?" I ask.

"They don't carry it here." Shay won't even look at the display.

"I liked this when I was a kid." I grab a yellow box and raise an eyebrow.

Two pairs of round eyes blink at me.

I fake putting it back on the shelf. There's a flicker in Mia's eyes. I drop it in the cart.

"You ladies are very easy to shop with."

Shay hoists her nose into the air. "You're going to pay almost five dollars for a box of cereal."

She says that like it's unreasonable.

"How about you let me worry about how much things cost?"

Shay has her mouth open to tell me off when a voice rings out from behind us. "Kellum?"

Shit. Elizabeth.

Since when does she go grocery shopping? She always did parcel pick up before.

I didn't have a plan for this yet. Obviously, I'd have to have a conversation with her sooner or later. But not before things were more settled with Shay, and we'd decided how to tell Mia.

I turn slowly.

"Elizabeth."

Mia shuffles a step closer to Shay.

Elizabeth stares at them, smile frozen on her face. She must have come straight from work. She's wearing one of her green news anchor dresses, and she hasn't removed her on-air makeup.

Shay tightens her grip on the cart.

I clear my throat. "I was going to call you. About the Harvest Day Parade. I got your messages."

She arches her eyebrows and waits. I set my jaw.

She deliberately moves her gaze to Shay, her forced smile now utterly mismatched with the rest of her face. This could get ugly.

"And who is this? I don't think we've met." She offers her hand. Shay eyes it with suspicion as she presses it quickly.

"This is Shay and Mia."

Her eyes round. She remembers Shay's name.

She never mentioned it after that one phone call, but there were always veiled references during fights. How I couldn't claim the high ground because I wasn't perfect, was I?

"Shay Crowder." Elizabeth blinks. "You've come back to Stonecut."

Shay jerks her chin.

"I was sorry to hear about your grandfather." Elizabeth was always good at keeping up appearances and saying the right thing. "I never met him myself, but I understand he was quite a loss to Stonecut Farms."

Shay nods warily. "Thank you."

"I didn't realize you still had family here in Stonecut."

Shay shrugs.

Elizabeth's eyes are flying from her to me and back again. Gears are turning.

"And who is this?" Elizabeth coos, finally turning her gaze to Mia. It's not a surprise she didn't pay her any attention before. Elizabeth never had much interest in children.

I can see the second it hits her. The unmistakable resemblance. Her blue eyes go blank as she does the math. Her body goes rigid. I edge forward.

"Mia is Shay's daughter," I say.

"Shay's daughter," Elizabeth repeats, blinking. A flush creeps up her neck.

I half expect her to turn on me, unleash her rage in a flurry of profanity like she grew accustomed to doing by the end of our marriage. I brace myself.

There's a long silence.

Elizabeth's gaze settles on Shay. "The resemblance is uncanny," she says, almost to herself.

I open my mouth to say this is not the time or place, but Shay interjects. "Not here."

A flash of temper crosses Elizabeth's face, but then she clenches her jaw.

"You were hiding this?" Elizabeth looks to me. "The entire time?"

Again, before I can respond, Shay speaks. "He didn't know. And I'm telling you—not here."

"He didn't know," Elizabeth repeats. Her mask is slipping.

Goddamn it. We're in the middle of the grocery store. Elizabeth doesn't lose it in public, but this is huge. It's not how I would have handled it. Not in the damn cereal aisle. Not by the side of the road, either.

I've tried to do the right thing, and I've managed to hurt all of us.

I step forward, trying to draw Elizabeth's gaze to me. She's staring at Mia, an awful look on her face. Shock. Pain.

"I'll call you," I say. "Later."

"Kellum—" Her voice breaks. "How could you?"

Shay shuffles in front of Mia. She hoists her backpack purse higher on her shoulders. "He didn't know." Shay's voice is calm. Gentle even. "Not here, though. Later."

Elizabeth drags her gaze away from Mia to rest on Shay. Shay offers her a small smile.

Elizabeth straightens her spine. "She's beautiful."

"Thank you," Shay murmurs.

"The family is losing their minds, aren't they?" She smirks at me. Then she turns back to Shay, sobering. "Watch yourself with them, Shay Crowder. They're a real mixed bag."

"Eliz—" I start, but she raises her hand.

"I'll talk to you later. About the Harvest Day Parade." She spares a last look for Mia, and then turns on her heels, and stalks off.

Shay watches her go, face inscrutable. Then she sighs and says, "We like the kind with flakes and raisins."

What?

She gestures at the shelf behind me. "That kind. The box with the sun on it."

Then she grabs the cart and wheels off in the opposite direction, regal and unruffled, Mia trailing in her wake.

I'm left alone in the aisle, unsettled. I'm missing something.

I shake it off, snagging two boxes of the cereal Shay pointed out. It's done now. Elizabeth knows. It could have been worse. She's capable of making a scene if she wants.

I should feel relieved, but there's lingering uneasiness in my gut. I replay the interaction, and I can't put my finger on it.

I've been a cop for over a decade, though. There's something. It'll come to me.

I put it aside and go find my girls. I want to swing back to the produce section before we leave. Grab another carton of the strawberries Mia was eyeing.

12

SHAY

These past two weeks, Kellum, Mia, and I have fallen into a routine. He makes us breakfast before he leaves for work. I make dinner except for a few times when he grilled outside. I bought some workbooks at the Family Discount, so after Kellum leaves, we review Mia's math facts, and she practices her handwriting.

Then we spend the rest of the day outside. The heat is unrelenting, but there are plenty of shade trees. Sometimes we hike along the horse path downhill, away from the Lodge, but mostly we stay in the yard. Mia loves playing in the sprinkler. When we need a break from the sun, we explore the workshop and the house. Mia's fascinated by the idea of a bat in the attic. She likes to sneak up the stairs, but we haven't caught sight of the critter yet.

If Kellum called Elizabeth, he must have done it at work. When he's home, he spends every waking moment with us. His phone is off.

He takes us up to the barn to visit the horses, or we drive into town to the playground. Early on, he came home with a big ol' car seat for Mia. Once he installed it in his truck, we went for a joy ride on the dirt access roads that wind through the property. We saw a family of deer: a doe and two big fawns who hadn't headed off on their own yet.

Everything has been very low-key and mellow. I'd almost consider relaxing. Move the clothes from our bag into an empty dresser drawer. Let my guard down a little bit.

Except for the kisses.

Kellum steals 'em every chance he can get. In the pantry. When Mia runs off after a flying bug of some kind. At night, when I go to put Mia to bed, and she's already upstairs, but I'm lagging behind on the bottom step. He grabs me by my wrist, tilts my head, and kisses me.

A strong hand cradling my jaw. Firm lips taking mine. His clean, spicy scent surrounding me.

Quick and done. He never takes it further.

It has me squirming in my skin.

But I don't tell him to stop.

I can't. It'd be like sinking your teeth into a rich, creamy chocolate, and it tastes so good, better than you ever imagined it could, and then you spit it out. It goes against every human instinct.

I don't care anymore if it's foolish. I go looking for things in the pantry sometimes. Things I know he keeps in the kitchen cabinets.

If he doesn't follow, my stomach twinges with disappointment.

I'm not this thirsty woman. I never used to be, at least. I've done lost my mind.

I can't be mad at him, either. Because while he's stealing kisses from me, he's spoiling Mia rotten. He figured out she loves fresh berries. Unless they were buy one, get one, blueberries and raspberries have always been a once-in-a-while treat.

Apparently, there's a farm stand on Kellum's way home. Every night, he brings her a carton of something. Strawberries that aren't huge and pale like in the grocery store, but small and red and sweet. Fat blackberries. I've had to freeze half because we can't eat them all.

He's also going to the stores at lunch and buying her toys. He says it's only right since she has nothing to play with at the house.

Chapter 12

He's bought her a few new tubes of plastic critters, but he also bought her a bike.

The bike is sitting in the workshop. It's pink with a white basket, a bell, and pretty rainbow streamers coming from the handlebars. It's a dream bike, the kind that would show up around the trailer park when the tax refunds came in.

Mia doesn't want anything to do with it.

Packs of kids back home roamed the streets on their bikes, popping wheelies, playing chicken with cars. Mia showed no interest in them then, either. She's not a very physical kid. She'll walk as far as you want without complaint, but she's not one to climb a tree. She's never tried a cartwheel. I show her, but she's not inclined to give it a go. She's a sturdy enough kid, but she's not coordinated.

Kellum asks if we've gone bike riding every night when he gets home, face lit up with anticipation. I tell him it's too hot. I do try to show her, wheel her along. She refuses to pedal. It's a sorry thing to see.

Last weekend, Kellum took us for a drive up to Anvil. We hiked around the state park, and then we had dinner in town. On Sunday, we rode horses again. Mia's taking to that like a duck to water. She won't ride with me anymore. I make the horses go too slow.

Now it's Saturday again. He has plans for us. A surprise, he says. He brought a basket up from the root cellar, and he's making sandwiches and wrapping them in wax paper, so I'd say his surprise is a picnic.

He tells us to put our bathing suits on under our clothes. Mia has one I bought from the Family Discount, but I don't own one. He says to wear something I don't mind getting wet and to bring a change of clothes.

I hope this is a sprinkler, hose, wade-in-a-creek type thing. Neither Mia nor I can swim.

We take the truck. After he buckles Mia in the back, Kellum wraps his hands around my waist and lifts while I climb aboard.

He insists. I don't need the help, but my body still heats, and my innards go squishy.

And he knows. He preens, almost imperceptibly. Same as when he kisses me. He knows what he's doing to me, and it'd be insufferably irritating if it didn't seem to make him so happy.

When Kellum gets himself settled in the driver's seat, I try to distract myself. "Are you going to tell us where we're going now?"

"You don't like surprises?"

I shrug and try not to stare at his legs. He's wearing black boardshorts, the kind that double as swim trunks. They've crept up, and I can see his thigh muscles. His legs are shredded. Sprinkled with fine, dark hair.

I've never seen him in shorts before.

It's weird to gawk at a man's legs.

I force myself to look out the windshield. I can feel Kellum's eyes on me. He does that. Tracks my every movement. It's embarrassing. It makes me squirm, but the squirm kind of feels good.

"The A/C is up as high as it'll go," he says. "But it's not a long drive."

I nod and gnaw on my lower lip. Of course, he caught me looking. My cheeks burn.

"I hope you girls are hungry."

I saw how much food he packed. We'll have leftovers.

"You hungry, Mia?"

He glances in the rearview and flashes a wide, white smile. Mia's playing with critters from one of her new tubes. Animals of the savannah. She's playing with three critters that are obviously supposed to be different species but they all look like the ferret mold.

Mia deigns to give him a small smile in return.

Over these past two weeks, they've developed a way between them. Mia still doesn't talk much—about as much to him as she does with me—but he *always* talks to her.

He'll ask questions or tell her little things about the farm or town or what he was like as a boy. When he's done, he pauses and

Chapter 12

looks at her, and she'll give him a sign. A smile, a blink, a cocked head. He takes it as a totally satisfactory response.

We need to tell her soon that Kellum is her daddy. I just don't know how. She's not gonna ask questions. I have to get it right the first time.

She's going to wonder where he's been all this time. I think. It's so hard to sort through.

If Mama sat me down and told me Willie or whoever was really my daddy, what would I think? I'd want to know where he'd been and why he'd never been around and what I'm supposed to do with a daddy now. And all I'd be is angry.

I asked Mama who my daddy was every so often until I was thirteen or so. She always put me off, but then I caught her at the wrong time. She was tired. Drunk. She said she couldn't be sure, but none of the men were around anymore, and I'd been an accident besides.

I asked for names, and she said it was a long time ago. I couldn't get anything else out of her.

Mia's not me, though. Mia's never asked about a daddy.

How do I put it?

I could say there was a misunderstanding. That sounds like bullshit. It might hold while Mia's young, but that explanation has an expiration date.

I could make it a fairy tale. Bad men convinced me I had to take my baby and run. In the end, though, the prince found us, and everything turned out happily ever after.

But what if it doesn't? It's all strawberries and bicycles now, but we're in the middle of the same kingdom. The bad men who wanted us gone? Daddy goes to work with one of them every day. They live up the hill. I've seen one from a distance a few times now, staring down at us as we play in the yard, hand shielding his eyes from the sun.

What if we have to bail, and I've told her that her daddy is a prince?

I don't want to ask Kellum about it because I know he wants to tell her, and if I open the door, he's not going to be okay with waiting much longer to walk through it.

So I fret about it. That and how school is starting soon and how I need to find a job because come fall, I can't spend all day alone worrying. And if I'm gonna be turning down payouts, I need cash of my own. There's no such thing as a free ride despite how this feels now.

Kellum's casting me concerned looks now. I make an attempt to smile. He grimaces.

"You okay?"

"I'm fine."

"We're almost there."

I try another smile. Must be better. His focus shifts back to the road.

We were headed toward town, but right before the "Welcome to Stonecut" sign with the Stonecut Farms logo at the bottom, Kellum turns and drives along the river, upstream, tracing its path up the slopes that become hills and then rise into the mountain in the distance.

After ten minutes or so, he pulls off onto a rutted, unmarked road. It's been seven years, but I recognize the place. My heart flips, and my stomach clenches.

This is where the bonfire was.

Kellum is studying my face.

He did this on purpose.

This was the surprise.

I've got my backpack in my lap. It's holding a change of clothes for Mia and me, some toys for her, and a library book on fall crafts for me. I grab the fake leather and dig my fingers in.

I was only ever here the once, and it was pitch dark when we arrived. Pandy drove. I'd already had two beers in the car, and I was a lightweight. I never really drank until I fell in with Pandy and her crowd.

Now, in broad daylight, I can see we're on an access road to a farmer's backfields that happens to run along the river. Trees line the river here, except a few clearings.

At a wide break by a bend in the river, Kellum pulls off the road. There's a fallow field here, crisscrossed with tire marks. More than a few crushed beer cans, too. It's clearly still a party spot.

What are we doing here?

Kellum clears his throat. "A little ways up, there's a great swimming hole. There's no place to park, though. We'll have to hike. It's not far."

He's frowning.

There's a lump in my throat.

"We can go somewhere else," he offers.

"No. We're here now." I draw in a breath, swing open the heavy door, and hop down.

Reality slides across memory, and it's jarring, and it doesn't fit. Despite my sunglasses, it's bright. Not that strange dark when moonlight outlines everything.

The rock ring of the bonfire pit is still down on the shore. That's where Kellum and I danced. Where he led me off into the woods. It was cool that night. There was a breeze.

Now, I'm dripping sweat. I'm wearing my black tank top and khaki shorts. Both are damp and sticking to me.

This whole place is smaller. Have the trees grown closer?

That night, it was magic. I floated away on it. Let go of my good sense, and how could I be ashamed? I was under a spell.

That was the story I told myself. Kellum was a prince, and I was Cinderella at the ball, and if it didn't end with happily ever after, it ended with Mia, and that's just as good, better even in this world.

But that's bullshit, isn't it?

This is just a muddy clearing with a bunch of cigarette butts littered around, and is that—? That's an old red cooler turned on its side with a dirty T-shirt wadded up in it.

Why did he bring us here?

Something inside me sinks. Drops all the way to my feet. Makes my steps heavy.

"Shay?" There's concern in his voice.

Kellum's helped Mia down, and he has the basket. "You okay? Too hot?"

"It's fine."

"It's only a quarter mile or so." He gestures up the road.

"All right."

"We can go back home if you want." His brow is furrowed. I know he's remembering, too. His eyes keep flickering over to the fire pit.

"We're here now." I sling my backpack over my shoulders and stomp off in the direction he indicated.

My eyes sting. It's the perspiration. I have my hair pulled back tight in a ponytail, so there's nothing to stop the sweat from dripping down my forehead.

"Shay—" He tries to trot to catch up, but he has Mia's hand, and she has one speed.

I don't know why I'm mad.

We had sex.

It wasn't romantic. It didn't mean anything.

Yeah, I was young, but I knew better. I was either supposed to save myself for marriage or make sure I used reliable protection, and which was the best course of action differed by the health teacher, but definitely one or the other. And all the teachers—and the evidence of my life—were clear. Accidents can and will happen.

I happened, and I was an accident.

Why should the truth get me out of sorts?

That night wasn't some extraordinary moment out of time. It was a dirty fuck in the woods.

I swipe at my eyes. I can't even wipe my face with my sleeves 'cause I'm wearing a tank top, and my forearms are slick with sweat, too. This sucks.

"Shay."

Chapter 12

Kellum tromps up beside me. He's giving Mia a piggyback ride. She's clinging to him like a baby monkey, her face impassive, her thin legs wrapped tight around his waist.

Huh. She is not a clinger. She wriggled out of my arms when she was two, and she fussed like hell whenever I tried to carry her again.

I slow down my pace a bit, but I keep my gaze straight ahead.

"I would have picked another place—"

"This is fine."

"Clearly, it's not."

My jaw clenches. "Let's just eat."

I gesture for him to take the lead. He knows where we're going. He sighs under his breath. I stare on down the road.

We trudge along for a good while longer. The crickets in the fields chitter in waves. When they're quiet, you can hear the river lap the banks, but the trees are too thick to see anything but flashes of silver.

Eventually, we come to a trail that's been cut through a thicket. It's narrow, but well-traveled. Kellum goes first. The path is steep, and I have to watch my feet so I don't trip on a tree root. The shade feels good. I swear it's ten degrees cooler under the tall trees.

I hear the river before I can see it, a low rushing. We round a corner, and there it is. It's not so wide as it is in town, but it seems deeper. There's a grassy bank, more than enough room to lay out a blanket, and a pebbled shore. A grand willow looms overhead with a thick branch reaching out almost parallel to the water. There's a rope swing hanging from it.

It is a pretty spot. Like a lemonade commercial.

Kellum's eyeing my reactions. "Will it do?"

I jerk a nod and slide off my flip-flops. The grass is thick and cool on my bare feet.

Mia wriggles to be let down. Kellum squats, those thigh muscles bulging, until her feet touch the ground.

"My mom would bring us kids here in the summer for a change of scene. My older brother John hung that rope swing."

I don't remember John. He must be a lot older.

"I didn't know you had an older brother." I settle myself on the ground, running my fingers through the dark green blades. Mia wanders down to look at the river. It's shallow at the edge. Even from here, I can see tadpoles zipping back and forth. She's gonna go nuts.

He starts digging in the basket. "He lives a few counties over."

"I figured you were the oldest."

"Why's that?" He snaps a thick flannel blanket a few times before he spreads it out. I stay where I am. The grass is nice.

"You act like an oldest."

"Responsible?"

"Bossy."

"Woman, you haven't seen bossy, yet." He grins, his eyes crinkle, and my belly flips. Stupid belly. "Come sit on this blanket."

"It looks scratchy."

"It's not."

"I'm fine where I am."

"Okay, then." He reaches in the basket and takes out sandwiches and three bottled waters. Then he reaches deeper and takes out two plastic containers. I didn't see him pack those. "If you stay all the way over there, you won't get any of these."

He pops the lids. There are chocolate-covered strawberries in one and slices of red watermelon in the other. Red, not pink.

Mia notices what's going on, and she dashes over. She sees those strawberries, and her eyes nearly eat up her face.

"Whoa. You need hand sanitizer." I rummage in my purse. "Come over here."

She's kneeling on the blanket, though, marveling over the strawberries. She's not crazy for chocolate, but she's human. And huge dipped strawberries? She's in heaven.

I huff a sigh and haul myself over to the blanket. "Hands." She shoves them at me, and I give her a squirt.

I look to Kellum. He cups his palms. I give him a squirt, too.

Mia grabs a strawberry in each hand.

Chapter 12

"Should we have her eat a sandwich first?" Kellum asks.

"You think you can stop her?" As I answer, she's gobbling a strawberry whole, chocolate smeared around her mouth.

"I bought them for you. From that French store on Main Street."

I know the one, but I've never been inside. I thought it only sold table clothes and soap. "Thank you."

I reach out and snag the watermelon container, dragging it closer. Kellum tracks me.

"I should make you eat your sandwich first," he says.

"Too late." I've sunk my teeth into a slice. Juice dribbles down my chin. It's super sweet and the tiniest bit grainy, just like I like it. I moan.

Kellum's throat bobs. He's sitting with his legs straight, bracing himself with his hands. He's very casual. Crisp white T-shirt with a construction company logo and his boardshorts.

His biceps are in sharp relief, though, and the cotton of his shirt clings to his sculpted shoulders. His shorts are tight across his thighs.

He's kicked his shoes off. Even his feet look strong.

I don't know how feet can look strong, but his do.

He unwraps a sandwich. "Did I make these for nothing?" he asks.

"We'll get to them."

I finish nibbling the rind. Delicious.

Mia's eaten half the box of strawberries, and she shows no sign of stopping. She'll make herself sick.

"Last one," I say.

I try to be a good model and take a sandwich. It's ham. Not my favorite, but I'll eat it. I keep half and pass Mia the rest. "Finish this and you can have one more after."

I'm not sure what gets the nastier look: the sandwich or me.

Bargaining doesn't work as well with Mia as I've seen it work with other kids. She knows her own mind and sees no reason to change it. I'm lucky that her particularities aren't usually hills I'll die on. If she wants to play with her critters for hours or wander around the backyard poking bushes with sticks, it's no skin off my teeth. She's gonna eat this sandwich, though.

She scrunches her face. She intends to look mean, but she only manages to look like a sad, wrinkly puppy. I keep my expression bland. She takes a long-suffering bite of ham sandwich.

Kellum chuckles softly. The sound sets off prickles dancing across my skin.

I focus on my sandwich, and when it's done, I help myself to some more watermelon.

Mia polishes off her dessert strawberry and hops up to go exploring again. I don't think Kellum has any idea how long Mia can be entertained by critter watching. There's a real danger that she'll have a meltdown when it's time to leave, even if we stay for hours.

"After we let our food settle, we can go for a swim." He stows our wrappers and the Tupperware in the basket.

"Mia and I can't swim, but we could wade."

"You can't swim?"

"Nope." Where would we have learned? Can't swim in a marsh or a creek.

He's watching me. Like always. I lick my fingers, sticky from the watermelon. He sucks in a breath. My nipples bead into stiff points. I swallow hard.

"I'll teach you both."

"Okay." What are we talking about? Swimming.

Yeah, Mia should learn. I know it's important. And swimming now wouldn't be at all like the night at the bonfire.

Mia's here. This is different. And I don't need to dwell on memories. Now is okay. Better, in a way.

The awful feeling that filled me earlier has worn away until it's only a faint, bitter aftertaste. I stretch my legs and flex my feet. The river burbles in the shallows by the edge, and somewhere nearby, a woodpecker's having a go at a tree trunk.

Mia squats at the edge of the river, poking stick in hand.

I lean back on my elbows and stare up through the willow branches. They sway lazily, the delicate leaves fluttering in the slightest breeze. A few leaves are constantly being blown loose, even though it's nowhere near fall, and they drift down slowly, floating on currents too gentle to feel against your skin. It's pretty. Like slow motion confetti.

On the other side of the basket, Kellum leans back, too.

"What are you looking at?" he asks.

"Same thing you are."

He lowers himself to lie flat and turns on his side to face me, propping his head in a hand.

I lower myself to lie on my back, too, resting my hands over my squirmy, nervous belly.

"Not now, I'm not," he says.

I keep my gaze trained in the treetop. "Why are you always looking at me?"

"Because you're beautiful." He doesn't miss a beat.

"You're full of crap."

"It's the truth."

I slide him a glance. His face is relaxed. His blue eyes are sparkling.

He doesn't strike me as the sweet-talking type, but I guess he picked it up somewhere.

"Don't bullshit me under this lovely tree when I'm full of delicious watermelon. That's just wrong."

"I would never bullshit you under this tree."

"Well, good."

He breathes out, and there's a pause before he speaks. "I'm always looking at you because you're beautiful and because I'm terrified I'm going to fuck this up."

My throat tightens. "I'm not going to take Mia away."

"I know. That's not what I mean."

He falls silent.

I should leave it. We've salvaged the day. No need to make it heavy.

Still, I ask, "What do you mean, then?"

Despite the blanket, the ground is hard on my back. I bend my knees, keeping them pressed together.

"You know. You feel it, too."

I turn my head to face him. The blanket is scratchy against my cheek. Feelings swirl in my belly and chest, and damned if I know what they are. My eyes prickle. I'm happy I'm lying down, and I don't have to figure out what to do with my body.

"Feel what?" I ask.

"Why were you upset when we got here?"

"Why are you changing the subject?"

"Humor me." His eyes bore into mine. It's too much. It makes my breath come shallow, but I can't break contact.

I don't want to.

"The bonfire site is trashed," I say.

I gnaw on the inside of my cheek. He waits.

"Well, did you want to rub it in my face? It's all trashed. It's trashy. What we did was trashy. I was trashy." I blink quickly until my nose stops tickling.

It takes me a few seconds to notice his expression. It's stormy. There's no other way to put it.

"Don't say that. Ever again."

"Well, it was."

"Until I met Mia, it was the best memory of my life."

I mean to laugh, but it comes out a strangled, bitter croak.

"Do you know how many times I've thought about that night?" His gaze breaks from mine and he raises his eyes to the treetops. "I was a married man. I knew it was wrong. I tried not to. Still." His eyes find mine again. "I've never been able to stop thinking about you."

"Why?"

"You know."

"I don't."

He sighs, frustrated. "You remember that night?"

I could deny it. Say it's a blur. In a way, it was. But not 'cause I was drunk or my memory's failed me. It's because I've wandered back to it so often in my head and then yanked my thoughts away, I've turned it into mush in my brain.

"What do you remember?" he presses.

"I don't know. We danced."

He smiles. Shivers fly across my skin.

I go on. "You asked me if I wanted to see the moon."

He chuckles, deep. "That was an awful line."

I press my lips to stop myself from grinning. "It was. I went anyway."

"It was so hard to wait to kiss you."

A pang of shame cuts through the riot going on in my body. "Why didn't you kiss me by the bonfire then? In front of everyone?"

"I needed you alone. It wasn't going to be just a kiss."

"How did you know?"

Because I was dressed in that skintight skirt I borrowed from Pandy? Because of how I must have looked at him? Like he was famous, and I'd do anything with him?

"Same way I know now," he says.

"I don't understand."

"Hell, Shay. I don't either." He reaches for me, but stops short, leaving his hand on the blanket, resting a few inches from my side. We're not that far apart. Two feet maybe. I can smell his soap. "But it's real. Back then, I—I had these ideas about what was the right thing to do."

I shift. He reaches over and puts his hand on top mine as if to hold me still.

He opens his mouth as if he's going to make a confession, but he seems to get stuck. Finally, he simply says, "I had the wrong ideas."

I don't understand him, but I'm too scared to ask. I'm walking on a balance beam, dipping my toes on either side, lower and lower, fully expecting that I'll never make it to the end, but somehow, I keep going, and I don't fall.

This conversation feels like that. Like I'm holding my breath, somehow keeping my footing through nothing but dumb luck, and he's waiting for me, palm open, oblivious to the fact that I'm a hair's breadth away from tumbling over.

"I don't regret being with you," he says. "I regret everything after."

I close my eyes. His palm is warm on the top of my hand.

"Shay, I'll go on however long you need with you and Mia in the guestroom, but you belong in my bed."

"How can you say that? We hardly know each other."

He shrugs. Confident as always. As if it's obvious.

"What wrong ideas?" I ask.

His brow knits.

"What wrong ideas did you have?"

He's searching for words, but I cut him off. "'Cause it seems to me if you had all these wrong ideas before, who's to say you don't have them now. This is all about doing the right thing, isn't it?"

I pause for breath. He opens his mouth, but he's not quick enough.

"You're the sheriff's deputy. You do the right thing, yeah? And playing house with the mother of your child probably feels pretty close to the right thing to you, doesn't it? Picnics and bikes and kissing me like you're my boyfriend."

My stomach knots. It's awful and mean, but it has the ring of truth.

"You don't have to make this something it's not, Kellum." I look back up into the branches. "You don't have to rewrite history so it fits with your white picket fence."

I expect him to move his hand. I ruined the moment. I feel like crap, but I'm not sorry.

He doesn't miss a beat. "Bullshit, Shay. This isn't about me doing the right thing."

"Yeah?" It comes out bitter.

"Yeah. 'Cause the things I want to do to you are very, very wrong."

Chapter 12

My cheeks flare. Anger. He can't make light of this. Not when I feel this way.

I snort. "That's an awful line."

"Shay." It's a command. My gaze finds his. He twines his fingers between mine, curving them until my palm is a fist. His blue eyes darken. He seems to be searching for something. Eventually, he says, "I want to come home now."

My brow knits.

He goes on. "I haven't wanted to come home in years. These past two weeks, I can't wait. It's Mia. And it's you. That's the truth." His jaw tightens. "I know you're not there. Yet. Ever. I don't know. But as long as you give me a shot, I'm taking it."

On the inside, I'm wobbling. Careening. Tumbling, scared as shit.

"Okay?" he prompts.

I screw my eyes tightly shut, listening to the river and the leaves flutter in the breeze.

"Okay," I say.

I'm not. I'm not, I'm not, I'm not. And I never have been.

But I want to be.

I want.

And for the first time since that night seven years ago, for a little while, I stop shoving everything down. I let go. I exhale.

~

LATER, Kellum spends an hour squatting next to Mia, looking at tadpoles. He catches her a crawfish, and she's in heaven.

She says, "Look at its antenna! It's wiggling." I store the words. *Antenna. Wiggling.*

He tries so hard to find her another one, but no luck. Eventually, he's drenched in sweat. Patches of his T-shirt and the bottoms of his boardshorts are wet, and his hair is mussed from him running wet fingers through it.

He looks happy. Younger. The authority he wears as naturally as his uniform is fading, and he's more like the boy I remember bolting down the football field on Friday nights, twisting and dodging, utterly self-assured but still joyous when he crossed into the end zone.

Everything is perfect when Kellum suggests we go swimming. It's getting hotter, even in the shade. Mia has to be roasting. I've slathered her in sunscreen three times, and now she looks like a wild thing, striped with dirt and smears of white.

She peeled off her clothes when we first arrived, so she's ready to go in her navy one-piece with the anchor.

I've got a decision to make. It's gonna suck getting these khaki shorts wet. We're definitely all alone. My tank top is relatively long. It would cover what it needs to. And my panties are black cotton.

I'm not getting my bra wet with river water. I don't have so many that I can be cavalier with the ones that fit.

While I'm debating, Kellum pulls his shirt off, two arms crossing overhead, biceps bunching like a lifeguard in a TV show. He's tanned. His chest is chiseled and covered with the same fine, dark hair as his legs. It's thicker on the ridge between his cut abs, and it disappears into his shorts at the button.

My fingers twitch.

He slides a glance at me from the corner of his eye. Then he stretches, all exaggerated, and his abs and his obliques ripple. He rests his hands on the back of his head. He's showing off. And grinning.

Sweet lord.

He knows exactly what he looks like.

I roll my eyes, turn my back, and shimmy my bra off under my shirt. Do I keep the khakis on? They're gonna chafe. Heck. Live dangerously. I drop my shorts, tugging down my top. It's stretchy, so it stays.

When I turn back to the river, Kellum has dropped the pose. He's staring at my body, making no show of hiding the fact. His eyes glint.

The devil gets in me. I stretch just like he did, arching my back.

My top rides up to my hip. I don't show any midriff or anything, but his gaze is glued on me, his playfulness gone, hands clenching like he needs to stop himself.

My heart pitters-patters. I toss my ponytail, hiding a smile as I sashay to the river's edge.

"Hey." He catches up to me in two strides and grabs my hand. We join Mia where she's crouched in the shallows, swirling her fingers in the water, watching the ripples. She doesn't pay either of us any mind.

"Mia?" Kellum offers her his free hand. She squints up at him. "Let's go wade in the river."

She immediately returns her attention to the water.

"I don't think she's interested." She gets like this when she's into something. She's definitely gonna have a meltdown when it's time to go.

"Come on, Mia," Kellum says, oblivious to the mulish cast of her jaw. "I'll be holding your hand."

Mia ignores him.

"Mia?"

Nothing.

His face falls. My heart aches for him. So far, Mia's treated him differently than anyone else, but this is more in keeping with her normal behavior. She lives in her own world, and she is set in her ways. She doesn't have a use for most people. It can hurt if you're expecting her to react like other kids.

"If we go out further, we could see some real fish." He tries again.

No reaction.

"I'll carry you. Want to piggyback?"

She squats down further, frowning.

"Why don't you want to go into the river, sweetheart? Are you scared?"

Silence.

Kellum glances down at me. I lift a shoulder.

"Come on, Mia. It'll be fun." He offers Mia his hand again. This time, she scoots away. Gives him her back. His face falls even more.

There's a twinge in my chest. Even I take it personally sometimes. It's hard not to.

"Come on." I tug him into the water. "She'll just have to miss out."

Thankfully, he comes with me, and I pick my way gingerly across the sharp rocks until the river bottom becomes silt, and it's soft and smooth. The water is cool, but not cold, and it's running fast enough that you feel it against your legs, but not strong enough to threaten your footing.

It's wonderful. I go deeper, step by step, until it's lapping the underside of my boobs. It hits Kellum at the hips where those V-shaped muscles disappear into his trunks.

I forget about Mia's recalcitrance, distracted by the water, until I glance up. Kellum's staring back at the bank, brows knitted together.

"She'll change her mind when she sees us having a good time," I say. It's a long shot, but it's possible.

He sighs. "She likes the water. Why doesn't she want to come out? Is she scared?"

We're far enough out that if we speak normally, she can't hear us over the river. Besides, she's oblivious, totally intent on whatever's caught her attention.

"She just wants to do what she wants to do."

He thinks for a long minute and then scrubs his face. "Dina is like that."

He squeezes my hand under the water, hesitating a second, and then asks, "Does she have an autism diagnosis?"

My belly knots.

Ugh.

He was going to ask. I've known it's coming. Still. Ugh.

I hardly ever talk about it.

Whenever we get back from the clinic, Mama always says, "Did you ask them about it?"

I always do. Of course, I do.

Mama will say, "Well?"

She'll huff impatiently as I tell her about the visit, and then she'll grunt and drop it when she realizes nothing's settled. She thinks I could get SSI benefits for Mia with a diagnosis. I don't think so.

And then, during IEP meetings, the school asks, "What does the pediatrician say?"

There isn't a pediatrician. There's whoever is working that day. And they say different things. Let's wait and see. They know a specialist who takes Medicaid; they'll talk to him and call me back. I should really switch to wholegrain, gluten-free carbohydrates.

There's no diagnosis.

And I don't really want one. Mia is Mia. She's not the easiest child, but I'm not a perfect mother, either.

I've always thought God made her just for me. I had nothing, and he gave me everything. The child best suited to me, and me to her. We both keep to ourselves. We're both quiet. We're both stubborn and serious.

If she loses her shit when the world gets to be too much, too loud and crazy? Maybe the world needs to settle down.

Maybe there's nothing wrong with her except people wanting something else. Something more like everyone else.

Kellum has turned us so we're both facing the bank. He's waiting patiently, watching Mia back on shore. The sun is at our backs, baking my arms.

I draw in a deep breath.

"No. But—" It's hard to sum it all up. "The doctors have mentioned it. They've given me checklists. A few times. Some things fit. Some don't. And the doctors change a lot."

And some of them are in a hurry, and there's no time. And some are so sure, and then the next one says, "Let's not rush to judgment."

Kellum tugs me closer until my side brushes his. He waits, listening.

"She doesn't do the flapping, but she lines things up. You've seen her. She'll make eye contact, but not a lot. She didn't talk until late, and—you know. She's quiet."

I draw myself up. "There's nothing wrong with her."

"No," he says. "She's perfect."

I glance up. He's intent on her, a soft smile playing at his lips. My shoulders relax.

He clears his throat. "Dina—Dina has a diagnosis."

"Autism?"

He nods. "The doctor says that before they made it a spectrum, what she has? It was called PDD-NOS." He takes a beat. "Pervasive Developmental Disorder – Not Otherwise Specified."

"Before? But not now?"

"Now it's under Autism Spectrum Disorder. So Dina will say she has ASD."

"She tells people?"

"Yeah. If she deigns to talk to them, and it comes up. Dina doesn't have use for many people."

"But she works on computers?"

"Yeah. Coding. She works from home."

"And she talks?"

"If she likes you."

"A lot? Or only sometimes?"

"If she likes you, you can't shut her up."

"She likes you?"

He grins sheepishly. "Yeah. She likes Jesse and me. She can't stand Cash, and he's her twin."

Cash was a dick in high school. I can't say I blame her.

Kellum squints, still watching Mia. "Dina would line things up, too. She had every kind of doll. The little ones with big heads. The plastic ones with big boobs. She's the only girl. Spoiled, you know?"

He smiles, and his eyes crinkle. I love his eyes. They're such a pretty shade. More blue than the sky even. They're Mia's eyes. The same shape and exact hue.

"Mom bought her all these clothes to dress them up in. Accessories, cars, kitchens. All Dina wanted to do was line them up."
That was a waste of money.
"She was raking the sand," I say.
"Raking the sand?"
"That's what I call it. 'Cause that's what it seems like to me when Mia lines up her critters. You know those little sand gardens with the little rakes? That people put on their desks?"
Mrs. Ellis, Mia's teacher, had one. That thing must get knocked over all the time, but I get why she needs it.
"Yeah. I know what you're talking about."
"That's how I see it when Mia's lining things up. She's getting her mind in order, putting everything back to rights. Raking the sand. At least that's what it seems like to me."
Kellum thinks on this a minute. "Is that what she's doing now? Raking the sand?"
"No. She's looking at tadpoles. That's pretty much her favorite thing. Observing critters."
I tighten my fingers. We're still holding hands under the water, and it's strange, but also okay. "Don't take offense. There's no human alive she likes better than an animal in its natural habitat."
"I'm second fiddle to a tadpole?"
"Humbling, isn't it?"
He chuckles. "That it is."
"Fair warning. She's going to have a meltdown when it's time to leave."
"What do we do?"
Warmth suffuses my chest. He says it so quick, without thought. *What do we do?*
"Roll with it."
"I guess I'd have a problem, too, if you tried to take me away from the thing I love most in the world."
I know what he's talking about, but the words still fall heavy.
I stare down at the river. It gently pushes and tugs my middle, rippling where it flows around us.

It's so peaceful that before I really make a decision, I say something that's been on my mind. "I'm sorry I didn't try harder."

He doesn't make me say for what. He understands that I mean telling him about Mia. We're really different, he and I, but in a weird way, we're on the same frequency.

"You were seventeen," he says.

He draws my hand closer to rest against his thigh. His voice drops lower. "Do you—"

He exhales, stiffens.

"What I did. You were a minor. Did it—" He struggles with the words.

My body floods with something hot and spikey—shame, panic, I don't know. I don't want him to say this, ruin it, make it dirty once and for all.

His voice is stern. "It was against the law. The corruption of a minor statute."

I want my hand back. I tug. He won't let go.

He draws in a steadying breath, plunging ahead. "I guess what I'm asking is did I hurt you?"

I don't want to talk about this.

But don't I owe him?

Pandy said I was her cousin, a hairdresser, and that was a lie. I didn't prompt her to tell it, but I didn't correct her. And didn't it feel like I was getting away with something when he asked me to dance? Didn't that mean I knew—on some level—I was in the wrong?

It's the least I can do. Be honest. It feels like stripping naked—an awful, public, naked. But doesn't he deserve answers?

He owes me, and I owe him, and it's one huge mess. How much worse can I make it by speaking the truth? It's been ruined all this time. Ever since he left me by the side of the river to go help that guy with his truck.

Did it hurt?

"Only at first. Not for long."

He sucks in a breath. "Shay?"

Chapter 12

I shrug.

His body has gone totally taut. "Shay, why'd it hurt at first?"

I keep my eyes trained on the bank. "Well, I hadn't done it before."

"Jesus," he says, ragged. "Shay, why didn't you say?"

I close my eyes. "You would have stopped."

"Damn straight I would have stopped." He drags his free hand through his damp hair. There's a thread of anger in his voice. "Why would you have let me do that?"

My pride is pricked, and my gaze flies up.

"Pandy lost hers in the Ready Mart men's room to the clerk who works nights. Angie back home lost hers in the loading dock."

I yank my fingers hard until he lets me take them back.

"Where'd you lose yours? A hotel suite at the Ritz?"

Shit. I bet he did. Prom night. Rose petals strewn across the bed. I bet it was picture perfect, and then he married her.

"The Riverside Inn."

I didn't think he'd actually answer. "Prom night?"

"Homecoming. Senior year."

"Congratulations. I hope it was everything you'd dreamed."

I'm going back to shore. I lunge forward, but as I do, Kellum grabs me around my waist. He lifts me, splashing, and settles me in front of him, so we're both facing the bank. He wraps his arms around me. There's no give. He's crazy strong, even when he's not trying.

"Not so fast, prickly pear."

I squirm, but he's not giving an inch.

"I want to go back."

"You want to avoid the conversation."

"Exactly."

When he chuckles this time, I feel the vibrations against my back. A shiver zips up my spine.

"I want to know why." He nips at the tip of my ear. I wriggle. Then I feel a hard poke right above my ass, and he smothers a groan. "Why did you let me, Shay?"

"I was curious."

"Bullshit."

"What do you want to hear, Kellum? What'll make you happy?"

"The truth. Always the truth."

He says that like it's the simplest thing in the world. Like I have no pride.

I make my body as rigid as a board.

"I don't owe you shit." With Mia, yes. With me? No.

"I guess you don't." He sighs, but he holds on tighter. "But I wish you'd let me in. I wish you'd trust me just a little bit more."

A little bit more. He knows I do. Trust him. Not much. But more than I trust anyone else ever so that little bit is huge, and out here in the middle of nowhere, no emergency in sight, I can admit it to myself: it's scary as hell.

It feels as dangerous as a fresh razor. You can cut yourself and not even know it until you're dripping blood down your leg.

I don't do dangerous. Or risks. Those are for folks who have a soft place to land when they fall flat on their face. I can't afford trust.

But it's not all or nothing, is it?

I let him take us to his house. That's been okay, so far. I let him get me on that horse. After the debacle with the lawyer, I told him what happened, and however he handled it, Mia and I have been left in peace. So far.

Even that night in the kitchen. I would have gone farther, but he stopped. And I don't think it was because he was ashamed to be hot for me, or whatever garbage thoughts my low self-esteem was peddling. I think he stopped for the reason he said. He wanted to do it right. His version of right.

He wanted my trust.

I could give him a little more.

It wouldn't be much in the long run. He couldn't use it against me in any kind of concrete way. It'd only cost me pride, and so many things do. I'm used to paying.

Chapter 12

I cough, clearing my throat.

"Well, I had a crush on you."

He retightens his grip. He's surprised. "You did?" I can hear the smile in his voice. It softens me all over.

"Yeah."

"You knew me?"

"Everyone knew you. You were the star quarterback."

"You watched me play?"

"When I'd come up to visit my grandparents. They went to the games every Friday night. Religiously."

He rocks me against him. "Which games did you see?"

"The ones where you threw a ball to another guy at the end of the field."

He chuckles. "Fair enough." He tucks his chin into the crook of my neck, grazing me with his stubble, sending shivers zinging across my skin. "As soon as I saw you, I had a crush on you, too."

I snort and squirm. He presses a kiss to the place he's nuzzling.

"You were beautiful."

He rests the tip of his nose on my pulse point and inhales. "You *are* beautiful."

"You don't have to sweet-talk me."

He chuckles, and tingles fly. "Yes, I do."

"I don't take you seriously."

"Maybe not. But maybe you will one day."

"You're putting a lot of pressure on this, you know. You could—I don't know. Ease off."

I don't want him to. If he stopped holding me, if he stopped talking to me like this, my heart would slip under water and drown. But the words are almost automatic, almost like I have to test if he'll hold. If only in this moment for a little while.

"I'm not going to."

He says it with a hundred percent certainty, and damn, but I don't understand him at all.

"It's getting late." It's true. The trees are casting longer shadows on the river.

"You want to head home?" he asks.

"Yeah." I pull away, and finally he lets me go. "She's gonna have a meltdown."

"Maybe not."

Kellum smiles down at me, somehow happy, as we trudge through the water back to shore. He's a mystery, but when I smile back—small, polite—his face lights up and his blue eyes sparkle.

I did that. And damn if it doesn't feel like magic.

∼

MIA DOES, indeed, have a meltdown.

I give her thirty minutes and count down the time. While she studiously ignores us, Kellum repacks the basket, and I duck behind a tree to put on my change of clothes. When I come out, he's grinning my way. He couldn't have seen anything, but my belly still swirls.

I join Mia at the river's edge and give her a five-minute warning. She plops flat on her ass, digs her claws into the sand, and screws up her entire face.

I still give her the five minutes. Kellum has the good sense to hang back. He's fretting, but there's nothing you can do once she's set on her course.

I talk to her about how we're going to have dinner when we get home, and she can have the last of the chocolate-covered strawberries, and how tomorrow we'll have another day with Kellum. She's unmoved.

She makes her body so rigid that when time is up, and I have to lift her, she holds her shape. And then she starts flailing. She gets me good in the hip.

Kellum starts forward, but I shake my head. I've done this before. Transitions with Mia are hit-and-miss. You can do all the things they say—countdowns and simple directions and visual cues—and it can still go to shit. Or you can run out of time, say "get your shoes on," and it's fine.

With Mia, honestly, it's usually fine, but today has all the trappings of a meltdown. She's really into those tadpoles, she's overheated and tired, and she hasn't had one in a while. I swear she stores them up.

I manage to swing her so I've got her belly-to-belly, and all she can do is make herself stiff as a board and hard to haul. Tears are streaming down her reddened cheeks.

"We'll come back another day," I promise. I know it's not registering now, but I want her to know. If tadpoles are important to her, they're important to me.

She kicks her legs and loses a flip flop. Kellum ducks to scoop it up.

It's a long walk back to the car. Mia loses her oomph half way, but she finds her voice. She wails, wordless and brokenhearted.

"I know, baby," I whisper in her ear.

Mama always takes me to task when Mia has a meltdown. She says I coddle her. That I should whup her good just once when she kicks a fuss like this, and she won't do it again. Other people, too, will stare and judge. Spare the rod, spoil the child.

Is that what Kellum's thinking as I wrestle Mia along, and he trails behind us?

You can't beat what a person is out of them. Well, you can try, but that's evil as hell.

Mia's not a brat. She picks up after herself. She does what she's told. But when she gets into something that speaks to her, it's like she rearranges the whole world. That thing—watching tadpoles or lining up critters or whatever—becomes the tent pole holding up everything in her world.

Life is fine and wonderful, and then I come in and say, "In five minutes, I'm gonna yank this pole and pull everything out from under you, turn your day topsy-turvy, and most likely also loud and unpleasant, and there is not a damn thing you can do. Five minutes."

And folks want me to whup her on top of that when she doesn't act with perfect grace? No. I give her time to mourn the way she wants. Folks can get bent.

By the time we get to the truck, she's dangling listless in my arms, and my biceps are burning. Kellum opens the back door, and I slide her into her car seat. He sticks the basket beside her and opens my door.

I finally take a peek at his expression.

If he's judging, I'm gonna tell him where to get off.

He's smiling. He gently rubs my thigh where a bruise has already blossomed. "She got you good back there."

"I'll live."

"I could have carried her."

"I'm used to it."

"My skin is thicker. You should let me next time."

Next time? Yeah, there will be a next time. My eyes prickle. I shake off his gentle hands and hoist myself into the passenger seat.

"Maybe," I say, over my shoulder.

He shuts both our doors after checking that I've got my feet all the way in. I feel like a princess, which is stupid, but it also warms something inside my chest that has been thawing for a little bit now.

It's like I had a muscle all clenched tight, and it's loosening, and now there's movement inside me that I'm not used to, and it's distracting, and terrifying, and fascinating, and it's all mixed up somehow with this man in the seat beside me, his elbow propped on his rolled down window, sunglasses on, the wind ruffling his hair.

He's as handsome a man as you'd ever see in real life. That's pure fact. He's not bodybuilder stacked, but every one of his muscles is honed. His veined forearm as he grips the steering wheel. His thigh as he shifts.

He glances over and tucks a piece of hair that was whipping my cheek behind my ear.

"Want the air on?"

I shake my head. I like the windows down. It's past five o'clock now, and there's the slightest hint of cool.

In the back seat, Mia is already zonked out, her head lolling to one side. She'll be cranky when she wakes up. She always is if she naps late in the day.

We drive in silence to the turnoff onto the main road, past fields of tall corn, and almost all the way home. I take in the scenery. With his sunglasses hiding his eyes, I didn't realize Kellum was lost in thought.

He clears his throat as we drive past town. "Was it a terrible day, then?"

His gaze is on my face, but I can't see his eyes. "What do you mean?"

"You didn't like it at first. We didn't swim. Mia's meltdown. I should have taken you somewhere else. Cash's cabin up on the mountain."

He firms his jaw, returning his gaze to the road.

He's really bothered. That thing in my chest softens even more. "We can't swim."

His temple tics. Shit. I'm not saying it right. And it matters. To him. To this perfect man in this fancy truck. It matters if Mia and I had a good day.

"Mia loved the tadpoles and the strawberries."

He gives a short nod. Like he thinks I'm placating him.

"I loved the watermelon."

He nods again.

"And wading in the river."

He manages a wry smile. Damn. It does sound like I'm humoring him.

I exhale, and I unclick my seatbelt. His gaze darts down. "Shay?"

But I'm quick. I lean over, steal my own kiss, and I'm back in my seat in a split second.

His smile cracks his face wide open. I wish I could see his eyes. "What was that for?"

"You know."

"Was it for taking you on a mediocre picnic?"

"And then fussing about it afterwards."

"Stick with me, kid. I'm a hot date."

"I'm not going anywhere," I say, offhand.

He eases into a four-way stop, and then he's grasping me by the back of the neck, and he's unbuckled, leaning over, taking my mouth, plunging his tongue past my lips, owning me, letting me feel how much raw strength there is behind his reserve and restraint. Heat floods my core.

It's over in seconds.

We're both breathless when he accelerates.

"Damn straight, you're not," he says.

We finish the ride in silence.

It's been a long day, and my mind is slow and dull from the heat, but my body is a live wire. When we pull up to the house, I don't wait for Kellum to come around. I jump out and stick my head in the back, trying to wake Mia.

She's out like a light.

"Let me." Kellum hands me the basket, and he unstraps her and gathers her to his chest. He leads the way. I follow, digging the keys from his pocket when we get to the front door.

The sun won't set for another hour or so, but the shadows from the maple trees in the front yard are getting long.

When we get inside, Mia finally stirs. Kellum sets her down so gently in the foyer, and she scrubs her eyes with her fists, glaring around, pissed at the world for existing, until she decides to set off upstairs, most likely to find her critters.

"We should start dinner," he says.

"I'll make it." I need to do something with my hands.

We both head into the kitchen, and we're like bumper cars. He's unpacking the basket. I'm rummaging around to see what I can whip up with the least amount of fuss. He reaches past me into a cabinet. I brush against him as I open the fridge.

Chapter 12

I don't think he minds. I think he's getting in my way on purpose.

I settle on reheating some tortellini I made last night. I cut some lettuce and tomatoes for a salad and heat some rolls. It takes fifteen minutes.

Kellum's done, but he hangs out, watching me. He offers to help, but it's a one-person job.

He's making me nervous.

I rinse the tomatoes and the cool water rushes over my fingers, and because he's watching, I can *feel* it. I'm feeling everything.

I take down plates from a high cabinet, stretching my spine, and my breasts lift, and because he's propped against the kitchen table, phone in his hands but his eyes on me, I'm a hundred percent aware of my body—the sway of my back, the tightening of my nipples.

He's driving me nuts.

But I don't want him to stop.

After I set the table and call Mia down—three times—we sit and eat. Kellum talks. He tells Mia about catching crawdads with his older brother John and younger brother Cash. John had a knack for finding them, but Cash had no patience, so he'd always go in too quickly, lose the critter, pitch a fit, and stomp his feet, scaring the rest away. Sounds like the guy I knew in high school.

Mia listens, patiently, yawning in between bites. It's going to be an early night; she's tired and ready for bed.

I don't want to go to bed.

I'm the opposite of tired. Restless. Antsy. But Mia actually lays her cheek on the table when she finishes.

"I'll clean up," Kellum offers, smiling at sleepy Mia, grazing fingers across her matted hair. She's gonna fight me so hard when I hose her down in the tub, but she is not going to sleep this grubby, not sharing my sheets.

"Thanks." I start for upstairs. "Coming my way?" I ask Mia when she doesn't follow.

Mia shakes herself off, drags herself up, and stumbles after me. You have to give her space when she's at her limit like this.

Upstairs, I run the bath water and pray. She peels off her clothes and climbs in, squats in the tub, and scrunches her eyes closed while I give her a once over. It's my lucky day because she covers her face with a washcloth and cranes her head way back without me asking. I shampoo and rinse her hair as quick as I can. This is normally a source of great consternation.

She must be absolutely exhausted. She doesn't even pet the feet of the clawfoot tub like she usually does.

She lets me dry her, but she sways against me as I comb her hair. All tuckered out. I help her into her pajamas and under the covers. She rolls onto her tummy and falls straight to sleep.

A rush of warmth fills my chest. This is a good day.

We're well fed. The air is cool. The house is clean and quiet. Mia's tired, but she's okay, and we have a big, soft bed. Nothing is looming. Nothing urgent needs figuring out.

And there's Kellum.

Kellum, who thinks nothing of all of this luxury, so he buys bikes and chocolate-covered strawberries and takes us on day trips.

Kellum whose heavy tread is on the stairs.

Usually, after Mia falls asleep, I sit in the rocking chair by the window for a bit, flipping through craft books from the library, or watching the stars come out over Stonecut Mountain. I worry about what I need to do next—apply for jobs, figure out a car.

Kellum heads to his office after dinner to finish work. I don't usually hear him come to bed.

But tonight, I hear him. There's no rush in his steps.

He's here. Close. And I'm not tired at all.

I don't even think. I hurry out of the room on my tiptoes, easing the door shut behind me.

Kellum's at the end of the hall. His eyes were on my door. They come alive when he see me, the blue piercing the shadows. He reaches out a hand.

Chapter 12

I don't walk. I run.

I hit him, and he goes oof, and he wraps an arm around me, firmly, under my butt, lifting me, pressing me to his chest, and his other hand is scrambling at the knob behind him.

We're breathless.

This is where I want to be.

He kisses me, demanding, hungry. I open, let him in, moan as the taste of him floods my mouth.

We're through the door.

We're kissing, drowning, devouring each other, but in between, we're frantic. My top. His pants. My shorts. His shirt. His boxers.

There's no time to touch, only move. He palms my breast, fingers digging into my ass. I propel him back to the bed. He's too tall. I can't reach what I want.

"Shay," he gasps, falling back, drawing me on top of him, and now, *this* is how I want it.

He's hard. His skin is burning. Everywhere he touches me, I'm on fire, and somehow he knows how to stoke everything hotter.

I'm straddling him, but he's lifting himself to kiss me, and his crunched abs are rock solid, the plane of his chest hot and hard against my aching nipples.

He's got my hips, and he's urging me to grind down against his cock. He's thick. Long. My panties are still on, but they're wet and wedged between my pussy lips. His heat seeps through, and the pressure when he rocks, it feels so good, better with every stroke, and if he stops, I'll die, and if I don't get more, I'll die.

If he hesitates, I'll fall apart here, drop into a black hole, my heart crushed. I know it. The danger is there. Instinctual because my brain isn't thinking—it's feeling.

Panic swells, but it's too mixed up in his hands, his body, his spicy scent, and his raspy urging.

"That's right, baby. Oh, yeah. Oh, fuck yeah. Shay, don't stop. Don't stop."

He hooks his thumbs in my panties, tries to drag them down, but that would mean I'd have to draw away, and I don't want to.

We're kissing, lost in each other, our tongues twining, our arms winding, holding on, mine around his neck, his around my waist.

It's so *good*.

He growls, and we're flipping. I'm under him. He's pushed up over me, the kiss broken, and we're gasping for air, and he's looking down, stock still. Why's he not moving?

No. I want more.

I reach for him. He grabs my forearms, pins them over my head, but gently, fingertips stroking the soft skin of my inner wrist, and I shiver everywhere.

"Beautiful," he murmurs. "Stay." He means leave my arms where they are.

He means let him.

My body kicks up to another level. The wanting is still there, throbbing, demanding, but my flushed skin is also cool and waiting, and the anticipation has prickles, sensations all its own.

What's he going to do? It's going to feel good. I *know* it.

He drags my panties down. He eases my knees apart. He looks.

My pussy clenches on air.

I whimper. He strokes my belly. Reassures me. And he's still looking.

His stiff cock bobs, veined and purple.

And his gaze dips back to my face, and he smiles. "You're so fucking beautiful."

I flush hotter.

He means it. He wants me as much as I want him.

"We're gonna do this, yeah?" He's smiling.

"Yeah," I breathe.

He leans over, notching his cock between my legs. He's hot against my entrance. He drags higher, lathing my clit with the velvet of his skin and the hot precum beaded at his tip.

He's panting. My chest is rising and falling fast, too, and our eyes are locked. His blue has almost been eaten up by the black of his pupils.

He pushes in. There's a pinch. It's tight. I whimper.

His brow furrows. He was thrusting in, but now he slows down. He smooths the hair from my face. "Okay?"

Yes. He's filling me. Testing my walls. It's a good pinch. An amazing tightness.

"More," I growl.

"More," he repeats, groaning in victory, sliding home.

I have no choice but to open for him. My knees fall wide. I grab weakly at his shoulders. All I can do is hold on. He drives into me, stroking my pussy, hitting an angle that cranks the dial, and now I'm nothing but a wave rising higher and higher, about to crest, so close to cresting, and he's doing this to me, he's making me feel so, so good.

I whine.

"You gonna cum for me, baby?" he murmurs in my ear.

He's sweating, thrusting hard and fast with perfect control, and he's watching me, a hundred percent tuned in. I know because when my gaze focuses, he's always right there.

This is for me, but he loves it. His muscles are straining; his face is etched with restraint.

I want to pop the bubble. I want to see him go flying. Like I am.

"Cum in my pussy, Kellum," I pant. I don't know where it comes from, but I know before I say it that it'll do the trick.

He lets out a strangled shout, gone, tipped over, and heat fills me, sending me over the edge, too, tumbling, pure pleasure exploding from my center and sweeping out to the very tips of my fingers and toes.

I collapse, limp, sinking into the mattress. I was right. I feel so, so, so good.

I can't help it. I giggle.

Kellum looms over me, chest heaving, and he's still smiling. Bashful. Beautiful.

He bends, nips my neck, and drops a kiss on my swollen lips.

He's inside me. Still pulsing a little. I'm sticky. Wet. We didn't use a condom.

"I'm on the pill. For cramps and PMS." He doesn't seem worried, but it's not like we ever talked about it.

"Okay. Good. Yeah." His face scrunches. I don't think he thought about protection, not until now. "I guess we should have talked about that."

"Probably."

"I got carried away," he says, rueful, but not sorry.

"Me, too."

He kisses me again, taking longer this time, going slower. He softens a little inside me.

We're so close. Our faces. Our bodies.

I've never been this close to any other person in my life. I've never *let* anyone get this close. It's so strange. I can smell his powder fresh deodorant. And I can see where he nicked under his chin when he shaved.

He's so superhumanly handsome that until you're this close, you miss the human things. He has a silver filling in a back molar. His left eyebrow has a swoop to it that the right doesn't have.

Now we're staring at each other.

My face heats. Is he categorizing all my weirdness, too?

He tugs me, resettling us on our sides, belly-to-belly. He strokes my back. I rest my cheek on my upper arm.

"Are you okay?" he asks.

I murmur yes.

He coughs, clearing his throat. "Was—was this okay?"

My lips quirk. "It was all right."

His arm firms around my waist, molding me to him. His cock twitches. "All right?"

I shrug. "Nice."

"Nice." He sighs. "I guess we're going to have to go again, then."

"Yeah?"

I'm a limp noodle, but he's already kissing me again, draping my leg over his hip, his cock hardening against my tender pussy. The wanting perks up inside me.

He wraps my arms around his neck and slides me onto my back.

"Hold on, Shay."

"Yes," I exhale as he teases my clit with his finger and slides inside me where I want him, where he's supposed to be. Where he belongs.

He fits so well it's terrifying.

13

KELLUM

I don't want to leave her. I don't want to leave this bed.
And to go hunt coyotes and confront my uncle? Not nearly a good enough reason to untangle myself from Shay's slim limbs and soft skin.

Since last weekend, Shay comes to me at night, but she makes sure she's back in her room with Mia well before sunrise. I don't know how she wakes up without an alarm, but she does.

She's sleeping now. It's almost three in the morning. I'm supposed to meet everyone up at the Lodge at four. Coyotes howl at dawn and dusk, and if we want a bead on them, we need to be out and listening.

There's no part of me that wants to be anywhere but here.

Shay sleeps on her side, facing the room. She's not a natural cuddler. I wait until she drowses off and then I gather her up. After a while, she kind of melts, and then she starts snoring softly. Even asleep, she's got walls.

Not when I'm inside her, though. Not when my tongue's in her pussy. She's wild then. Demanding. Like I have what she wants, and she's taking it, and I can come along or not, it's all the same to her. I fucking love it.

Almost as soon as she comes, she bricks herself off again, but

Chapter 13

for a few moments, she looks at me with round eyes as if I hung the moon.

I'd hang the moon for her.

But at the moment, she doesn't want anything but my body. She's been talking about places she can apply for a job. Places that don't require a high school diploma. I'll be damned if she's working late shifts at the Laundorama or the Ready Mart.

I tighten my grip and draw her tighter. Dad could find her something to do on the farm. Helping Bill with paperwork. There are a lot of other folks I could ask for a favor—a few of the boutique owners are always looking for part-time help, and bitching about how high school kids don't want jobs anymore—but she wouldn't like me interfering. She'd see it that way. Interference, not help.

The woman has more pride than anyone I've ever known. I love her pride. I love when she lets it down for me.

I kiss her neck and inhale her scent—sex and shampoo and the body wash she bought from the grocery because it was on sale. It's peach-scented supposedly, but it's a powerful smell, less peach and more like a man in a lab was told to make it smell like fruit. Unspecified.

It's my favorite smell. It's on my sheets. In my truck. Everywhere.

I sigh and stroke her belly. She's not a deep sleeper. She's gonna wake up. I'm not sorry. I want to see her brown eyes before I go. I want to find out if she decided what she and Mia are doing today.

This hunt has always been on the calendar. We go after the coyotes once per season, always have since my grandfather's day. He said in his grandfather's time there were gray wolves, but when folks over-hunted them, the coyotes moved in. They harass the horses. Go after the dogs.

Really, it's a chance for us to get together and get outside. Test out new gear for deer season. I always look forward to the day.

Not this year. Van and I have a reckoning coming. He's gonna need to come to Jesus.

He will.

Shay and Mia are part of this family, now. Period. End of story. No more bullshit.

I stroke a sensitive spot, the divot at the base of her spine, and Shay whines, wriggling against me. She's naked. If I exhaust her, she passes out before she remembers to put her yoga pants and tank top back on. If she sleeps in clothes, I know I got to work a little harder.

"Hi," I whisper in her ear.

She makes a sleepy, indignant squeal and rocks her hips back, thrusting her tits forward. I palm them, tease the already hard nipple. She's already ready to go.

I lift her leg, prop it up in the crook of my arm. I test her slit with my cock. She's wet. Plump from last night.

She reaches back, grabs my cock with her slender fingers. Her grip is tight. I'm hard. I'm always hard for her.

She notches me in her pussy. The angle's not quite right. She mewls and wriggles.

I don't think she's even opened her eyes. I keep massaging her tits. It drives her crazy. She's writhing. Whining.

I slip my free hand between her legs and tease her clit. It's popped from its hood, stiff. I circle the bud, slow and steady, the way she likes. She's shaking. I readjust myself and slide home. She's sticky from last night. From me.

One day, I'm going to put another baby in her belly.

"How does that feel, baby?" I ask. I don't really need to. She's bucking her hips to take me deeper, moaning, her fingers digging in my forearm hard enough to leave nail marks.

"Good," she pants.

"Are you gonna cum on my cock?"

"Yes," she gasps, and she's already tightening around me like a vise and squeezing. My spine tingles, and I'm knocked off kilter by the power of my release, the waves of ecstasy, the satisfaction as I spend deep inside her. I'm left reeling like I am every single time with her.

She's so delicate in my arms. So beautiful.

She's trying to catch her breath, and she's keeping real still so the cum doesn't dribble out of her pussy on her side of the bed. She hates getting the sheets wet.

We're quiet for a moment as our heartbeats calm.

Eventually, she clears her throat. "You have to leave soon?"

"Yeah. In a minute."

I told her about the hunt last week. She made her face blank and said, "Poor coyotes." Then, she wouldn't talk about it.

"What are you and Mia going to do today?"

She's stiffening in my arms. I don't like it.

"I thought we'd take the truck. Go warn some coyotes to get gone."

I know she's joking, but my muscles still tense. "Don't go into the fields today. We'll probably be up north of the Lodge, but just stay close to the house or the barn. Okay?"

"I don't know. I figured Mia and me would dress up in little ears and tails and go frolic in the woods."

"Smartass." I slip out of her. She squeals and squeezes her thighs together.

"Kellum! Tissue!"

But my hand's already there, cupping her pussy. I spread the wet and sticky mess through her curls, over the C-section scar in her hairline, and then I circle her belly button until she's scrunched up and giggling.

"Be straight with me, woman."

"I don't know." She swats my hand away. "We'll probably go visit the horses. Do school."

Shay spends about an hour with Mia every day on workbooks, practicing math and handwriting. She tries to get her to read sight words aloud, but Mia's not inclined to participate most days, so Shay has come up with a thing where she puts words on one index card and pictures on another, and she has Mia match them.

Reminds me I have to pick up more index cards. She's used all the ones I had in my office.

Shay's an extraordinary mother.

My mom is great. She's the stereotype, the mama bear. Lives for her kids. PTA president, head of the Booster Club. Over indulgent. Blind to our faults. Especially Cash's.

Shay's different. She sees Mia very clearly. She worries about her deeply. But she's laser focused on making sure Mia is okay, and she's always pushing her a little farther—try the broccoli, now see if you can figure out this problem—but with a gentle touch. She doesn't get frustrated. She accepts Mia as she is.

Mom was always butting heads with Dina. Mom wanted her to go to sleepovers, do dressage, leave her damn room. Dina's more stubborn by half, though. She'd always win. Flat out refuse to leave the car or get on the horse. Mom would sulk and feel like a failure. I don't see that dynamic with Shay and Mia.

Shay rolls with the punches. And she's had a lot of punches to roll with.

I tug her closer, nibble on the sensitive nook where her shoulder and neck meet. I love it when she shivers and giggles.

I don't want to leave her and Mia today.

"I'll try to be back before you fall asleep."

She settles and sighs. "Okay."

She's drawing back from me. She's still letting me hold her, but she's gathering up her defenses, tucking herself away.

I sigh. "I need to go. I need to have some conversations."

"I said okay."

"I know you did." I brush another kiss across her shoulder, and she squirms, struggling to sit upright. I guess the moment's over.

She bends over and grabs her pants off the floor.

"I need to straighten things out. Once and for all."

She gives me her back and ducks to fish her shirt from under the bed. "I didn't say anything."

I chuckle. "You're saying all kinds of things."

She casts me a look over her shoulder, narrow-eyed. I grin. Her prickly doesn't faze me.

"I know me going bothers you. I'm telling you it shouldn't. I'm going to set things straight."

"It doesn't bother me. You're a free man."

"I am." I hook an arm around her waist and tug her back. She's made herself as stiff as a mannequin. "And I'm not gonna live forever with my families at odds."

"Families?" Her voice is laced with suspicion.

"My folks and you and Mia. My families. Mia is going to have doting grandparents and uncles and aunts and cousins. That's happening for her. This shit is not so far gone that it cannot be rectified."

We haven't talked about it since the lawyer. I know how Shay sees my family, and I know they've given her every reason. But these are the people who raised me. They're good people who made mistakes. I also know I have no reason to ask Shay to give them a chance, but they can ask for themselves.

Mom calls every day with a different excuse. Can she bring Mia my old toy chest? Would Shay want some canned pears? I can hear Dad in the background, hollering, "Ask if she has a bike. I can run into town later."

I don't put that on Shay. I say no. Later. Give us space.

Mia will have a family, though. She's not less than. She's going to have big Thanksgivings at the kid table and family cruises and folks trying to outdo each other at her birthday party. She's going to have what my nieces and nephews have, all that love.

I don't know how to explain that to Shay without hurting her.

She doesn't speak much about her past, but the best I can piece together is that she was raised by a single mom. No dad in the picture. No aunts or uncles nearby. She doesn't talk about friends. I've got her set up with a new phone on my plan, but she doesn't use it much. No social media or phone calls.

She keeps to herself, which is fine by me because it's my natural inclination, too.

You need a family, though. Even when they fuck up as bad as

mine. You need back-up in life. Mia deserves that.

Shay deserves that.

She hasn't responded to me. I can't tell if she's mulling it over, or if she's blocking me out behind her high walls. I tighten my grip around her waist.

"I'm going to make it right."

"They tried to buy me off."

My chest constricts. "It was Van. You have to understand about him." I search for the words. It's not forgivable, but if you know the man, it's...fathomable. "It's money with him. There was a time— My grandfather mortgaged the farm. Put it all on a stud. Patterson's Revenge."

"That's the name of a horse?"

She hasn't relaxed, but she's listening. She's accepting my arm.

"I know. There was a story behind it. I've forgotten. Anyway, the horse was a full-blood brother to a Derby winner. He had an injury early on, but when he was young, there was talk of a Triple Crown. At the time, there was only this house. The old barn. The fees would have put us on the map."

I pause. She's still listening. Her fingers are resting lightly on my forearm.

"Patterson, uh, got into some leaves he shouldn't have. Red oak. He died."

"Van killed the horse?"

"No. That was on the old barn manager's watch. Anyway, my grandfather was ruined. He was going to have to sell the farm."

"'Cause a horse ate some bad leaves?" Her eyebrow quirks.

I lift a shoulder. The way the story's told at the dinner table is that Grandpa took a bold risk—noble, even—and fate dealt him a dirty hand. Shay doesn't seem to see it that way.

I go on. "Van was in college. He'd been day trading with his allowance. Teaching himself. He convinced my grandfather to liquidate what was left of his savings. He dropped out of school and played the market. He was good at it. He saved the farm."

That's what earned my father's respect. Dad is a self-made

man. He busted his ass learning the horse business. He got a leg up when he married the boss's daughter, but he's never shirked from a hard day's work.

On the surface, he and Van have nothing in common but Mom and the farm. They're as close as brothers, though. Dad respects what Van did to protect the family. Van could have gone his own way, but he didn't. He was loyal. That means something to Dad, and it means something to me. Even now.

"Van has the wrong idea that you're going to try to take from the family. He doesn't get it. He will."

I can feel Shay's muscles tense under my forearm. She presses forward, and I have to let her go. She stands, yanking down the hem of her top. It was the wrong thing to say.

Her mouth is open like she's searching for words, and they're failing her. I sit up. Raise my hands. It was not my intention to start shit.

"Van doesn't know who you are," I try again. "I'm going to make it clear. It's gonna be settled."

"He doesn't know who I am," she repeats, her voice tight. Pissed. "See, I disagree. He knows exactly who I am. That's why he tried what he tried."

"You don't get it. He sees it as the family versus the rest of the world. He is going to understand that you and Mia are family."

She jerks her head, side to side. "No, you don't get it. It's not *versus*. It's *above*."

"What does that mean?" I stand. My blood's flowing, but I'm not angry. Not at her. At the situation, yes. She takes a step back.

She sniffs and shakes her head; her walls are all the way back up. "It means go hunt your coyotes. Have a conversation. Clear things up. And when you come back—"

Her face is flushed. She's furious. It's not the time, but damn, my hands twitch to grab her. Throw her on the bed. Touch her until she lets me back in. Until she fucking *trusts* me again.

Her voice cracks. "When you come back, he's still gonna think Mia and I are trash. You can't change how people think."

She doesn't understand. She doesn't have a close family. How could she?

"Shay, I'm going to make this right."

Her eyes soften, and her lips curve down before she fixes her tough, hardened mask.

"Kellum, I'm sorry. You can't."

She turns and leaves, and I don't go after her. She's not going to believe me because I say so. But she's wrong. I know these people, and in time, she will, too. She'll learn to trust. It's a matter of time and patience.

And I'm a patient man.

~

WHEN I ROLL up to the Lodge, everyone's there, including Mom. She's in her robe, but she's made cinnamon rolls and a plate of bacon. Bacon's mostly gone.

Dad and Van are leaning against the tailgate, sipping from thermoses. The air is damp and hazy gray, but the sun will burn that off in an hour once it rises past the mountain.

Cash is squatting, testing his calls. Between his ranger work up in Stonecut Mountain and his hunting guide work during deer season, he's got more gear than any man should.

"You calling 'em here so they can get themselves cinnamon rolls," I ask, swatting the back of his head.

He half-assedly swings at me and misses. "Nice of you to show up."

I kiss Mom on the cheek, and she passes me a roll on a plate. "Smells good."

Dad clasps my back, and Van gives me a deliberate nod.

"Jesse says go without him," Dad says. "He's up with that new mare."

If it wasn't that, Jesse would've come up with another excuse. He can hunt, but it goes against the grain for him.

I look around. My cousin Branch is in the cab of the truck,

scrolling on his phone. He looks less than thrilled to be up this early.

"Where's West?"

"He chose to stay at his mother's this week. To get ready for school." Van's face is tight.

West's mother was Aunt Rachel, Van's first wife. She had no problem stepping to him. She fought him hard during the divorce. She ended up with fifty-fifty custody and alimony.

Branch's mother was much less assertive. They were together for a decade, but Van never married her. She lives out in Aspen now, I think. Branch lives with Van full time.

There was some overlap. West is six months older than Branch. They're both eighteen now. I guess West, at least, is making his own decisions. There is no way Branch wants to be up this early. At eighteen, honestly, I was here out of duty. Cash was the one waking up extra early to make sure we didn't miss any dawn calls.

"Hear anything?"

Cash waves at the woods to the north. "Same place as before. I might set some traps. They're almost to the property line."

"Too smart for traps," Dad opines.

"Not my traps." Cash stands, hoisting his pack.

"Snare wire won't hold a coyote if you give him time to figure it out." Van moves toward the driver's side. His truck. He drives.

"Fuck snares. Catch and release." Cash hops into the bed, offering Dad a hand up. I clamber up behind him and shut the gate.

"Where you gonna release a coyote around here?" As deputy, my interest is piqued.

"Not around here. I'll drive him up the mountain."

Sometimes Cash is oddly decent.

"Stick him in Briceson's garage," he goes on. "Little present." Cash snorts a laugh at his own cleverness.

"You're an asshole."

Cash shrugs. "Yet Briceson loves me anyway."

"He's the only one."

"Sad, but true."

It's unclear how Cash met Briceson Carroll. They're the same age, but the Carrolls homeschooled, if you can call it that. Every weekend, though, Cash would want to go up to the mountain. Dad and Van taught us to hunt—shoot a deer and take it to Miller Meats for processing and Lou Ingle for taxidermy—but the Carrolls taught him to skin and butcher and tan.

"How are the Carrolls?"

"Good."

"Everyone good on the mountain? Haven't gotten a call to go up there in a while."

It's an odd assortment up there. The Carrolls, whose people have been there since Civil War times when they migrated up from Georgia and settled in their hollow.

There's a religious group. A cult, some would call them. Or a hippie commune. It's not clear. Del says all they do is grow weed and sell crafts on the internet, so leave them be. And there are a few vets who threw in together on a parcel of land on the north-facing side.

Calls generally come from weekend warriors with hunting cabins who get nervous when they run into the kind of folks they aren't expecting to see in the woods.

"Folks are fine, far as I can tell."

Van puts the truck in gear, and we all get thrown a few inches. There's an access road a few miles up that'll get us close to where we've had luck before. The trek from there is short, but it's slow going since the terrain is thick with underbrush.

"How's your girls?" Dad calls out over the crunch of tires as we head down the drive.

My heart warms. My girls. Damn right.

"Good."

"Home sleeping, I guess." Dad hasn't pushed like Mom to meet Mia, but he's definitely curious. Hopefully, we settle shit today and move forward.

Chapter 13

"Mia was in bed when I left. Shay was up making coffee."

"So, you tapping that or what?" Cash calls out, smirking, confident he's out of range on the other side of the bed.

Dad reaches over and slaps him in the head.

"Obliged," I say.

"I raise you to talk like that?" Dad's pissed. Cash pushes his buttons like none other.

"It's just us." Cash makes an exaggerated show of rubbing his head.

"That makes it worse. That means you know it's wrong, so you wouldn't say it if it wasn't just us. Integrity, Cash. Jesus Christ." Dad shakes his head. "Where'd I go wrong?"

Cash's eyes glint. I see what he's thinking. He went wrong when he ran off the mother of my child.

I wasn't expecting to speak my piece, bumping around the back of a Ford, but it seems like now's the time.

"To be clear, Shay's the mother of my child." I point at Cash. "You let another foul word leave your mouth in relation to her, I'll knock your teeth out."

I turn to Dad. "And, yeah. Integrity. Jesus Christ."

Dad works his jaw. I bet he's got a plug in his cheek. Mom doesn't allow it, but when we go hunting, he lets himself off the chain.

"Son, I understand what I did." His eyes shine. "And trust that your mother will not let me forget for a moment."

"Did you know that Van had Don Prescott offer Shay three hundred fifty thousand to leave town?"

Cash whistles. Dad's face goes bright red under his gray beard. "He wouldn't."

I lift a shoulder.

We all know that's not true.

"I'll speak to him," Dad says.

"Not necessary. I will."

Dad hangs his head back, staring at the lightening sky. The birds are up, and the woods chitter as we drive through.

"This is such a goddamn mess," he says.

"So we fix it." I see the unshakable doubt in Shay's eyes, but I have to believe that this family can come back from this. Dad did raise us right. This can be remedied, and I can give Mia what I had. Family. Stability. Bedrock.

When we get to where we're going, we park and gear up. As we start the trek to the grassy clearing where we had luck last time, we fall silent.

Cash sights some scat along the way, but we don't hear any calls. Branch is bringing up the rear, head in his phone, tripping over tree roots. He's no help, but at least the kid never bitches.

He's an odd duck. Has a penchant for numbers like Van. Genius level IQ and no discernable emotion. He's not like Dina where his reactions are atypical. More like he has one register, and it's profoundly disinterested.

He doesn't cause any harm, though. And growing up as he did, splitting his free time between here and the city, shuffled off to boarding school every fall, you can't hardly blame him.

When we get to the field, Cash takes some rabbit carcasses from a bag and stakes them on an incline, a stream to the north, and a ravine to the west. We hunker downwind. Dad takes Cash and Branch to the tree line, and Van and I take position in a shallow ditch.

We wait in silence for a quarter hour, and then Cash uses his rabbit squealer.

We settle in on our bellies, rifles cocked, up on our elbows.

It's always strange seeing Van in camo. He's a suit guy. His camo is pristine, his hat crisp. Brand new. His boots are unscuffed. He looks like a tourist, but he's been hunting his whole life.

He chews and spits. Dad must have shared his chaw.

A buzz starts up when we've been quiet long enough. Insects flit in clouds above the long grass. The heat rises.

Van takes out a silver flask, takes a swig, and passes it to me. Whiskey. The good shit.

"I suppose you have something to say to me," he murmurs, eyes trained on the decoys.

"I do."

"Don called as soon as she left. He said she turned down the money."

"She did."

"She told you about it?"

"Yeah."

He exhales. "To be honest, I didn't see that coming."

"Why?" There's no good answer, but the question needs to be asked.

"Because if this is a grift, if she's playing on your good heart for a payday, and she's gonna tear everything out from under you, we need to know now. Before shit gets too deep. Before that kid can get really hurt."

"It's not a grift."

"Do you know that kid is yours? I know, I know. Kelly swears she's Dina's spitting image. But do you *know*?"

"I know."

"But no paternity test?"

"No paternity test."

"Why not, Kell? We're talking a lot of money."

"Because trust goes two ways."

"Trust, but *verify*, son. You think I didn't have paternity run on Branch? Sure as shit I did."

"It's not your call."

He exhales and takes another swig. "Maybe not, but you can't act like this doesn't impact the rest of us. You understand the terms of the trust. An even split between direct descendants. You're taking money from your cousins, and if the kid is yours, that's fair. Mazel tov. But if she isn't?"

My muscles are tensing. "She is."

"But you refuse to find out for sure. If you won't, I have to look out for this family."

"Bullshit."

"The trust isn't make or break for me, but you have to think about your brothers. You'd really take from them if you didn't have the right?"

"*You* had no right."

He huffs. "Right? There's nothing right about this. We're all trying to handle it the best we know how. Put yourself in our position. Someone's saying Jesse banged an underage girl. Threatens his reputation. His livelihood. You would have handled it. Someone might be scamming the family. You'd handle it."

"You should have come to me."

For a moment, it looks like he's going to bark back, but instead, he slowly exhales. He slides his sunglasses to the top of his head, and turns his head to meet my gaze.

"I should have. It was a mistake."

I didn't expect him to come around this easy. Van never folds.

"You have to accept how it is. Shay and Mia are family. End of story."

A muscle in his temple flutters. He searches my face. "You won't be swayed to reason? No paternity test?"

"I've made up my mind."

A flash of something crosses his face, but it's gone in a moment. "Well, then. I accept that."

He awkwardly offers his hand, and I contort myself to take it.

We spend the next couple hours in silence, listening to Cash's calls, looking for a rustling in the tall grass. We see a groundhog, but we let him amble past. This far out, he's no danger to the farm.

At one point, Van rolls onto his back and dozes off.

The heat and humidity are rising. When we took position, we were in shade, but the sun has risen, and we're baking now.

I pass the time lazily flipping through recent memories. Shay shuddering as she comes around my cock, a rosy flush rising on her chest. Shay sliding a dinner plate in front of me and standing there, hands defensively on hips, until I take a bite and tell her it's good. Shay and Mia in the backyard, bent over a stick bug while Shay narrates how it munches on a leaf.

Mia padding softly down the hall in the morning to watch me put my uniform on. Cocking her eyebrow just so when I forget to get the syrup down for her pancakes. Mia running out to the front porch, knight tucked in her fist, when she hears my car in the drive after work.

I didn't understand how full a man could feel. When I was married, we went through the motions. Elizabeth cooked dinner. We had date nights. She'd set it up to take couples photos every holiday season, and she framed them and hung them on the wall going up the stairs. A daily reminder of how happy I was supposed to be.

I was fucking miserable.

None of it can compare to Shay tiptoeing down the hall after Mia's asleep, tapping on my door, but too impatient to wait for me to open it.

I love her. And I love Mia. And I had no idea what a bite love has. I thought it was an "of course." But it's an "I do."

Around noon, we break for lunch and switch positions. Despite our morning luck, Cash swears this is the place. He points out the scat. Can't argue with that, though Van tries.

In the afternoon, I doze off. I'm awoken by the crack of a rifle. A peppering of shots toward the decoy. In less than a minute, Dad and Cash take out four from the pack. The rest scatter.

Later, as Cash and I are field dressing the animals, Dad says the pack was at least eight strong. With numbers like that, they'd be getting bold. Dad makes a note to walk the fence and make sure there's no easy entrance to the fields since the last repairs.

When it's time to head back to the truck, Van makes sure Branch carries a carcass. It's an obvious attempt to toughen the kid up. Branch accepts the animal with a blank face. The kid is tough already. Just not in the Price way.

He lags behind, and I fall in step beside him. I feel for the kid. In his skinny jeans and plain designer T-shirt that probably costs more than my camo, he's got to be hot and uncomfortable.

"You got that okay?" I ask. I've got my own slung over a shoulder, but I could manage both.

He grunts.

"When are you heading back to the city?"

He shrugs. "Whenever Dad says."

I usually respect a person with little to say, but today, for some reason, I press.

"You headed back to school soon?"

He grunts.

I drop it, and we continue on in silence. At one point, he stumbles on a root and loses his grip on the coyote. It hits the ground with a thump. He glares at it, fists balled, chest heaving.

I stoop and grab it by the scruff of the neck. It's a female. Thirty pounds or so. I continue on. Let him collect himself.

He catches up soon.

"I can take it back."

I hoist it over to him.

Dad, Van, and Cash are so far ahead, we've lost sight of them. It's not far to the truck, though, and we left enough sign coming out. We'll get there.

I'm genuinely surprised when Branch clears his throat. "Is it true you have a kid?"

"Yeah. Her name is Mia. She's six."

He's quiet for a few steps. "Maybe I won't be headed back to school soon."

I'm not following. "No?"

He casts me a look. It's unreadable. "That seven percent's gonna have to come from somewhere."

"What do you mean?"

He rolls his eyes at me. "The trust. Cousin Mia's going to take Dad from forty-three to thirty-six percent. And, in, uh—" He looks up and squints. "Four months? Dad loses control of West's share. And then mine. Come the new year, he's going to be down to thirteen percent."

Branch shakes his head. "You kind of feel for the guy. He saved the trust, and he's been working for it all these years, and he's losing it."

He shrugs. "Sucks."

I flash back to our conversation in the field. My mind's reeling, but I keep getting stuck. The numbers don't add up.

"You've got the percentages wrong."

"Nope." He's unfazed.

"Your dad doesn't have control of forty-three percent. It's divided evenly among descendants. God, if you count John's youngest, that's how many—?" I do some quick math. "Twelve. Thirteen with Mia."

Branch snorts and tosses his head to get a styled curl out of his eye. "You're out of the loop, aren't you? John had him and his kids written out of the trust."

I had no idea.

John's so much older that we aren't as close as I am with Cash and Jesse, but we see each other at holidays. We go hunting. I drop in for dinner if I'm down by Petty's Mill. We're close enough. How did I not know this?

But yeah. John works construction. He runs with a motorcycle club, Steel Bones, that is more or less legit. Now. He has a nice house, but it's not flashy. Mona stays home with the kids. I thought, like me, he needed a job to keep sane.

"Why?"

Branch shrugs. "Dad thinks he's fucking nuts."

John's one of the simplest, sanest men I know. He and Mona had a rough go of it there for a while, but he's steady. He waited years for her to take him back.

"What do you think?" I ask Branch. He seems to know a hell of a lot more than me.

Branch licks his parched lips, and he's about to shrug again, but he stops himself, shoulders lifted. "Maybe he didn't want to be beholden to anyone besides himself."

Branch shakes his head. "Yeah, like principles." His voice is soaked with derision. "The minute I turn eighteen, I'm taking the cash and blowing town."

Branch has never been this blunt with me before. Honestly, though, it's been years since we had an actual conversation. His head's been in his phone since he got one when he was ten or eleven.

"Where you gonna go?"

"I don't know, man." The coyote is slipping. He hoists it back onto his shoulder. There's blood on his pale blue T-shirt. "But wherever it is, I'm not waking up at three in the morning to bake my ass off all day and fuck my clothes up carrying dead fucking coyotes."

I bark a laugh. Luckily, it doesn't seem to offend him. "Fair enough."

Much later, after we have some beers and steaks at the Lodge, retelling stories of hunts from when we were kids and listening to Dad and Van recount tall tales of their own exploits, I head back down the hill to Shay and Mia.

They're both in bed, asleep.

I'm careful, but the creak of the door startles Shay awake. She blinks, her eyes shiny and dark in the moonlight.

I can see the fog clear, and her lips curve as she sees it's me. She slips from under the covers and comes to me. I take her hand and pull her down the hall, my heart as light as it's ever been.

"I'm sorry I wasn't home before you fell asleep."

"That's all right."

"Did you miss me?' I pull her into my room, tugging at her night shirt.

"Some," she laughs softly and lets me lead her to bed.

My heart eases. I'm where I want to be. The past is settled.

I don't expect it's going to be easy, but there's a path forward. Shay and Mia are part of the family, and we're going to make it work.

14

SHAY

Kellum and Mia are standing at the back door, matching expectant expressions on their faces. Kellum's holding the riding boots he bought me. Mia's wearing the miniature version of the same style that Kellum ordered online. They're cute as hell, but there is *no* way.

"You can go on. I'm not coming."

I busy myself at the sink. The pan from breakfast is still soaking.

"Come on, Mama," Mia trots over and tugs my hand.

"No, thank you."

The two of them hatched this plan together, Lord knows when. They want to go on a ride. Not around the enclosure, but a hike on one of the trails that runs through the woods north of the Lodge. No, thank you very much. That's where Kellum went coyote hunting last week.

"It's broad daylight," Kellum says. "And Dad says he hasn't heard howls since last weekend."

He reads my mind sometimes. It's disconcerting. But I like it.

"You two go on. You're sharing a horse, right?"

"Yes. Bronc."

Bronc is Kellum's horse. He's got a mismatched name. He's very mellow. Lazy even, truth be told.

"Well, have a nice time."

Mia taps her foot and looks to Kellum as if he needs to change my mind. I pity him. Mia's looks have weight. They can make you squirm.

"You're going to be lonely here all by yourself for hours."

"I have my books."

He shrugs at Mia. She narrows her eyes at him.

He's about to try something else when my new phone rings. It's the elementary school. Mia starts really soon. We got a welcome packet in the mail with the bus number and pick-up time. We're all set except I'm terrified.

I assume it's one of those incessant robocalls reminding everyone about the start date for varsity conditioning or whatever, but when I tap, it's a live person. A woman.

"Miss Crowder? It's Ms. Averly. From Stonecut Elementary."

"Yes, ma'am." My heart kicks up a notch. It's probably nothing. A change in the bus number or something.

Except it's never nothing when they call you in person.

"Do you have time to talk?"

"Yes, ma'am."

Kellum has stepped over from the door. Mia huffs in irritation and ducks outside, probably to look at the anthills she found by the garage. She loves tracking their maneuvers.

"Miss Crowder, we've finally received Mia's exit paperwork from South Carolina."

She pauses, as if she expects a response.

"Okay."

"Well, we see in Mia's IEP that she was placed in the self-contained program. You neglected to tell us that when she enrolled."

My blood drains. I did neglect to tell them that. Because she's not going into a room at the end of the hall past the boiler room again.

Kellum's frowning down at me. I wave him off.

"That was not a good program for her. I want her put in the normal class."

I steel myself for the explanation that there is no normal class. "Miss Crowder, all of our classes are designed to meet the needs of the students. We have an excellent CALS program in Stonecut County. It's housed at Anvil Elementary, but transportation is provided, of course. I'm going to have Barb Renfro reach out to you—she's the head of the program up there—and she is going to walk you through everything. She'll answer all of your questions."

"No. She's not going to some other school. I said I don't want her in that program anymore."

I'm so pissed, I jerk when Kellum takes the phone from my hand, puts it on speaker, and sets it on the counter between us. Ms. Averly's talking.

"Unfortunately, Miss Crowder, as you know, the IEP has the weight of law. We don't provide the services that Mia needs, so we would be out of compliance with the law if we were to enroll her in a regular education classroom."

Regular. That's what they call it. Mia *is* regular.

"Then call a team. Change the IEP." I signed a paper; I can sign another one.

Ms. Averly's voice thins. "And it is absolutely your right to call a team, and we will accommodate that as soon as possible, but Miss Crowder, to be frank—looking at these assessments—I'd really like you to talk to Barb Renfro about the services her program provides. I think it's a really good fit. Mia will get the kind of support she needs with language and regulation. It's a good program."

That's what they said back home. Hell, it might have been true if Bryce Adams hadn't been in her class. But he was, and I'm not chancing that again.

"No."

"Miss Crowder, by law, we have to provide the services in the IEP, and we don't offer them at Stonecut. We can look into a change of placement, but that's going to take time. School starts in nine days. We're in a legal bind here. I would really suggest you talk to Barb Renfro."

There's a pounding in my ears. My fists are balled. I don't know what to say. Mia's starting school. We bought her a backpack and a matching lunchbox. She's excited. She's reorganized her pencil case about a dozen times.

I'm searching for words, panic making me stupid, when Kellum clears his throat.

"Hey, Soph. I put you on speaker."

"Kell? Hi." She laughs, high-pitched. "How are you?"

"Well, Soph, not as good as a few minutes ago, truth be told."

He doesn't sound anything like himself. It's like a schmoozy actor took over his mouth. A flirty actor who'd be more than happy to give you his autograph.

I don't see how, but it seems to charm Ms. Averly. "Yeah, I know. This is a real sticky wicket," she sighs.

It's a sticky wicket now. Not a legal bind.

"Talk me through this, Soph. Shay's an old hand, but this is all new to me, you know?"

"Oh, of course. Yeah. So, ah, Mia's IEP—that's Individualized Education Plan—it's a document that has the force of law. It mandates the services she needs to meet her goals, which are determined by the ed and psych assessments. Okay?"

Kellum says, "Okay."

"And Mia's plan specifies that she receive seven and a half outside gen ed hours a day, and that's what she'd get in CALS. Speech, OT, OG probably looking at her phonics goals, SEL for self-regulation. All that good stuff."

Kellum's looking at me, eyes wide, brow quirked. Yeah. It's fifty percent gibberish. You get used to it, though.

"And you're saying you don't have that at Stonecut?"

"Well, we have each of those services individually, but not as a comprehensive program. And we don't offer the whole day self-contained. Those students go to Anvil for CALS or Beaver Dam for FALS."

Kellum mouths "FALS." I shrug.

"Soph, Anvil is a forty-five-minute drive."

"I know." She sounds very sorry. "But based on the assessments in front of me, it's really what Mia needs."

My temper spikes. Bullshit. I know what Mia needs. "She's not going to Anvil."

Kellum reaches out, grabs my hand, and squeezes.

"Soph, that isn't going to work for us. I have total respect for your professional opinion—you know that—but you understand this is a special situation. I can't have Mia almost an hour away. You understand."

"Of course."

"What can we do?"

There's a long pause. On Ms. Averly's end, there's a rustling of papers.

Finally, she sighs. "These papers came through on the fax this morning. I happened to be here, getting things ready."

Kellum chuckles. "I was wondering why you were working the weekend. That's dedication, Soph."

You can hear her preen. "What can I say? If I don't do it, it doesn't get done."

"Exactly. Anyway, you were saying?"

I feel like I'm intruding. Kell and Soph need to get a room.

"I'm just saying that no one but me has seen these yet. Mia's already enrolled. I can slip these under the big stack in my inbox, and we can call a team for as soon as we can. It'll give us some breathing room."

"That's sounds great, Soph. We really appreciate it."

"Oh, anything for you, you know that, Kell."

"Don't work too hard, Soph."

"Oh, you know me." She titters. "Elizabeth was saying you'd agreed to marshal the Harvest Day Parade?"

"I wouldn't say 'agreed.' Gave in."

"Elizabeth knows how to get her way."

The wistfulness in Ms. Averly's voice would make me cringe if I weren't so busy trying to coax my heart rate back down. *It's going to be okay. Mia's going to be in a normal class.*

Of course, this is total bullshit. Kellum can hop on the phone and get his way without hardly asking, and if I were a better woman, maybe I'd fight instead of letting a man fix it for me. Fight, and lose.

Kellum's chuckling. "In this case, it was Del. He said I needed to take one for the team."

"And it's so hard riding in the back of a convertible waving to the fans."

"You want to trade places, Soph?"

"Nope. I'm happy on the Stonecut Elementary float."

"What are y'all doing this year?"

"Same as always. Apple orchard. I'll be sitting on an overturned bushel basket with my ass numb, yelling at kids not to fall off the back."

"Cash fell off the back when he was on the float."

"I believe it."

"I sat on my bushel basket like a good boy."

"I believe that, too."

"Well, thanks again, Soph. It's appreciated."

"Oh, anytime, Kell. You have my number if you need anything."

"Will do."

Kellum taps to end the call, and it's wild—the Hollywood heartthrob act drops instantly. His whole face changes.

He looks at me, his eyes crinkled at the corners in worry.

My arms are crossed, my jaw clenched. The panic has receded, but I'm a bit wobbly on my feet. I lean a hip against the counter.

"Explain this to me," he says.

I squeeze my folded arms to my chest. "Which part."

He draws his shoulders back. "All of it."

Chapter 14

"Mia was in a special class back home. It was bullshit. She doesn't need to be in a special class."

"Shay—"

I can't tell if he's chiding me, or if he's at a loss. I don't really care. He's not the one who's been dealing with this all along. Must be nice to swoop in, turn on your gravelly voice, and get your way.

"What?"

He sighs and tilts his head back. "We can't pretend that Mia doesn't need extra help."

My fingers dig into my upper arms. We?

"You don't know what you're talking about."

"Then *explain* it to me."

There's a knot in my chest. I force myself to breathe. "They convinced me to put her in the special class. They said she'd get help talking and with the meltdowns. But she didn't talk anymore than she did in the other class, and there was a little boy in there, and they couldn't control him, and they wouldn't get him an assistant, and he terrorized her. He *beat* on her."

It comes tumbling out.

"His own mother would apologize to me when I saw her around, but what could she do? She'd stop him if she was there, but she wasn't, and the teacher and her helper had too many kids to keep an eye on every single one at every moment. She came home with bruises, Kellum. All the time. Fingerprints on her arms. Marks on her shins where he kicked her."

His entire demeanor has changed. He's bristling with anger.

"Shay—" This time it's ragged. Powerless. Furious.

I know.

"I don't want her in that kind of class."

"That's not *ever* going to happen again. No one is going to lay a hand on her."

"Saying doesn't make it so."

"It sure as hell does."

"It doesn't matter. *Soph* buried the paperwork. We're fine."

He exhales, and he paces to the fridge. He opens it, thinks a minute, and then shuts it without taking anything out.

"Mia does need extra help. Dina had all kinds of support. I remember she had speech, definitely. Mom took her into Pyle. There was a doctor at the Bell Adelman Institute that Mom swore by."

He thinks I don't know she needs help?

I can't snap my fingers and get someone to say "fuck the law" for me.

"Okay. You know it all. What do we do, then?"

"I don't know it all."

"No shit."

"Shay, we're not enemies in this."

"Yeah? We're not friends. Like you and *Soph*."

He freezes. He's pissed. Tense. But he just turns on a dime, and the corners of his mouth curve up. His eyes sparkle.

"What?"

He stalks toward me, folds me in his arms, wraps me so tight I can't even think of jerking away.

I'm mad. I don't want a fucking hug.

"What are you doing?" My voice is muffled by his shirt and his hard chest.

"I'm holding you."

"Why?"

"Because you're jealous."

I snort. Not going to dignify that with a response.

"You care about me." His breath warms my cheek.

"We're not talking about that. We're talking about Mia."

"We'll talk about Mia after."

"After what?"

"After I've had a good, long minute to enjoy the fact that you're jealous."

"That's a messed-up thing to be happy about."

"It is, isn't it?" He kisses the top of my head. I squirm. He lifts

Chapter 14

my chin, ducks down, kisses me. He tastes minty. My insides turn to mush.

"I've known Soph Averly since I was a kid."

"I didn't ask."

"She's Elizabeth's best friend."

"Good for her."

"I like you a thousand times better."

"Makes sense."

He's dropping kisses along my jaw. "I love it when you're stubborn and grouchy."

"My best traits."

"I can't wait until Mia goes to bed," he growls in my ear.

My skin heats, prickling all over. I rise up on my tiptoes to get another kiss. He smiles against my lips and slips his hands down to cup my ass. My gaze darts to the window. Yup, Mia's crouched by the garage, watching the ants on parade.

I slip my tongue into Kellum's mouth. He moans. I love it when I make him moan.

"After we tell Mia, we won't have to wait. We can plop her in front of the TV with a movie, and tell her Mommy needs to help Daddy upstairs."

I freeze.

He groans and closes his eyes. "Shit."

He gently lets me go, but he doesn't step back.

He brings up telling Mia every few days. Sometimes teasing like just now. Other times serious. Sometimes I roll with it better than others.

Some days, I think yeah, we should talk about how to tell her.

And then a paralyzing fear grips me, and I'm certain that if we tell her, it'll all fall apart. That will be the worst that can happen. Mia will know she has a father, and he cares about her, and then his family will swoop in and fuck things up—or I'll fuck things up—and she'll know for the rest of her life that she wasn't enough.

Not gonna happen. Not on my watch.

But I can't tread water forever. Kellum doesn't deserve that.

"Killed the moment, didn't I?" he says.

"No. I did."

"We have to talk about it."

"I know. Put it on the list."

He grabs my hand and leads me to the window. He sets me in front and wraps his arms around me again. "She's happy here."

"I know."

"We will figure out school. And the other stuff."

"Okay."

He sways with me, not much, only rocking from foot to foot. My muscles relax. I crack my jaw.

"What are you most afraid of?"

For a second, I'm going to say I'm not afraid. It's too close to a bold-faced lie, though, and he'd know it.

"You'll change your mind about wanting us. Wanting Mia. Your family will convince you we're garbage. I don't know. They'll make you pick between us or them, and you'll choose them."

"I choose you two."

I sniff. "Of course, you'd say that. But people pick money over blood all the time."

"Not me."

"No. But them. They do."

"Shay, they don't. That's not how they raised me. That's not who they are."

He calls me stubborn, but I'm nothing to him. He has this way of seeing the world. I'd call it rose-colored glasses, but it's not only what he sees, it's what he believes *despite* what he sees.

He thinks his people are salt of the earth. Ordinary folk. They have a goddamn *bridge* named after them, and the arts center on the square. But they're a simple, God-fearing family.

He thinks Stonecut is the perfect place to raise kids, and I'm sure it is if you have money. If you look like everyone else, which I do, you can get by. But there's no bus. No place that takes EBT, so if you need groceries, you're walking the highway. And Kellum likes to talk about how there's no opioid epidemic in the county, and

Chapter 14

he's right as far as it goes, but hanging with Pandy back in the day, booze was everyone's drug of choice.

Stonecut's great. If they let you in. If they don't run you out. And he really believes his family is as upstanding as he is. Never mind the bribe to leave town. Never mind running me out when I was expecting. Those were misunderstandings. Honest mistakes. Not the predictable machinations of folks who think they're better than you and will lie, cheat, or steal to stay on top.

I read the paper. I know what the sheriff's accused of doing. Kellum talks like it's some hassle, some inconvenience that's going to be resolved, and all will be right again.

From what I read, the noose is tightening. Del Willis sold the surplus military equipment he got under that federal program, and he pocketed the cash less the shipping he was obliged to front. And then he doctored the books to make it look like he was paying maintenance, and he pocketed that, too. He's going to jail.

I'm not going to be the one to tell him, though. His boss is his godfather. He taught him how to fish. He helped him save a man, and that's why Kellum's a police officer.

We talk at night before I fall asleep. Usually about stupid things like whether we were good at home ec in school, but I've told him about Mia's birth, and he's shared other things.

Sometimes, I want to shake Kellum. Other times I want to protect him. He has a good heart. He deserves to live in a world where other people do, too.

"You have to trust me," he says.

"All right." I sigh. "You know them better than I do." I twist and kiss his chest. I leave my cheek resting there to listen to the steady thud.

"I want Mia to meet her family. If we're not going to tell her yet. Nothing serious. Lots of people. Kids she can play with."

"You have something in mind?"

"My parents always have a Labor Day picnic. John comes up from Petty's Mill with his family. Mia could meet her little cousins. We barbeque. It's outside. Very casual."

"I don't know."

"Mom asked me to invite you. She said to assure you everyone will respect boundaries. It'll be low-key."

"Where is this thing?"

"Just up the hill. At the Lodge. We can leave whenever you want."

"No one is going to say anything to Mia?"

"I guarantee. It'll be fun. Some burgers. Horseshoes. The pool will be open."

"Horseshoes, eh?"

"I mean, obviously." He grins down at me.

Outside, Mia's rolled onto her stomach in the grass so she can spy on the ants even more closely. She's swinging her legs, kicking her own butt.

We can't stay in this holding pattern forever. It's not fair to Kellum, and it's not fair to Mia.

But I'm not ready yet. I'm too much of a coward.

A picnic is a nice compromise. It's only a few hours. A big group. If things turn bad, Mia and I can walk home.

What can go wrong?

"Okay," I say.

Kellum hugs me and swings me around. "You won't regret it."

I smile, but my blood runs cold.

"Since you're saying yes, does this mean you're going on the ride with us?"

"No can do," I say. "I have to figure out what dish I'm gonna bring to this picnic. Can't possibly take the time to die by falling off a horse."

"I'd never let you fall," he says.

He means it.

And he cannot possibly make that guarantee.

∽

Chapter 14

Labor Day breaks hot and hazy. It's calling for thunderstorms in the evening. I make sure Kellum understands that we need to be back before that happens. I do not want Mia freaking out in the middle of a bunch of strangers.

My nerves are jangling. I made deviled eggs. I asked Kellum what I could bring, and he said whatever I wanted. Very little help, that man.

We're in the truck, and I've got the eggs balanced on my lap, but they're slip-sliding into the plastic wrap and getting all messed up. Story of my life.

Kellum decided to drive up so if the storms roll in early or sudden, we can bail and be back home in a few minutes.

Even having to backtrack to where the driveways split, the ride is less than five minutes. Not nearly long enough.

Mia senses my unease. She's got her shutters closed; her face is blank, her lips pressed in a thin line.

I dressed her in a pretty red-and-white gingham sundress from our Family Discount haul, and I made her let me tie her hair back in a ponytail with a red ribbon.

I have her swimsuit in my backpack purse in case she wants to get in the pool, but I doubt she will. She doesn't like splashing.

"You okay?" Kellum glances over to me.

"Better than the eggs."

He eases up on the gas and downshifts. "This better?"

He hits a pothole, and we go into and out of it in slow motion. The eggs pile up on one side. Most of the paprika is smeared on the plastic now.

I giggle. High-pitched. Nervous. "Not at all."

"How about this?"

He speeds up, and the eggs shift the other direction.

"What are you doing?" I shriek.

"Makin' them scrambled."

"It's not funny!"

"No, ma'am."

He reduces speed again as we approach the Lodge. There's a

half dozen vehicles parked in front of the four-car garage. A fancy SUV. A silver convertible. A minivan that looks like a spaceship. Each of them is shining, not a smudge or ding or chip in sight.

Kellum parks behind another truck. It has a lot of racks.

"Looks like everyone's here," Kellum says, turning the key. It's silent in the cab. Mia's watching us. She's gonna take her cue from me.

"All right, then. Let's go say hi." I shove open my door, and the eggs teeter on my other hand.

"I got these." Kellum grabs them, then comes over to help Mia and me down like he always does.

My nerves settle a touch. I don't know how this situation is going to go, but I know Kellum. Yeah, it's only been a short time, but you don't need more with a man like him. What you see is what you get. It seems strange considering how he came up, but he's a simple man.

When he takes my hand, I let him keep it. I grab Mia's. We head toward the voices drifting from behind the house.

House isn't really the word for the Lodge. It's huge. The shrubs alongside are pruned into perfect boxes, and the flower beds are definitely more than one person can weed. We pass a koi pond. Luckily, Mia doesn't notice, or we wouldn't get any farther.

There's a cute stone path that curves through all the landscaping, through a gate, and then we're on the patio, but it's not like a deck with a table and chairs. It's a whole *place*.

There's an in-ground pool with a diving board and chaise lounges along the side. There's a gazebo. An outdoor kitchen made of stone and wood with a built-in grill. There's a fire ring surrounded by bright white Adirondack chairs facing the mountain, which somehow seems taller and clearer than it does in Kellum's house down the hill.

And there are a lot of people. Some women bustling in the kitchen area. Men and kids in the pool. Other men drinking beers around a wrought iron table. A kid scrolling on his phone in a

Chapter 14

chaise lounge he's moved as far from the rest of the people as he can get.

Mia's palm is sweaty. She doesn't like this one bit. Neither do I.

When they notice us, there's a momentary lull. Everyone stares. But it's only a second. These folks have good manners. Immediately, everyone continues what they're doing, and it's really awkward.

Everyone except the tall woman I've seen staring at us when we're at the barn.

She strides over, wiping her hands on a red-and-white-striped apron, a wide smile on her face. She moves with purpose.

Mr. Wall reaches for her when she passes his table, but she sails on by.

For a second, I think she's going to hug one of us. She's coming in like that. She stops, though, rocks back on her heels, her hands kind of fluttering at her side.

"Shay. Mia." Her voice warms. "I am so happy you came."

She searches my face for a second, and then all she can see is Mia. Mia's more or less staring at her knees.

"Oh, Lord, Kellum, she is the spitting image of Dina."

He grunts. He's sliding glances at me. I keep my mouth shut. This is gonna go how she decides. We're here now.

"Hi, beautiful. We are so happy to have you here. I've been wanting to meet you for a long time."

She chokes up a little, but swallows it down.

"I want you to know that you are so welcome, and I cannot wait to get to know you."

She brushes her eyes. "And Shay, the same to you. *Thank you*."

This is where Kellum gets it from. You can hear it in her voice. She's sincere.

I relax the tiniest bit.

"You brought deviled eggs!"

She takes them from Kellum.

"They, uh, moved around a little on the ride."

She chuckles. "Kellum, I'm holding you to blame."

"I drove very carefully."

She snorts. "Likely story."

She reaches out and smooths his shirt. He's wearing a blue button-up with jeans. It's the closest to dressed up I've ever seen him except in his uniform.

"I'm so happy you came," she says again, and then shakes herself. She's still smiling so wide her eyes are crinkled nearly shut. "Oh, I should let you get settled. Say hello to everyone. Get something to eat!"

She looks to me. "Dina is a very picky eater. I have bread for sandwiches, and there's butter and American cheese slices if Mia doesn't want brisket. Oh, and we have berries!"

She squats down. I can hear her knees pop, but her smile doesn't dim in the slightest. "I went down to the stand on Brummelstown Road, and I got strawberries and blackberries and...." She draws it out, but Mia is shut down for business. There are too many people, too many new things.

In my mind, when Mia gets like this, I picture a guy pulling down the metal gate on his storefront at the end of the day. Clank, clank, slam. Come back tomorrow.

I expect Kellum's mom to look to me to prod Mia into reacting. That's generally how this goes. But she doesn't.

"Raspberries. Bigger than my thumb." She holds it up and wiggles it. "I can't lie. I taste-tested them all. Sweetest of the year so far."

She doesn't seem at all disappointed that Mia won't respond. She just seems happy to look at her.

My eyes prickle. Me, too. More when she was a baby, but now, there's not a day that goes by when I don't stare at her in wonder. Search her face for clues as to how in this wicked world something so good can be made so easy.

Kellum's mom switches her gaze to me, and rises up to her full height again. She has at least a half a foot on me.

She sticks out her hand. "I'm Kelly, by the way."

I have to shake with my left. Mia's got a death grip on my right.

Chapter 14

"Hi." I look at Kellum. He's taking it all in, a small dopey smile on his face. "You're named after your mother?"

"In a way. Mom was named for her dad, Kelly Wall, Junior. She's the third. She thought Kelly Wall the fourth sounded pretentious, so she changed it to Kellum."

"My oldest, John, is a junior. I thought two Johns and two Kellys in one house was too much." She's examining my eggs closer now. A twinge of embarrassment heats my cheeks.

Nope. If I start feeling less than about eggs, around these people in their fake country mansion, there's no bottom to sink to. I'll just keep going.

"I'll take care of these. Kell, why don't you take Shay and Mia to meet Dina?"

"I don't see her," he says.

I don't either. There's only three other women, now that I'm taking it in. One has a baby on her hip, and she's ladling potato salad into a bowl from a plastic carton.

The other two could be models. There's a blonde in a white bikini, and a brunette in a red one-piece cut up past her hips. They're sunning themselves side-by-side next to the pool, playing on their phones. Now that Mia and I are drawing less attention, the men are sliding glances their way.

Neither of them looks at all like Mia.

"She's in her treehouse. Go grab a water for her if you go. She didn't take a plate when she made a beeline out there."

"When Cash showed up?"

Kelly chuckles. "She made it until John showed up with all those kids. Then, she was in the wind."

Kellum checks with me. "You want to?"

"Yeah. Let's go check out the treehouse."

Mia is happy for me to lead her past everyone, through a pristine yard with unnaturally dark and even grass, toward a line of trees an acre or so away from the Lodge.

Kellum's grabbed my hand again. "Is this okay so far?"

"So far."

I'm expecting a platform in a tree with a rope ladder dangling down. I should have expected a *house*.

It has wooden steps. And a porch. And windows made of glass. It's not so much *in* the tree as built *around* the tree. It's a miniature version of the Lodge, down to the steep-pitched roof and the horseshoe hanging over the front door.

There are two thin, white legs swinging over the side of the porch balcony.

"Hey, Dina," Kellum calls. "Can we come up?"

There is a very long pause. The legs stop swinging.

"The woman and the child can come up. You can fuck off."

"Dina." Kellum slips into his police officer voice. "Don't curse in front of children."

"I'm sure she's heard the word before. My house, my rules. If you don't like them—" She waits a beat for emphasis. "Fuck off."

Kellum's jaw tightens. He's about to let her have it. It's cute, but she's not wrong. Mama and Bill and every person I know back home—they all say "fuck" as a matter of course and worse when they're mad.

I stopped cursing so much when I lived with Grandpa. First because Connie made a stink about it, and then because Grandpa took me aside. He had a whole lecture about being a lady, which was garbage, but he cared. And I cared about him, so I toned it down.

I can sense Kellum working himself up. I'm curious, though. This is the woman who's supposedly just like Mia. And she doesn't seem to have a problem talking.

"We'll meet you back at the pool. Go get something to eat."

Kellum's brows jump. "Are you sure?"

"Yup." I give his hand a squeeze. He does not look reassured. He'll get over it.

I lead Mia to the stairs. She follows with no complaints. Her body's less wired away from all the people. And she can't tear her eyes away from the treehouse.

Kellum waits until we're up on the porch to wave and turn

Chapter 14

back. He shoves his hands in his pockets and squares his shoulders. I don't think he's used to being turned away.

"You're Kellum's kid."

Hold up. Jesus. Fuck.

I should say something.

This is not how we planned this. We didn't plan this.

Mia has walked up to Dina and is staring at her.

Dina is sitting on the porch, legs stuck through the railings, head cocked. She's wearing cut-off jean shorts and a tight, ratty T-shirt. She has a pixie cut, but her hair is not cooperating. There are random tufts sticking up. She still looks like a fairy.

She looks *just like* Mia. It's uncanny.

"You can sit," she says to Mia.

Mia kicks off her flip-flops, plops down about a foot away from Dina, and sticks her legs through the railings. She starts swinging her legs.

What do I do? What do I say? Did it even register with Mia?

"You can sit, too," Dina says. Both she and Mia have their foreheads pressed to the wooden slats as they stare at the party across the lawn.

I slip my flip-flops off and take a place next to Mia. My thighs aren't sliding through the slats. I sit crisscross.

You can see everyone pretty clearly, but you can only hear them when the breeze blows this way. It's very quiet except for the birds high in the pines. It smells like pine needles, too. Earthy with a bite. There's shade. It's nice.

My brain is too broken to figure out the next step, so I don't say anything at all.

After we've been quiet together for a long time, it's Mia who breaks the silence.

"Kellum is my daddy?"

I open my mouth, searching and stuck, and Dina beats me to it.

"Oh, yeah."

"He's nice."

"He's very nice," Dina agrees.

"Why didn't my mommy tell me?" Mia's staring straight ahead. My heart cracks in two. I rest my hand on her back. I can feel the bumps of her vertebrae.

"To protect you."

"But Kellum is nice."

"He is. But most people aren't."

Mia is silent, but it's clear, she concurs.

"I don't understand," she finally says.

Again, I try to find the words—decide on a story—but Dina beats me to it.

"She took you away to protect you from the bad guys."

"Kellum's not a bad guy."

"No, he isn't. But there are bad guys around him."

"Does he know?"

"No."

"Are those people down there bad guys?"

"Some are. Some aren't."

"Do you know which are bad?"

"Some I do. Some I don't. Some haven't decided themselves yet."

I don't think this is the way the conversation is supposed to go. I don't want Mia to feel about Kellum's family like I do. But Dina's not lying, and she's woven some kind of spell over me. She's just so identical to my daughter. Like Mia's come back from the future to have this conversation.

"Why doesn't Kellum know who the bad guys are? He's a police officer."

"How do you know who the bad guys are?" Dina shoots back.

"I don't."

"Exactly. People use a lot of words. Words are confusing."

"I don't talk much."

"I didn't either. I listened."

"Me, too."

Chapter 14

"And I watched. I still watch. I watch what people do. You watch, and you know who the bad guys are."

"I watch ants by the garage."

"Are they fire ants?"

"Black ants."

"I hate fire ants."

"I don't hate them."

"Respect." Dina leans back on her arms and stares at the canopy overhead. At first, I don't realize she's talking to me. "Don't trust them."

"Okay."

She raises her thumb to her mouth and chews at the nail bed. "You can trust Mom. And Jesse. Kellum, obviously. He's oblivious, though."

"And you?"

"Yes, but I'm working on something. I might not be there to help."

"Should I—?" I can't say *leave* in front of Mia. Especially not now.

"No. I'm going to make things right. But it's going to take a little time."

"What's wrong, Dina?"

Does she mean the bribe? Is there more?

She drops her head all the way back. Her neck is so delicate; it curves like a swan's. She doesn't answer right away.

While I'm waiting, I notice her hand has inched close to Mia's. Their pinkies are touching. As I watch, Dina tucks hers over Mia's. My daughter observes the people like she does the marsh rabbits or the tadpoles or the ants. And she lets Dina—her aunt Dina—hold her hand.

"There's a bridge in town. Over the Luckahannock. You know it?"

"Of course."

"Everyone calls it the town bridge or the Main Street bridge, but Dad and Van helped fund it. There's a plaque that says it's the Price-Wall bridge."

"Yeah." Everyone knows this.

"It's mostly good. You don't have to drive out to Route 5 to the girder bridge. They block it off for the Summer Arts Festival. There's a walkway. People like to stroll across it in the evening."

For the first time in the conversation, Dina turns her head to face me. She gazes past my shoulder. "It's mostly good. But sometimes a man throws his baby off it."

She immediately tightens her grip on Mia's pinky. "Don't worry. Kellum saved the baby."

"How?" Mia asks.

"He leapt into the air and caught her. Then he protected her with his body when they hit the surface. His bones broke, but he kept her above water until they were rescued."

"Wow," Mia breathes. I should have known she wouldn't be upset. Still, I'm going to need to tread carefully. Dina does not know how to talk around children.

"Your daddy's a hero. A real one. He had no reason to think he'd come out of that river."

"Dina—" It's true, but I don't want that in Mia's head.

Dina's lips turn down. "Am I being too forthright? I'm too forthright. It's one of my shortcomings." She's absolutely serious. And right.

"Yes. A little."

"I'm sorry."

"I prefer it, but, uh—" I nod slightly toward Mia.

"Understood."

"But what were you saying, about the bridge?"

"Oh, yeah. My point. This family? We're like the bridge, you know? Mostly good. But we can do horrible things, too. You know that."

"I do."

"We haven't changed much in seven years. Or seventeen or seventy. We won't unless someone makes us."

"I don't want to change your family."

"You already have." She smiles. Her pointed incisors make her look even more like a fairy. "You're gonna have to fight, for you and Mia."

"I don't want to fight, either."

"You're gonna have to. Kellum's not the kind of hero for this kind of trouble."

"What trouble, Dina?"

She shrugs a thin shoulder. "'The falcon cannot hear the falconer; things fall apart; the center cannot hold.'"

"I don't understand. Is that a Bible verse?"

"It's a poem. Yeats. It's about what happens when good people let bad things happen."

"Your folks let bad things happen?"

"You know they do."

True. But what happened seven years ago doesn't seem to be what Dina's talking about.

"What are you trying to tell me, Dina?"

She huffs and rises to her feet. Mia blinks up at her as if she's waking up from a nap.

"I'm saying I'm going to fix it; I'm going to put things right. But don't put your defenses down until I do."

Her blue eyes are blazing, her pointed chin is hiked. She's so slight and delicate, but I have no doubt she'd shank a man. She has a half-mad energy that's utterly unlike Mia's calm. Even if she weren't the adult version of my child, I'd be fascinated.

"I don't put down my defenses ever."

She nods in agreement. "Wise." She starts for the stairs, but stops before taking the first step down. "You can trust Mom. Jesse. John, but he's never around. Dad means well, but he's like Kell. He doesn't believe anyone he knows can be bad at heart. Keep her away from Van and his kids. Keep away from Del Willis."

"What about Cash?"

"To be determined."

She blows her bangs so they stick up spikey like the rest of her hair. "Mia, there are slugs in the garden by the tomatoes. They have optical and sensory tentacles."

She takes a step down. "I always wished I had separate optical and sensory tentacles."

Mia's face lights up.

Dina raises a hand and trips down the rest of the stairs. She must head off through the woods. She doesn't cross the lawn.

I wait. Mia must have questions, but she just keeps watching the people gathered behind the house.

"Do you want to ask me anything?"

She doesn't respond.

"I love you. Kellum loves you." He hasn't said the words, but there are things a person can't deny. "If he could have been there for you before now, he would have been."

Like that. It's as true a thing as I know.

"You don't have to worry about anything. Dina is—she's very dramatic. Everything is going to be fine."

Mia slides me a glance. She thinks I'm full of it.

"Slugs?" she says.

I sigh. "You're wearing a dress."

She narrows her eyes.

I try to make my face firm, but I'm knocked over inside, and I have the fortitude of a limp rag. "Okay."

"Kellum?"

"We'll get him. Maybe he has a T-shirt in his truck you can put on over the dress."

I'm not getting mud stains out of that fabric without tearing a hole in it. Family Discount isn't known for quality.

She pops to her feet and offers me her hand. I take it, grabbing the railing to hoist my weight.

"I like Dina," she says as she leads me down the stairs.

"Me, too."

"She looks like a swan."

I blink. "I noticed that, too."

"We look alike, but her hair is messy."

"It is."

"Like ruffled feathers."

I snort. "Bet she ruffles feathers a lot."

"No, Mama, *she* has ruffled feathers."

"Okay." I squeeze her hand. It's not until we're halfway to the garden that I realize I haven't stored any of the words. *Slug. Swan. Messy. Ruffled.* I tuck them away, my heart rate kicked up from the close call. I almost forgot. I almost got distracted into forgetting.

I can't afford that. I'm going to need them all one day, at a conference table where people try to put Mia away somewhere she doesn't belong.

Dina was right to remind me. I cannot let down my defenses.

∼

KELLUM DOESN'T HAVE A T-SHIRT, but his mom hears what we're planning to do, and she runs into the house for one of her aprons. She slips it over Mia's head herself, tying the string in a big bow, her heart on her sleeve and her eyes shining.

I ask her if she wants to come with us, and a tear dribbles down her cheek, mussing up her foundation. She doesn't even mind when we spend nearly an hour slug watching. She sends Kellum for buckets for us to sit on, and she tells me stories about him as a boy.

I've never really met a woman like her before. From what Kellum says, she grew up on the farm, but she's not country. She's suburbs all the way. Short, styled, silver hair. Crisp jeans high above her waist and a tucked in, collared shirt with embroidered initials on the chest that aren't hers.

She's tentative, but friendly. She doesn't ask me anything, and she doesn't pry about Mia although she watches her like she wants to eat her up. The bucket's hell on my behind, but I relax.

The strange conversation with Dina fades. As the sun rises higher in the sky, it gets hot, but not miserable, and there's plenty of shade trees dotted around the property, including a tall elm next to the plot where Mrs. Wall grows green beans, peas, sweet corn, and zucchini.

While we're still in the garden, a sedan with dark tinted windows pulls up. Del Willis steps out. My blood runs cold.

It's the first time I've ever seen him out of uniform. He helps a woman from the passenger seat. She's not that old—late fifties maybe—but she's moving slow. He holds her elbow and guides her around back. He doesn't seem to notice us.

My chest tightens. They're all here now. Mr. Wall, Van Price, and the sheriff.

Mrs. Wall sighs and stands, brushing imaginary dirt from her thighs. "I better go make sure Lil doesn't need anything."

"She looks better," Kellum says.

"Amen," his mother says. "Breast cancer," she tells me. "She just finished chemo—what was it? Three weeks ago?"

"Four," Kellum provides. He's squatting with Mia in the dirt.

"She's doing great. The doctors are very optimistic." She squeezes Kellum's shoulder. "Del and Lil are this one's godparents."

"Mom and Lil have been best friends since they were kids. Del and Dad were neighbors growing up," Kellum explains.

"Del and Lil introduced my husband and I." Mrs. Wall's lip curves.

I smile politely.

"Take your time, but come back to the party. I want you to meet Lil."

I give a short nod.

To be honest, I'd be okay with slug-watching the rest of the day. These people put me on edge. This whole scene makes me feel like I'm wearing someone else's clothes.

I don't have godparents. Except for Uncle Pete, my mom's family is all over. The rare times we went to visit an aunt or uncle, we'd maybe go to a park or cookout. It was beers on a back porch, not a pool and a buffet. This all is nice, but it's not what I'm accustomed to.

Chapter 14

I've got no reason to feel out-of-place except that I am.

It's not my day, though. Mia plays five more minutes, and then she tells Kellum, "Hungry."

Makes sense. She hasn't eaten since breakfast.

"You want some of those berries my mom mentioned?" Kellum asks.

She starts for the back. Yes, I'd say she does. We both follow. Most folks are gathered around two long tables now, digging in. They're eating off of china with wine and water glasses. In the middle of the tables, there are huge arrangements made to look like wild flowers.

The kid on his cell phone is still scrolling by the pool, and one of the pretty ladies seems to be napping, a bottle and empty glass on the ground beside her chaise lounge, but everyone else is chowing down and chatting.

Dina's not there, but at some point, it looks like Cash's friends showed up. There's a handful of people my age sitting by him, nearly falling out of their seats laughing while he tells some story all loud. The empty seats are at that table.

My stomach clenches. It's like I'm back in high school, and the only place to sit is with the assholes.

"I've got to run to the bathroom," I murmur to Kellum. "Mia, do you need to go?"

She shakes her head. "Well, you're coming anyway. We need to wash those hands."

"There's a sink over here. I got her," Kellum offers. "Bathroom's through the kitchen, down the hall on the left. Can't miss it." He brushes my cheek with his thumb, a whisper of a touch, then gone. I shiver.

Did anyone see? Probably not. Everyone's carefully not staring at us. Or maybe they honestly don't care, and the tension is all in my head.

"What was that for?" I scrub my cheek. "Dirt?"

"Because." He doesn't elaborate. He's grinning, all goofy, as content as I've ever seen him except for after sex. He wants this. One big happy family.

It is picture perfect. Except for the lady by the pool, I don't see anyone getting wasted and passing out. No one's likely to start a fight or whack their kid for nothing. I can see why he wants Mia to have this.

I give him the best smile I can muster and head inside. He made it sound like a hop, skip, and jump, but the house is massive. The kitchen has zones. There's the cooking area. The oven has two doors, the fridge has four—two horizontal, two vertical.

There's a breakfast bar, but it's as wide as a table, with six stools. Then there's an eating area with a dining room table and six more chairs. There's the door to a pantry that looks bigger than my room back home. The hall has several doors. I pass a sewing room, the laundry room, and a closet before I find what I'm looking for.

You can't miss it because after the bathroom door the whole place opens up into a huge, high-ceilinged hall with wood rafters. There's stuffed leather furniture, mounted deer heads and fish, and a goddamn bear on a pedestal. A stone fireplace takes up an entire wall, and the opposite wall is windows from floor-to-ceiling.

And a bunch of paintings of horses. Of course.

I duck into the bathroom. Good thing Mia didn't have to go. I'm not sure how she'd feel about that bear. Not sure how I do. Do we have that many bears that we can be shooting and stuffing them? I don't know. Mia would.

I do my business and take a long time washing my hands. I check my makeup. I put on earth tone eyeshadow and mascara. It doesn't show much, so it doesn't smudge either. Kellum noticed when I came down this morning.

He said, "Your eyes are beautiful." And then I had to pour my cereal like my face wasn't burning up.

After procrastinating as much as I figure I can get away with, I head back. It won't be so bad. I'll make myself a plate. Sit next to

Mia. Stuff my face so no one expects me to talk. My stomach's queasy as hell, but I can fake it.

They probably don't want to talk to me anyway. Cash and his friends seem very into each other's company.

I'm so worried that, at first, I don't notice him at the breakfast bar. Not until he speaks, his deep voice startling me. I freeze, my fists clenching.

"Did you go for the jewelry, or should we count the silver after you leave?"

Van Price is leaning on the marble counter, all casual, leg crossed, hand on his hip. There's a glass of liquor beside him. His slacks are light tan, his pale-blue button-down isn't done up quite as far as it should be, and he has a thin white sweater thrown over his shoulders. He looks like the professor from that TV show where they're stuck on an island. If that guy was an asshole.

"Screw you." I keep walking.

I'm almost to the door when he says, "Mia is so happy. It'll be such a shame..."

My heart drops. I don't want Mia's name in this man's mouth. I turn and spit, "What?"

He swirls his glass and takes a sip. Drawing it out. My pulse pounds in my ears.

"A girl that young. She needs her mother."

"What are you talking about?" I glance around, but we're alone. The windows are airtight. You can't hear the people outside at all.

"A smart woman takes the money. Just like you took my money seven years ago. Cash out and disappear. But I guess you're not a smart woman, are you, Shay Crowder?"

"Smart enough. I don't keep throwing my money at folks who won't take it."

"It's almost like you don't care about little Mia at all." He narrows his glittering eyes. "A smart woman would understand who she's up against."

"An old man who needs to mind his business." I stare him down, tensing my muscles so I don't shake.

"Oh, I am minding *my* business, Shay. You need to attend to yours. Who's going to take care of Mia when her daddy's at work?"

"Stop talking in riddles. Say what you mean."

He sets down his glass with a clink. "When you're gone, who's going to watch her?" His lips curl, showing his too-white veneers. "Actually, my sister will be delighted to take over as little Mia's mommy. She always wanted more girls."

My pulse is racing. Is he threatening to kill me?

"Spit it out, Mr. Price."

He runs his tongue inside his bottom teeth, sizing me up. I steel my spine and force my arms to stay straight at my sides.

"This is mine, Shay Crowder."

He gestures out the French doors to the folks crowded around the tables.

"The farm. The trust. This town. This whole goddamn county. It's mine. I earned it. I bought and paid for it. You don't get to spread your legs and take from me."

"I don't want your money."

"Bullshit."

"Believe what you want. Leave Mia and me alone."

"Or else?"

He waits, but he knows damn well I don't have an "or else."

Eventually, he barks a laugh. "Don Prescott thought you were some kind of hillbilly savant because you negotiated him up to three hundred fifty thousand. But you aren't, are you? You were bluffing."

He stalks forward. I stand my ground. He's taller. Wiry and athletic for his age, but all he's doing is trying to intimidate me. He'd never actually touch me. That sweater draping across his shoulders would fall off.

He stops a foot away. He smells like brandy and old man aftershave.

"I don't bluff." He lowers his voice, even though we're all alone.

"You're going to take that mistake you insisted on keeping and crawl back into the hole you crawled out of. Or *else*."

"Are you threatening me?"

"Yes." He works that tongue in the back of mouth as if he's worrying a loose molar. It contorts his expression, makes him gruesome. Like an old plastic doll. Hair thinned. Skin stained from years of tanning and unnaturally tight, like it's been smoothed and tugged over his skull. He's an ugly man.

"I *am* threatening you, Shay Crowder."

"With what?"

He actually smiles. He blinks, and then he gestures around him. "With this."

"I don't follow."

"Of course, you don't. Look around, Shay. Everything belongs to me. Everyone works for me, whether they admit it or not. John plays with his horses. The kids pretend their hobbies are jobs."

He casts a quick, scathing look at the kid on his phone by the pool. He's still scrolling.

"*I* sign the checks," he goes on. "The sheriff is eating food paid for with the money *I* made, next to his wife whose cancer was treated by the top-of-his-field oncologist who *I* engaged. Later, he's going to meet with his lawyers who *I* bankroll."

He's pointing outside, jabbing his finger in the air. "Cash's hunting guide business. Whatever Jesse's doing with those bad-tempered horses that should be put down. The jewelry on the women. The vehicles out front. This is my world, Shay Crowder. It only exists because of me. If I want you out, you're gone."

"You realize you sound like a real asshole, right?"

It's all bravado. My blood has drained from my head, and my thoughts won't move; they're stuck in mud. He's telling the truth. My grandfather said as much.

"I listen to your grandmother, then God, then Mr. Wall and Mr. Price," he used to say. Grandma would laugh. It was funny 'cause it was true.

Mr. Price's lips peel back. "You've got a mouth on you now,

don't you? I liked you better when you sat on that ratty couch with your tongue tied."

"I'm not seventeen anymore."

"No, you're not." His gaze flicks to my breasts, and my stomach heaves. "But whatever power you think you have over my nephew, think about how that stacks up to what I can do."

"What are you going to do?"

He drags his eyes down my front, speculatively. "I haven't quite decided yet. Maybe I'll catch you spreading those legs for some bigger fish. That's true to type."

"You're disgusting."

He shrugs. "Or maybe I'll catch you stealing Grandmother's jewelry from Kelly's dresser."

He clucks his tongue, reaching into his pocket and pulling out a tangle of gold chain and pearls. He dangles it in front of my face. I don't move.

"I didn't touch that. Kellum won't believe it."

He slips the necklace back in his pocket. "Maybe not. Everyone else will. They'll start keeping a close eye on you. Whispering. And then maybe Kellum will find pills in the house. Where Mia could easily get them." He shakes his head. "You'll deny they're yours, of course. But didn't you steal that necklace?"

Cold spears my chest. "You don't go anywhere near Mia."

"I won't have to. And Kellum won't let you near her either, if he thinks you're a danger. He's a boy scout, that one. Very into doing the right thing, even when it's hard."

"I'll tell him. I'm going to repeat this to him word for word."

He ignores me. "Or maybe he never finds the pills. Only gossip. Late night phone calls where whoever it is hangs up. Money goes missing. It'll be a tragedy, really. When little Mia finds you in that charming clawfoot tub. Everyone saw it coming." He fakes a frown. "But you can't help people who won't help themselves."

"You're a sick son of a bitch."

He levels his gaze at me. "I am. Take the money, Shay. Call Don Prescott. He'll have a cashier's check ready."

Chapter 14

"Kellum's gonna kill you when I tell him about this."

"You're not going to tell him."

"Oh, yes, I am."

"No, you're not. You're going to take a minute, and you're going to decide if I'm bluffing. If I am, go ahead. Tell Kellum. He might believe you. But if I'm not bluffing, Shay? What might I do if you tell him? Think it through. You're not actually stupid, are you, Shay? You can count."

He cocks his head. My skin crawls. For a second, I can see Mia in him. It's there. In the chin. The eyes. That angle of the neck while he waits for me to figure it out. My stomach churns. It's obscene.

This whole thing is obscene.

"It's all about money." I startle. I hadn't meant to say it out loud.

He quirks a lip. "Everything is about money."

And that is the truth, isn't it? He wants us gone, but it's not because we're trash; it's because we're not good enough for the family. It's about cold, hard cash.

People will do anything for it. If he sees Mia as a threat, it's because she'll cost him money he can't afford to lose. And I don't know the particulars, but if he's so pressed that he'll resort to this, he's in a bad way.

What if he went after Kellum?

Kellum wouldn't see it coming. He's strong and brave and good, and he has utterly no concept of what the world is really like.

If I told him right now, word for word what his uncle said, what would he do?

He'd "have it out with him." He'd "make it right."

You can't make it right with a man like Van Price. He's a master of the universe, the king of all he surveys. He does what he wants because he can. It's not a *sense* of entitlement. He owns it all. He *has* the titles. It's reality.

Van Price has me cornered, as much as when he had me

surrounded back in Grandpa's trailer. The fact is, I don't know what he's actually capable of, but through the window, I can see his helicopter on the pad beside the mansion on the ridge above us.

I can see the infinity pool glinting in the sun. The mansion that they insist on calling the "Cabin."

I remember him squeezing my ass when I worked at the diner, and I remember how if Miss Denise was working, she'd take the table and tell me to go in the back and roll silverware.

"Come on, Shay," he says. "You aren't stupid. Am I bluffing?"

No. He's not.

"I want four hundred thousand."

He chuckles, and his face shifts, smug and superior.

"Tomorrow. Go to Don Prescott's office." He does some mental math. "There will be a cashier's check and some papers for you to sign. I'll arrange a car that'll take you where you want to go."

I feel sick.

"What papers?"

"You'll need to renounce any claim on the trust. Swear out an affidavit that Kellum isn't Mia's father. Sign a standard nondisclosure."

My chest tightens.

"You disappear. You understand? You come back—you make a phone call, send an email—I'll know. You'll forfeit the settlement, and there will be nothing holding me back."

I try to swallow, but my mouth is dry. "Are you going to tell Kellum that Mia isn't his?"

"I'm not going to say anything. But for his sake, I think *you* should."

"She is his."

"It doesn't matter. Does it?" He raises an eyebrow, clicks his cheek, and he saunters off toward the front of the house, cocksure and whistling. He got what he wanted, and soon Mia and I are going to be back where we belong. Somewhere else.

We don't matter.

The truth doesn't matter.

Only power. Only money.

My fingers tremble. I shove them in my pockets. I stand in the middle of the huge kitchen, gulping air until the shakes rack through me, and then I grit my teeth and go back outside. Everyone's involved in their own business, but Kellum's gaze flies to the door as soon as I slide it open. He smiles. I lift my chin so I can't see him.

I walk to the far table and slide into the open seat next to Mia. Kellum's filled a plate for me. Hamburger with mustard and tomato. Five slices of watermelon.

I sit there, as quiet as Mia, a rock in my guts as everyone gossips and laughs. Cash's friends try to draw me into the conversation a few times, but when I don't say much, they give up.

I stare at my food, and none of it feels real except the awful weight that's descended on my shoulders once again. It's familiar, but I've grown soft since I've been with Kellum. It hurts like it never used to.

Is it going to crush me this time?

God, help me.

And God forgive me for what I'm about to do to Mia and Kellum.

~

KELLUM KNOWS SOMETHING'S WRONG. He suggests we leave shortly after dessert.

Mia senses something's off, too. She sticks by my side. When Mrs. Wall asks if she wants to see the worms in the compost, she ignores her.

I let Kellum say our goodbyes. Mrs. Wall makes us stand there while she runs off to get the plate the eggs were on. She's washed and dried it and put it in a pretty, reusable fabric bag. She asks if we'd like to come over after school and swim sometime. I tell her sure. There's no sense in disappointing her now when we'll be gone in a few days.

We ride back to the house in silence.

I don't want to send Mia to a brand-new school just to yank her out in two days, but there's no way around it.

I don't want to leave, either. I don't want to take her away from Kellum. I don't want to never see him again. I don't want to lie to him and break his heart, and I don't want him grieving over his child, not knowing where she is, if she's okay.

How can I do that to him? Or her?

I can't.

I'm amped, and I'm bone-deep exhausted. Kellum keeps trying to catch my eye, but I stare out the window. Thankfully, he doesn't press it.

When we get home, I say I'm giving Mia a bath. I let her play until she's shriveled like a raisin. Then, we go through her backpack again and make sure she has everything she needs for the first day. She loves school supplies. So do I. We spread everything out on the bed. I write her name on everything with permanent marker, adding cat ears to the "M" and whiskers to the "i."

Kellum bustles around downstairs, making sure we hear him. After a while, the scent of sausage and peppers filters through the cracked door. He's making dinner.

"Let's pack this back up," I say. We stow everything carefully. Mia puts the backpack next to the dresser where we've laid out tomorrow's outfit. She's going to wear a pink shirt with a sloth on it and a matching pair of pastel checked shorts. Kellum bought the clothes from one of the boutiques on Main Street. The shirt is the softest cotton. The price tag said thirty-five dollars.

"Ready when you are!" he calls up the stairs. I take a deep breath. I can't keep giving him the cold shoulder. He'll think something's wrong—more than he already must.

I let Mia go ahead of me. He's waiting for us in the entryway.

I try, but I can't hold his gaze. I've never done anyone dirty. Not as bad as I'm gonna have to do to him. He doesn't deserve it. He's done everything he can to do right by us. He's a decent man, and that's saying something in this world.

And I don't want to never see him again.

My eyes prickle. I blink.

He pulls my seat out like always. "You okay?" he whispers in my ear.

I nod. "Thanks for cooking."

"You didn't eat anything earlier."

"It was too hot."

He brushes his fingers along my shoulder and sits across from me. "Are you coming down with something?"

"Maybe," I say, grateful for the out.

"How about you?" He presses the back of his hand to Mia's forehead, and she doesn't even flinch. "You feel fine."

He frowns. I can see the wheels turning. "Dina didn't—Dina didn't say anything that bothered you, did she?"

I'd been so stuck in panic and hiding it, that I hadn't thought about that strange conversation. Not so strange now.

"I like Dina." It's not what he asked, but it doesn't seem to register.

"She's different." He smiles fondly, and he reaches over to cut Mia's sausage. She's managed to hack it to pieces, but they're too big. Her cheeks are bulging, and it looks like she's chewing cud. I didn't even notice.

Lord. With everything that happened, I forgot how Dina dropped the bomb. It hasn't seemed to throw Mia off, but she's got a lot on her mind with school starting tomorrow and her mom being weird. Besides, she's one to mull things over.

Kellum deserves to know, though. I should have taken him aside right away when we got home. Well, the opening is there. And time is running out.

"She told Mia that you're her dad."

He drops his fork with a clatter. His gaze flies between Mia and me. His lips part. I want to grab his hand. I want to squeeze real hard. I grit my back teeth.

"She did?"

I nod.

"What did Mia—how did—" He kind of gives up, and leans over, cupping the back of Mia's head, and he lowers himself until he's eye level. "I am so happy to be your dad, Mia. If I could have been there all along, I would have. I swear that to you."

Mia finishes chewing her sausage and swallows. "That's what Mama said."

He casts me a glance, his eyes shining. Then he presses his forehead to hers. "I love you, Mia. I'm always going to be there for you. I'm gonna make it up to you. I'm just—" His voice breaks. "I am so happy to have a daughter like you."

Mia contemplates him, and then she draws back slightly and pecks his nose.

"Okay," she says, and then she finagles another forkful of sausage between them somehow, and slides a bite in her mouth. She's really hungry.

I'm sniffing back tears, and my heart twists in my chest. What am I gonna do? I can't take them from each other.

Kellum straightens back up, but he can't tear his eyes off Mia. "I can't believe Dina would do that."

He's completely sincere. Knowing her for only a half hour or so, *I* can completely believe Dina would blithely drop a secret like it's nothing.

"I'll talk to her tomorrow," he says.

And there it is. His solution to everything. Which does *nothing*.

"Cat's already out of the bag," I point out. A rush of rage fills me, heating my skin. Makes my pulse pound in my ears. All of this is so fucking unfair.

In this moment, I hate him.

He's the most honest and upstanding man I've ever met, and I can't trust him. He simply can't fathom a world that doesn't arrange itself for him so he'll never understand the danger Mia and I are in.

If I told him right now that his uncle threatened to kill me, he wouldn't believe it. Oh, he'd go talk to the man. And he'd listen to whatever story Van spun, and he'd come back with reassurances that I'd misunderstood, and it'd be the first wedge because he wouldn't believe me.

There's no doubt in my mind that is how it would go down.

No matter what he whispers in my ear at night—how I'm beautiful, how he wants me, how good I feel—I'm not from his world. I don't get the automatic benefit of the doubt. The assumption of rightness.

Back when I was pregnant, I called him. We'd fucked, the condom broke, and I called him out of nowhere a few months later, and he cut me off and hung up on me. And then he comes across Mia and I on the road, and he's bowled over. Completely mind blown that he's got a kid.

I know I'm ginning up my anger so I can stop feeling the hole in my chest, but I'm not wrong.

His ex-wife manages to open credit cards in his name after nearly bankrupting him, and it's an earth-shattering discovery. But he's suspicious enough to follow me when I went to Don Prescott's.

"Soph," who's never spent any time with Mia, says she belongs in a special program, and I've got to argue all the reasons she doesn't.

It's the way the world works, but it's bullshit all the same.

"Shay?" His forehead's furrowed.

I push my chair back. It scrapes the floor. "I'm not feeling well. I'm going to bed early."

He stands when I do. "Do you want an aspirin?"

"No. I'll be fine after I lie down." Mia's shoveling the rest of the peppers in her mouth. "Will you bring her up when it's bedtime?"

But Mia hops up and grabs my hand. Kellum's face drops.

"It's been a long day," I offer. He nods slowly. "When are we leaving tomorrow?"

"I thought seven-thirty."

"Okay."

There's a bus to school, but Kellum figured it'd be better to drive Mia until she gets settled in. If I could have done that back home, I would have. The bus was loud on the way home, and it always put her on edge.

This isn't going to be a worry past tomorrow, though.

The day after, we'll be gone. I need to figure out how to do it. It actually shouldn't be hard. I'll walk back to town, take Mia out of school early, and then get the check and the car. We'll be gone by noon.

Adrenaline mixes with the riot in my guts, and I feel sick and flushed. I clear my throat, but I don't know what to say, so I head upstairs without saying another word or meeting Kellum's eye.

I help Mia into her nightgown, and I watch her brush her teeth.

"Brush, don't chew," I remind her, like always, and she ignores me, like always.

Tomorrow, I'll need to find a suitcase with wheels or a big backpack. We have a lot more stuff than we came with. But if I'm walking back into town, I can't be hauling bags. It's a small town. People would notice. I wouldn't put it past folks around here to call the sheriff about a suspicious bag lady.

We'll have to leave almost everything. Unless I come back for our things after we get the car. Kellum's parents might see a strange vehicle and wonder. Would they call and tell him? He's a cop. He could put out an APB or whatever. I can't risk that. But I don't want to give up all these clothes and toys. I don't need to take that from Mia, too.

My head's pounding. I hate this. I hate all of it.

I read Mia her book, and when I'm done, I have no idea what the story was about.

She's out of sorts, squirmy and huffy. She knows something's wrong. It takes her a long time to fall asleep, and she doesn't roll onto her tummy. She stays on her side, facing me, her little hand clutching the hem of my shirt. Eventually, her lips part, and every so often, she lets out a tiny, delicate snore.

All this talk of how she looks like Dina, but to me, she favors

Kellum. She has his collected way of carrying herself. The shape of his eyebrows. His cheekbones.

I'm going to steal some pictures tomorrow. There have to be some in his office or somewhere.

That'll make it better, won't it? I'm taking her daddy from her, but she'll have pictures. She'll know what he looks like. That's more than I do.

My chest constricts, and I force my lungs to expand.

I can't do this.

But what's my choice?

Tell him.

Tell him and hope he listens. Hope he believes me. Hope he chooses me over them. It feels like a massively foolish bet. Why would he do that? Because we're fucking? Because he's a stand-up guy, and he sees Mia and I as a package deal?

You cannot trust that.

What did Van Price say?

Am I bluffing?

No, he's not.

So what do I do?

Put my money on the long shot or the sure thing? Only it's not money. It's my life. My child.

I uncurl Mia's fingers from my shirt and get out of bed. I can't lie still, the same train of thought looping in my brain, coming to the same awful conclusion. I need to *do* something.

But I can only stand in the middle of the room, paralyzed. After a few minutes, I hear Kellum's foot on the stair.

I go to him every night.

He'll expect me. He'll get suspicious if I don't go.

But I can't. I can't even look at him. There's no way I can fall into him, tangling our limbs, kissing as if we haven't for years, losing ourselves until we're muzzy-headed and sighing and laughing like we're drunk.

It felt like magic, like time we stole, and I guess we did.

His steps stop at our door. My body tenses.

He'll keep going. He won't risk waking Mia. Tomorrow, I'll say I was asleep. Not feeling well.

He raps ever so lightly on the wood. I hurry silently to the door.

"Shay." It's a whisper. The door's heavy. The only reason I can hear him is the slight crack underneath from the house settling.

I rest my fingertips on the porcelain knob.

"Shay," he says again.

I can't slip out. I can't lie to his face. Not so late at night, in the dim light, when I want so bad to throw myself in his arms, and let myself believe he can take care of it all.

I want to open the door. I want to press my finger to his slightly chapped lips. I want him to step back on his heel with the slightest pressure from me.

He'd wrap me up, snuggle me to his chest. He'd tell me everything will be okay. He'd believe it.

And he'd be wrong.

I stand by the door until I hear his steps head down the hall, and then I drop my forehead to the cool wood.

My heart cracks.

I breathe through it, and I go back to bed. I don't sleep a wink. I lie on my back, staring at the white-washed ceiling, tears dribbling down the side of my face, dampening my pillow, as I force myself to think of states and towns I've heard of, discarding them one-by-one because they're not here, and somehow a summer of Kellum Wall has made me weak.

15

KELLUM

Something's wrong.
Shay's always a touch somber. Her smiles are small and quick, and she's always watching. Waiting. Bracing for impact. Maybe she'll drop her guard as time goes on, after a few months, but it's just as likely this is how she's made.
I don't mind. Her toughness kept Mia safe and cared for when I wasn't there. Besides, it's a gift every time she softens for me. A little giggle-snort. Or when she wriggles under my arm, tucking herself into my side in bed, and I'm the king of the damn world.
It's not out-of-character for her to be standoffish. Quite the opposite.
Still, something's wrong.
She doesn't need to come to me every night, and I get it—yesterday was intense. Dina overshared. Shay had to suffer through a meal with Cash and his groupies. And she did say she was feeling poorly.
She's got to be worried about today. I'm sweating bullets.
So far, so good, though. Mia woke up early. She ate her breakfast. Shay didn't touch hers.
Mia let me take her picture in front of the maple tree out front. Apparently, first day of school pictures weren't a tradition for Shay

growing up. I made Shay join Mia for a few shots. She hated it—they both did—but they humored me.

The plan is to drop Mia off at the elementary, and then I'll bring Shay back home. Until I get her a vehicle, this is going to be the routine. I don't mind. It's only a fifteen-minute drive, and it's time alone with her.

Maybe I can get her talking. Or I can walk her inside. Stay a while. My cock's gotten accustomed to Shay every night. *I've* gotten accustomed. I didn't sleep well without her cold feet on my calves.

The drop off is smooth. They've got it down to a science. Soph saw me coming, and she was there to open the back door and help Mia out. You're supposed to stay in your vehicle, but Shay hopped out anyway. She buckled Mia's backpack for her, and they shared a look.

I was a little worried there'd be a meltdown, but Mia follows Soph without complaint. No enthusiasm either, but I wasn't much for school myself until I started playing ball.

Shay's silent on the ride back to the house. She has her phone in a tight grip.

"Mia's gonna be fine."

She grunts.

"They'll call us if there's a problem."

She jerks her chin.

"Soph is going to keep an eye on her."

That gets a reaction. "You asked her to?"

"She reached out and offered. She's a decent person, Shay. She cares about the kids."

Something flashes across her face, but it's gone in an instant. She turns to stare out the window.

I sigh. We pass the sign for Stonecut Farms.

"What's wrong, Shay?"

She presses her lips. "I'm worried about her first day, is all."

It's like she had the words prepared. I'm worried, too, though. I already have plans to roll past on my way back to the office. And at lunch.

"It's gonna be fine."

"Yeah."

When I pull up in front of the house, she already has her seat buckle off.

"I'll come get you around three to pick her up?"

"Okay."

"You'll be fine all day on your own?"

"Yeah." She has the door open and one leg out. She can't wait to get away from me this morning.

I don't think I did anything. Unless she's pissed that I made her go to the picnic. If she'd said no, I would've taken that for an answer.

"Shay." I grab her arm before she can bolt. "What's wrong?"

She stares at my hand gripping her forearm. I let go. She won't meet my eyes. "I told you."

"I can't help if you won't talk to me."

Her chin wobbles for a moment before she grits her teeth. "You can't help me." She sucks in a breath. "I told you. I'm just worried about how things are gonna go. After a day or two, it'll be fine."

"It will. Stonecut is a good school. Mia's a great kid. It'll work out."

Shay squeezes her eyes shut, and then she blinks a few times. She summons up a truly raggedy, half-assed smile.

"Don't worry," she says. "I'll pull it together."

She kind of wiggles her fingers at me, and then she's gone. She raises her hand on the porch, another attempt to shaft me off, the weak smile already replaced by a haunted look.

What happened yesterday?

I replay the day on my drive back into town. She was hesitant with Mom, but she warmed to her later when we were in the garden. Mom kept it light. Stories about Halloween costumes and trouble Cash and I got ourselves into.

Shay was definitely deep in her head when she came back after hanging with Dina. For good reason.

Is Shay pissed because we didn't get to tell Mia in our own way? Shay put me off a dozen times. I know she was nervous about how it'd go. I figured rip the Band-Aid off. There's no way to make what happened right. We have to rely on what we do from now on.

Was there some reason Shay didn't want Mia to know I'm her dad?

Is she unsure about me? Does she think she's trapped now that Mia knows who I am to her?

Maybe she's having cold feet now that it's getting real. It's a lot in a short amount of time. Especially for a woman like Shay. I don't think she's ever had a relationship. None she's mentioned. And she seems genuinely surprised every time I open a door or bring home something for her.

Tonight, once Mia's in bed, I'll talk to her. We'll get it out in the open. Whatever it is, we can deal with it.

When I get to the office, it's nearly empty. Del's running later and later these days, and folks are taking advantage. Bev's making coffee in the back, but Nancy's nowhere to be seen. The phone's ringing.

"Get that, would you, Kell?" Bev hollers. I oblige.

Deb Karwacki wants to know when the signs are going up to block off parking for the Harvest Day Parade. She doesn't want her son's car to get towed. I tell her forty-eight hours in advance, same as always. She calls three times a year like clockwork. Fourth of July, Saint Patrick's, and fall.

She asks after Lil and Mom, and then I get lucky and her dog starts howling to be let out. Bev shuffles in with two mugs of coffee, passes one to me, and then rummages on Nancy's desk.

"You've got messages. What's this woman done with them now?"

I snag the slips from under her keyboard. Bev huffs. "Who'd think to look there?"

"Well, I am the deputy sheriff."

She snorts and settles herself in her chair.

"What's that for?"

She powers on her computer and takes a sip from her mug.

"You're more Steve McGarrett than Frank Columbo."

"Who?"

"Exactly." She stares intently at her email and starts click-clacking. "Mia do okay at drop-off?"

"She did fine." When I took a detour past the school on my way to the office, everything was quiet. There were kids on the playground, but they were too big to be in Mia's class.

"She'll do great."

I grunt, tap the counter, and head back to my office. The first message is from Deb Karwacki about the no parking signs. The second is from Ed Houser.

I spoke to Sarah a few weeks back. I thought it was settled. The message says he wants to know if I've heard anything about Rory. I haven't.

I don't have anything else pressing today. Not until Del rolls in and foists whatever he's got onto me. I might as well go patrol. Stop by the trailers and talk to Pandy. See if she's heard from Rory. Then I can swing by the house. Make sure Shay doesn't need anything.

I check my email to make sure, but there's nothing there that needs doing.

"I'll be on the radio," I tell Bev. She waves me off.

I take a half hour or so driving around town through the alleys. I check for broken windows and gates left ajar. Crimes of opportunity are about ninety percent of our caseload. Public intoxication and domestics make up the rest.

After checking the alleys, I do a lap on the main drags to be seen. Then I take another pass by the elementary. There's a new crowd of kids on the playground. Smaller, but not short enough to be first graders.

I could text Soph and check in. Shay wouldn't like me doing that; she's not Soph's biggest fan, for good reason. Besides, Soph has my number. She'll call if there's an issue. The weather's clear. Mia hasn't had a meltdown since the day at the river. There's no reason to think she won't roll with this like she did the picnic yesterday.

If I'm being honest, I'm a little letdown that she doesn't seem phased to find out I'm her father. She hasn't spoken to me since she told me she was hungry at lunchtime yesterday.

She could be turning it over in her head. Or maybe it's not a huge deal to her. I have to remind myself sometimes that she doesn't know what a real family is like. She's been living with her mother who didn't have a father. And her grandmother who seems more like a landlady than blood. She might not know enough about how it should be to feel hurt.

My chest aches. That's not any better. That she wouldn't know enough to be hurt that I haven't been around.

When I get to the turnoff to Stonecut Farms, I resist the urge to take a right at the fork and check on Shay. I take the rutted lane that runs down to the gully. I shift down to first. There's no avoiding some of these potholes. You have to just take 'em slow.

I'm banking that Pandy will be home. She's been working the late shift at the Gas-and-Go. She could have a second job, though.

I pull up in front of her trailer. Her vehicle is parked out front. Lonnie's truck isn't there. That'll make things easier. Lonnie's a blowhard.

I spare a look for Buck Crowder's place. I came back after I moved Shay and Mia up the hill to make sure the place was secure. It looks the same as I left it. I turned the porch light on in case Connie straightened things out with the electrical company, but the bulb's dark.

Honestly, the whole thing should be hauled to the dump. Pandy's place and the one next door are in better condition. Probably because they're further from the creek. Grandpa Price bought the trailers before I was born for the seasonal workers, and clearly no one's spent much time or money on upkeep since his day.

How does Dad not know? He's busy. I suppose he has no call to come down the hill. I don't think he's pressed about the rent. Most the folks that live down here have for decades, or they moved in

Chapter 15

with grandparents and stayed when the older generation passed. Does he even collect? If he did, I can't believe people wouldn't be in his ear about making repairs.

Shit. I need to talk to him about it. Feels awkward telling him his business, but with the rusting and the way the doors are hanging and how the porches are misaligned, some are sinking. Half these places are going to be uninhabitable sooner rather than later.

That's tomorrow's worry, though. I take off my sunglasses, put on my hat, and go to knock on Pandy's door. By the time I hit the porch, she's leaning in the doorframe.

"I didn't do it, officer," she says through the screen. Her hair's in a messy bun, she's braless under a white undershirt, and the elastic of her panty legs peek past her cut-off shorts.

"Good morning, Pandy. Is Lonnie home?"

"He didn't do it, neither." She cackles. "Shit. He probably did." She digs a crumpled pack of cigarettes from her pocket and holds it toward me.

"No, thanks. Mind if I come in?"

"You got a warrant?"

"Nope."

"Well, all right then." She nudges the door open with her toe. "Lonnie ain't here."

"It was you I wanted to talk to."

She brays a laugh. "Is this gonna turn into a porno, Deputy Wall? I'm gonna warn you now. I ain't shaved in days."

"Not a porno."

She gestures to the sofa, and I take a seat. It sags in the middle, so I perch on the edge. She props herself cross-legged on a chair across a cluttered coffee table.

"This about Shay Crowder?" She's smirking, her red-rimmed eyes showing a spark of life. She's got gossip.

My heart rate kicks up. I have a hundred questions. A thousand. But I'm in uniform, and that's not why I'm here.

Shay's not exactly forthcoming. If I don't ask, there are things I might never know.

Shay would hate me talking about her behind her back.

I clear my throat. "It's about Rory Evans."

Pandy leans back, her eyes rounding. She takes a long drag. "Really?"

She glances at the door as if she's expecting someone. Or checking to make sure there's no one there.

"Ed Houser says she was living here before she left town."

Pandy's gaze shifts over my shoulder. "Yeah."

"There some kind of falling out back home?"

"You know Sarah Evans."

"Was that it?"

"Ain't that enough?"

I suppose it is. Despite Sarah—or maybe because of her—Rory never ran with the kids we'd bust for possession.

"So she moved in here? When was that?"

Pandy leans over and taps her ash in a beer can. "She's fine. Talk to Del Willis. He'll tell you."

"I'm just trying to tie up loose ends."

She sucks in her cheeks and raises her pencil-thin eyebrows. "Talk to Del."

Why is she stonewalling me? Pandy's the type who'd blab her pin code if you talk to her long enough. The back of my neck prickles.

"There a reason you won't answer my question?"

"I did answer. I said talk to the sheriff."

"Pandy."

"Kell." She cocks her neck, all attitude, but the way she's flicking the butt of her cigarette…she's nervous. Scared even.

"Pandy, what are you afraid of?"

"Not you, Dudley Do-Right."

"Who?"

"Never mind."

I grind my teeth. Try a different tack. "Where's Rory Evans?"

Chapter 15

"New York."

"Do you know how I can get a hold of her?"

"Ask. Del. Willis." She drops her cigarette in the beer can with a hiss.

I lean back, rest an arm along the back of the couch. I raise my eyebrows.

She rolls her eyes.

I wait.

She breaks after about ten seconds of silence. "I'm not saying shit."

"About what?"

She huffs, drawing another smoke from the pack. "She won't talk to you."

"Why not?"

"The—" She snaps her fingers. "You know. The paper she signed."

"What kind of paper?"

"You know. The kind where you won't say anything. PDA. NWA."

"NDA."

"I don't know, Kell. You're the law."

"Why'd Rory Evans sign an NDA?"

"For the money."

I exhale. "Pandy. Come on. What happened?"

For her, she's put up a valiant fight. She breaks, though, blowing out a breath and leaning forward. "You're not gonna believe me."

"I'll believe you."

She purses her lips. "Okay. We'll see. You know that Rory was cleaning up the hill, right?"

I nod.

"You know your uncle's handsy, right?"

"Van?" I didn't know that. My stomach knots.

"So, you know, it's a hassle, but the pay's good. I always told him to fuck off. Made it a joke. Told him Lonnie would kick his ass. But Rory...she's shy."

"Why didn't you say something?"

"Hey, Deputy. Your uncle grabs my ass. Arrest him. Seriously, Kell?"

"I would have talked to him."

"Oh, well, then." Pandy snorts. "Anyway, Rory never said anything, so he kept pushing things, and then one day, when Rory's dusting the living room, he, you know—" She lifts a shoulder.

She can't mean—she wouldn't be telling it so calmly.

"He what?"

"Forced her."

My guts heave.

"I mean, he didn't beat her up or anything, but she told him no. Rory's not really a fighter."

"Jesus Christ."

"She was gonna quit and try to get a job at General Goods, but —I don't really understand how it went down—but there turned out to be video. Like not from the inside of the house, but from the security cameras outside."

"Where's the video?"

"I'm not the cops, Kell. I'm just telling you what I heard."

I force myself to take a breath. My muscles are bunched, and my chest feels caught in a vise. This can't be true. Pandy's telling the story so casually. If it were true, she wouldn't be recounting it like a TV episode.

"So, then what happened?"

"Well, that lawyer from town came out, and he said if she signed the papers and kept her mouth shut for two years, she'd get fifty thousand dollars. And he gave her a thousand down to get started somewhere else. I don't know why it's two years, and not, like, forever, but Rory's not stupid. She signed. She knows she's done here."

Acid scores my throat.

Chapter 15

Two years is the statute of limitations for civil sexual abuse cases.

"Why didn't she report it? You know me, Pandy. Why didn't you tell her to talk to me?"

For a second, she's baffled. "Kell, Del Willis was here, too. Came with the lawyer. In case she wanted to press charges, he said. He told her that even with the video, there wasn't enough to make it stick. 'Cause there was no sound. He said to anybody watching, it'd look consensual."

"Why—" All of a sudden, my head's a dead weight. It's an effort to keep it high.

"Why, what?"

I clear my throat to play for time. I can't sort my thoughts. "Del believed her, though."

"Oh yeah, he believed her." She laughs, bitter. "You think this was the first mess he's cleaned up for his old buddy Van Price?"

I catch myself as I begin to shake my head. It has the power of instinct. To deny it.

It can't be true.

I've known these men all my life.

We've spent hours in tree stands and by campfires. I sat with Del in the hospital waiting room when Lil was in the hospital with pneumonia. I smoked my first cigar on the patio with Van when Branch was born. I was maybe thirteen. Mom had a fit when she smelled it on me.

I *know* these men.

Yeah, they're a product of their times. Del says shit he shouldn't, and Van's always been a little too friendly with pretty women, but they aren't bad men. They're family men. They care about this town.

"It must have been a misunderstanding."

Pandy's jaw drops, but only for a second. Almost immediately, her lips curl into a cynical smile. "Yeah. Must have been."

"Who has the video?"

She shrugs, and then she narrows her eyes. "So, you'd believe it, then? If you saw it with your own eyes?"

"Or give me Rory's number. I'd like to talk to her."

Pandy laughs, rough and low from the cigarettes, and shakes her head. "I remember when Shay Crowder called you to tell you she was knocked up. You blocked her. She was gone the next week."

"This isn't that."

"I don't know. Feels a lot the same to me."

I'm going to argue. My mouth is open. My body is alive with adrenaline, a sickening stone rolling in my guts. The words are on my lips. Van and Del would never do something like this. She's talking about my family. She's talking about the men who raised me.

I don't *want* to believe this.

If it's true, who are we?

Who am I?

"Why didn't you come to me, Pandy?" I ask. It's not an accusation. I keep my voice even. I hold her gaze. I need to know.

"About Shay or about Rory?"

"Both."

She takes a drag, and her brow furrows. "Well, I mean, what good would it have done?"

"I would have handled it."

"Oh, Kell. Sweetie." She rounds her eyes and slowly shakes her head. "No, you wouldn't. You're part of the problem."

She falls silent, letting the cigarette dangle from her fingers. She's waiting for me to speak, but I've got nothing. Shame I haven't felt since I was a boy heats my face. My uniform chafes, the duty belt is heavy cumbersome around my waist.

I don't think she's lying. I don't think there's been a mistake.

I've chosen to be blind, but I'm not stupid.

Pandy rises and awkwardly jerks her chin toward the kitchen. "Want me to make a pot of coffee?" There's pity in her voice.

"No." I stand. "Thank you." I fumble for my wallet and take out a card. "Will you pass my information along to Rory. Tell her I'd like to talk to her. If she's willing."

"She's not risking that money, Kell."

"We'd keep it private."

"No such thing in Stonecut County." Pandy smirks. "On your way out, will you tell Tycho Anderson he needs to put that dog on a leash?"

"I thought his dog died."

"He found himself a new one. Meaner than the last one. Almost bit me when I went for the mail."

"All right." I'm heading out when the thought occurs to me. I don't want to ask. "Why haven't you called my dad about the dog?"

"Why would I call him?"

"Isn't he the landlord?"

"I don't think so. We make the check out to some management company in Pyle. I think your uncle owns it. You can call and wait for them to send someone, but there's better ways to waste your time. You'll have a word with Tycho?"

"I will."

"If you don't, Lonnie's gonna," she warns.

"I'll straighten it out."

She sees me out. She stands there watching me behind the screen door as I head over to Tycho's. He's not there, and neither is the dog. I make a note to drive by tomorrow after I drop off Shay.

Pandy raises a hand as I roll past on my way out.

When I came out, I had the idea to check on Shay, but I decide against it. She'll be fine at the house. I take the long way back to town. The radio's silent, traffic is light, and there's nothing to distract me from the ugliness crowding my brain.

There was this time once when I was in high school. Van, Cash, and I had gone fishing. We'd stopped at the Over Easy for a late lunch. Van flirted with the waitress. This was well before Shay came to stay with Buck. I knew the girl. We weren't in the same class, but she was in my grade.

He touched her back. Slid his hand down so it almost rested

on her ass. Then, he brushed her boobs handing her his credit card. She blushed bright red. I was embarrassed.

When she picked up the check, she was happy with the tip. Van joked around. She giggled. I was relieved. He's harmless. It was an accident. No hard feelings.

It's like I was too close, but I took a step back—got shoved back—and now, I can see all the details. Everything I missed. Everything I should have wondered about and never did.

What exactly did they say to Shay to send her running?

Why didn't I ask her?

That's why she doesn't trust me. Why she didn't want to tell Mia that I'm her father. And always slips out of bed before dawn. Why she'll let me in, but only so far and no further.

She can't trust me.

I'm supposed to be the good guy, but how good can I be if I make excuses and pretend I don't see? Isn't that what a coward does?

I pass the elementary on my way back into town, easing onto the shoulder. Everything looks peaceful and in order, but how would I know?

Soph would call if there's a problem.

Soph, who got drunk and grabbed my dick at my wedding.

Who was giving Shay the runaround before I strolled into the office.

Who let me cheat off her in Calculus, which is the only reason I didn't have to retake the class in summer school. Who had to be treated for smoke inhalation when she didn't evacuate the time the kiln went up in the art room because she was searching for Tommy Dorney. When we found him scared out of his mind in the boy's bathroom, she broke down.

I blink my eyes. They're dry as hell. I got to pull it together. I need to do something. This can't stand.

But what do I do? Where do I start when things are this fucking rotten?

Chapter 15

I drive aimlessly back toward the office. Del will be there by now, for sure, even if he had an appointment with the lawyers.

Shit.

Did he do it?

Dad swears it's political. All the folks from the city moving out here. We're dealing with problems we never had before. Zoning. Setback issues, noise complaints, all kinds of proposed ordinances that get people up in arms. Used to be that town council meetings were Dad, George Hardt—Elizabeth's dad—Del, and Jim Ellwood. Now it's a full house. People bring lawyers. They livestream it on the damn internet.

A lot of the new residents don't like Del's plain speaking. They want him to jump when they say, and he's not gonna do that. And Ken and Glenna Dobbs, our resident lefties, break the story? When the hardest hitting news Ken's done in twenty years is when maintenance accidentally cut down that white oak?

Del Willis really sold military surplus and pocketed the proceeds? It beggars belief.

This is Stonecut County.

It's crazy.

Right?

My temples are throbbing. I'm crossing the bridge, and I just pull over. I need a minute. I need to *think*.

I get out, stretch my legs. I'm a few yards from where shit went down with Billy McAllister. The river's glinting silver in the midday sun. It's so far down, its rushing is muted. If you strain, you can hear it, but so high above, it's easily drowned out by the breeze that's finally kicking up and the occasional traffic.

It was a one in a million shot.

If I leapt now, with no pressure, no blind panic—if I had all the time in the world to calculate—I'd hit the water and be dead on impact. There's just no way a person can jump from this height and survive. Let alone a baby.

I didn't think. There was no conscious thought in my mind. Afterwards, when I was in the hospital, Mom suggested I should talk to someone. Everyone else was happy to call me a hero, and eventually, that's how she saw it, too, but when I was in that bed, she did the same math I had done.

There is no way I could have expected make it.

Blood drains from my face, and I lean my forearms on the wall. The concrete's warm from the sun.

I wasn't suicidal. I just didn't care enough to think twice before I made the leap.

If I had died that day, Shay and Mia would be alone. Shay would've come back here, and Mom or Dad or Van would've eventually noticed the little girl who's Dina's doppelganger. They would have figured out that Mia was mine.

Mom would take them under her wing. No doubt in my mind.

What would Van have done?

What would Dad?

There are no answers. Only questions and ugly what ifs, one after another, none leading to a solution, no way to make it right.

What does a good man do when he realizes he's not?

I stare at the river, and all I can think is that it's so far down.

That's what I'm doing when an SUV pulls off behind my cruiser. There's the rip of an emergency break, the slam of a door, and the clip of high heels. I draw myself up.

It's Elizabeth.

Not now.

It's such a goddamn small town.

I'm expecting her to call out, launch into whatever it is that made her pull over instead of driving on by, but instead, she sidles up to me and peers down into the river as if she's trying to see what I'm looking at.

"You drop something?"

I slide her a glance. She's on her way to work. Solid blue dress. Hair pulled back. No make-up. They do that at the station.

"Too soon?" She arches an eyebrow.

I sniff and go back to surveying the river. "What can I do for you, Elizabeth?"

"The Harvest Day Parade. I need a firm yes."
"Now?"
She sets her jaw. "I need a Grand Marshal."
"Come on, Liz. I've got shit going on."
She sucks in her cheeks and starts chewing the insides. It's a tell. She's trying to keep a grip on her temper. Next, the cords in her neck will pop. I don't have the time or inclination for this today.
"The car seats four plus the driver. You can bring your —whoever."
"There has to be somebody else."
She kind of sputters and tosses her head back. "For Chrissake, Kell, can you give a shit for just once in your life?"
I bristle, turning to her. I'm not doing this right now. I open my mouth, but she hasn't stopped.
"I realize you're perfectly happy with your head up your ass, but if you haven't noticed, this town is falling apart. The sheriff's going to jail. The gentrifiers are suing the locals; the locals are boycotting the gentrifiers. A half dozen people I know are working themselves up to run the Dobbses out of town."
"Stonecut is getting gentrified?"
"We've got a place on Main Street that sells soap and tablecloths, Kell. What do you think?" She sucks down a breath. She's joking, but she's also serious.
"That's all petty shit. It'll sort out."
"You cannot be this oblivious."
My temper flares, and I go for the cheap shot. "You found it convenient for me to be "oblivious" when we were together."
She has the grace to blush. "We're not talking about that." She exhales gustily. "I know what you think about my committees, but you should show up once in a while. Things are getting heated."
"At the Stonecut County Coordinating Council?"
"Yes, Kellum. At the Coordinating Council. And if I were you, I'd start thinking about what you're going to do when Sue Acheson

sues Mr. Henry for harassment. She's already complaining that the 'local yokels' won't do anything."

"She rides her bike on the sidewalk."

"And Mr. Henry squirted her and her husband with his hose. She's calling it assault and riling up her friends. She's already sent a mob after him on social media. What are you gonna do when someone puts a brick through his window?"

I'm about to brush it off. It's such second nature. But I stop. "What do you think I should do, Elizabeth?"

She's on a tear. She doesn't recognize my change of tone. Which is fair enough.

"I know you're only useful for pulling cars out of ditches and rescuing ladies tied to railroad tracks, or whatever, but I really, really need you to sit in the back of a convertible and wave to people for two hours on a Saturday morning."

"What is that gonna do?" I know how it sounds, but it's an honest question.

Still, the muscles in her neck striate, and her nostrils flare. "Show people," she grits out.

"Show people what?"

"That there are good guys left. And maybe they should pull it the fuck together."

"I'm not a good guy."

She doesn't bat an eye. "You're decent. These days, it's good enough."

A stiff breeze blows in from the east. The temperature's dropped at least five degrees since we've been standing here. It's a relief.

"You think it'd make any difference?"

She's checking her watch, tapping through messages. She doesn't even look at me when she replies. "Not as much as you denouncing Del, or hell, writing the Achesons a damn ticket, but Stonecut isn't gonna get the hero it needs, so we'll take the hero we can get."

"You're great for my ego, Liz."

Chapter 15

"Your ego has always been just fine, Kell." She pats my shoulder. "I'm gonna be late. You're a 'yes,' right?"

"Sure."

"Wear your dress uniform. And the star."

"Yes, ma'am."

She glances up toward the mountain. I follow her gaze. A bank of fluffy, grayish clouds is rolling in. "Looks like it might be blowing up into something."

"The weather didn't call for anything."

"You get your forecast from channel thirteen?"

"Of course."

"Well, that's where you went wrong." She presses her key fob and her SUV beeps. "Cal Winstop can hardly read the map."

"Seriously?" He's new since we split. I never had to hear about him at length at the dinner table.

"They hired him 'cause he's a pretty face. And unlike me, that's all he brought."

"Your ego's doing okay, too, eh?"

"You know it." She winks and strides off, a swish in her walk.

I watch her roll off and fail to come to a complete stop at the sign at First Street.

I cannot think of two people more ill-suited for each other than Elizabeth Hardt and me. The whole town thought we were meant to be. Even folks like Bev who can't stand her.

I was gonna make that square peg fit in that round hole, though, wasn't I?

It's amazing how a person can make such God-awful decisions doing what he thinks he should.

The only time I ever really followed my gut was that night at the bonfire with Shay.

She's been alone in the house a few hours now. She's probably getting restless. It's clear she's used to being busy. When I get home at night, she's always done something around the house. The laundry or the dusting. I can only imagine what she'll get up to without Mia to watch.

Would Shay get lonely?

She's not keen on people, but she's not accustomed to being alone, either.

My pulse kicks up.

Nothing in my brain is settled. It's all a buzzing mess. Thinking isn't making it better, though.

I want to see Shay.

She was so out of sorts last night. I'm gonna sit her down and make her tell me what's wrong. And then I'm gonna fix it. And that'll be one thing put right.

My body loves the idea. I've got a surge of energy as I return to my vehicle and call in. Bev says it's all quiet on the home front. I check my messages real quick before I head back out of town, but there's nothing that requires an immediate reply.

The clouds have stalled over Stonecut Mountain, dimming the blaze of the sun and cutting the humidity. It's mild enough that I drive with the windows down rather than the AC cranked. Looks like the forecast was right. Anvil might get some rain, but it doesn't look like it's heading down into the valley.

The awfulness, the shame, it's all still crowded in the corners of my mind, but there's a buoy in my chest. A beacon. Shay.

It didn't start right with her—*I* didn't start right with her—but I haven't fucked up this second chance. She's prickly and wary and suspicious, but she comes to me. She trusts me some, and that trust is earned. Not because I'm a Wall or whatever else.

Whoever I am, I'm the man Shay Crowder trusts. It's a lifeline in the dark. Everything can't be lost—this is all salvageable—if that is true.

16

SHAY

I should have been gone an hour ago, but I can't find any pictures. I found wedding pictures shoved in the back of a hutch in Kellum's office, but nothing from when he was younger.

There's plenty of pictures on my phone of Mia and Kellum, but what if she wants to know what he looked like when he was her age?

Who doesn't have pictures of themselves as a child? Even Mama started an album of me when I was little. She gave up when I was in fourth or fifth grade, but she keeps it in pride of place on a shelf in the entertainment center.

I've searched his office, the living room, and the downstairs closets, and now I'm in his room, digging through his dresser. I was being careful, but now I'm shoving things around and not bothering to put them back as they were. It's nearly 1:30. I need to go.

The car's packed. I just crammed everything into trash bags and filled the trunk. I spent longer than I needed to disassembling the front wheel of Mia's bike so it'd fit in the cab if I recline the passenger seat.

Van Price spared no expense on the promised car. When I got

the cashier's check from Don Prescott this morning, there was a used compact with crank windows waiting for me. At least I didn't have to walk back home. The hike into town was miserable enough. The heat was broiling, I kept having to shake asphalt out of my shoes, and every time a car passed, my heart lodged in my throat.

Now, I'm just flinging undershirts around. I force myself to focus. I'm looking for a box. Maybe an envelope. People don't keep pictures loose in their underwear drawers. Shit.

What am I doing?

Kellum will be here in less than an hour so we can go pick Mia up from school. I need to have her and be heading out of town by then. I don't need pictures. How are they gonna make things better? When Mia asks me why I took her away from her daddy, is a picture going to make up for what I've done?

I need to go, but instead I sink onto my butt. The wood is hard. The house is silent except for the whirr of the air conditioning.

My eyes burn. I cried on the walk into town. I was sweating so much, it's not like anyone driving past could tell. Even if they had, they'd have stared straight ahead and pressed on the gas. Back home, if someone saw you trudging along, they'd offer you a ride. This is not that kind of place.

Doesn't matter. I wouldn't have said yes. I didn't back home, either.

I let my eyes drift shut. Kellum's room smells like him. Clean and musky. I breathe deep, try to imprint it on my memory. I love his scent. It's not a cologne or an aftershave. I'm not ever gonna be able to walk into a department store for a reminder if I forget.

The papers laid it out very clear. There's no coming back. There's no waiting until Mia's eighteen and reaching out. I cash the check, and it's done.

The papers said that Mia is not his child, and I signed it. I didn't hesitate. I'd do it again.

When I walked into Don Prescott's, there was a cop leaning on a cruiser across the street. Even from a distance, it was clear it wasn't Kellum. The car was black-and-white, not brown, and it didn't have the sheriff's logo on the side. It read POLICE. The cop was young. My age. He rested his hand on the butt of his gun, and kept his gaze trained on me as I mounted the steps and knocked on the door.

While I waited, he held up an orange prescription bottle. He shook it, raised it up bold as day in the middle of the street, sneered at me, and then slipped it back into his pocket. The block was empty. By the time Don Prescott himself opened the door, he was leaning there, cool as a cucumber.

Mr. Prescott gave him a nod. The cop touched the brim of his hat.

My blood was still running cold when I signed. I wouldn't have bothered to read the papers, but Mr. Prescott insisted on going through the terms. I had to initial next to every messed-up thing.

I assert that Mia Crowder is not and cannot be Kellum Wall's biological issue. I hereby surrender all claims on the Price Trust. I agree not to disclose the terms and conditions of the agreement under penalty of forfeiture of all considerations provided to me.

There's something like a stone lodged in my throat, suffocating me.

I did the right thing.

I can live with the guilt choking me. I'll give it a minute, and I'll suck it up, haul myself off the floor, and go get Mia.

It's gonna throw her, me coming alone to pick her up early. Kellum made a point of talking through her day several times. He's good like that. I don't need to coach him, not that I would. He remembers from seeing how his Mama was with Dina growing up.

Please Lord, don't let her have a meltdown. It would only serve me right. I'm screwing with her schedule on the first day of school, and then I'm gonna upend her life—again—and she *should* lose her mind on me, but I'm gonna break into pieces if she does.

If I could take this all on myself, I would. If it were only me, I'd spit in Van Price's fake-tanned face.

He doesn't want *me* gone, though. He wants *us* gone. He's

threatening me now, but I know if I shrug him off, he'd be on to her next.

That's it. I need to get up. I squeeze my closed eyes, blink a few times, and drag myself to my feet. There are no pictures. That's that.

I'm stiff. I crack my neck and rotate at the waist to stretch my back. I can do this. One foot in front of the other.

A car door slams.

Who is that?

Adrenaline shoots down my veins. My heart slams against my rib cage. I rush to the window.

It's Kellum. He's loping toward the car. Peering in the window. Now he's sprinting for the porch. I race from his room.

What do I do? What do I do?

My phone's charging on the kitchen counter beside my purse. There's no back way out. I've got no lie prepared, and I'm shaking so hard, I couldn't tell one anyway.

"Shay!" The word rings through the empty house.

I freeze in the hallway.

He takes the stairs three at a time.

"What the fuck is going on, Shay?" His voice booms.

Then, he's there. Uniform. Radio. Hat. Shiny black shoes. Belt. Gun.

I'm panting although I've only made it a few feet. His chest is rising and falling, too. He looks through the open door into the room where Mia and I have been staying. The bed's made. There aren't any toys in baskets on the floor or crap on top of the dresser.

"What are you doing, Shay?" His face hardens, the muscles in his neck tensing. His blue eyes spit fire.

"Are you leaving me?" His voice raises. There's a rawness to it I've never heard. He doesn't look like himself, and I'm afraid. I didn't think this through. I step back on instinct. He lunges.

"Are you taking Mia away from me?" He seizes my upper arms. It hurts. He's hurting me. I'm paralyzed.

Chapter 16

He hauls me into the room, holding me in a punishing grip with one hand while he flings opens drawer after empty drawer.

"You're running off? What are you doing?"

He grabs me again by the arms, fingers digging into my skin, and I think he's going to shake me or throw me. He's vibrating with rage, out of his mind. I've never seen him like this.

He hates me.

Fear floods me, saps my strength, and I sway, and then it's like something inside me bursts, ugly and huge and out of control. It hurts. I hurt, and I hate him. I buck, catching him unprepared. His fingers dig deeper, but I knock him off balance. On instinct, I drop so that my whole weight is yanking me out of his grasp.

"Let me go!" I scream.

He does. Instantly. My knees slam into the hardwood. I taste metal. My tongue throbs. I scramble to my feet. He stumbles back.

"Jesus. Shay—"

"No!" I scream it. The word echoes off the ceiling. I gasp for air and point my finger at him. "No."

This time it's ragged. From deep in my chest.

His hands are fisted. I dare him. I *dare* him.

"We're leaving," I gasp.

"*No*," he booms. He's between me and the door. His stance is wide. He's taller and stronger and he has a gun. I'm no match for him.

It's not fair.

None of this is fucking fair.

"Yes," I say, strangled, broken. I'm crying. When did I start crying? The tears are hot, dribbling off my chin.

What is he going to do?

Whatever he wants.

He glares at me. I drop my gaze to the floor.

For a long minute, the only sound is our ragged breathing.

Then, he exhales. It's not a sigh of frustration. Not quite anger. It's not a giving up sound. It's something else.

He walks away from the door—away from me—toward the bathroom. There's a clear path out now.

He's faster than me. If I run, he'll have no problem catching me.

He stops next to the dresser. What's he doing?

He's unbuckling his duty belt.

I turn to face him, inching closer to the door, my back to the wall. He's not looking at me. Not even in the mirror. His shoulders are rigid, his back ramrod straight.

He sets his belt on the dresser. He undoes his radio holster and puts that down, too. Then he runs his hand through his hair and drops his head back, and he closes his eyes for a second.

Then he walks calmly over to the bed and lowers himself to the edge. He inhales, rolling his shoulders. And then he turns his head to face me. His expression is grim. Unreadable.

"What are you doing?" I stutter.

He swallows. His Adam's apple bobs. "I'm listening."

I wait.

He sits there, still and tense and scary as hell. I know what he's doing, but it can't work. He can't make himself safe and unthreatening. It's not possible.

I ease back until I'm right beside the door. He doesn't move a muscle.

The keys to the car are in my purse. I don't have a play here. It doesn't matter that he's across the room, that his gun's not in arm's reach. Even if by some miracle I got to the car, all he'd have to do is call the school and tell Soph not to release Mia to me. Or put out an APB.

I'm trapped. Rock. Hard place.

Fucked.

I sink, sliding down the wall. I draw my knees to my chest. Kellum jerks, but he sees what I'm doing, and he stays where he is.

"I don't want to go," I say, quiet, but it's loud in the silent room.

He's not gonna believe me, but it's true. And I want him to hear it.

Chapter 16

There's a beat. He seems to struggle for words. "I don't want you to go, either."

"I don't have a choice." I force myself to meet his eye.

Again, it seems like he's going to say something, but at the last second, he thinks better of it. There's a pause, and then he asks, "Why don't you have a choice?"

I can't tell him. He wouldn't believe me if I did.

But what am I gonna do?

I'm not lying for that motherfucker Van Price. Not when my back is literally to the wall, and I have no way out.

"Your uncle wants us gone."

"It's not up to him," he growls.

I laugh, but it comes out mangled. Like a sob.

Kellum's jaw clenches. He inhales deeply through his nose. "He said something to you?"

"Yeah."

His forehead furrows. He stares a moment out the window, up the hill. "At the picnic?"

"Yeah."

"I didn't see him speak to you." He presses his lips. "He talked to you when you went inside."

I nod.

"What did he say?"

I feel sick. Ashamed. Still scared.

He's not gonna believe me.

He's gonna twist it until it lines up with the way he sees the world, and then this impossible thing between us will crack and shrivel and die.

There's something worse than sneaking away and never seeing him again. It's cowering in this room, telling him the truth, watching him weigh up the value of people and their word, and living through the exact moment when he ranks me less than.

It's keeping my head up while he breaks my heart, and I'm already wrung out and so damn tired.

I don't know where to find the strength.

But I will.

I've picked myself up off the floor before.

It's cold comfort, but it's enough.

He's turned his back on me before. I survived then. I'll survive now.

I clear my throat. "He gave me four hundred thousand. I signed papers that say you aren't Mia's father. We have to leave and never come back."

I'm tracking his expression, and it goes so hard, so ice cold, I tremble. I go on. "And if I didn't take the offer, he was gonna set me up so everyone thinks I'm an addict. He'd make it so you'd take Mia away from me, or he'd kill me and make it look like an accident."

I can hear it myself. It sounds crazy. No one would believe it.

Kellum leans forward, rests his elbows on his thighs, and lowers his head in his hands. He won't look at me.

This is why Van Price bothered with the bribe. I had wondered. If he's willing to do what he said, why offer me money?

Because it makes an instant liar out of me. What makes more sense? A gold digger with a wild story? Or an upstanding pillar of the community threatens to murder the woman who shows up out of nowhere with a kid in tow?

I want to take it back. I want to say that I'm sick of him. I want to be a bitch or a flake. I don't want to be whatever he must think I am.

My mouth is dry, my mind's numb, and my heart feels suspended high in the air, dangling on a split thread.

I can't bear it a second longer.

"Kellum?" It comes out a raspy croak.

He straightens, but he doesn't look at me. He stares at the empty wall above the dresser. "Why didn't you tell me?"

"I—"

He raises his hand, and then his fingers curl before he drops it to his lap. "No. That's not what I want to say. I'm going to—" He stops again, abruptly.

Then he squares his shoulders and turns his head, catching my eyes, holding my gaze.

"I believe you, Shay."

My heart flips. "What?"

"He's done." There's a finality in his voice, a barely banked violence, that sends shivers down my spine.

"What are you going to do?" I ask, breathless.

"The right thing." A look flashes across his face. I've never seen it before. It's bitter, jaded, world-weary. And stone-cold. "You don't worry about it. Or him."

He rises. A low rumble sounds in the distance. Is that thunder? A truck?

"Do you trust me, Shay?" He steps forward and holds out his hand.

How can I answer him? I don't trust anyone. I don't know how.

His expression darkens, and his lips turn down. I think he'll give up, but instead, he lowers into a squat until we're eye-to-eye.

"Trust me, Shay," he says.

There's another rumble. This time, the window frame shakes.

"Is that a storm rolling in?" I ask.

He glances over his shoulder. "Yeah."

"Mia." I struggle to my feet, grabbing his hand. He startles, but he takes it.

We rush downstairs. I grab my purse and keys. He goes ahead and starts the car. There's no rain yet, but the sky's turned yellowish-green. It's coming from the north. We're a few minutes ahead of it.

Mia's classroom faces the river. The thunder is a growl, not a boom. If she's into something, she might not have noticed the sun dim. I didn't.

Kellum left the passenger door open for me. I slide in, swing it shut.

"Ready?" He's already pulling out. "Buckle up."

I'm fumbling with the latch, trying to catch my breath.

"She's probably fine."

He nods. "We told everyone how she is with storms. If she freaks out, they'll handle it." His knuckles are white on the steering wheel.

"She won't bolt. She only did that back home because she knew where to hide. She doesn't know the school well enough yet."

Am I trying to reassure him? Or myself?

"She's run from the teachers before?" He accelerates.

Shit. I'm not reassuring anyone.

"It'll be okay," I say.

He grabs my hand and squeezes. There's another rumble of thunder. The rain starts, a gentle patter on the windshield, not a deluge. I force myself to take a deep, steadying breath.

This isn't Mia's first storm at school.

Worst case scenario, she's melting down in the cloak room. Unlike back home, her classroom at Stonecut Elementary doesn't have a door that opens to the outside. She can't get out easy.

She's not racing down Main Street, dodging traffic, or any of the other wild thoughts that were popping in my head like scenes from a horror movie. I'm overwrought, and I'm letting my imagination run wild. I know my child. She ran from Bryce Adams. She hides from storms.

She might not even be freaking out. There's no lightning. It seems like we're only getting the edge of something that passed to the north.

"Check my phone," Kellum says, breaking the silence. He sounds a little chagrined. Like I'm starting to feel. "Soph said she'd text if there was a problem."

I reach in his pocket, grab his cell, and swipe. No texts.

My chest loosens a little more. "Nothing."

"See, it's fine," he says.

I let out a light snort.

"What?" he says, turning onto Bank Street.

"That's what I told you."

We pull up in front of the school. Everything is peaceful. The rain is no more than a misting now, and the sun's breaking through the clouds.

I check his phone again.

"Anything?" he asks.

"Nope."

"Mia probably didn't even notice," he says. "Those walls are thick. And if the blinds were down—"

"Yeah." I swallow. Now that the panic has passed, everything else crowds back in.

"There's only forty-five minutes until dismissal." He slides me a glance. I nod. "I'm going to drive down a few blocks. I don't want anyone to think something's wrong."

"Okay." He makes a U-turn and pulls off by the square. The rain has totally stopped, but no one's ventured out again yet.

Kellum reaches into my lap where I've clasped my hands. He tugs one loose and draws it to his lips.

He brushes kisses across my knuckles, and then he presses my hand to his hard pec, holding it there. I can feel his heart thud, fast but steady. My chest warms.

"I swear, if you stay, I will protect you and Mia. With my life, Shay."

"*If* we stay?" He'd let us go?

"You'd be taking everything I love from me. But yes. If you don't believe I will handle this—if you *can't* believe that—yes. I won't stop you."

"I know you love Mia." My voice cracks. "I don't want to—"

"—and you," he interrupts.

I—what?

"I love you, Shay. You damn well better know that, too."

My mouth snaps shut. He tightens his grip on my fingers.

My brain doesn't know what to do with that. I change the subject. "What are you going to do? With your uncle?"

"What needs to be done. Will you trust me, Shay?"

I'm still trembling. My head is swimming. I'm scared. Lost. I don't know what to do.

But yes. I can trust Kellum Wall.

"Okay," I say.

He presses a kiss to my temple.

After a few minutes, he turns on the radio. I lift my face, and he brushes his lips across mine. I cup his neck. He unbuckles me and drags me onto his lap.

He's solid and strong and quiet and sure.

"I love you, too." I whisper in his ear. My heart races like I've run a mile.

I'm terrified.

But I'm done running. I'm right where I want to be.

~

I DON'T KNOW what I expected. More hissed phone calls on the back porch, I guess. Another sit-down at his parents.

I go along with him because of the expression on his face. He's changed. I can't make it out exactly. Grief, maybe. Rage. Resolve. Regret.

It only lightens when we pick Mia up from school. Soph makes a point of sticking her head in the window and telling us Mia had a great first day. No mention of a freak out. Mia's a little wired like she always is after school before she gets her snack and spends some quiet time with her critters.

Kellum asks about her teacher and her lessons, and she ignores him, but she holds her backpack on her lap like it's precious.

I think it went okay. She's not wiped or agitated.

It's not until we're close to home that I realize all our stuff is in that car.

Shit, shit, shit.

I'm about to say something when Kellum takes a left at the fork past the Stonecut Farms sign.

"Mia, I know we didn't talk about this, but your mama and I have some errands we need to run. I was thinking you could have your snack with my mom."

Mia frowns, but she doesn't complain. I exhale.

When we pull up at the Lodge, there's no cars in the drive, and the garage doors are closed.

"Are you sure she's here?"

He gives a slight shrug. "One way to find out."

He honks, and by the time I've got Mia untangled from her backpack and out of the car, his mother's coming around the side of the house, wiping her hands on her jeans. She's wearing a wide-brimmed straw hat and dirt-stained knee pads. Guess she was working in the garden.

"What a delightful surprise!" She hugs Kellum fiercely, and then she flashes me a huge smile. "Hello, Shay."

I smile back. She's a lot. Mia eyes her under lowered lashes.

"How was the first day of school?"

"Good," I answer.

"Good," she repeats. Her smile doesn't fade in the least. After a few seconds, she seems to shake herself. "You all hungry? I bet Mia's hungry after a long day of learning. How about some cookies? Or ice cream?"

Kellum cuts her off. "That would be great, Mom. Actually, we were hoping Mia might be able to hang out with you for a few hours. Shay and I have to take care of something."

His mom's face blanches. You can tell she wants to ask. She chews at her lip. "Of course. Anytime. Mia and I will have a snack, and then maybe she'll help me in the garden."

Mia perks up a little at that.

"We can feed the koi, too."

"She'll love that." I relax a bit. Mia could feed fish for hours. It won't take but twenty minutes to unpack the car. She'll be fine.

If—

Where's Mr. Wall? Who else is here?

Suddenly, I tense. Kellum glances down at me.

"Where's Dad?" It's like he reads my mind.

"Up at the Cabin. They're all up there. Cash, Branch, Van—"

I stiffen. Mrs. Wall doesn't seem to notice.

"Dad. Jesse. Van's heading back to the city tonight. They all decided yesterday they were gonna teach Branch how to shoot a crossbow or something. Poor kid. I think it's an excuse for them to make the long weekend longer." She shakes her head, but there's no real criticism in her voice.

Beside me, Kellum is bristling. I grab his hand. His mom's gaze flicks down, and her smile broadens.

"You two get on now. Miss Mia and I will be just fine. Won't we?"

Mia looks to me. I give her a nod. She trots over to Mrs. Wall, dragging her backpack across the asphalt.

"How about I take this?" Mrs. Wall asks. She waits until Mia hands it over, and she slings it carefully over her shoulder.

"Don't worry, Mama," she says to me. "I'll clean out her lunchbox so nothing gets too ripe. I remember how it is."

I mumble thanks, and I watch them walk with measured steps to the house, Mrs. Wall chatting, Mia listening with a somber face.

Dina said I could trust her.

I don't know why I put so much stock in what Dina says. Maybe because of her resemblance to Mia. Maybe because she's the only one who doesn't even pretend to buy the bullshit.

I breathe through my unease, and I get back in the car.

"Okay?" Kellum asks.

I nod. "We won't be long."

The calm expression he's been keeping drops as he puts the cruiser in reverse. "You don't have to come."

"What do you mean?" We're headed downhill toward our house.

"I'm gonna change, and then I'm gonna take the truck and go to the Cabin. Can you unpack the car?"

"Yeah, but—" I'm thrown. "What are you going to do?"

"I'm not a hundred percent sure. But I don't need to be wearing my gun." He sets his jaw. "You can stay at the house. I'll drop by and pick you up after. We'll get Mia. Take her for pizza. Does that sound good?"

I guess."

We're at the house. He squeezes my knee, and then he jogs into the house. I head for the car. It only takes two trips to unload everything. After he changes into jeans and a gray T-shirt, Kellum helps me put the clothes away. It hardly takes any time at all.

My heart's pounding.

I don't ever want to see Van Price again.

And I'm terrified of what he'll say to Kellum. What lies he'll spin.

I pile the last of Mia's critter tubes into the laundry basket I've been using as a toy chest, and Kellum waits for me in the doorway.

I go to him.

He skims his rough fingers down my cheek. "Trust me, Shay," he says.

"I will."

"Will you come?"

"You want me to?"

"No. I don't want you anywhere near him. But, uh—" He seems to struggle. "I think you should hear what I have to say."

I nod slowly. "Okay."

We walk to the truck in silence, side by side. I'm amped with adrenaline. He opens the door and helps me up. He's amped, too, but it's not like earlier. He's in total control.

We head up the winding drive to the Cabin. I've only ever looked up at it before. It's at the highest point of the property, on a ridge. The infinity pool overlooks a valley filled with pine, Stonecut Mountain rising behind. The helicopter is on its pad. A brown and tan cruiser with SHERIFF on the side is parked in front of a four-car garage.

My stomach clenches. Of course he'd be here, too.

There's a flat field beyond the garage where the men are gathered. There's a target on a bale of hay at the far end and Adirondack chairs around a stone-ringed fire pit closer to the house. The grass is unnaturally green, thick, and even. More like a golf course than a backyard.

The men all look relaxed. Cash, Branch, and Jesse seem to be taking turns with the target. Mr. Wall, Van Price, and Del Willis are relaxing in the lawn chairs, beers in glass mugs on the tables beside them.

A woman in a white apron is lingering at the sliding doors, wiping them down. It looks like she's waiting to be asked for something. Van Price has a maid? Of course. He has a helicopter.

Kellum sees where I'm looking, and his face goes white.

"What?"

He shakes his head. "Let's do this. You ready?"

"No."

He barks a surprised laugh. "Me, neither."

They've noticed us. All eyes are on the truck. Mr. Wall raises his hand in greeting.

Kellum hops out. I wait for him to open my door.

I keep my eyes on Van Price as Kellum helps me down. I'm wearing the same thing I have all day. Khaki shorts, a purple V-neck top, and my flip-flops. I wish I had dressed up. I wish I didn't feel like an awkward kid as soon as I'm around these men.

Jesse and Mr. Wall's faces are friendly. No one else's are.

Van rises to his feet and sets his glass down. Del Willis follows his lead.

"Thought you had to work," Cash calls out, aiming the crossbow and pulling the trigger. There's a zing. He hits a bullseye.

Cash seems oblivious to the rising tension. Kellum ignores him. He takes my hand, and we walk to the fire pit. Mr. Wall belatedly realizes everyone's standing but him, and he stands, too.

The gang's all here.

Van glares daggers at me, but his stance is relaxed. Unconcerned.

"Kellum. Shay. Would you like a drink?" He lifts his hand, and the woman at the door slips inside.

"What the fuck do you have to say for yourself?" Kellum bites out.

His father chokes on a cough. Del Willis shifts to stand behind Van. Backing him up.

Van sneers.

"No." Kellum stalks closer. Cash and the others are paying full attention now. "I don't want to hear it. I'm going to tell you what's going to happen."

He draws a breath, and Van leaps in, projecting too loud for how close we are to each other, his tone dripping condescension.

"What did Miss Crowder tell you now, eh?"

"The truth."

"Sure." He glances around, eyebrows as high as his hairline. "And what's that now?"

"You know." Kellum's tensing, his muscles bunching, his grip on my hand growing painfully tight.

"I really don't, Kell. I know that ever since she's come back to town, it's one thing or another. Lots of stories. Lots of drama."

"You're done," Kellum grits out. He's almost shaking with holding it back.

Van casts a sad, embarrassed look around the group. "This is your family, Kell. What are you doing?"

I almost shrink in my skin. There are six of them this time. They loom, tall and arrogant to a man, each in his own way, looking down their noses at me as if I've ruined their fun.

As if *I've* done this to them.

I wriggle my fingers until Kellum loosens his hold on my hand, and I take a step forward.

"He's telling you—" I don't know what I'm saying, but the words still spill out. I drag my gaze from one man to the next, and I don't linger. I don't care what they think. They're gonna hear me.

"He is telling you that *I* am his family. Mia and me. We're done with you." I point at Van. "And we're done with any of the rest of you who can't wrap your brain around that."

I stride forward until I'm arm's length from Van Prince. He smirks. "And if you threaten me or my child again, I'll kill you."

Van looks to Del Willis, but Del's gaze is pinned behind me. I glance back. Kellum is there, right by my shoulder. Cash and Jesse have joined him.

Mr. Wall has backed away. He's watching his sons.

Van shakes his head and clicks his cheek. "Kellum, you're really going to take the word of this trailer trash slut over family?"

There's a shout. I'm shoved to the side.

Kellum's fist cracks into Van Price's jaw, and the man goes tumbling. A table tips. A hand gently grasps my wrists, pulls me further away. It's Jesse.

Cash has tackled Kellum, and Mr. Wall is in front of him, arms back, using his chest to block him as he fights to get free. The black of Kellum's pupils have eaten the blue. He's lost it.

"Don't let him go!" I try to go to him, but Jesse tightens his grip.

"They've got him. Don't worry."

Del's helping Van to his feet. He wobbles, but his sneer's in place. "Look what she's turned you into. You whore," he says to me.

"You don't talk to her. You don't look at her. You even *think* about her, and I will kill you," Kellum shouts, struggling. Cash uses his whole weight to hold him back.

Van rubs his jaw. "You're lucky you didn't break it." He spits. "John, get your kids in line."

Mr. Wall turns, slow, deliberate. "You got him, Cash?" he asks.

"Yup," Cash pants.

Mr. Wall takes a few stiff steps toward Van. "Like the lady said. You threaten my kids—or my grandkids—again, I'll kill you."

Then he swings out of nowhere, and drives his fist into Van's belly. Van folds with an "oof."

From a yard away, Branch Price snorts. He's got his phone out, and he's taping.

"All right, Uncle John," he says.

Mr. Wall shakes out his hand. Del Willis offers Van his arm. Kellum's stopped trying to break loose.

"You all forget who signs the checks," Van spits, drawing himself back up to full height. "You forget who you owe all this to."

"Which is it, Van?" Mr. Wall asks, his voice heavy. "We family? Or are you the landlord?" The creases at the corner of his eyes deepen. "Didn't have to be like this." He looks to Del. "You comin' or goin'?"

Del avoids his gaze.

"Del?" Kellum's eyes are shadowed.

Del shakes his head.

"My gun and badge will be on your desk in the morning," Kellum says. There's pain in his voice. And determination.

"Come on, son." Mr. Wall claps Kellum on the shoulder, and Cash eases back. Kellum reaches for me. I slip my hand in his.

We walk away, Mr. Wall in the lead, Cash and Jesse behind us. I'm surrounded by large men, all of them at least a head taller. It feels strange.

Kellum tucks a strand of hair that's sprung loose from my ponytail behind my ear. His fingers trace down my cheek. "Thanks for having my back, Shay Crowder."

"Anytime, Kellum Wall."

EPILOGUE
SHAY

"I really don't want to do this." I tug my dress down. It's a decent length when I'm standing, but sitting on the back of this convertible, it's creeping up. I don't want all of Stonecut County to see my dimpled thighs.

"Would you feel better knowing I don't either?" Kellum's sweating bullets in his dress uniform. It cooled down the past few weeks, but this weekend, it's gotten up to eighty-five in the afternoon, even though it's early November.

"I wish I'd stayed back at your Mom's with Mia."

"I wouldn't have minded."

"I know." I wriggle a little closer to him. We're in a line of cars, waiting, and have been for almost an hour. Even though we're in the second brigade, the parade goes at ten miles an hour and all the fire engines stop for the railroad track, so it runs late almost as soon as it starts.

That's what Elizabeth says.

She's been coming over to chat between putting out fires. Apparently, she organizes the parade every year, and it's always almost a disaster. You get the sense she loves it.

I don't actually hate her. She made a point of coming up to me when I was alone at the refreshment table at a PTA meeting. She was there helping her friend Soph.

She was nice. I don't need more enemies, so I didn't turn my nose up at the olive branch.

Kellum never had a chance at bailing on the parade. He's the acting sheriff now. He never had the chance to quit before Del was put out on leave. He's in deep trouble.

A few ladies from the hospital auxiliary walk past and call my name. I wave. Kellum's mom has recruited me as her apprentice, understudy, and jack-of-all-trades. I take meeting minutes, sort donations at the food bank, tag along on visits to the homebound. Kelly Wall is the unofficial mayor of Stonecut, and I love being useful. The days had been getting long with Mia in school and nothing to do.

The car jerks forward and my stomach sloshes. I can't believe I'm gonna be in a parade. I don't know what I'm doing.

"Do I wave?"

"Yup."

"Like this?" I move my hand side-to-side like the Queen of England, and the sun glints off the diamond on my left hand.

It's ridiculously big. Kellum slipped it on my finger while we were watching Mia wade by the banks of the Luckahannock.

He hadn't asked me. He'd said, "Do you like it?"

I told him it would do.

"Should I do more like this?" I wave my hand back and forth like a windshield wiper.

"You do it however you want, baby." He grabs my hand and drops a kiss in my palm.

I giggle. "That tickles."

He leans over. "Wait 'til we get home," he whispers in my ear. "I told Mom and Dad we'd get Mia after dinner."

"But we'll be done by noon." I bite my lower lip. His eyes drop to my mouth.

"We have all afternoon."

"What did you have in mind?" I murmur.

"We'll get out of these hot clothes."

"Yeah?" I don't point out that my white sundress with the blue and red stars is actually quite cool.

"We'll take a shower."

"You'll scrub my back?"

He groans and takes a quick nibble at my ear. A shiver zips down my spine. "Anything you want."

"And then?"

"I'm gonna lay you back on the bed, sling this leg—" He squeezes my left knee. "—Over my shoulder, and I'm gonna lick your pussy and swirl my tongue around that sweet little clit until your knees fall open and you blush from your neck to your waist."

My face flames. That's exactly what I do when I cum from oral. I slap his shoulder. "Watch your mouth. We're in public."

"No one can hear."

That's certainly true. If he weren't right next to my ear, he'd have to shout to be heard over the engines and the crowd.

"Still."

"All right." He straightens until there's an inch or two between us. I don't like that, either.

A few vehicles roll forward, the marching band clumps, and I catch a glimpse of the banner the majorettes are carrying.

"Oh, look." I point it out. Now it's Kellum's turn to blush. It's a list of the parade sponsors. *The Wall Family* is written at the top in the biggest font. *Family Discount* is half the size underneath. I can't make out the other names below.

I imagine that in other years it said *The Wall-Price Family*. My mood dips, and my smile fades. There's a lot of reminders around this town.

After that afternoon at the Cabin, Van Price got on his helicopter and left for the city. He hasn't been back. He hired some people to cover his furniture and drain the pool. It's like a ghost hovering over all of us.

Kellum's flown down to New York a few times, trying to sort it out, but my sense is he's hitting a wall. He can't tell me everything.

Apparently, Van's crimes run deeper than his offenses against me, and there are privacy issues. Kellum's frustrated. He wants justice, and the world's not falling in line.

He's doing what he can, though. Kellum told his folks everything. Mr. Wall fired Don Prescott, and he hired a woman from Anvil. Kellum had me meet with her, and we went over the papers I signed. She said most wouldn't hold up in court. She explained how you can't legally sign away your child's rights because they don't belong to you. It makes sense.

I still felt awful. I tried to dodge Kellum that night, but he ducked into my room after Mia was asleep and lured me out with watermelon sorbet.

The Walls have decided to dissolve the trust. It's with the lawyers now. Sometimes I feel guilty that I caused all this consternation, but then I remember that I didn't. I've got plenty to regret, but Van Price made his own bed.

"What's wrong?" Kellum's shaken off his embarrassment, and I guess he's noticed my distraction.

"Nothing." I hurry and kiss him so he doesn't pry. The car lurches forward, and I almost tumble forward into the back seat. Kellum's got me, though.

"Whoa." He draws me tight against him. "I got you."

"You do." I smile into his handsome face. It's a beautiful day. The sky is robin's egg blue. There's a crisp breeze. Every so often the drum corps gets bored and launches into a song, and all the bored folks waiting to parade down Main Street hoot and holler.

"It's a good town," Kellum muses.

I nod. As good as any.

"You like it here?"

"Yeah."

He reaches across my lap and takes my left hand. He rubs the diamond with his thumb.

"Do you really like the ring?" His heart's in his eyes. All that confidence. All that natural swagger. It's deserted him. He's hanging on my words. He needs to hear my *yes*.

Somehow, I became the most important person in someone's world. It's a miracle and a gift and a dream.

"Yes," I give him, no hesitation.

"You sure?"

"A hundred percent."

He exhales, and a smile breaks across his face, transforming him. He's not the football star. He's not the golden boy, the favored son, the hometown hero.

He's Mia's father. My first and only love.

The best man I know.

A NOTE FROM THE AUTHOR

Want an invitation to Kellum and Shay's wedding?

Sign up for my newsletter at **catecwells.com** and get a bonus epilogue to *Hitting the Wall* as well as other freebies, news, and special offers.

ABOUT CATE C. WELLS

Cate C. Wells is the author of the Stonecut County and Steel Bones Motorcycle Club series. She writes gritty, real, emotionally satisfying romance. She's into messy love, flaws, long roads to redemption, grace, and happily ever after, in books and in life.

Along with stories, she's collected a husband and three children along the way. She lives in Baltimore when she's not exploring America with the family. #allfiftystates

She loves to connect with readers! Check out the The Cate C. Wells Reader Group on Facebook.

Facebook: @catecwells
Twitter: @CateCWells1
Bookbub: @catecwells

BOOKS BY CATE C. WELLS

STEEL BONES MOTORCYCLE CLUB

Charge: A Steel Bones Motorcycle Club Novel (Book 1)
Nickel's Story: A Steel Bones Motorcycle Club Novel (Book 2)
Scrap: A Steel Bones Motorcycle Club Romance (Book 3)
Plum: A Steel Bones Motorcycle Club Romance (Book 4)
Wall: A Steel Bones Motorcycle Club Romance (Book 5)
Forty: A Steel Bones Motorcycle Club Romance (Book 6)
Dizzy: A Steel Bones Motorcycle Club Prequel
Twitch: A Steel Bones Motorcycle Club Novella

STONECUT COUNTY

Hitting the Wall

Printed in Great Britain
by Amazon